Photo by Reg Gordon

KEN BRUEN

"The next major new Irish voice we hear might well belong to Ken Bruen."
Chicago Tribune

"Bruen is a brilliant, lyrical, deeply moving writer who can make you laugh and cry in the same paragraph and whose characters are so sharply portrayed that they almost walk off the page at you. If you like Ian Rankin, Dennis Lehane, Pelecanos, and the like, Bruen is definitely a writer to reckon with."
Denver Post

"Even in barrooms, 'there are poets among us,' and sometimes their voices are fierce."
Marilyn Stasio, *The New York Times Book Review*

"Bruen writes tight, urgent, powerful prose . . . his dialogue is harsh and authentic . . ."
The Times (London)

"If you haven't discovered Bruen, it's time you did."
Ali Karim, *Crimespree Magazine*

"Reading Ken Bruen, as anyone who ever has will tell you, is like playing with fire; you know that your feelings, your emotions and your sensibilities are apt to get burned, but you just can't resist the almost primal allure of the heat and flame."
James Clar, *Mystery News*

ALSO BY KEN BRUEN

Jack Taylor novels

The Guards
The Killing of the Tinkers
The Magdalen Martyrs
The Dramatist
Priest

Brant novels

A White Arrest
Taming the Alien
The McDead
Blitz
Vixen
Calibre

Other crime novels

Rilke on Black
The Hackman Blues
Her Last Call to Louis Macneice
London Boulevard
Dispatching Baudelaire
Bust (with Jason Starr)
American Skin
Tower (with Reed Farrel Coleman)

Limited edition short stories

"The Dead Room" (published by A.S.A.P. Publishing)
"Murder by the Book" (published by Busted Flush Press)

A FIFTH OF BRUEN

EARLY FICTION OF KEN BRUEN

Busted Flush Press
Houston 2006

A Fifth of Bruen

Published by Busted Flush Press

ISBN: 0-9767157-2-4

Design & Illustrations: Greg Fleming
Layout & Production Services: Jeff Smith

BUSTED FLUSH
PRESS

P.O. Box 540594
Houston, TX 77254-0594
www.bustedflushpress.com

A FIFTH
OF BRUEN

A FIFTH OF BRUEN: EARLY FICTION OF KEN BRUEN.

Funeral: Tales of Irish Morbidities
Originally published by Terrance Publishing, Pittsburgh, PA, 1991

Martyrs
Originally published by Minerva Press, London, 1994

Shades of Grace
Originally published by Images Publishing (Malvern) Ltd.,
Upton-upon-Severn, 1993

Sherry and Other Stories
Originally published by Adelphi Press, London, 1994

All the Old Songs and Nothing to Lose
Originally published by Minerva Press, London, 1994

The Time of Serena-May & Upon the Third Cross
Originally published by Adelphi Press, London, 1994

INTRODUCTION

ORIGINS OF AN ORIGINAL
By Allan Guthrie

Imagine, if you will, the time before Jack Taylor, the time before Brant & Roberts, the time before Serpent's Tail published *Rilke In Black* and *Her Last Call To Louis MacNeice*. Picture a bar in the west of Ireland. It's evening. Smoke hangs thick in the air. Laughter bounces from table to table. It's the Galway Arms Bar, and there's the young Ken Bruen, smiling and joking as he hands over a copy of his latest book to a brand new reader. That reader was one of the lucky ones.

Ken Bruen's early works have been much sought after in the last few years, and they've been virtually impossible to obtain.

Until now.

You have in your hand, *A Fifth Of Bruen*, an omnibus edition of those early works, four short novels and two collections of short stories which Ken Bruen used to sell by hand in the bars of his home town.

The first of the novels to be published was *Funeral: Tales of Irish Morbidities*. Published by Terrance Publishing in 1991, it tells the story of a young Irishman who is fascinated by funerals. So much so, that his life is spent frequenting one funeral after another. What's intriguing about this novel is that, as with most of Bruen's very early work, it isn't a crime novel. Oh, there are crimes, sure, but it's a literary novel, no question. Highly contemplative, introspective, but even then, I'm glad to say, Bruen didn't "do scenery", and the plot has a pace to it that's often frequently absent from the typical literary novel. And, of course, it's full of Galway humour.

In *Funeral* we find the following appearing in (to borrow a Bruen phrase) jig time:

> America
> Books
> Irishness
> Alcoholism
> Fathers
> Poetry
> Quotes

And of course:

> Lists

Bruen aficionados will recognize in the above list some of the obsessions which have gone on to drive many of his subsequent novels, creating the idiosyncrasies which make the Bruen novel stand out from the crowd, and make his books horribly imitative for us, his poor colleagues. Bruen is the one writer it's not recommended to read if you're writing a novel yourself. His style is so easy, fast-paced, elegant, it's hard not to find yourself emulating it.

Shades Of Grace, published in 1993, is a love story, but of the sort that only Ken Bruen could write. The central character is, like many Bruen protagonists, a literary-named figure: Ford (after Ford Madox Ford), a social worker who should really have a social worker of his own. Ford is an Irishman abroad (London), who falls in love with an American, Grace (Bruen temporarily amalgamates the two countries with his use of the acronym, CIA, to mean Catholic Irish Alcoholic). Yes, Ford has a drink problem. So much so that a client tells him, "You drink and you drink and you fall over every time I see you."

This novel has some terrific observations, from the anti-authoritarian "The police arrived about midday. In plain clothes, they had that politeness that slaps your face," to the more general aphoristic rhetorical wit of "How dangerous could someone called Cecil be?" Bruen wasn't writing noir yet, but Ford bears many of the hallmarks of a noir protagonist.

Martyrs, originally published in 1994, has more emphasis on plot, more twists, more surprises, more suspense. But without sacrificing any characterization. It's here that Bruen first quotes a crime novel, the protagonist, Stephen Beck, saying, "If you had to quote a writer, make it a crime writer". Beck is a loser. He has a degree in sociology, runs a market stall, has "an ex-wife, an ex-child, and no excuses." And his alcoholic brother is in a hospital for the "dipstick dysfunctional."

Even back in 1994, Bruen was giving mothers a hard time. This novel is where the darkness in Bruen really starts to take hold. There's a scene which takes the reader's breath away with the startling speed and unexpectedness of the violence. One of those instances where you say, aloud, "What?" Then re-read the paragraph and say, "Jesus, he really did just do that." But I'm giving nothing further away. Read on. Martyrs can't be beaten for full-on bittersweet irony.

Danny Taylor (distantly related to Jack, I wonder?) is the vigilante protagonist of *All The Old Songs* and *Nothing To Lose*. Here we're firmly in crime fiction territory. Danny's wife and kid were killed by a joyrider, and Danny's sense of outrage has led him to seek to serve his own brand of justice. For all kinds of wrongdoings. Danny's a complex character. He breaks arms at the slightest excuse, yet loves Larkin and MacNeice. And his idealized sense of justice is offset by a keen cynicism. His friend Richie describes the effects of ICE (amphetamines): "you don't eat, sleep. And it lingers for about three days," and Danny's response is: "Bit like love, is it?" With typical Bruen wit, Danny is surely the first vigilante hero with a bad back.

Of Bruen's many short stories, "The Time Of Serena-May" is the author's favorite. And understandably so. Bruen is renowned for making the reader laugh and cry, manipulating our emotions like a conjuror. This stunningly moving story is shot through with emotional honesty: "They said a Downs Syndrome baby had one chromosome too many. Maybe it was everyone else who had one less." But there are also wonderfully subversive moments, such as this definition of nuns:

"women in hoods who do a lot of polishing."

Bruen demonstrates a sleight of hand that all writers would love to have, and the dexterity with which he delivers, time after time, is awe-inspiring. Some further examples include this piece of succinct characterization from *Funeral* where Bruen describes the barmaid, Eileen, thus: "mebbe she'd had a head of hair once"; and this pithy aphorism from "Upon The Third Cross" that slams home with the ineluctable truth of a speeding bullet: "You left prison but it never left you."

Like "Serena-May", "Upon The Third Cross" is another long short story, this time using the kind of multiple point-of-view that's reminiscent of the Brant novels. This, though, is not a police procedural. It's perhaps better described as a criminal procedure, with an ex-con protagonist, his grief-crazed sister, a couple of "bone breakers" and their unsavoury boss. This is an excellent revenge story with some very nice twists.

"Where do you stand on homosexuals?"

"Well clear." ("Priest")

"Priest" was originally published in the collection *Sherry and Other Stories*. Only Ken Bruen would give a later novel the same title, but it just goes to emphasize the extent to which the priesthood is a key theme in his work. "Priest" opens with a desecrated alter, and introduces us to Father Morgan, the kind of priest who delivers a drunken sermon and then bites a Rottweiler, and whose thinking is "all below the waist". He battles with his demons as best he can, belting back Jameson to stem the sexual desire he feels towards Sera and Kate, two women who've recently entered his life. But along with the sexual attraction, there's an air of malevolence about the place as memories of the dead Father Malachy are reawakened . . .

***

With the huge success of *The Guards* (nominated for seemingly every crime fiction award under the sun, and winning the Shamus), Ken Bruen is fast becoming a legend in his own lifetime. But that wasn't always the case.

Back in the bad old days, Ken Bruen published a novel called *The Hackman Blues*, one of the most important books in the crime canon. And it was published against seemingly everybody's wishes. Even after its publication there were anguished cries from the House of Lords to have the book banned. To have created such a commotion must have been both bemusing and amusing for the young author. There must have been times when he wondered if he made the right choice. He did, despite strong pressure not to. *Hackman* is a book that tells it like it is. A book about AIDS. A book where everything doesn't fit neatly into the pigeon-holed template of redemptive crime fiction, where order and justice prevail, no matter what. That's Ken Bruen. He writes noir. There aren't always happy endings. There isn't always redemption. There is often chaos. The unexpected happens for no reason. Life sucks, but it's a ride, folks, and with Ken Bruen, you're hanging on by your fingertips for dear life.

FUNERAL
TALES OF IRISH MORBIDITIES

"Waste . . . Remains?"

Learnt
All there was to learn
of the wasteful
and
the wasted
what remains
isn't always
the worst
that's left behind.

Funerals can be fun. How's that for a positive attitude. I was thought-feeding this when a shadow loomed above my dwindling pint (of stout). Sean, a second-hand bookseller. I knew him well . . . well in the Irish sense. I'd buy him a drink, and he'd tell me some secrets of the trade. The following one nigh on destroyed me. His name was Shaun after his year in America . . . but he's over that now. I don't remind him of it . . . often.

"A fella brought in five hardback Graham Greene's today."

"In good condition?"

"Pristine! Like they were never opened."

"And?" (I had to ignore that pristine.)

"He was in a fierce state from drink. I offered him a fiver."

"Did he take it?"

"He hemmed and hawed . . . sweated . . . shook, then snapt the fiver."

"God bless Graham Greene. I suppose it's a complete coincidence that he was a convert to Catholicism."

Sean gave me a worried look. Vaguely satisfied I wasn't needlin' him, he continued. I was, but that's neither here nor there.

"I was checking through the third book, and on page five there was a fiver . . . on page ten there was a tenner . . . on page twenty, a twenty . . ."

"Stop! Stop for Godsakes . . . I know alcoholism is a progressive disease, but this is cruelty itself." Sean idled with his pint. I dunno what visions the glass yielded. An endless line of first editions . . . mebbe. I could stand it no longer.

"Okay . . . okay . . . tell me just this. How many pages in the book?"

"Two hundred and fifty," and he laughed. Deep. I didn't like him a whole lot then. But I had to know. Damnit. He knew that.

"Tell me the title then."

"*The Human Factor.*"

"Oh, sweet Lord above . . . that's vicious."

I allowed myself to notice him sucking on the glass. Do it. Go to it, I thought. I knew I'd hear a story like that on the day of a Monday funeral. What else! I looked at my watch. I should be moving for the 6:15. A crowd would already be gathered at the morgue. I hate the Monday funerals. But I knew I either give this thing my whole attention or forget it. Due to my own naivety, I'd missed the nine o'clock removal from the church. Recently, I'd been practicing a bracing honesty. Deadly stuff! I had also neglected to touch the talisman I'd written above my bed. It's a favourite G. K. Chesterton paradox. The one describing Elizabeth Barrett's life at home with her bullying father.

> "She took a much
> more cheerful view
> of death than her father
> did on life."

Mighty stuff. But I'd forgotten to touch it and paid the price. The Irish town I live in is undergoing a crisis of identity. Who isn't? It's large enough to warrant the dubious title of city but retains a provincial flavour.

I had hardly hit the main street when I saw O'Malley. It was too late to avoid him. So we did the Irish dance of polite verbal hostility.

"How are ya, Dillon?"

"Not bad. And yerself?"

"Fine, fine! Have you time for a coffee?"

Everything in me roared – No. No way – not ever . . . so I said, "Yeah."

I was suffering from a glut of self-improvement books. A galaxy of inspirational tones were having an adverse, not to mention perverse, effect on my behaviour. Terms like *confrontation*, *face your fears*, and *best your neuroses* had me dizzy with integrity. I bought the coffee. Black for O'Malley. . . like his nature. Whoops! A negative attitude. True though. O'Malley could never stand me. I decided to cut right through to this.

"You never liked me . . . did you?"

He nearly dropped the coffee in his lap. "Wot?"

"Let's face it . . . (good, positive approach) you hate the living sight of me. Would you like me to tell you why?"

"Cripes! Have you taken drink? . . . anyway, why do you think I don't like you?"

"Because you can't understand why I don't need a crowd, why I hang out on my own. My independence grates on your nerves. But the reason you most dislike me is because I never mention the money you owe me."

"Ary . . . you're as mad as a hatter. Everyone knows that."

"What's more, I can also tell you the reason I don't like you. It's a lot simpler . . . "

"Who the hell cares, you're a bloody lunatic."

"I don't like you because you don't like me."

I got up then and left. Timing: it's all in the timing. By evening the story would be all over the town. T'was too late now to catch the nine o'clock hearse. I heard O'Malley roar, "Ya bollix," after me.

I notice nowadays that they like to spell this "bollix" in an up-market fashion. I'm a traditionalist and like the old forms. At least O'Malley had given me the old usage. Why didn't that make me feel better. The story by tonight would lack the financial aspect. By now O'Malley might even have converted it to me owing him the money. My father operated on a different type of diplomacy. He'd have taken O'Malley behind the guards' barracks and beat the living daylights outa him. One thing is certain, there wouldn't have been any roaring of names after him. Traditional, up-market or otherwise. They buried my father in 1980. Shortly after I began my first faltering steps on the funeral philosophy, my Irish instincts ensured that logic would play no part in the formation of this. Obvious works of reference like *The Tibetan Book of the Dead*, I completely ignored. I knew instinctively that if the philosophy was to be practical, I'd have to steal, adapt, and plagarise wholesale. This I've done. The beauty was that familiarity could seem like the ring of truth. I had two fathers. The one who actually existed and the one I wish he'd been. In June 1980, I buried both. My mother is a non-runner. She died when I was three and is buried up in Louth. A fierce enough epitaph in itself. Drink killed my father. But in Ireland, very few died from drink. They die pist in car crashes, in drunken brawls, fall drunk from bridges, under cars while footless. But . . . the death certificates list coronary failures and other euphemisms which leaves other drinkers free to the business at hand. My father died in the horrors . . . screaming of funerals he'd never attended. This was relieved with rats and various low-life forms coming through the walls to him. I think he mentioned bank managers in there. He was sixty-two years of age and, moments before he died, he sat bolt upright, like the best clichés. I moved near for words of wisdom . . . words of comfort . . . mebbe. He grabbed my wrist. Many's the one since who regrets the last error of judgement. He should have gone for the throat. The stench of his breath was woeful. But I was going nowhere. The grip was ferocious. Betwixt a mixture of spittle and venom he roared, "Get to the funeral . . ."

My then-girlfriend wasn't big on funerals. Marisa. Not your usual Irish name. Her mother had notions of grandeur and some gothic romance she'd been reading lodged in her memory. Her brother was less fortunate. He's Raoul Darcy. Try telling the knackers in the school yard you're Raoul. . . .

I met her 'round about the time I'd got my first funeral notched up. I was a novice then and fairly shaken by the grief of the family.

No stranger to drink myself, I went to The Weir for some oblivion. I was building towards heaven when she sat down. I took note without interest. Early twenties, blond hair, dark eyes, roughly 5'2" and thin to the point of anorexia. Turned-up button nose and a "friendly" mouth, as they say here. The hair was fresh washed and with new leather and baked bread, my favourite fragrance. I dismissed her.

"Bit early . . . is it?"

"Wot."

"Early, like early to be getting legless. Don't you have work then?" I played the gamut of responses,

> – mind yer own business
> – wot's it to you
> – silence
> – a belch.

So I said,

"I've just come from a funeral." She didn't disappoint. Her face was a mix of concern and curiosity.

"Oh! I'm sorry . . . oh dear . . . am . . . was it someone close?"

"Close enough."

"Let me get you a drink. Is that Jameson?"

"Paddy."

"Oh right . . . I mean, sorry . . . I'll get it."

I watched her order the drink. I liked the air of calm she had. How far wrong can you go with a girl who'll get the drink? A coffee for her. I was reaching immunity and little cared.

"I'm Marisa."

"Howya Marisa. . . ."

"And you?"

"I'm fine, thanks."

"No, I mean . . . what's your name?"

"Well, while my father was alive, I was always called young Dillon. Since he died, they dropped the 'young' . . . which I'm not . . . am . . ."

"Not what?"

"Not so young either . . . anymore."

I was becoming befuddled. As this was the point of the exercise, I didn't struggle.

"Well, okay then. Dillon, so . . . highly trendy."

"What! What are you on about?"

"Bob Dylan . . . Dylan Thomas, you're right in there."

"I have to go now."

She looked startled. Good, I thought, and left.

A week passed. I slotted in ten funerals. I still hadn't come to grips with my vocation. Back to The Weir. I was putting down the first part of the funeral thoughts on paper. This was slow. Three glasses of Paddy were whispering "Why write, let go . . ."

"Howya." I looked up. Her again.

"Oh . . . hello . . . Maura . . . ?"

"Marisa."

"How are you?" She was staring at the empty glasses.

"Keep passing the empty glasses."

"What?"

"Do you want a coffee . . . a drink . . . a sandwich . . . a slap . . ." she asked.

"A coffee."

I nearly left then as she brought back two coffees.

"So . . . are you well?"

"Mar . . . i . . . sa, yea, what do you want?"

She was caught. I wasn't into confrontation those days, only drink. It spoke loudly. You can put anything to the Irish except direct questions. The devil mend you, I thought . . . in your grief it might help you to talk.

"You're a counsellor, are you?"

She could have given me a hiding there.

"I'll go. . . ." I wanted that so I said, "No . . . would you read this . . . please?"

I passed the first part of "Funeral" to her. The title got a jump from her. I had written:

"Funeral"

"England"
Funeral . . .
was the face – constrict
it took me years
to put together – crazed
a mix
of tragedy small played
upon a smaller stage
blend with
the farcial events
a random fate
believed not random
pushed my way
in England
all the years I
wandered thru
I never heard
not once
a funeral took place
with advertising

"Ireland"
But Ireland – always
we go the route
for melodrama
hoarding death
to mingle with
the welcome – back
your business first
to ask
the why
– mere information
they'll with the deadliest
of smiles – free-set
remark

"Response"
Your funeral
it is
a race that mocks it
to its very face
yet *lives* on dread

of what
it might not hold
three days
on walking slow
I feel the fear
beneath my very feet
recede.

***

It was early days. She laughed out loud.

"This is hilarious . . . oh, I love that . . . the notion of funerals with advertising."

I had expected scorn. Was I hoping for it? Her reaction meant we might have a chance.

"Don't you think it's a bit insane?" I asked.

"But of course I do . . . that's why I love it. Can I have a copy?" Magic words.

I told her about my cousin then. He was twelve years in London. He never heard hint nor hide of funerals. He returned home and in his first month, went to eleven.

"Do the English not die?" she asked . . . laughing.

"Well," I said, "like everything else they do it with the minimum of fuss. The Irish roar at it. They thrash it, shout at it, try to strangle it. It's as if by keeping it loud and brash, they can keep it controlled. Death has a fierce job of sneaking up on us." She was hooked. I continued. "The Irish greeting is 'how-yah, do you know who's dead.' I often feel like asking people if they've been to any good funerals lately. I hear people remark of funerals, like football matches – there was a good turn out."

Marisa was nodding furiously. On I went, cruising now, the drink nearly forgotten.

"Watch any Irish mother. They're full of chat, tea, and vitality. They get to the daily newspaper and straight to the obituaries. Never mind what's huggin' the headlines. They zero in and want to know who's dead. You get asked in complete seriousness, 'Is anybody I know – dead!' Then, 'Been to any good funerals lately?' A bit like going to the cinema. How long before they start reviewing them. I'm not coddin' you [which is the Irish preface to a lie], but I heard a woman say that a friend of hers died. Her companion asked the cause . . . 'Oh, nothing serious'. . ."

Marisa said, "Death, where is thy sting."

I had a bad moment when she did. Lord, I tried to blot it out. Our fragile communication was near beached on that. Roll with it. She hadn't yet mentioned Dylan Thomas's hackneyed poem . . . hope lived, if you'll excuse the irony. I continued.

"I heard an American ask where he could find a real 'wake.' I think it was probably listed under the 'not to be missed section' of his guidebook. I dunno of any other country where the corpse gets to be the guest of honour . . . the final entertainment. Our whole vocabulary hinges on the closeness of death. Sick aren't just sick, they're at death's door. To describe the pits, you only mention you felt like death warmed up."

9

I was whacked, so I took a hefty whack of the Paddy.

Mistake! It let her commit the dreaded one.

"Did you ever hear of the Dylan Thomas poem on the death of his father?"

"No." Very quiet I said that.

"Oh . . . well it goes, 'Do not go gentle into that good night.'"

"I see." My heart was pounding.

"I must get you a copy," she ended.

Worse and worse. Visions of her reading this to me over open caskets began to shape. I stood up.

"All the best now . . . goodbye." And I fled.

A measure of my terror was the glass of whiskey I left behind. Did you ever? I knew I'd dream of her mouthing "Rage rage against the dying of the light. . . ." No amount of whiskey would remove that taste. I did what I could. I crawled into the nearest card shop and, sure enough, a flurry of Desideratas were scattered expensively. It's my heritage to try to erase nausea with saccharin. The platitudes induced the inertia . . . not the ideal solution, but I couldn't crawl into a bottle if I was to work later. My mother left one legacy. A leather-bound copy of Thomas Moore's "Irish Melodies." The dialogue between living and dead is captured in "O, Ye Dead" . . . which lines I memorized:

> "It is true, it is true, we are shadows cold and wan;
> and the fair and the brave whom we loved on earth are gone; . . .
> That ere, condemn'd we go
> To freeze 'mid Hecla's snow.
> We would taste it awhile and think we live once more! . . ."

I spoke to a fellah who frequented the early morning houses by the docks. He had no doubts about resurrection. According to him, the dead lined up each morning. No conversation. Absolute quiet. An hour after opening, the "curses" took effect and the "dead" indeed came back to alcoholic life.

All through Joyce is the theme of the dead returning. In *Ulysses*, Stephen sees corpses rising from their graves like vampires . . . to deprive the living of the joy. Like the Inland Revenue. "The Dead" begins with a party and ends with a corpse. Like *Finnegan's Wake*, you get the blend of "funferal" and "funeral." America sags under the weight of Joycean study. My own favourite piece of Joycean lore was uttered by his daughter Lucia. Hearing of her father's death she said . . . in disbelief:

> "What is he doing under the ground, that idiot. When will
> he decide to come out? He's watching us all the time."

Who's to say.

I work as a security guard. It's not in preparation for better things. I have no aspirations to act or better myself. The shift system is ideal for my funeral timetable. When I told my father, he laughed.

"It takes you all your time to mind your own business."

Neither of us noted the significance of his next remark.

"Anyway, it's your funeral."

The Weir and Marisa were now indistinguishable. Over the bar, I knew I had to change my behaviour. For the moment I settled for changing my drink.

"A Jameson please?"

A fellah was nodding into his pint. He looked up.

"Did you ever see God?" he asked.

"I'd say you saw him recently," said the barman.

"Fruggit," he said.

A new obscenity or more of the same, but slurred . . . perhaps.

I'd just ordered the coffee. She arrived.

"I got you that," I said.

"Thanks." Whoops, the ice dripped from the gratitude. Murder with manners.

"Will you sit for a minute?" I asked.

"Okay," . . . I had to ignore the tone of sulk. I'd go for broke. I began.

"I like you a lot, but I'm woeful in the beginning. If you could suspend the surface stuff. Bear with me for awhile till you see if mebbe we have something going here. Could you ignore the outside while, as Donne wrote, 'our souls are in negotiation.'"

She smiled. Donne is an unfailing hook. I waited. Fiddled with the nigh on empty glasses. I was on the verge of laying out the gist of Lowry's *Dark as the Grave Wherein My Friend Is Laid*. That nervous I couldn't throw the ole "don't care switch." She spoke. Phew-oh.

"I dunno what to make of you. The most I see of you is your back . . . rushing away. You have me mystified. I'd like to take the chance. I read that funeral thing you gave me so I'm going to ask you the same. Then I'll leave and I'll meet you here on Saturday night. Is that okay?"

I nodded. She gave me a sheet of paper, smiled awkwardly, and left. I read:

"And Dark Rain"

Out of the rain
a suitcase full of show
contains
a sandwich turned
to staler expectations . . . eating
slow
un-relished most
is eaten sat
at but another departure
have put in motion
hurt . . . I feel intense
these hours – lull

of cheered conversation
buzzin' clear, breathin' agonised
"the rain itself was dark"
if you I might part ways
have freed from this
I'd travel . . . whoa
that twice it back again
if you'd be un-affected
stand!
to grant me un-afraid
the moment
in our loss.

And what was I to make of that. "Fruggit," I said and got me another one of them Jameson. Marissa and I would be okay, I reckoned. As long as she kept out of the funerals, we'd have a shot at it.

***

Family!
"Will you come to the house?" she asked.
We were sitting on the Square. Side-steppin' the winos, we'd wrestled a bench from a stray tourist.
"No," I said and said nothing else. Long pause. The winos had put the make on the tourist.
"Is that it . . . blunt and no explanations?" she fumed.
I considered carefully.
"Right."
"Just come once . . . and I'll never ask you again." It was now a point of principle. I had to make a stand. All sorts of un-spoken freedom rested on my not submitting. True to my heritage . . . I said, "Okay."
"What . . . janey mack . . . will I ever understand you . . . cripes, thanks. Call tonight so . . . am . . . at eight."
Dazed . . . she left. The head wino bowed graciously as she passed. Preoccupied, she neglected to give him anything. Her turn towards the town was orchestrated with a hail of abuse. The type that begins, "I know your ould wan," and trails off in spittle and, "God blast all belong to you . . ."
Few have the hallmark in abuse like the Irish. The Americans have an elaborate style which prefaces their obscenities with *mother.* . . . This may be a by-product of a matriarchal society. The essence of their swearing further involves the addition of an initial to various deities as in Jesus H. Christ.
Growing up, two names held complete power. You knew you were in deep stew when an adult described you as a "pup." And the ultimate trouble . . . was when teeth-grit they whispered, "You young pup" . . . you could prepare your will on that.

Second only to this was a "blackguard" used to describe low-life of every type.

A wino sat beside me.

"How-yah," he croaked.

"Fair to middlin,'" I replied.

I knew he wouldn't ask for money as his greeting hadn't included, "Sur."

"We'll hardly get a summer now," he said.

"Right enough," I said.

The fact that it was November was neither here nor there. Neither of us remarked on it. He produced the Cyrus and gave it a fierce wallop. It took him places as he twitched and jerked to silent melodies.

"Ar . . . gh . . . ah . . . orh . . . whee."

I took this to be appreciation of the desired effect. I took my leave and left him to his visions.

I tried not to project the visit to Marisa's home. I owed her on two counts:

1. She hadn't yet mentioned Elton John's dirge "Funeral for a Friend," despite flaunting a battered copy of Genet's *Our Lady of the Flowers.*
2. She hadn't commented on my not commenting. (Dare one Irish phrase it, that this spoke volumes.)

I went to work. I was then the security guard for Traders' new supermarket. The usual mausoleum. My brief was to prevent people borrowing the trolleys. I had yet to apprehend one of these criminals. The chances of so doing were remote. The customers usually greeted me by name. Familiarity here definitely bred conspiracy. The security firm sent a van round on Sunday mornings to collect errant trolleys. The blind-eye arrangement was maintaining us in employment. How bad was Traders hurtin' . . . ?

Being Irish means never having to say you don't know. The accuracy of the reply is purely a wing-shot. Despite the video revolution, going "to the pictures" is still a prerequisite in courtship. I hadn't yet escorted Marisa to them and was mystified as to her bringing me home to meet her parents. This was stage eight, at least, in the game. "Why," I wondered during my shift at Traders. "Dunno," I said as yet another neighbour greeted me and wheeled Traders' finest into a sunset.

Back at my place, I washed slowly and drank quickly. I had a bottle of Metaxa brandy for special occasions. Taste didn't matter. Anything that walloped the back of your eyes like this had to be quality. The vague headache I was entertaining testified to the quantity I was having. Next I'd be humming! I put on a black tie. This was in heavy current use . . . for work and the funerals. I'd miss a funeral today but I could double up on Saturdays. My quota was high . . . what else . . . I hummed.

***

Tear apart
the artificial lines

of ill-defined
communication
would you . . . like
me as much
if
close . . . as in the
nearness of a situation
we had been
– Lord strive
that near related

Blood ties
had brought . . . the
ounce of tolerance
have heard it claimed
as part the heritage
on the birth-right
now obscured
thru pain observed
in Ireland . . . family
have seen
more sure-d-ly
is peace the licence
to . . . to hurt
without the consequences
care?

Care I
a murmer less
to mutter twice
blood is
and it has seemed
to long have been
that thicker is
than sense
I might have known

or broach
the furthered cliché
is
to hurt – sign-full
the ones
you're closest to . . . I think
on that

could only pray
this cliché then, I hadn't understood
a family
to plead the years
thru waste
to plead . . . is given
what is given
un-explained
am better in
the strands of old
denial . . . here
I don't apply

and sure
it is
if it is . . . that far
from what I wish
it might have been
can live
in rough-shaped harmony
with what
it is for now
begin
deliver . . . from myself
an own
with equanimity can't say example
– no
from myself I guess
on illustration.

***

Her family lived in Maunsells Hill. The sort of area where they deposited their rubbish in designer bins. My anticipation wasn't eased by the brass name plate "La Rosario." I rang the bell. Worse . . . chimes, and unless I was badly mistaken, did I detect the strains of "Viva Espana."

Add my Greek-brandied level, and Europe was thriving. Marisa greeted me. There was no effective way of ignoring the chimes. If she'd greeted me in Spanish I'd have fled.

"For whom the bells chime," she said.

There is no reply to that. Her parents were lurking in the sitting room. Tunnel vision helped me block out the various bullfighters and flamenco dancers lining the walls.

"Bill and Irene," said her father.

I'd call them a lotta things. Their Christian names wouldn't be included.

"A drink?"

"Whiskey," said Marisa and shoved what appeared to be half a bucket of it into my hand.

"You're in the Security business," Bill said.

"I am."

"The coming thing," said Bill.

"Tell us about yourself," said Irene.

I knew of few conversation killers to rival this. I took a near-lethal swipe of the whiskey. Marisa was a huge help. She said nothing. Irene produced the photo albums. I was almost relieved. Double vision obliterated the first two volumes. I muttered "Who" . . . "Where" . . . "Surely not" . . . "janey mack" . . . at staggered intervals.

Bill told me about the insurance game. He took as given that I knew nothing, and after a brief background, he recounted his coups across the country.

"You're insured?" he said.

I didn't know in my floating state, did he ask "You're innured" . . . to what . . . to grief . . . did he know about the funerals? The whiskey lashed over the brandy. A supremacy struggle. The upper hand was definitely with the whiskey, and I didn't throw up. I looked at this small plump man in his plump suit. Who the hell was he? I'd read that when you're threatened by a person, try to see the child in them. I concentrated . . . and saw a fat kid in a fat suit.

"I renewed," I said.

Irene was making ferocious hand signals from across the room – to me?

"Do you dwink . . . no . . . am . . . do you drunk yirself?" I asked.

"Never . . . never touch it . . . not a drop . . . nor does my wife. Not that we're against it . . . in moderation."

Would he say it . . . he did!

"Moderation in all things . . ."

I made a gigantic effort.

"Clen . . . clendii . . . dee . . . cleanliness is next to . . . whoa . . . to Giddiness."

A total silence.

"Have you met Raoul?" Irene gasped.

Who the hell was Raoul? In fact, who the hell were these people?

"Raoul is our other child. He's an English language teacher," she persisted, "and Marisa is heartbroken since he left again."

Two thoughts collided. The explanation for "And Dark Rain."

The second thought I verbalized . . . sort of.

"His . . . hiss . . . hiss there a big demand for . . . fur . . . English langua . . . uage here."

Marisa jumped up.

"We have to go."

I was thinking "I'll miss them" when she grabbed my hand. I was half-way down Maunsell Hill before I knew what had happened.

"Jay-sus," she said. "Oh sweet Lord . . . oh God."

"Where's the fune . . . fun . . . the fun-eral?"

Marisa hailed a taxi.

"Where do you live?" she asked.

A long complicated word struggle, as first I had to remember myself. Sharing the information wasn't easy. With the help of the driver we pieced it together.

"Langers," said he. Pist in other words.

The driver helped me into the flat. I offered him tea.

"Well, I wouldn't mind a bit of whatever put you in orbit," he said.

I lashed the last of the Metaxa into a mug. He threw it back.

"Paint off a friggin' gate," he said. "Well, goodnight to ye now."

Marisa was building some form of fatal coffees. I slept. Raging thirst pulled me awake. The flat was dark. A litre of water later, I looked into the bedroom. Marisa was snoring lightly. Between spasms of nausea and remorse, I shuddered beneath the shower. Missing the funerals today was bad, but a line blazed thru my head. "And never to Maunsells Hill go no more."

It was easy to slip quietly into bed. Noise of any volume was pain personified. It crossed my mind that less drunk, I might even now be slipping into Marisa. Drink is a rough mistress. She woke me with a coffee. I felt as if someone had slept – very badly – in me.

"You look like shit," she said.

Ah . . . I thought. Not exactly soothing, but probably accurate enough.

"Well . . ." she said.

I figured this wasn't an enquiry – gentle – into my health.

"I liked the taxi-driver," I said.

"Do you know what you said to my parents?"

Was she insane; sure, wasn't I part-time there? I didn't.

"I'm sorry."

I don't have a hang-up with apologies. I make them unconditionally and let the flak settle where it will.

"My father asked you what you were in. Do you know what you said!" I didn't.

"M . . . m . . . ph . . . not the exact words . . . no."

"Words!" she roared. "Word . . . you said, 'Bits.'

"When he asked later how you're parents are doing . . . you said . . . or worse . . . you slurred, 'Dead, thanks.'"

Sick as I felt there in the bed, I marvelled at my manners.

My stomach shuddered when the coffee hit.

"Good coffee," I ventured.

My mouth wasn't benefitting any better. Marisa was pacing the room. A fine recall she had. Though this perhaps was not the time to compliment it. She continued.

"My mother managed to ignore you dribbling on the photo albums. She even offered to show you Raoul's wedding album . . . and you asked, 'If she had any good mortuary snaps' . . . God above."

I tried to look cowed.

"Well . . . come on, Dillon, what have you to say?" she seethed.

"What I have to say . . . Mau . . . am . . . Marisa, I already said but I guessed you missed it in there. At the beginning it was, and what it was . . . was 'Sorry.'"

Hands on hips, she stared at me. I was impressed with the amount of words I'd strung together. In light of my present state of non-health.

"Okay . . . Dillon. What is it you want from me? What do you bloody want." So I told her.

"Two aspirin."

Var . . . oom . . . hinges off the door. I knew she wasn't gone to seek aspirin. Sometime today I'd have to see Julie. The best friend I had. The only friend I had.

"And there's always Julie," my father used to say. . . . "You could do worse and, knowing you, you probably will."

Parental blessing.

I think I've always known her. She grew up in our street. Despite hidings from her mother, I was the friend she got and kept. At twenty-nine now, I had a year on her and absolutely nothing else. She was 5'1" . . . dark haired, blue eyed, with a strong body as witness to a hard rough life.

"Never show them how they've hurt you," was her total credo. It was said about her that she feared neither man nor God. Brazen was the common judgement. Julie encouraged that. She worked for a travel agency. For three years she'd been based in Greece. Hard years for me. I didn't even have the funerals. She'd married a Greek, and this had lasted two years. Back home she kept her relationships on a fling and fly basis.

I faced a dilemma! If I was to see Julie, I'd miss the 6:15. Could I risk two days without attendance. My post contained the November Dead List. A "Who's Who" of the local dead. Murder erupted in most families with its arrival. Resentments lived far beyond the grave. People were highly indignant about the company they kept . . . even in death. In-laws were a point of bitter feuds. The names of the dead appeared on this list, and masses were said for them. Families were highly sensitive to their names being linked to in-laws they detested. In Ireland the final leveler was regarded as a right chancer. The grim reaper had one hell of a cheek. Cemetery Sunday was the day to flaunt your status among the dead and in front of the living. The weeks prior to this were the busy season for the stone masons. Polish, improve, and sheen them headstones. My father was there, top-tenned. A list he loathed – "Compiled by gombeens for the benefit of gobshites." I put it beneath the only photo of him I possessed . . . he glared as always. I tossed betwixt Julie and the funeral. Julie lost, so I went to see her. The travel agency was the principal eyesore on the main street. Julie took early lunch.

"The pub?" she asked.

"Sure." She wasn't big on the "how-yah doings . . . the how-yah bin." She reckoned you'd get to that. She ordered Guinness and sandwiches. I nursed the drink. The sandwich was out of the question.

"Like that, is it?" she said.

She lit the first of what would be a chain.

"What . . . I'm alrite," she said.

"Dill, you look like you've got religion or AIDS."

"I've been dreaming of my father again. And then this morning, on top of a hangover – ferocious mind you – I got the November Dead List."

She ate some of the sandwich. Another cigarette. I reckoned she was running the Irish belief:

> "If your dead father
> comes to you in a
> dream, he comes for
> bad news. If your dead
> mother comes . . . she
> comes for good news."

"So, any show from your mother?" she asked.

"No."

"Well, let's get to it, Dill. What have you been at. Apart from minding the business interests of the town."

"The funerals . . ."

"I don't want to hear that dead stuff today. Sorry! I just can't get into that. What else? Anything that doesn't stipulate that friggin' black tie of yours."

I finished the Guinness, and my stomach eased. Not a whole lot, but the broken glass feel was ebbing. I told her about Marisa. The slight up-step in health encouraged me. The Maunsell Hill visit came out, including Marisa's version of it. Julie whistled . . . low. I got some more Guinness.

"Okay, Dill. Do you want some advice, comfort, or a decent lashing?"

"A smatterin' of them all," I said.

She knocked the colour off the second Guinness. The head went way down. The cigarette took a hammering. Time to die.

"O-kay, Eddie. . . ." I knew from the rare mention of my Christian name that this was serious business.

"This funeral crack is weirding you out. You won't tell me what's involved there. How much do I want to know, I ask myself. Most of the time the lights are out inside your head. You're getting to be one strange fellah. I don't care if you keep chasing the kinda women who put the 'R' back into reptilian. Will you come round to me after you've finished work?"

"I will."

We sipped the Guinness dregs. I took one of her cigarettes. Her eyebrow raised a touch. She knew the crucified battle I had to quit. It tasted woeful. Thank God . . . nip back up on the cross for a spell.

I managed to get to work. The draw towards a dedicated piss-up teased and shimmered. The funerals would take a drastic beating then. Work it had to be. I bought the pack of cigarettes without too much of a struggle. Before hitting out that evening, I coerced myself to get some food down. Two eggs on a base of chili beans . . .

hot as I could raise them. When I got to Julie's, I'd be fit to kill for a beer. Whatever state the eggs had been in, they sat in dismay in my bewildered system. My breath would oil hinges. Only as I prepared to leave did I notice the small yellow envelope . . . match the eggs I thought.

> *"Sorry . . . will you meet me on Friday at 8? I'll wait on the Weir Bridge. Love in warmth, Marisa."*

The makings of a haiku, her . . .

> eggs in chili
> love in warmth
> Now . . . beat well.

I passed O'Malley outside a pub. He was footless. He muttered a string of obscenities, and I'm not positive, but I thought I recognised "Bollix" in there somewhere.

I smiled in what I think they call fellowship. I figured he was not the person to lay my haiku on. I think the seventeen-syllable requirement might have thrown him. Julie answered on the first ring. She was wearing a grey faded track-suit. Dressed to run, I thought.

"Beer or what?" she asked.

"Oh, beer, I'm chili-d out."

She handed me a stein . . . relic of her travels, and I gave her Marisa's note. She snorted. I drank – deep. I repeated the haiku. "That's atrocious," she said. The note . . . the haiku? Both I guess.

"I have Chesterton for you," she said. I read:

> "There are no words to express the abyss between isolation
> and having one ally. It may be conceded to the mathemati-
> cians that four is twice two is two thousand times one."

She sat on the floor where I had half-folded. Her hand moved along the inside of my thigh. Just that and I was sparked. I kissed the top of her head . . . fresh washed hair . . . lemon fragrance. She eased the zipper on my jeans, and her hand went inside. I moved direct to ready.

"You're sure ready?" she said.

I turned and she lay back. Sliding the tracksuit bottom off, she gave a rare and rarer smile.

In Irish style, we got to bed after. I sat, half-propped with beer, a cigarette, and Julie . . . not necessarily in that order.

"Care," she said, "is the difference between sex and making love."

"I'll have me some of that."

To maintain the edge I smoked . . . and whacked down a week's worth of beer.

"When a woman asks you what you're thinking about, especially in bed, always

– get that ALWAYS – reply 'I'm thinking about you, dear.' Stick relentlessly to it. Bearing this seriously in mind Dillon, what are you now thinking of?"

I ran the limited replies a bit. I wanted to tell her the only requirement for a haiku was your quality hangover. I said, "I'm thinking of you."

"And . . . did you want to add anything?"

"Oh right . . . dear."

"You know, Dillon, I odd times think you might be the only company I need . . . and that's got to be real close to love."

"As close as you might need."

"But . . ."

But! My heart lurched. Even the beer sagged. What's this "but" crap. Yer shot of pathetic fallacy . . . lean heavy on the ole pathetic.

"The truth is . . . I can live without you . . . in Greece. I thought of you all the time but abstracted. You're a deep vital part of me, but you don't of necessity have to be part of my life."

I lit some fags. The psychic kick to the cobblers. Nicotine seemed a kind alternative. What I was thinking was, you callous bitch. I hated her full then. The pure hatred nurtured on love. Accept no other. I nearly hummed, "My Sentimental Friend." Go for broke. I reached for her breast. The love we made was slow and with more tenderness than I'd ever now concede. The cigarettes burned slower in the ashtray. Without care, they burned regardless.

Before she slept she asked, "What are you thinking of, my love?"

I stretched with what must have appeared total contentment.

No contest.

"I'm thinking of you, dear . . ."

She chuckled way down in her throat.

The refrain played a long time as she slept. It whispered cruel – sex is . . . is sex . . . sex is.

Julie hadn't a whole lot of say in the morning; I had less.

"Will you meet yer wan on Friday?"

"Yeah."

"I've got to meet a fellah . . . how about a double date?"

Was she mad! Flick the range of morning melodramas. Reply with the lash:

1. Screw you lady.
2. I'd rather borrow money from O'Malley.
3. What the hell – is the hell going on with you.

To prepare myself, I spooned the dead eggs before me . . . go. "Fine . . . see you in The Weir at 8:30."

We left the flat without any post mortems. No fuss. Wasn't it grand to be free of the kiss on the cheek . . . the "Have a nice day, dear" rigamarole. I didn't mention I was going to be in fine time for the 9:15. At the canal, Julie said, "Bye." I said much the same. Would a morsel of warmth be so dangerous. I looked at the Chesterton

plaque she'd given me. High above the water, I hurled it. I didn't wait to see it hit.
My closest friend. Close . . . yeah.

***

"Close"

Age
itself is solving . . . most
the dreams
I'd longed for . . . bad . . . and
fear
of course ensures
the present ambitions
elusive do remain . . . that
close
I've been
to knowledge – I evaded
all my skirmished life – on
near
is near enough
for what
I'd need to know.

***

My hangovers had an echo of Samuel Pepys about them. While watching a
living man about to be castrated and disemboweled, he said, "The man was looking
as cheerful as any man could do in that condition." I felt that kind of cheerfulness.

The 9:15 was a small affair. The deceased was an old-age pensioner. The casket
was open. I looked long into the dead face. Shriveled and decrepit. Of the small
crowd, maybe four of the people actually knew him. A man, remarkably similar to
the corpse, tugged my arm.

"Did you know oul Kearns?"

"Yes." In the grave tone.

"He was a sour oul bastard, the same fellah."

"M . . . m . . . ph," I mumbled.

Decipher that, you wasted fart.

"He was a blow-in – he's from Kildare."

Not any more, I nearly said. The death hadn't caused any furor in Kildare.
Come to the West and get yerself a begrudged send-off. The coffin was closed, and
we shambled towards the door. Let's go Mr. Kearns. . . .

***

22

The manager of the clothes department in Traders dropped dead that afternoon. In the fruit section. They didn't appreciate that. He had no business down there. A massive stroke threw him across the vegetables. During the confusion, the clothing department was nigh-on cleaned out of its winter woolens. Those shoplifters nearly ran me down as woolen-laden they headed for the hills.

I was to guard the body 'till an ambulance arrived. The manager had been a Dubliner. Dead among the cabbages, I noticed his socks were from Dunnes. What a betrayal . . . and him in the clothing section, too. Mind you, he was in a no-win position on every level. If he'd been wearing the Traders brand, they'd say he'd stolen them. The fruit section staff had gone to the pub. Grief has to be liquified. I wondered if they'd jettison the cabbages. They were a sick-looking collection, though. I guess the corpse wasn't doing anything to enhance the presentation.

The suit appeared to be a Penney's pin-stripe. Some years ago Penney's had a super sale on these, and did that item move . . . Jeez . . . oh. They had a particular sheen. A snag was that every tinker in the town had invested in them. T'was rumoured that even the beggar on the Weir Bridge sported one as he made his pitch. No matter how much you paid for such a suit now, be it gilt-tailored or not, it was seen as a Penney's special. It didn't matter a rat's ass to me what a person wore. I did feel that he might have lain in some dignity in any other type of clothes.

The ambulance arrived, and when the doctor finished, they hauled him off. One of the attendants winked at me and slipped some oranges into his jacket. The store closed early, and we were asked to try and show for the funeral. Good grief! A legitimate reason to attend a funeral. I didn't know if this one could be notched up in the total. On the way home, I kept seeing the dead manager. His suit looked as if he'd finally disappointed it.

I decided I'd get a mass for the manager. I dropped into The Old Franciscan church. They gave masses at the old rates and V.A.T. hadn't yet featured. The Jesuits now were right up alongside inflation. You could call them Jack and Tom . . . your buddies, so to speak. You'd be sure of a modern, sparkling mass and a right good whack out of your wallet. The only thing the Franciscans called was your bluff. You still had to call them "Father." Confession was the wallop and skelping form. None of the sacrament of reconciliation for them. You took the licks and got the blast of forgiveness. The other crowd, they'd hold your hand, dispense understanding, and apply the probation act.

Father Benedictus came out to see me. He was nearing eighty, gruff and fearsome.

"Wot do you want . . . I was in the middle of me dinner. . . ."

That it was four in the afternoon mattered not at all.

"Would you sign a mass card for me, Father?"

"Is it yerself, young Dillon . . . are you not at school."

"Finished for the day, Father."

He peered at the name.

"Who's this fellah?"

"A manager up at Traders."

"He's not from town?"

"No, Father . . . he's . . . am . . . was . . . a Dubliner."

"Smart-alecs them crowd, they know everything. They'd lift the eyetooth outa yer head . . . you couldn't watch them. And dirty footballers, too."

I didn't feel a comment was required for any of this. So I didn't offer one. I had heard the same tirade from him with regard to the English . . . and Northern Irish . . . and Nuns.

He signed the card, and I handed him the toll. I'd put a pack of Afton with it. Strong, unfiltered, and basic cigarettes . . . to match his faith. We both acted as if I hadn't.

"How's yer father?"

"Am . . . he's doing as well as can be expected."

"A martyr for the drink. It will kill him. You tell him that for me. Do you hear me!"

It would have been hard not to. He was roaring like a bull. I was about to leave when he grabbed my arm.

"I hear great things about that drink crowd . . ."

"The Pioneers?"

"Ary not them lunatics . . . the A.A. fellahs. Alcoholics Anonymous."

He was lost in thought. What's he seeing I wondered. Tee-totaling nuns on a football pitch perhaps. He returned . . . his hand rooted deep in the folds of his brown habit.

"Give this to your father," he said. And he headed back for his dinner. I looked at what he'd given me. A silver Saint Jude medal. The patron saint of hopeless cases.

My father would have appreciated the grim humour. Weaving through the winos, I slipped into the public toilets on the Square. I fitted Saint Jude onto the chain Julie had sent me from Greece. Emerging with this new protection, I was besieged by winos.

"Gawd bless ya, sur . . . have you a few coppers, sur . . . and a happy Christmas to all belong to you."

Under such a concentrated assault, I parted with a few bob. They clapped me on the back, shook my hand. If I was to receive half of what they wisht me, I could run for local office. Jude ruled indeed.

Julie's father was in that A.A. He was a drinking partner of my father's in the old days. A taxi-driver. I knew he hadn't touched a drop for five years. On impulse I walked to the taxi-rank . . . he was there.

"How are you doing, Mr. Brady?" I said.

"Well be the holy! Young Dillon, how are you son?"

"I'm fine, Mr. Brady. I wonder if mebbe you had time for a drink . . . oops . . . I mean . . . am, a tea . . . you know."

He smiled . . . a little sadly, I thought.

"Wotever, Dillon, I'm due a coffee break. Let's go over to The Central."

Nice compromise, I thought. A hotel was neutral ground. We got a pot of coffee, and I the shock of my life at the price of it. I tried to pay, but he wouldn't hear of it. I didn't struggle. I could have kept a wino for a week in blessings with the money. Mr. Brady looked marvelous. He had to be over sixty but he looked forty. There was a glow in his face, and the eyes were hopping with vitality. I had seen those eyes leap with lunacy in the days he beat Julie's mother along the length of our street. In the old days, as I said.

"Any sign of the young wan?" he asked.

Julie. I took it for what it was. They weren't reconciled. Again, the flash of sadness in the eyes. I did the verbal dance of saying a lotta stuff and meaning nothing. He got that.

"Was there a specific idea you wanted to kick around?" he asked.

"I wondered . . . well, would your A.A. have saved my father?"

He poured some more coffee. The caffeine hit. My heart-beat moved way up. How much did I want to get into this area.

"Your father didn't want to quit. I tried to talk to him. In my own case, I just couldn't continue. I didn't give up drink . . . it gave up on me. I was sick and tired of being sick and tired."

"Do you miss it?"

"No, drink is great for removing stains . . . did you know that?"

I didn't . . . and said . . . "I didn't."

"Oh yeah. It will also remove your clothes, your wife, your health, your home, your sanity. Alcohol is the great remover."

I was tempted to laugh. I didn't know whether I should. I didn't know this man at all and I'd known him all my life.

"What about yourself, Dillon . . . any problems with the bottle?"

Did I? None I was gonna admit to. Okay, I felt threatened.

"No."

"If you ever want to talk . . . about anything, at any time, here's a number where you can find me."

"Thank you."

We stood up. A total air of calm characterised him.

"You know, Dillon, despite all the things you may have seen your father do, he loved you more than anything else."

I couldn't think of any reply to that. He asked quietly, "Do you believe that?" I didn't know.

"I dunno." He smiled.

"That's honest, anyway."

We parted there. Him in his calm and me in bits.

Near my flat I ran into a band of young tinkers. More thug than itinerant. Bands of these were a recent phenomenon, and they roved the town in part-time terror. Encircled, the chief thug stood before me.

"Give us a cigarette," he demanded.

"I don't smoke," I said.

We had us the eye-balling fandango. He shrugged and led his reptiles away. The blast of fear rooted me to the path. It wasn't 'till I felt the sharp pain that I noticed the cigarette which had burned the fingers of my right hand. Phew . . . oh . . . God, I said, very quietly. Time for a re-run of some "Dirty Harry" movies.

In the flat I looked at the empty Metaxa bottle. Julie's father or otherwise, I'd have lit into it (if it had been carrying). I checked my funeral timetable as recompense. I'd the Traders manager's funeral in the morning. With the word-association in full flight, I looked to see had I any fruit. I took an early night. The best solution to some days is to cancel them. I ran the thug scene by myself one more time. My father applied an inflexible maxim. "Kick before you are kicked. Wallop before you are walloped. ALWAYS retaliate FIRST." I thought about the lines I was attempting to write for him. At his sickest, mangled in a hangover, he'd look like an undertakers dream and mutter, "Winter waits." The bareness of his eyes discouraged enquiry. I'd nurture a hate. It didn't float. Then I'd try to build towards a flat indifference. I couldn't get a handle on that either.

"What the hell are you looking at?" he'd roar.

"Not bloody much," I wanted to roar right back. But I never did. At fifteen years of age, I'd sat with him on one of these mornings. I watched as he tried to put a shakin' cup to his lips. I'd said, "Can I hold it for you." A mighty back hand slap had lifted me out of the chair. Retaliate first. A practical application.

At school, I hadn't learned a whole lot. I was never tortured with "what was I going to be." I had trouble enough with "what I was." I remembered a word from French lessons. The sound of it hooked deep. It was the word of a nightmare. That night I had me one . . . a beauty of a "cauchemar." My father and old Father Benedictus were walking behind my funeral. I was sitting up in the hearse trying to get their attention. "Be quiet," they said. "Do one thing right in your life." At the cemetery, my grave was lined with cabbages, and I was dressed in the Penney's suit. "You didn't drink half enough," whispered Mr. Brady. "I'll give him no Benediction," said Father Benedictus. The band of thugs were kicking the coffin – "Come out – we know you have cigarettes . . ." I woke drenched in sweat. No Benediction. I looked on the bedside table. No cigarettes either.

***

"Benediction"

Never believed
in such as blessings
were
you threw
a make un-helped
upon the day . . . and
help available
was how you helped
yourself . . . a crying
down

to but a look in caution – stayed alert
reducing always towards
the basic front
in pain
– never
– never the once
to once admit
you floundering
had to be
such Gods as crost
your mind . . . if God
as such it could have been
you never took
to vital introspection
. . . He'd have an urgent set
of other obligations
such it was
from you
did know
the very first
in steps belief – form
framing
every reprimand
you ever force-full
gave.

***

The Traders funeral was huge. The store was closed for the day. A Friday! Phew-oh-d. A major trading one. Most of the mourners were dressed in Traders best. Less a mark of identification with the deceased as more the result of a late November sale.

I spotted some of the shop-lifters, and they looked appropriately grieved. He had been lax to prosecute offenders and was thus a huge loss to the thieving fraternity.

I hit the Square, and a rib must have broken in the devil. A shard of wintered sun. Cold of course but the illusion was sustaining. The bench there was vacant. I enjoyed the sight of the Bank clerks hurrying to their lunch. What an air of young gravity they worked for. A few more years, and they'd have the dead mackerel expression complete. Try getting them to a funeral. Their lives were geared to mutterings of grief on a daily basis.

A shadow fell. The head wino. I knew him as Padraig. The usual rumours beset him. He was supposedly from a good family. He was

a teacher

> a lawyer
> a brain surgeon
> a lapsed genius

As long as I'd known him, he was in bits and fond of the literary allusion. Today, he was but semi-pist. "And greetings to you my young friend. Are we perchance pertaining of the late winter solstice. . . ."

I smiled and gave him a cigarette. The tremoring of his hand we both ignored. He was about 5'5" in height, emaciated, with a mop of dirty white hair. The face was a riot of broken blood vessels, swollen now. The nose was broken, and more than once. Blue, the bluest eyes you'd ever get . . . underlined in red, of course. Ordinance surveyed. He mutilated the cigarette to get rid of the filter-tip. He smoked deeply of what remained.

"Well, young fellow, forgive me for the desecration of your cigarette."

"No mind, my father did the same."

"A man of subtlety and taste. Was he not?"

"He had his moments."

"One deduces from the use of the past tense that he's no longer with us – or worse – in England."

"Dead . . . he's dead."

At the top of his lungs, Padraig began to sing. Startling the absolute wits out of me.

> "Blindly, blindly at last do
> we pass away."

I looked furtively 'round, hoping he was through. He ate deep from the cigarette and in a cloud of nicotine . . . he bellowed:

> "But man may not linger
> for nowhere
> finds he repose . . ."

He paused and I jumped in.

"Will you stop if I give you money?"

He laughed, showing two yellowed teeth, the rest, obviously, were casualties of combat.

"Indeed I will."

I gave him a quid.

"Young man, you could have left, it would have been the wiser course in the financial fashion."

"I like it here."

"Pithy . . . you are not a man who gives away a lot . . . a lot, that is, in the knowledge department. What you have to say has the qualities of brevity and clarity."

Before I could reply to this, briefly or clearly, he was assailed with a series of gut-wrenching coughs. Up came phlegm and various un-identifiable substances. I gave him a handkerchief. He used it to dry him steaming eyes.

"I am indebted to you, my young friend. It has been many the mile since I was offered a fellow pilgrim's hanky. Might we indulge in a further spot of nicotine."

We did . . . I said, "Your accent is hard to pin down."

"Like a steady income, it has an elusive quality . . . not to mention effusive."

There was no reply to this. I didn't even try.

"At one dark era in my existence I was, I believe, from the countryside of Louth. Are you at all familiar with that barren territory?"

I had no intention of telling him of my mother. None! I said, "My mother is buried in it."

"A burden for any crat-ure. May The Lord Bless Her. She'll need all the comfort available in that forsaken land."

My concentration was focused on not talking like him. It was highly contagious. He rooted deep in his coat, a heavy tweed battered number. Lightin'! Lightin' with the dirt, as they say. Out came a brown bottle.

"A touch of biddy perhaps," he said.

He wiped the neck with the clean end of my hanky and offered it. I took a cautious swig. Ar . . . gh . . . oh God. Red Biddy, meths, and sherry! My eyes felt reversed and a punch like bad luck side-swept my stomach. It got your attention . . . fast. He nigh on drained it when I passed it back with no apparent ill-effects . . . no iller than he habitually was at any rate. Relief being how you drink it mebbe. He said, "The only advice I remember is it's better be lucky than good. . . ."

"And are you?"

"What?"

"Lucky." He laughed deep.

"It has been a long time, anyway, since I was any good. Whatever that means."

Across the square, we saw a bunch of winos emerge from the toilets. Padraig shook himself in artificial energy.

"My young friend . . . my people await me . . . perchance we'll talk again."

"I'd like that."

Not wild enthusiasm, but a certain tone of approval.

"I bid you adieu, and if I am to pray again I will mention your mater in the wilderness of Louth."

The next time I saw Padraig, he was close to Louth himself.

***

I got to The Weir at eight. Marisa was waiting. She was clad in skin-close denim jeans, a heavy grey sweat shirt, and a maroon leather coat. Just right for the drug crowd who infested this pub at weekends. The serious drinkers retreated to the pubs below the Square. She looked delighted . . . to see me?

"How are you, Dillon?"

Energetic joy always throws me.

"I'm doing okay. What will you drink?"

"A snowball." . . . in hell?

The Weir management knew their weekend trade. The barman had an earring and the attitude to match. Fixing his sneer, he fixed his attention to a point beyond my shoulder.

"Pint of Guinness, a Jameson, and . . . am . . . a snowball . . ."

"With a cherry?"

I was caught. I ran the range of immediate trade-offs. No. Too easy. At the same time, I reckoned I better get the ground rules down. He'd spew all over submissiveness.

"Yeah . . . but not in the Guinness."

He got it. Raised his eyes to mine. For a second, I felt I was my father's son. He got the drinks.

Marisa gave me a devastating smile. Was she smoking the weed?

"I missed you. . . ."

"What! Was I late?"

"No . . . no. I mean yesterday and, yes, today, too."

She was definitely on something. Who talks like that.

"Julie is going to join us and one of her suitors." Was I now talking like her.

"Oh marvelous. She's your friend . . . isn't she?"

I downed a quart of Guinness. Sour. Bolt it in place with a wallop of Jameson. Better. I hoped Julie would arrive . . . soon. Marisa did whatever it is you do with snowballs. The best you can, I guess. Julie arrived, looking wonderful. She had a knee-length denim skirt . . . Aran sweater and a sailors reefer jacket. The jacket had the soft worn appearance that money can sometimes buy. Her boots would have cost my week's salary . . . with overtime. A tall blond-haired guy held her hand. The type whom Woody Allen says "takes handsome lessons." Good teeth, good build, good clothes. Good grief!

We did the introductions. Julie's friend was Robbie. I got a round of drinks. Vodka for Julie and vodka for Robbie. Indeed a twosome. More stout and whiskey and a snowball for Marisa. There wasn't any way that repetition made that drink more accessible. The earring took the cherry as given a slight suggestion that hash now appeared. Julie did that scene sometimes. I liked my drug wet and in a glass. Preferably in a lotta glasses. But . . . there it is. The three were brisk in conversation.

"These are double vodkas," yelled Robbie.

"Yeah," I said.

"Here's looking at you, kid." He toasted Julie.

Now, what could I do. I got deep buried in my own drink. When in perplexity, run like hell. Spare me the Bogart drivel.

"Have you known Dillon long?" Julie asked.

"M . . . m . . . h . . ." from Marisa.

The aim of conspiracy she launched blended with the hash. I offered the cigarettes. As I expected – Robbie didn't. I waited for the inevitable and it came.

"Don't you know how dangerous smoking is?"

"I have a feeling you might be about to tell me."

He looked to Julie. She said

"Do you work, Maura."

"It's Marisa . . . actually, I'm hoping to be a teacher."

"Of what?"

"What . . . oh I see, well I was thinking of Montessori."

"Why?"

"Am . . . I want to do something fulfilling."

"Ah . . . the 'Total Woman.'"

Marisa to here had drank viciously from the snowball. T'would take something more lethal than that to stop Julie.

"*The Total Woman* . . . I have a copy. I haven't actually read it. Is it absorbing?"

"I dunno, I haven't read it."

Julie produced the black book and a wad of notes. Irish style, it was an indeterminate wad of bruised notes. All denominations. I saw a hint of drachmae in there. She pushed a flutter at Robbie.

"Get the drinks in . . . keep the vodkas doubled . . . Dillon will have the same and another yellow thing for Maire. . . yeah?"

"Oh yes please . . . and . . . am . . . it's M-A-R-I-S-A."

The black book was Julie's catch all philosophy. She'd had it for years and wrote in whatever grabbed her. Kazantzaki featured heavily, Cavafy usually took pride of place. I had once offered some Emily Dickinson and she'd withered me. If I wanted to talk American women poets, she'd said, go find Anne Sexton. I was working on it. It could have been worse. I'd nearly offered Sylvia Plath . . . phew-oh.

Robbie arrived back – beaming.

"Ted works here," he said.

Not receiving the ecstacy this warranted, he continued.

"Ted Joyce, he's working part-time here . . . we were at college together."

The Earring. It figured. The lash rose in me . . . did they take perhaps cordon bleu together. Julie shot me a look. I passed. Pity.

"What do you do, Robbie?" asked Marisa.

"I'm an articled clerk . . . at Boyd's."

Ol' Ted took English Lit. Took it where, I wondered. A long standing insult down our street was "You dirty article." I didn't need to look at Julie. I passed here again. Julie found the quote.

"Listen to this, Marcy."

Marisa was snowballing and missed the chance to give her name again. Julie read:

> "High up in the mountains of Crete, it sometimes happens a
> milk-sop is born into a family of ogres. The father is at a loss.
> How can this . . . this jelly-fish be his son? He gathers the
> family. 'This son is a disgrace. What can we do with him? He

can't be a fighter, shepherd or a thief, he's a disgrace."

Julie took a hefty belt of vodka. If not exactly enthralled, we certainly looked attentive. Julie concluded:

"He's a disgrace. Let's make him a teacher."

Robbie spoke first. "That reminds me of a joke . . . there was . . ."
"For chrissake," said Julie.
He shut up. Marisa went to the ladies. The Earring gave Robbie a shout. Julie snapt the book shut. I asked, "So Julie, how do you like Marisa."
I got the Emily D. look. "She says '*actually*' a lot . . . I can see you're taken with Robbie too – "
"Well Julie, I've been thinking of getting an earring . . . actually . . ."
"Do . . . and I'll help you put it thru your nose."
Truce . . . of sorts.
"In fact, Dillon, I have something of interest for you . . . Listen . . . listen to this . . . are you ready?"
"What's ready, I'm interested – okay . . . is it something about Greek security guards?"
Julie gave the bleak smile.

"The dead have their own sad grammar
– he was
– he said
– he did . . .
Poor young man, thinned to a single tense . . ."

I had some whiskey, ah that sucker was sliding down slow and ferocious. I gave what she said some consideration. Why not, I thought. I was near through with my time of Julie affirmations.
"Well, I think people are stupid by a tense alright. But it's not the past. Most people I know are crucified by the future . . . how the hell they're gonna get by. How to pay for things. Most funerals these days, I hear less and less of grief and more of the expense of dying . . . a costly business."
Julie looked furious.
"The funerals . . . His cock-swalloping funerals. You're gonna have to give up that garbage. . . ."
In her tirade, she took a slug of the snowball.
"Oh Gawd, am I poisoned? What the hell is this . . . yellow Biddy . . . Aher . . . gh . . ."
Marisa arrived back to see Julie apparently swiping her drink.
"Nice, isn't it?" she said.
"Yeah . . . so are funerals," Julie rasped.

Robbie came with a tray of drinks. "My shout," he said.

So shout, I thought. I was well the worse for drink now. I took off for the toilet. An indication of my condition was a friendlied roar I hurled at the Earring. He glared. The toilet was a hive of industry. The drug dealing has its centre in a fitting place.

Gurteen was centre toilet. A fellah my own age. He was 5'2" with eyes as black as his attitude. A victim of the peroxide craze, the hair was a sick yellow . . . long and lank. There wasn't a pick on him. He looked like a worm-fumbling crow. A particularly vicious one, he was one of the few very dangerous people I knew.

Even my father had said, "Don't turn your back on the fellah, particularly when he smiles. . . ."

When Gurteen smiled you could believe there was indeed a hell. Such as the old priests preached. Gurteen wasn't so much headed towards it as on an extended sabbatical from there. Solely by virtue of the length of time we'd known each other, he was "fond" of me. Fond if snakes can be credited with fondness. A small-time dealer in drugs of every strength, he greeted me.

"Dillon . . . you wanna score?"

"Naw, I'm doing fast and furious on the drink."

"Yeah . . . a piss-head, that's o-kay, I like to get maggoty meself . . . I hear you've moved in on the money . . ."

"What?"

"Maunsell's Hill; the Darcy one . . . Martha or whatever she calls herself. A bitch in her heart that one. . . ."

He paused to give a small envelope to a zonked client. A flash of notes showed . . . he gave me an indefinable look then continued.

"Do you know her brother?"

"Raoul."

"That's him . . . a bolix but quare as a Kerry sixpence."

"Odd – you mean . . . is he odd . . . or wot?"

"Jaysus, cop on, Dillon . . . *gay* . . . he likes it Greek style . . . you know what I'm saying."

"I didn't know . . . I didn't."

"Isn't that more of it, Dillon, you're always the last to know . . . do you want some speed . . . no charge."

"No . . . no thanks . . . I'll be seeing you . . . no, wait . . . will you take a look at a fellah who's here with Julie . . . Robbie, he's called."

"Give Julie my love, that wan would kill for you, Dillon . . . go on, you're not the worst. I'll let you know about yer man."

I tried to remember that what you got from Gurteen's smile was a view of his teeth. Anything above that carried a price. I'd felt warmer looking at the corpses in the morgue.

"Gurteen sends his . . . acknowledgements," I said to Julie.

"Who's he?" asked Robbie.

"A part-time psychopath," Julie said.

"And the rest of the time . . ." from Marisa.

"The rest of the time you don't want to know about. He used to hang out with your brother Saul."

"Raoul."

"Let me tell you, it's many the one perished on that rock."

Was I very pist or was Julie mixing a heavy batch of metaphors here . . . a heavy mix of aggravation if nowt else.

"Let's go Chinese," chirped Robbie.

"He means . . . do ye want to eat?" said Julie.

We jumped on this with way over the top enthusiasm. At the door, I felt my arm tugged . . . Gurteen.

"He's Robbie Fox . . . a gay . . . so tis easy three to one that you'll have company of some description in that bed of yours tonight. Oh yeah, I read today that bi-sexuality is socially okay . . . okay!"

Inscrutability is the Chinese byword. Our only Chinese restaurant has moved into active hostility.

Surliness with impeccable subtlety. The waiter dealt us four slow menus and a slower sneer.

Julie is in her element with strife. Being pist helped. She rattled off a crescendo of numbers. The waiter had to check twice. Some Oriental respect might perhaps have hit his eyes. We sat before Julie like children, indeed of a highly temperamental God. She said . . . "I ordered a rake of stuff, it's bound to have something ye all like, and I threw in two bottles of Beaujolais."

Robbie asked for chopsticks. Now how did I know he'd do that.

The waiter brought the wine. No pretence of tasting or pouring.

"Are you familiar with the I-Ching?" asked Marisa.

Julie snorted.

"Oh yes, I do it on a daily basis," said Robbie. I refrained from asking if it was some breed of Oriental dog.

"Did it tell you to be a montesorry – ?"

"Am . . . that's Monte-sorri . . . am . . . !"

Open bloodshed was deferred with the food. Plates and plates. Chop suey this, chow mein of sundry descriptions . . . bamboo shoots, curtain rails, rice, sweet and sour porks, all served with resentment if not panache.

Robbie flourished the chopsticks. The waiter flourished condescension.

Waving a chopstick in my face, he said, "I believe you attend funerals . . ." I was stunned. I looked to Julie who was opening a Chinese cookie.

"Confucius say, 'Shut your mouth, asshole.'"

Marisa spilt her Beaujolais over the mess before her soy sauce was available . . . but . . . !

"Yeah . . . yeah, I find them gay affairs," I said.

"Seems like a sick pastime to me."

"No . . . not sick . . . it's well past that stage; it's a dead pastime."

"Can't be a whole lot going in your life, is what I think."

I took a ferocious hammer of wine. My father would have taken the chopsticks and put them where they would forever have remained lodged. Some vestige of control tried to surface. The wine said, "The hell with it." Marisa said nothing.

"Well, Robbie, you consult the I-Ching, so you're familiar with the oracle of changes – resting on coins – "

"Yeah . . . so!"

"So why don't you and me toss for the bill, to sweeten it, I'll put a straight twenty alongsides!"

"Am . . . I dunno, can you afford to do that?"

"Can you afford not to?" asked Julie.

"Look, Robbie. It's more civilised than me asking you outside and wallopin' the living be-jaysus out of each other."

"Okay, the bill and twenty quid. Let Julie toss . . . I'll take heads."

He didn't put the money on the table. I put a new crisp note down. That's the way I was reared – foolish.

Julie took a coin, cleared the centre of the table. A flick high and slow. Marisa gulped wine. *Thunk* . . . nigh flat down . . . tails. I picked my money up.

"You're some latch-crow," he said.

"Does that mean I get paid?"

"I'm going to have to owe you the money . . . but I'll pay this bill . . . okay . . . is that okay guys . . . yeah . . . fair enough?"

"Well, Robbie, tis not the question of okay or not. . . tis – do you pay on bets? Let's go, Marisa . . ."

We stood up. The waiter brought the bill. Julie looked at it and her eyes lit . . . huge.

I was holding the door for Marisa when Robbie shouted something.

"What did he say?" she asked.

"I'm not altogether certain, but it sounded like 'baulox.'" She suggested my flat. I stopped en route to buy a bottle of Jameson. From my winnings you could say. The rain was lashing, cold . . . dark, and I felt . . . felt bedraggled inside. I gave her the makings of a dry tracksuit. She tried to fit into that, and I built some big hot whiskeys. I even had faded cloves. Whoa-hay, whack in the sugar, the cloves . . . no lemon . . . no problem . . . get that water hot . . . right . . . now put a normal sized whiskey outa your head. Lash in mad amounts. Gotta paste it. Now big mugs. Taste. Phew-oh, that's the kick. So who's bedraggled. A shot more and mebbe us can get into realms of befuddlement. Cruising home. I bring the mugs to the bedroom. She's sacked out in my battered sweat-shirt – going thru my books.

"You're very close to the canal here."

"Yeah, you can think of me lying here listening to the wino's roar."

"Is that a quote?"

"A Joyce mutilation – "

"I love Joyce."

The temptation was enormous. . . what do you love about him . . . but I'd had my tails streak already. Best not to lean on that luck. I said, "Cheers."

"Oh right . . . slainte . . . there's an awful lot of Hemingway here."

"Yes there is."

"I suppose you love all that . . . strut . . . and yes, all that macho stuff."

Ah . . . u . . . d, the whiskey chunneled down in a weltor of sugar and . . . did I swallow a clove? Who cared. My eyes moved into overdrive. I figured she'd been reading *Cosmopolitan*. Sure it heightened your awareness. So did hot whiskey . . . then the sugar kinda blinded your subtlety. Time to reply.

"No."

"What?"

"No, I don't . . . I like A *Movable Feast*."

"Will you teach me about him?" Was she lisping.

"What! . . . what's to teach. You read his books. You like or you don't like the way he writes. You get something from his view of the world . . . or you don't. That's what there is to learn. What I can tell you of real significance is nearer home."

"Oh please . . . tell me!"

"It's smart to drink hot whiskey when it's hot!"

. . . she did . . . and how, she knocked back a whack that my father would have had a cure from.

"Whee . . . ee . . . h . . . oh Dillon, that's lovely. Cripes, you read a lot of American writers. Do you like them a lot."

"Lemme show you something." I weaved towards the bookcase. I wasn't hurting now – at all. It took me some time to locate Ross Macdonald. I kept forgetting what I was seeking.

"Here it is. *The Ivory Grin* . . . written in 1952. He's describing an American woman. Listen to this:

> 'There were olive drab thumbprints under her eyes. Maybe
> she had been up all night. After all in my case, she looked
> fifty, in spite of the girlishness and boyishness.
> Americans never grow old; they died; and her eyes had
> guilty knowledge of it.'"

I forgot then why I was sharing this. Marisa forgot too.

"Do you want to sleep with me, Dillon"

"I do."

She stood and pulled off the track suit.

The whiskey receded a moment, and I didn't know – was it Julie before me. I said nothing. Then the whiskey got back to its mission. I moved close to her, and we forgot Ross Macdonald, Hemingway, Robbie, Chinese waiters . . . the whole shower.

***

Waking . . . on the better site of intimacy, we had gotten to the bed. A hangover hadn't yet decided on its strength. Marisa stirred. I lit a cigarette. Oh God, luck.

"What are you thinking about, Dillon?"

"I'm thinking about you, dear."

She smiled, deep. But there'd be more. Had to be.

"Do you think you might love me . . . a little bit Dillon . . . do you?" She was lisping.

"Well . . . I'm not in love with you . . . if I say I am, you'll want to hear it and hear it a whole lotta times. It's the first time that opens the dam. I like you a whole lot . . . let's not mess it about with that loaded term."

Far too long a theory. The hangover moved up. I headed for the bathroom. Morning prayer. . . on my knees to the porcelain. Sloo . . . sh . . . here went Robbie's bet . . . coloured gay. Twenty to the good.

Blast the shower . . . grief it meant to be. I chanced a glance to the mirror. Wet . . . I said . . . I look wet . . . right. M . . . m . . . mh.

A shade dismantled, alas. I managed to make some shook coffees. It's Saturday so . . . so perchance a jigger of that Irish. Morning drinking . . . hello, alcoholism. Back to the bed. Marisa was groaning.

"I'm ill."

"Have a hit on this." More of it, I thought.

"Ah, what's in this . . ."

"Sugar."

"Are you sure?"

"No."

She took a cigarette . . . coughed . . . coffeed and shook.

"Julie told me why you go to the funerals."

Good old chatty Julie . . . mebbe she could take out full-page advertisements. I savoured the coffee; no sugar there.

"She says you didn't go to your father's, and you've been compensating ever since."

"Could be . . . I might have me some of that line of thought."

" . . . and that you carry guilt because you don't recall your mother's burial. Is this very painful?"

"Hangovers are painful."

"Robbie said you were a death-freak."

"Ary, stop . . . I'm too ill for this . . . alrite."

"Why *do* you go . . ."

"I started initially because I had a dread of them . . . I was afraid to go . . . now I think I'm afraid not to go. . . ."

"I don't understand."

"Since I began to follow the funerals, nobody close to me has died."

"But that's crazy." She spilt the coffee in exasperation. T'would be a whore's ghost to remove coffee stains.

"Look, I didn't start out saying this was logical . . . did I? Why does it have to be rationalised. Where does it say this must make sense?"

"But you can't live like that."

"Why?"

" . . . Because . . . oh God . . . what . . . because it's weird. Julie says it's neurotic. . . ."

I moved. To ease the knife Julie was burying up to the flogging hilt in my back. How much whiskey was there yet in that bottle.

"I'm going to tell you about Julie . . . she lived in Greece for three years. Her father-in-law was in the army, and her Greek husband didn't understand a whole lot when she began sleeping with the colonel. Like a bad literary joke. They forgot to tell her no-one sleeps with the colonel." Marisa listened with the delight of the truly scandalised. The joy of the completely horrified. I could have stopped there. I saw her eyes again . . . as that coin spun in the air. Go to it.

"After a confrontation, the father-in-law leapt in his car . . . roaring . . . and an articulated truck put him and his guilt all over the centre of downtown Athens . . . that stopped the roaring . . . and his gallop – "

"Ker-ist."

"Julie got divorced and came back here. She gave me something she'd written and said it would explain everything and shed light on nothing. She called it – levels. Which she certainly wasn't . . . on the level I mean."

"Could I see it . . ."

My instincts said no.

My loyalty whispered . . . no way.

I said . . . "Sure. . . ."

***

"Levels . . ."

Ending school
at 17
as I was then . . . a
gutter-d level was
what they fore-saw
for me . . . I half-
elated
on some reputation tough . . . as I believed
believed thru years astray
should manic give me
bestow a mantle of
recklessness . . . from acceptance
lower

Second level
in Athens

on a Sunday
would you not
a day in sunshine say – near
had to be
and you'd be wrong
as wrong as I
descending
from a claustrophobic bus
witnessed
an army funeral
a silence thru the rain
you'd think
would you
I felt a sense
of something . . . something surely
that you could
describe – you'd be
on levels most
you'd be correct

Rising to the
third level
the level ultimate
is open to
the thousand interpretations
yet . . . a knowledge
only basic
is all I can
anticipate
have never once
articulated
that . . . as know
I mebbe know
mebbe
I almost might

The level fourth
it what it is . . . it
what you have believed
from me
and Lord . . .
amazing as it is
the rock belief
you placed . . . in me

might
bring
me . . . very near
towards
what I can but visualise
the level fourth
– beyond the words
mundane

Fifth and final . . .
dream . . . on
sacred fear itself
I've feared
you are
but what we dreamt
from aspirations
basked . . .
in urgency
My handicap it
is
my words out race
their meaning
every wasted time
and time
I never seem to get
to line your meaning
clear . . .
it clearly now
is at
the level fifth
near you
I have belonged
  "it only needs
  to read
  to where I am
  right now . . . you
  read these levels five
  five countries full
  from you
  . . . removed"

***

Outside the morgue. A smartly dressed middle-aged man kept sneaking looks at me.

"Did you know the deceased?" he asked.

"Not well."

"Ah, who did . . . who knows anyone.

"Ego . . . life is the constant search to define it."

I nodded. I couldn't rise to the verbal lunacy this morning. I wondered if he might be related to the head wino, Padraig. They attended the same speech coach mebbe! A three-day beard emphasized the crazed light in his eyes.

"You'll walk behind the hearse."

"Yeah."

"Ponder this, my silent friend, as we take the high road . . . ego is the sum of false ideas we have about ourselves."

"Piss off," I said.

I don't enter the cemetery. At the gates a wedding party roared past . . . horns blaring. I was too hung-over for irony. I mouthed the Beckett line and felt little solace. "They give birth astride of a grave." Hoot on. Who gives a diddly-fliggit.

I didn't see Julie for the weeks up to Christmas. I slept with Marisa at weekends and cut down on cigarettes. I didn't stop drinking because in Ireland you rarely do. I banged in a massive chart of overtime and kept to my funeral quota. The weather was bitterly cold, and I noticed Padraig no longer led the winos. Freezing-temperatured exposure keeps the numbers down . . . an expedient culling.

I thought of him a lot and, for a pound, a wino told me he was in the hospital.

I bought some roll-up tobacco, papers, and three pairs of thermal socks. The porter was obstructive as required by his status. Eventually I got the idea across to him.

"The oul wino, he's up in St. Joseph's ward; he's had his final blast of mello."

I didn't recognize Padraig, not only because they washed him but he'd shrunk.

"How-yah," I said.

"They won't let me smoke."

"Will I roll you wan?"

"I would be forever in your debt . . . they are not overly fond of me in this establishment. Do my colleagues on The Square prosper?"

They'd already forgotten him. He knew too.

"They were all asking after you."

He nearly smiled. I lit the rollie and put it in his mouth. Coughs and chest rumbles danced him in the bed.

"I needed that . . . did I ever acquire your name?"

"Am . . . no . . . it's Dillon."

"Suits you . . . I think. Lying here nicotineless and gasping for a drink, I pondered God. . . I think I heard once that he knew my name before I was born . . . what do you think of that . . . ?"

I had a furtive look round the ward.

People were point-d-ly ignoring us. The word was out on the wino . . . no sign of a nurse, so I lit a cigarette. Phey-oy, it tasted grand. Cutting down does magic for the oul want. I didn't know what I thought of God knowing a wino's name. So I said, "I dunno . . . isn't your name Padraig . . ."

"I think it is . . . on the other hand, it may be the remnant of a blackout. God knows . . . wot!"

He shivered again in the bed. The ward was roasting. I felt a slight perspiration break out on my forehead. I don't think . . . in truth . . . the heat was completely to blame for that. The tea trolley came . . . pushed by a middle-aged knacker. I knew him. Named Rooney. A small spit of a man who put the edge back into venom. My father, I believe, had once given him a hiding – he distributed tea and a dead biscuit to all the beds except Padraig.

"Hey . . . hey Rooney," I shouted.

He pretended not to hear me and the trolley accelerated as he reached the corridor. Cold. The cold flash of a killing rage. Blind. I caught him near the coronary unit. The rheumy eyes threw the challenge to me. The catering badge gave him status. The look said, "You can't touch me – "

I'm over six foot and weigh in at nigh 180 pounds. I felt like two of meself.

"Do you get to casualty . . ."

"No, I don't . . . I go to . . ." and he launched into a litany of saints representing the various wards.

"You're going to be in casualty in about five minutes because I'm going to break your left arm . . ."

"What . . . what's eating you, Dillon. I never did nothing to you. I was a great pal of your oul fellah's . . ."

"Go back up that corridor, wheel your bag of tricks into the ward, and offer that man a cup of tea . . . and one of them mouldy biscuits."

"Ary . . . the wino . . . what do you care . . . what's he to you. Tis not 'tay' the likes of him wants . . ."

As he finished, he looked into my eyes. Full. Then he turned the trolley round and he brought Padraig his afternoon tea . . . and two biscuits. I had a drop of tea myself as it was offered. I declined seconds.

"I won't make the Square for the New Year," said Padraig.

"You might . . ."

"No . . . I'd have liked to wear them new socks too. Do you think . . . do you think you could fit them on me now? I'm perished. . . ." He surely was.

The socks were a grey thermal from our clothing department. I rolled back the blanket and his feet grieved me. A serious novelist would describe them as gnarled.

Twisted, lacerated, and . . . old, very old. The socks were a size medium and enormous on his shrunken feet. He watched me watching them.

"How's that," I asked.

"Mighty . . . I'm the better of them already. I had a pair of argyles once or mebbe I just hope I did . . . you have a rare gift, my young friend."

"What's that?"

"You never probe or pry into a person's affairs."

"Thank you."

The nurse came and said I'd have to leave. A young dark-haired girl, she had huge brown eyes and what they call a homely face. Her name badge said "Nurse A.

Brown".

"What's the 'A' for?"

"Allison."

"Would you get in touch with me if he wants anything or if he gets a turn . . . I'll give you my address."

She didn't bat an eye or give me the current thought on winos. She said, "I've seen you up at Traders. Yes, I'll let you know. What's your name."

"Dillon . . . Eddie Dillon . . . thanks a lot."

Padraig tried to put some strength into his smile.

"What do you know about money, my young friend?"

"Not a whole lot."

"It's how they keep score," he said.

I rang Julie a few times. She was busy. Marisa mentioned to me that Raoul had attended Castleknock . . . as had Robbie. One of Ireland's expensive boarding schools. I thought of Saki's dictum:

> "To make a boy
> truly vicious
> you have to send him
> to a good school."

Christmas Eve materialised. My shopping list was brief:

- Julie
- Marisa
- Padraig

I was working a split shift and had the morning free. The town was hopping with cash and camaraderie. I bought Julie a boxed collection of Kazantzaki. By an incredible stroke of luck, I managed to get a recording of Richard Burton's reading of Dylan Thomas' *Under Milk Wood*. To keep the balance I threw in a copy of Adrian Mole. To lighten Julie's load, I added Stephens, *The Crock of Gold*. This selection of gifts proved I had a few bob if nowt else. I was buying some thermal long-johns for Padraig when I met Marisa's father. He was flush in a new sheepskin coat and deerstalker.

"Happy Christmas, Mr. Darcy."

"Well – well . . . well, young Dillon."

If there's a sensible reply to this, I don't know it. I gave him a smile – not too far removed from a grimace.

"I suppose you wouldn't object to a touch of something . . . the season that's in it. . . ."

"Sure, I'll keep you company . . . they have a coffee bar upstairs."

Ordering coffee was complicated. He wanted decaffeinated and the waitress reckoned he wanted seeing to. I was with the waitress. Sitting, I didn't offer the cigarettes. I lit one.

"Have you plans for the festive season," he asked.

"No."

"Mrs. D. and I have a lot of entertaining of course . . . But we try to get the few days in the Canaries. We hope to have Raoul home this evening. Are you . . . working?"

"Yeah, thieves don't have the festive spirit."

"How are the promotion prospects there."

"Almost nil I think."

"Well, I hate to run but I must look in at the office . . . the company have their 'claim' too."

T'was hard to say who was the more mortified with this insurance joke. It killed the conversation stone dead. How did you get the man's attention. Ask him how he was fixed for the few quid . . . what? I took a lone shot.

"Did you ever drink Mr. . . . . Darcy."

He sat back . . .

"I'm proud to say I joined The Pioneers take a pledge of total abstinence in order. . . ."

I had to cut in quick . . . he was off on a friggin seminar again.

"Yeah . . . yeah, I know what they are – I know that. But *why* did you take it."

He was well perplexed. I think he truly didn't get it. At least I'd shook some crap from the trees.

"The Pioneer Movement was founded . . ."

I hit the turn-off switch. You couldn't even call him a bolix. The lights were on. But who was home . . . I don't think he knew any better than I did. I tuned in again as he was looking into my face.

"Were you perhaps considering joining our crusade and getting yourself pinned. . . ."

. . . or nailed.

"No . . . I'd be more attracted to the militant wing of your organisation."

"To what, I don't understand that. . . ."

"A.A."

Enough. I stood up and wished him a merry Christmas. At the door I glanced back and he was fingering his deerstalker. What was running through his head. Decaffeinated probably. Avoid the kick. . . .

I got nicely scuttered at work. Customers passing through slipped me those minatures of spirits, packets of cigarettes . . . and even a turkey leg from one woman. I reckoned the Traders perimeter needed checking and patrolled. I chugged whiskey . . . brandy and gin. Whoa-hayed, I was getting the spirit. Our most persistent shoplifter extended the seasons greetings to me as I returned to the store's entrance. I spotted Robbie. Parcel laden, he scurried past. I hoped he spent my twenty wisely. I'd be seeing him soon. Come New Year. Gurteen roared past on a lethal looking motor-bike . . . and threw me a Hitler salute. Deference to the uniform. My supervisor showed. The worse for drink himself, he praised my diligence, my height, my attitude. I asked him if he'd my pay. Producing a rake of envelopes, he had to ask my name.

It included overtime and a Christmas bonus. Yip . . . feckin . . . ee! I nipped behind the store and toasted Christmas with something called, "olde England malte." Hoping it wasn't aftershave, I supped. M . . . m . . . m. I topped it. Glow full.

With an approximation of a step, I resumed duty. I was humming "little drummer boy" when a young woman marched up. Homely face but warm wonderful eyes and well shaped. A little excited though.

"Aren't you Eddie Dillon?"

"Yes, ma'am."

"Don't you remember me . . . ?"

"No, ma'am?"

"Allison . . . Allison Brown . . . I'm the nurse from the hospital."

"Uh yes, sorry, I didn't recognize you . . . in clothes . . . with clothes on . . . oh Gawd, I mean, out of uniform . . . am . . . you know . . . !"

"I hate to bother you at work but you said to let you know. Padraig . . . your friend . . . he died last night . . . and I only just got off work . . . I'm so sorry."

"Oh Lord. . . ."

At that moment, a "Biddy friendly" grabbed me. Her purse was stolen and she wanted "ACTION."

"Where is he?" I asked Allison.

"The morgue . . . at the hospital . . . "

"Thanks . . . thanks, I have to go . . . I'll go down later."

The woman pulled me into the teeming crowd. I could see her red face, yapping and shouting. I didn't hear it . . . any of it. I could put that down to "olde English malte." Immunised. I went through the motions with the woman and had her fill out the forms. Her own agitation blurred any reaction from me. I had a uniform. Right. So I knew the score. Right. Behave accordingly. Intimidate the daylights outa her. Eventually she left, in a medium cloud of shock. I kept humming that woeful drummer boy . . . beat on.

***

I called Marisa after work . . . and lied wholesale.

Emergency due to staff shortage . . . see her in a few days. An effective lie as I didn't care if she believed it. She wanted to grab it, and we buried our own sides of the fabrication. Yeah-oh, we threw some happy Christmases in there. The morgue was closed. I emerged from the off-licence with a crate of booze. Food . . . ? Food for thought . . . darkest of all. . . .

At the flat, I dredged up the track suit. A bottle by the neck. Jack Daniels. Did I buy that . . . and a mug. I sat on the floor and began to shape oblivion. Sip . . . ah . . . think . . . no . . . no thanks, not today buddy, I'm way through with analysis. Giving ole Jack D. a run for the money. Sour mash it said on the label. Better yet, the sourer the finer. The bell went . . . why not . . . ghost of Christmas something. Julie. Bearing gifts . . . beware of Greekophiles bearing! . . . what.

"I didn't expect to find you in – "

"Me neither . . . you wanna get yourself a mug and a bottle of somethin. . . . "

"I'll have whatever you're sailing with."

"No you won't . . . this personal . . . 'tween Jack D. and me. There's vodka . . ."

She handed me a gaily wrapped parcel and got the vodka. I had some coordination problems but got there. An Aran sweater. I gave her the Kazankatakis. Silence. She was dressed in a heavy black sweater. Black cords . . . black boots. The pale face looked luminous. The clothes were fitting on every level. Black as my attitude . . . levels indeed. The vodka took her onslaught stoically. Julie wasn't big on verbal gratitude but mebbe there was a smile in there when she opened the books.

"How's the romance, Dillon?"

"Do you care . . ."

"A whole lot . . . no! But we can open a conversation on any point?"

"I haven't been to a funeral for . . . phew . . . three weeks."

"Congratulations . . . welcome to the land of the half-alive . . . any withdrawal symptoms or side effects – "

"On your terms, no, life is hunky dory. How's Robbie?"

"Not too fond of you, Dillon. In fact, he's on the town with Powl or Rowell . . . your wan's brother."

"He's going to be meeting his obligations real soon . . . "

Julie was massacrin' the vodka. I felt a deep disturbance within and around her. I didn't know if there was friendship left enough to address it.

"I saw your father . . ."

"Screw him . . ."

And that closed that line of inquiry. The Jack Daniels had thrown the care-not switch, but I went again. She was hunched over on the floor. As near as rain and as distant as contentment.

"Julie, what's eating you . . . you're like a bag of cats . . ."

The smile. Oh, a bitter one, but you took the appearances.

Let's go Jack.

"Is it on meself but have you trouble in rising even to civility with me."

"Well, Dillon, you piss me off . . . but then everything and everybody does. I want out . . . and I've even got that . . . they want me to return to Greece. Lemme read you a bit of Cavafy."

Out came the black book. She lit two cigarettes and pushed one at me. She drew on it as if it also was irritating the hell outa her. Perhaps it was . . . why should cigarettes get exemptions. The piece was from Cavafy's *The City*.

> "You said, 'I will go to another land, I will go to another sea.
> Another city will be found, better than this . . .'"

She gave me the look. Did I want to comment. No. I drank and felt the inner cold. Someone didn't walk on my grave, they were having a full-blown jig on it. The vodka seemed to have no effect on her. She gritted her teeth and read the next piece in smart-ass American tone.

> "New lands you will not find, you will not find other seas.
> The city will follow you. You will roam the same
> streets. And you will age in the same neighborhoods;
> in these same houses you will grow gray.
> Always you will arrive in this city. To another land – do not hope –
> there is no ship for you, there is no road."

I'll be honest . . . I enjoyed the American twang . . . it blended nicely with the Jack Daniels. I poured the vodka. A tremor had laid hold of her voice. No amount of smart-ass-ness could disguise it.

"And here's the kicker," she said.

> "As you have destroyed your life here in this little corner
> you have ruined it in the entire world."

A conversation killer full. They said Julie cared and felt for nowt . . . 'cept Carlo. A dog. Three years before, we'd been standing on the Square after closing time. There's time and there's pub time. Rely on the latter. A dog was weaving back and forth across the road, bewildered by the traffic. A cross between a fox and a tinker's greyhound. "That ejit will be killed," Julie had said and called him. Coaxing and cursing, she'd lured him to her . . . and he'd moved into her life. The dog's eyes were brown. Pure affection . . . and it was all for Julie. "Someone forfeited love itself," she said, and she believed he had the appearance of an abandoned dog. "A crowd from Carlow dumped him here," she reckoned. To keep his imagined roots, he'd retained the county's name. That her father hailed from there wasn't mentioned.

"You'd have to leave Carlo if you go to Greece."

"I'm afraid . . . I think . . . afraid to go back . . . but am I more afraid not to. How does that sound to you, Dillon?"

It sounded confused. She wouldn't want to hear that.

"It sounds confused."

She asked if I wanted to take her to bed. I didn't. The Jack Daniels did. I guess we hit a compromise. I took her to bed but I don't remember it. I may have asked at one interval what she was thinking about.

"I'm thinking dearly . . . of you."

It probably wasn't like that but lacking a clear recollection, it's sufficient.
I woke to bells. Christmas bells . . . loud. I was not a well man. Julie had left a note on the Jack Daniels bottle . . .

> *"Dillon,*
> *I knew the first thing you'd want was Jack here . . . yeah. There's a drop*
> *in it . . . if you want feedin', call round this evening. I suppose I should*
> *wish you a happy Christmas . . . so some of that but primarily . . . a*

> *gentle-d hangover and a cure that takes. This explains everything, sheds*
> *light on . . . nothing.*
>   *X"*

Men with big hammers were whacking the be-damns outa my head. "I don't need that last bit of sour mash." As my mind played rationalisations, I drank – a shower cleaned me . . . a cure would take heavier consideration. I wore Julie's sweater and sneaked a mirror glance. The clothes looked new. The face wasn't lived in, no! Something very sick had died there, crawled in there and just died.

***

Not a soul on the street . . . save "Bad Weather." A fellah as old as the town, he was a drunkard who no longer needed drink. His brain was stewed in poison, and he was perpetually drunk. Without drinking. A final solution. To all greetings he said, "bad weather." He said this to me as I palmed him a few quid. I didn't want to examine too closely the fact he was wearing an Aran sweater and dirty jeans. Heading for the hospital, I kept repeating "Your jeans are clean . . . are cleanish . . . are . . ."

It had crossed my mind that ten months of the year, Bad Weather was correct in his forecast. I had Nurse Allison Brown paged. She displayed no surprise. "You look fierce" . . . an Irish adjective. Applied equally as in "fierce good" . . . or "fierce bad." I'd guess she'd opted for the latter. I passed on the happy Christmas bit. "What happens to Padraig now?"

She explained that if no one claimed him, he'd be buried by the State. The hospital would act for them. He'd get a funeral and be buried. If I were to go for it and claim him, I'd be buying myself a heap of bureaucracy. I'd have to claim a medical card for him, to prove he existed. That he no longer did was irrelevant. The relevant forms and claims were massive. It crossed my hung-over state that I could have a spree on his medical card. I felt Padraig would have cheered me on that. I didn't know what to do. I wanted to drink.

"I dunno what to do, Allison."

"Let the State bury him."

"I feel that I'm copping out."

"You are but I think you should."

I thought I shouldn't, so I said, "Okay."

"If you go down to our chapel now, the priest will be saying mass, you could ask him to mention Padraig."

"Thanks, Allison . . . I'll be seeing you."

She smiled and left. Wasn't I too ill to notice how brown these eyes were. Course I was. I tried to shelve how devastatingly attractive the uniform was. So . . . so mebbe I could take the uniform itself for a night out. I'll . . . she's got a lovely face.

I waylaid the priest before the mass. I asked him to mention the soul of Padraig. I thought that was the way to frame it.

"Padraig who," he asked. A small barrel of a man, he looked hungover too. I thought it diplomatic to omit that God would know who.

"I dunno his surname." I tried to look social worker-ish. Why I thought that would score points was even then a mystery. He muttered something and bristled away. No points. Padraig would be buried the next day. Funerals were kept to a minimum for the day it was.

Emerging from the hospital, I walked straight into Rooney, the trolley dictator. Was it on myself or was there delight in the ferret eyes.

"Did you hear about O'Malley?"

"No."

"He went mad down in The Weir last night . . . mad from drink . . . it took three guards to get him to the station – that will soften his cough."

I didn't even give him the look. I knew I should mebbe phone Marisa. I'm ill, I said, and headed for "The Post." An early morning house. My father was a known, if a less-than-valued client there. On the outside, it appeared closed. Shut down even. I knocked. The Irish speakeasy.

"Go away, we're shut."

"It's Dillon . . . young Dillon – "

"Oh . . . wait a minute."

Bolts sounded. Fat Willy came out. Over six foot he was and as thin as a spit. Not a pick on him. His father was over twenty stone in his time, and the son inherited the pub and the name. I'd need some big drinks if I was to visit O'Malley in the barracks. I knew enough to elevate rank. An ordinary guard you call sergeant . . . a nun is a superior mother and up you ascent. The vague flaw to this was my own experience in a security guard uniform. (People inevitably called "dumb-head" and ascended.)

The pub was packed and silent. The sanctity of serious drinking. Not a place for dabblers. You came here to get alcohol into the system, fast and with the minimum of pain. Talk didn't intrude. Later, when the cures were rampant, the crowd would loosen. Now it was hangover haven.

The holy atmosphere of the hair of the dog. Most attempted to ingest the whole flogging dog . . . if faces are mirrors, the crowd had been savaged by large animals. I took my place amid the silence. Whisper my order. Reverence is all . . . to all. A bus conductor I knew had the next stool. With both hands, he got his whiskey to his mouth. Tilt . . . the load, down. I felt the tremor. He bolted for the toilet. Returning, his face was green, a light coating of perspiration . . . and relief. "The next one . . . The next one will stay down," he said. The voice of experience. I dwelt on "Funeral II."

The bus conductor managed the next whiskey. Gregariousness was close behind.

"A happy Christmas to you, Dillon."

"And yerself, Pat."

"Would you join me in a drop."

"I would."

I put a cigarette on the counter for him to light in his own time. The shakes still hovered . . . his and mine. He swiped the second drink.

"Ah . . . stay . . . stay, ya bad bistard, ah . . . am I feeling better . . . !"

You find few finer examples of positive thinking. The cigarette was lit. A spasm of coughing nigh threw him across the counter. The fragile recovery near came up. Massive control; he won.

"There's comfort in the oul cigarettes."

"There is."

"I was off them there for the run up to the Christmas. Even the drink tasted flat. I had to give up beer, ya know. Only the spirits seemed to give me any bit of taste."

"I know what you mean."

I bought the next round. The temptation to spend the day was fierce. I was at the stage of recovery that a few more drinks might tip into paralysis. With the warmest of wishes, I left Pat to it. I felt reckless enough for the police barracks. This is a large granite building in the town centre. Grey and grim.

A young garda was tending the desk. The station was quiet.

"Good afternoon, Sergeant . . ." which he wasn't.

"Is it young Dillon . . . did you lose something?"

My nerve, mainly.

"I came to see how O'Malley was."

"—That blackguard. He's seeing the doctor . . . he fell down in his cell and might have broken his nose." We left that shift between us. The garda's eyes were a shade above blankness. Life was present there but not of any compassionate type.

"I wouldn't have thought that O'Malley was a friend of yours, Dillon."

"Well, would you tell him I called in."

He nodded. At the door, two huge guards were hauling a wino in. He was roaring like a bull and throwing his free hand to the free world . . . outside . . .

The guards said "happy Christmas . . ."

I hope I kept my peace if not theirs.

***

"Funeral II"

Ashen
was the way
I felt
when shunned again
by people
I had justi-
fied
didn't all
that all . . . much
really
warrant grief

– "tearing words beneath" –

Beneath
the anger . . . deeper
anger
ever lurks
. . . and wish
I wish
it weren't so
"so much now
Phew . . .
a sigh lifeless"

The saying less
that what I think
it is
the old triangle here
of . . .
think
I thought perhaps
of less
than I could
ever
start to say

A funeral
begins the move
up towards the hill
you know – beyond
the very plans
you'd power play . . . it
change you drastically
a choice . . . to change
was lined
behind the hearse

***

I didn't go to Julie's.
I didn't call Marisa.
I didn't eat.
    What I did was I drank . . . a whole lot. I didn't get to evening. I was cold on
the floor of my flat. I had me some rough dreams . . . French named or otherwise.
    The next morning was dues time. I had to die. Walk through the hangover. If

I had an inch of drink, I'd lose the next week. I didn't do it for Padraig . . . he'd have said, "Lose the week . . ." I didn't want to lose his funeral. So I showered and died. Drank shaky coffee and retched. I didn't shave.

At the morgue were the priest and the hearse and myself. Oh yeah, Padraig, too, but he wasn't feeling anything. Same priest . . . new hangover. I skipped the greetings. He gave me a seat to the cemetery. Padraig might have appreciated how we got there first. At the Square, I told myself, at least one of the winos will see the hearse. He'd pause and put his hand over his heart. If he'd had a cap, he would have removed it. Hail to the chief. That's the way I told myself it was. Indeed, I regretted not actually seeing it in full. But like I say, I was hungover and prey to anxious foolishness. I recognized one of the gravediggers. O'Hanlon . . . a former security guard. Over six foot, he was broad and had the look of being well fed. He rarely smiled. You got a look into those wet-blue eyes and all the smile you'd ever need was right there. From minding the living to burying the dead, an Irish success.

Padraig was laid in Billy's Acre . . . well away from the paying clients. In the days of the poor house, they took them here. To the present, your status could be destroyed if anyone belong to you had been put there. It veered on the Protestant graves, and those were the pits. On Cemetery Sunday, the priest blessing the graves ignored the paupers and the Protestants. The area of Billy's Acre was neglected and overgrown. The caretaker didn't bother with their upkeep, as who was there to complain. The Protestants were well known for their non-tending of the dead. I learnt that at school. They believed, "You passed on." Why visit the graveyard when no one was home. They didn't just chuck Padraig into the ground. But there wasn't a whole lot of ceremony either. The priest read that dirge in which "man has but a short time to live and is full of misery." T'was more fitting to us around the grave than the fellah within it.

Job, complete, the priest took off. I stood over Padraig and couldn't find any last words of enlightenment. I felt the last of the hangover, and that might have been the most fitting tribute. O'Hanlon put his shovel down and began to light a pipe.

"You knew the client . . . did you, Dillon?"

"I did . . ."

"Well, like the priest said, we bring nowt into the world and that client sure as spit didn't bring anything out . . . how's the job?"

"Monotonous. How did you get into this line of work?"

"It's a corporation job, so I'm secure. I like the hours. In winter it's a whore's ghost to put a shovel in the hard ground. We have to get it heated first. Did you know Rod Stewart was a gravedigger once?"

I didn't. I fought the inclination to inquire if O'Hanlon sang. I was afraid of the answer. That O'Hanlon was over fifty wasn't relevant. I think. He was in the grip of his dream.

"And that fella is worth millions, Dillon . . . millions . . . with blond women fighting over him morning, noon, and night."

"You never know, alright . . ."

O'Hanlon nearly embraced me for the breath of my vision. "That's it . . . you've said it all there . . . you have to be ready . . . you'd never know who'd show up in a graveyard. . . "

I left him spinning out his dream. I phoned Marisa, and icicles hung on the line. She agreed to meet me at The Weir for lunch. I debated returning to the flat to collect the Dylan Thomas reading by R. Burton. Presents seemed a travesty right then. The wren boys, dressed in colorful rags, were calling house to house . . . hollerin' and shouting. A group of them saw me and in nigh chorus chanted, "How's she cutting, Dillon?"

I wisht I'd know.

The Weir was deserted. I ordered a tomato juice. I think I hate the stuff. As ill as I was, it made little matter. I was glaring at it when Marisa breezed in. In fur. A new mini-length coat. She turned her cheek to be kissed. Not being Halian, I passed on this.

"Will you drink something?"

"Yes, Dillon . . . a g & t . . . and sour. Seasonal Greetings wouldn't be entirely amiss."

"What happened to your voice. Did they give you a vocabulary for the Christmas. Nobody talks like that. . . or are you pist? Does 'g & t' mean gin?"

The look. I got the gin and a tonic.

We sat for combat.

"Just who do you think you are, Dillon? You stood me up over Christmas . . . and you don't have the decency to give me a present . . . even some perfume. My father says you tried to suggest he belonged to Alcoholics Assembly – "

"Anonymous . . . that's Alcoholics Anonymous," I said.

"For Godsake, who cares. I think you care more for that old wino than you do for me . . . I don't think I can take much more of this."

"Do you like tomato juice?"

"What?"

"I'm gonna let you have that tomato juice there . . . okay and I'm going to go now . . ."

"If you leave now . . . it's . . . it's over . . . I'm warning you."

I had the feeling she'd use that line. Why does it always sound more sad than threatening. I got up and left. I thought a bit about the stranger in the fur and the new voice. Who was she? No one that I thought I'd ever get to know. It wasn't till a lot later that I realized I was now the possessor of the Dylan Thomas record. I didn't expect I'd be playing it a whole lot. But you never knew. I was glad I hadn't drunk the tomato juice, for I was far too ill for that. Control is over-critical these days.

I was reading *The Crock of Gold* and even Stephens was failing to rally me. A bottle of scotch stood on the fridge. A stand off. Course the scotch held all the shots . . . punned or otherwise. The sun was over various horizons . . . yard-arms . . . and I kept postponing the inevitable.

The door-bell went . . . insistently. I opened the door to a complete stranger. A tall blond guy . . . over six foot and built like trouble. The kinda face women said was too pretty. I don't follow that but he had that expression; he'd heard the women say it too. In his left hand was a brown paper bag . . . a bottle. Mebbe muggers did house calls. The clothes belied that. Rich knacker-ish. A worn suede jacket. Quality worn. A maroon sweat shirt that never heard of Traders, and the faded jeans that cost cash money for that fade. Was it on mesself or did he have a tan. In Ireland? At Christmas . . .?

"Yeah . . ."

"Are you Dillon?". . . an accent to match the jacket, money ill-disguised.

"Yeah . . ."

"I'm Raoul . . . Marisa's brother . . ."

Sure. He had the cut of her. What I thought was . . . he's gay . . . what does he want. I ran my reactions slow.

"Piss off" or "So . . .!" or "What do you want . . .?" or "Hoppit . . ."

I was kinda fond of the last one. It would get the job done and it had a ring to it. I said, "Come in."

He handed me the bottle. Inside, I looked at the label. Glenfiddich . . . m . . . m . . . mph. Pull out the oul mugs. . . they were on active duty these days. I tried to run the number, "Well, I'm not drinking alone," but it didn't float. I poured freely, gave him the mug.

"If this is sippin' whiskey . . . just don't tell me . . . alrite."

"Oh right . . . you're probably wondering why I'm here."

"I was wondrin' . . . about a friend of mine . . . Padraig."

"Well, Marisa asked me to come . . . am . . . I wanted to meet you as I've heard some fairly diverse opinions on you. Marisa says you love a lot of literary things . . ."

"I dunno if I would put it like that. It happens that things which make sense to me happen to fall into the literary can . . . well, sometimes – "

"My father says you're never sober."

We took this as a cue and had us some Glenfiddich. Not bad at all. I figured he was figuring me. So we let that dance about a bit. My stomach had howled initially . . . now it was working towards a purr. I was chugging up that road to some recovery.

"—I ran into Robbie last night, and he says you cheated him outa £20 – "

"And a meal . . ." I said.

"Yeah . . . and Ted . . . you know him?"

"I've met him . . . his earring anyway."

Raoul smiled. It looked real enough.

"Ted says you're a psychopath . . ."

"M . . . m . . . m . . . I dunno how much of that I would want to be denied. Psychos get fast service in pubs."

Smiled again, and he reached for the bottle. Poured some more of that good stuff.

"Marisa seems keenish . . .!"

"Did she tell you about the funerals?" I asked.

Now he looked uncomfortable. But there was a limited range of places to look. He looked at me. I had his attention . . . and of course . . . the bottle.

"She did . . . she said it's what you do most. So, you see, I've heard a lotta . . . diverse reports."

"Lemme ask you something . . . why on earth would you call to visit a drunken psychopath who steals money and likes funerals . . . are you mad is what I want to know – "

A guffaw . . . threw his head back and roared laughin'. Sure, how could I not like this guy. I sloshed in more drink. I was way past recovery. Indeed, I was into the area of having answers. A very drunken place. That takes big drinks.

"Well, Raoul . . . Raoul . . . cripes . . . what do I know about you. You're Marisa's brother and you seem to know a right bunch of maggots" . . . phew, the slow developing had nearly popped "faggots."

He began then – "I'm supposed to be a teacher. But of the itinerant kind. If you wanted to see the world, you became a sailor. I wanted to see the world and teaching English was a new way to do it. For nearly ten years I've done that, all over the world – "

"You don't much have the cut of a teacher."

"They say English language teachers are failed actors and big drinkers."

"And do you fulfill those requirements?"

He laughed again. There was nothing at all wrong with this guy's sense of humour.

I reached for the bottle. Nowt . . . zilcho, zip-oh, and out. Raoul looked as if he hadn't had a drop for a week. I was flying. The scotch on the sink was roarin', "Hey, guys, lookit me" . . . and we looked. Raoul jiggled the mug . . . dead zone! So I said . . . "I think we should be sensible . . . I mean, I think we should wink . . . drink, I mean, something but . . . wot . . . what do you think, Rouly?"

"Definitely . . . 100 percent . . . all the way." Agreeable guy. Right? And how much can you dislike that type of affability.

We made hot whiskeys . . . there could have been cloves, but we dispensed with the mickey-mousing around. Sugar, boiling water, and scotch. Plain and deadly.

"Here's to Wilde's view of Ireland . . . a nation of brilliant failures – he said."

T'was like a slap of cold water to me. He caught the change . . . I said then, "Yeah . . . well, Rouly, he also said that in failure there is a great strength to be earned."

This rang all sorts of lights in Raoul's eyes. . .

"Are you familiar with Wilde?" he asked.

"I've read him . . . does it say he's not accessible to security guards. But intimate."

No . . . I wouldn't be that . . . at all . . . no! . . . The lights moved up to shove. The anger was kindling. Stay on it, Raoul, I thought . . . he did.

"You know, Dillon, I'm gonna have to ask you to explain that. If you've got a snide lash in there . . . let's have it."

The anger now was full. He stood up. I was attempting to try something along familiar lines. The punch took me under the jaw and half-way across the room. Books and records went flying. He walked over and took a wide-angled kick to my ribs. Got me.

"Stay down, son," he said.

Son! I acted stunned to get some breath and leverage. Wait for my father's voice.

There are no rules in fighting . . . you hurt or get hurt. Put the fellah down hard, and make sure he doesn't want to continue. Doesn't matter dicky-birds who begins it. Be sure you finish it.

"I'll want an apology, too . . . for myself . . . for Robbie . . . for Marisa . . ."

Throw in the feckin government of the day, too. I stayed down . . . it wasn't difficult. He took the scotch and poured a large dollop. For one. No class. Putting it on his head, he began a victory gurgle. Beneath my hand, I noticed a broken Dylan Thomas record. Coming straight up, I hit him with my shoulder in the belly. Then swing to bring the elbow in. Hard. The half turn and chop his knees. Two kicks to the face. It was over. I got him by the scruff of the neck and hauled him down to the street. It was freezin'. I walked to the phone kiosk and reported a loud and vexatious spirit and location of this.

Odd how the lines of that Desiderata will intrude. There was half the scotch still. I broke yer man's mug and put it in the garbage. Alongside Marisa's record and his Glenfiddich bottle. Mebbe it was sippin' whiskey after all. Breaking the mug leant a bit to the melodramatic but I figured I could afford one. It crossed my mind that old Rouly must have forgotten his Wilde . . .

> "In manners of grave importance
> style
> not sincerity
> is
> the vital thing."

Violence requires a cold and deadly style.

The flat was a shambles . . . or was that my life. No matter. I took too aspirin and took to my bed.

***

I'm not much for premonitions. I don't see anything as a portent of the future. The past has a full hold on haunting and absolute hallalluas without completion.

In the present, I drink . . . and have a fragile being. When I dreamt of Julie's mongrel being mangled by a truck, I put it down to drink. No food either. My father was in there, too, but he was a featured player. The dog, Carlo, was a guest appearance. Drenched in sweat, I fell from the bed. The nightly horrors had helped sweat a lot of the booze out. So I told myself – a raging thirst, I nigh-on died of shock when I saw the ransacked flat. Burglars . . . what? Oh God . . . think . . . big blond dope . . . yeah, yeah and . . . threw him out. "*I* threw him out. Fair bloody play to ya, Dillon." I was in no shape to work. Few in the town were. En route to Traders I met "Bad Weather." He said his words . . . "and isn't it me that bloody knows it," I thought.

56

Rain lashed down and it was the all-encompassing freezing kind. My hangover was shrieking for help. No. I crawled into my uniform. I didn't have to worry about the supervisor . . . he'd be answering his hangover for at least another week. The replacement for the clothes department manager had arrived. A thin length of efficient misery, he was sporting a pioneer badge. Pinned. The shop wasn't open but a full staff was due to prepare for the January sales. A quarter had showed. The pleas of flu were rampant in the personnel office. There are no hangovers in Ireland. You get the "bad dose of flu."

"The nerves act up."

"A relative . . . any relative . . . dies suddenly."

"You catch that oul bug going round . . . everyone has it . . ."

For all of the above . . . for none of the above, we'd three-quarters of the staff out. I stalked out along Traders perimeter. The car park hadn't been nicked in my absence. Walk point. I gave a cigarette a lot consideration. But I couldn't get to it. The thought increased my nausea. T'was one of the most conscientious days work I ever did. I patrolled like a thing demented. Walk that sucker off. And had me a whale of positive thinking. "Sick . . . I'm not sick . . . whoops, nigh puked there . . . no . . . good good . . . walk. Cramp . . . no . . . retch . . . argh . . . I'm well, I'm well but . . . on the other hand."

For lunch I had two Alka-Seltzer. Get that goodness down. Ah. My shift ended at four. The guy relieved me had the dog patrol. Was it on meself or was the dog the worse for wear drink-wise.

"He has that oul stomach bug that's doing the rounds," I was told.

"How's yerself?" I asked.

"Well, Dillon, I have a touch of the flu . . . I wasn't going to come in at all."

I watched man and dog limp off. A fearsome duo. Mainly to themselves. I met Gurteen agitated . . . and extremely so.

"I need to talk to you, Dillon."

"Okay."

"Let's go to Nestor's, and you can buy me my Christmas drink."

Nestor's is a spit and sawdust pub. They only serve natives. They'll serve a wino if he's a local . . . and even women.

Mrs. Nestor is as old as Guinness and as black. From dirt. I dunno if she hates everyone but she sure fakes it well. Locals get a kinda tempered hostility.

"Lads," she said – you're a lad till you marry. Then you advance to yolk.

"Howyah, Eileen," said Gurteen. No one . . . absolutely no one called her that. But Gurteen was missing the few dots from his dice. Exempt from all regulations.

"Give us two pints of Arthur J," he said. She shuffled off to do that. She was a huge Connamara woman who'd married a local. Her eyes gave malice a bad name. Mebbe she'd had a head of hair once. Rumour had it she'd got the first ever hair net in Ireland. It sure appeared as if she'd never felt the need to once remove it. It fit like a bonnet . . . like dead glue. She dressed habitually in black.

The pints came. I paid. We sat at the counter and sipped gingerly. M . . . m . . . ph, nothing alive in there . . . yet.

Gurteen winked and we lashed half them home.

"Same again, Eileen . . . give us a fag, Dillon."

I did that. The Guinness settled on me like gloom. I was off again.

"You're in trouble, Dillon. I was in The Weir at lunchtime and I heard a conversation between three fellahs."

"Do I know them?"

"Marisa's . . . is that her name . . . yeah, her brother, the queer . . . and Robbie Fox . . . and the part-time barman, Ed of something."

"Ted."

"The queer looked like someone walked on his face. The Raoul fella. Someone did him!"

He looked at me. I nodded.

"Good on yah . . . well, them three were fixing to fix you. Soon."

I thought about that. Not hard but I thought about it. Two more pints arrived. I paid.

"I wouldn't like to think of them thundering shites beating up on you, Dillon."

I didn't like to think of it either. I said, "Me neither."

"Them scuts have bin pissin' me off for a while now. They're meeting again this evening in The Weir."

"I'd better take a look in so."

"Good man, good . . ."

I drained the pint. My cigarettes were on the counter. I left them. Gurteen gave a big smile.

"I'll keep our Eileen company for a bit . . . eh Eileen, come out here and I'll throw me leg over. C'mon . . . it's Christmas . . . and who's to say."

How do you dress for a hiding. Your worst clothes? Clean underwear in case hospitals feature. That stirred a thought. Wearing dirtied jeans, sneakers, and a dying sweatshirt, I threw an old oil-skin over me. Banish the thoughts of shrouds. I rang the hospital, but Nurse Allison Brown was off duty. Trucking down the canal I wondered how worried I should be. The first thing I saw in the Weir was three thugs. At the counter. Dressed in those black biker leather jackets, and chains weren't decorative. I knew those three by reputation. The guards avoided them. They were standing at the bar . . . drinking shorts. No one was standing within a wallop of them. Not a word was spoken by or near them.

My three laddy-a-bucks were down at a far table . . . and boisterous. Howls of laughter. I ordered a large scotch. The thugs continued to stare at nothing. Ho-kay . . . let's walk and talk. When I got to the table, I pulled a stool over and sat. The three had stopped laughing. Raoul's face was a mess. Ted was tittering, and Robbie whispered something to him. The table before us was covered in glasses.

"You're looking for me . . . are ye . . ."

Before any reply, another stool was pulled up and Gurteen sat between Robbie and Ted. He spoke to Raoul directly.

"Do you see them three fellahs at the counter. They want to talk to you now."

Oh, like right now.

Raoul looked at me . . . then his friends. He stood up and sauntered to the counter. A few brief words were said by the first thug . . . who then tapped Raoul gently on his bruised bone. Raoul turned and walked smartish out of the pub.

"And then there were two," said Gurteen.

Ted gave another low giggle.

Flash . . . Gurteen head-butted him on the bridge of the nose and grabbed him from falling.

"Piss off now, horseface." Ted, dazed, got shakily to his feet and did exactly that.

Gurteen turned to me.

"Dillon, get the drinks in, will you . . . Robbie here doesn't want anything."

I ordered two doubles. When I returned, Robbie was holding out a fist of money to me. I took it.

Robbie made to leave. Gurteen put a hand lightly on his chest.

"Ary don't go, Robbeen, you're great crack . . . sit and watch us drink a bit . . . alrite?"

Robbie nodded.

Gurteen then proceeded to tell me a lengthy story about his initiation to sex. This was a long crude mechanical tale. He kept winking at Robbie. I finished my drink and said I'd be going.

"Sure, Dillon, thanks for dropping in, me and Robbie will stay on for a while and I'll tell him a few more stories . . . Okay . . . Robbeen? I'm getting to like you . . . would yah credit that. Hop up there and get me a drink like a good lad."

I left. There wasn't any sign of Raoul or Ted. But I wasn't expecting there would be.

***

A shoplifter ran smack into me the next morning. The sales had begun. If bargains be what you don't want your neighbour to have, we had Big Bargains. The stampede was in full swing. I was standing sentry outside the main door. Well outside. Teeming with people. A man erupted from the door like the bat outa hell . . . and hell for leather he was traveling. He was laden with unwrapt clothes. I tried to move out of his way. Too late. Colliding, we went sprawling. Clothes littered the wet ground.

"You have me," he said.

"Not if you run like the hammers – "

". . . God bless you, Dillon," and he snapt a permanent crease trousers and lit out. I gathered the remnants and entered through the fire door. The vegetable department lay just beyond. Like a haunted place, it was not in the "sales category" and thus shunned. Standing over the fruit counter was Julie. An indifferent melon in her right hand. Her gaze was up and over the whole area . . . and preoccupied. I snuck off with the wet contraband.

I began to plan my funeral.

How to phrase the invitations.
A black border naturally.
A simple white card to read . . .

> *"You are cordially invited*
> *to the funeral of*
> *Edward A. Dillon*
> *Late of Traders Security Patrol.*
> *Dress informal.*
> *A reception will be held afterwards in the New Cemetery."*

I wasn't sure about the R.S.V.P.

I stuck the initial "A" in there after Edward as that strikes the right note of sincerity. So one of the better cheque passers in Traders had told me . . . dud cheques, I should add. People don't expect duplicity from middle initial people. I wondered about a black tie obligation. Naw, that would exclude winos. Best to keep it a quiet informal affair. The guest list. M . . . m . . . mp.

> Julie and Carlo.
> Marisa (why not, let her flaunt the oul Dylan T. number)
> Gurteen
> The three thugs (I kinda owed them)
> "Bad Weather"

I wish the Wilde opinion of George Bernard Shaw hadn't leapt into my mind just there.

> "he hadn't an enemy in
> the world
> and
> his friends didn't like him either."

Whoa-hey. Lighten up, Dillon.

Clothes. Julie's Aran sweater and the fading track suit bottom. I'd forego the black tie, I reckoned I'd given enough service to the necktie brigade. A pair of strong warm brogue's. New shoes would bring out the begrudgers. I knew from my own funeral experience the emphasis people placed on a good pair of shoes. Yea, worn but solid. A Timex watch. They last for years and set the right tone of unpretentiousness. No jewelry; let's keep this simple. I'd see if Father Benedictus was available to do the service. The words of farewell over the grave . . . something by Chesterton perhaps . . . none of that other shuffling off of mortal calls. It always reminded me of a drag artist. Before John Berryman jumped from the Washington Avenue Bridge, one of his students wrote that he had lately found his own faith in God. But, since it was a changing time . . . he said "this may change too. But I hope not." Berryman liked that a lot.

I visualised a plain slab of granite on my grave. No dates or name. Just "I hope not."

With my luck they'd figure it was a comment on the weather. I called Julie at work. She had a piece of my hungover hide for disturbing her.

"Good to talk to you, Julie, I needed to be ate and I sure called the right place . . ."

"Look, Dillon, don't you have funerals or something morbid to be at?"

"You're right, Julie, I thought I should ring to ask something truly weird as 'how yah doing' . . ."

"How am I doing . . . How am I doing what . . . "

I hung up. I'm right there for the oul wisecrack. Tis many the stretch I'll make to grab a crumb of humour. Bad friggin manners is something else. My friend Julie. Probably I should have gone the distance and hoped the friendship would be sitting further down the line. I reckoned she was wasted in the travel business. She ought to sit down and write a good vicious book. Coming out of the phone kiosk, I met O'Malley. A subdued version. His eye was blackened and he had a limp. The clothes were clean and fresh, round about Christmas Eve when he'd put them on.

"Will ya buy us a drink, Eddie?"

Ribs broke in devils, hell freezeth over, Eddie! The shock shocked me. Rigid.

"Come on . . . so." We went to Nestors.

The dirt remained the same. Lodged thick. Mrs. Nestor gave us the evil eye.

"Pints . . . is it?" We nodded. I gave O'Malley a cigarette. He shook like a bad lie.

"I'm in quare street," he said. What's new, I thought but kept in a thought. The drink came. Mrs. Nestor waved the money away . . . "yer Christmas box . . ." She fixed a look of granite on O'Malley.

"Aren't you the right pup . . ."

He flinched but said nothing.

"I hear the guards beat the lard outa you . . . I knew yer mother, God rest her, if she were alive to see this . . . she'd . . . she'd turn in her grave. One peep outa ya in here, mister, and I'll blacken yer arse for ya . . . do ya hear me."

He sure did . . . and half the town I would have thought.

"Yes, ma'am." She threw the eye towards me.

"You're not the worst of them, Dillon, I'll give you that."

We drained the pints in a silent penance. I ordered two more.

"What will I do, Dillon, my case comes up before the judge next week . . . and if it's Carty, I'm fecked . . ."

"I dunno, what can you do . . ."

"The Weir are looking for five hundred pounds damage. I know . . . look, Dillon, I know I owe you twenty-five quid but . . . but will you lend me £450."

"What . . . I thought you said they wanted £500 . . ."

"Ary, not to pay them crowd of ejits, to skip . . . you know . . . flog off to London . . . I know a fella in Kilburn High Road . . ." I didn't quite get it. I didn't see why he needed that amount.

"I don't see why you need that amount."

He sighed tolerantly. I was real glad he was going to be patient. The Guinness was chugged noisily. Mrs. Nestor even heard it as the living net on her head turned.

"If I'm going to London, I'll need a bit o' gear. Shoes, suit, and things. I saw a grand jacket in the sales."

So steal it, I thought, they're all at it. He was working on fervour now . . .

"And I thought like . . . as I'm going . . . forever . . . I'd give a bit of a do before I left . . . nothing fancy . . . just a few of the lads . . ."

He gave a loud cackle. Not a pleasant sound to hear. Worse, up real close. An actual slyness showed in his un-blackened eye. I saw it root.

" . . . oh . . . of course, you're invited, Dillon . . . give us more drink, Mrs . . . hey, Mrs . . ."

I wondered was he on somethin'. Apart from total insanity. Mrs. Nestor brought two creamy pints.

He leapt into it. I toyed with selecting my reply . . . thought carefully. Then the hell-with-it switch.

"I can't give you the money."

He hopped on the stool. This was a man whose life's plans had been snatched from him.

"What . . . what are you saying. I'm feckin' depending on you . . . if you break your word . . . if you let me down, I can't go . . . I'm dependin' on you, Dillon."

The roarin' of him brought Mrs. Nestor.

"What the blazes . . . O'Malley, finish up yer drink and clear off . . . or I'll put my boot in yer arse."

He didn't hear her. A man with his visions in ruins. The vision ruiner felt a beat of sympathy.

"O'Malley . . . I could mebbe give you thirty . . ."

"What . . . thirty, I wouldn't piddle on thirty. STICK IT. Do you expect me to do the rounds asking gob-shites for dribs and drabs. Is it coddin' ya are. STICK IT where the monkey stuck the peanuts . . . thirty . . . ha . . . ha . . . ha . . . come out here, Nestor."

I took my leave. On the street I could hear him roaring at her as to how she was fixed for thirty. I hadn't got my traditional blessing of "ya bollix." Mebbe some caution told him that in itself would have "Eileen" blacken his arse. I doubted that too. Caution that is.

The next five days were a blur of work. I doubled up on shifts. I dunno was I trying to raise cash for O'Malley. Probably not. The sales were in full blast. I was standing well clear of the entrance. On my third day of this double-shifting and reading double-visioned, I saw the Chinese waiter. He was with a wizened Chinese woman of similar height. Which wasn't a whole lot to start with. Hammering words to the dozen, he was attempting to push a large box into her unwilling hands. She was having none of this action. It vaguish crossed my mind as to what clothes he'd buy. Something in surliness to match his attitude no doubt. We did a slow line in kung fu apparel. The local muggers made do with a basic iron bar. Nothing fancy and they rarely drest for the occasion.

A voice behind me said, "I wouldn't mind a little nip . . ."

Gurteen! Nigh covered in contraband. He was one of the professional shoplifters. A craft to him and never a game. Always done with the utmost seriousness.

He'd wear absolute rags to a clothes shop. Into the dressing room and emerge resplendent. When shops mentioned their "write-off of acceptable losses," I think they had the Gurteen factor to the fore. The last shop assistant to challenge him found the three thugs perched outside her house for a week. She'd withdrawn the charges and Gurteen withdrew the three.

"I was in The Weir with ole Robbie last night . . . and he told me these days were the worse days of the worst of his life. What do you think of that?"

Could I say I'd head worse. No. Best not to ever encourage him.

"I'm teaching him all I know," he said.

Is there a reply to this? The mind didn't boggle, it threw somersaults. He popped a pill of some description. Into his black-toothed mouth.

"Do ya want something, Dillon? I've got . . . lemme see . . .

> . . . uppers
> . . . downers
> . . . chasers
> . . . levellers
> . . . alter-ers
> . . . shapers
> . . . bombers
> . . . maggots
> . . . coders
> . . . flyers
> . . . out-of-it-ers
> . . . destructers
> . . . high-fliers . . ."

I switched off. This would take a while. I sometimes felt he got off more on the names that the contents. The litany was a great comfort to him. Eventually, it wound down.

"No thanks."

"Clean, Dillon, eh . . . you're the last decade alrite. Did you hear about O'Malley?"

I hadn't.

"No I didn't . . . "

"He stole a car last night and ran it into a wall. Footless he was . . . absolutely paralytic, and he tried to drive. He's in the hospital now, and not badly hurt they say . . . the guards will have him as soon as he can walk."

Kilburn High Road would have to wait. Whatever Gurteen had popped seemed to mellow him. A hint of near warmth touched his eyes. A flicker . . . then was gone. A signal that Julie was next.

"Have ya seen much of yer wan . . . you know . . . Julie . . . "

"No . . . no I haven't."

"Well, do me a favour . . . would yah . . . I hear she's out of it . . . ya know. A bit off her game . . . and acting like . . . a zombie . . . would you go round to her place and see she's alrite."

"Yeah . . . yeah, I'll go round after work . . . thanks for telling me."

"Oh, hey, I don't care man, jeez, it's no skin off my nose . . . she never talks to me anyway . . . I think she's a jumped up snot . . . but well, she's yer friend . . . and what also have yah got . . . huh . . . wat-also."

"It's all there is, Gurteen – "

"You're all right, Dillon, you're a bit straight . . . but fecket, one of our own . . . aren't yah . . . I have to do . . . business . . ."

The visual I got of him was him slinking off behind the Chinese waiter. Going Chinese perchance. It wasn't nice to dwell on Gurteen's activities . . . I didn't know but I was already then the recipient of a legacy . . . or victim rather! On the way home, I stopped for something to eat. I ordered me a double toasted ham and an elephant coffee. Get that caffeine down. I needed stimulation? I was feeling good. Nigh five days without a drink. Phew-oh, I had that licked. Five full days. Mighty. That impressed the hell outa me. Food, lookit, I had my appetite wham'd back. Smoking only a little. See, a shot of discipline and you can kick-shape your life to where you choose. The Gods were chuckling deep. Vicious bastards.

I opened *The Daily Mirror* and was a man content. My horoscope confirmed it all.

"Nothing can stop you now. You are scaling new heights of achievement. Money is foremost and the future is bright."

I bit deep into the sandwich. M . . . m . . . m . . . Delicious; was that good or what. Lay another one of these suckers on me, please. A hint of tomato, and we'd be cruising. Sip the coffee . . . creamy . . . m . . . m . . . hm with a hint of bitterness . . . perfect.

A man sat opposite. Sit . . . sit, my friend. I was full of fellowship . . . more importantly . . . cash. I'd gotten paid and had converted it at lunchtime. Two hundred smack-aronies massaging my ass.

"Thank you . . . am . . . for your assistance the other day . . ."

I looked at him. The shoplifter who'd crashed into me. An educated one by the tone. You can't beat an education, seems to stand to you no matter what your calling. I could rise to moral indignation and demand to know what he was suggesting. My humour was too fine for such nonsense. I gave him a toasted-hammed smile. Encouraged, he said,

"Would you be a betting man?"

"Not very often . . . no."

"I'd like to suggest the name of a horse to you, he will win."

"Fine . . . fine . . ."

He looked at his watch.

"If you go now, you'll get the bet down. It's the last race in Limerick, the horse is called Carlo's Choice . . ."

I am as open as the next ejit to the call of coincidence. Stretch a point and you could build a case for the stray dog Carlo choosing Julie. Why not. The shop-lifter looked like a photo-fit. Ordinary features of no note. Plainly assembled. The eyes mebbe you would recall. They had a type of weeping sadness. Something had crushed him early and he'd never emerged from beneath the hammer. He was about forty-five and I'd say each year was hard earnt.

"Okay . . . I'll do it . . . thanks."

"You are very welcome; go as much as you possibly can on it. It *will* win."

Betting shops are as numerous as churches and nigh on as prosperous. They just don't advertise so blatantly. The Bookie's was drab. Depressing and silent save for the radio doling out results. Dire results. To look at the customers, you'd know pencils are a flourishing industry. The stubs of them anyway. Emotion was forbidden. How much to bet. Be sensible. A slight flutter. Lose only what you won't miss. The voice of practicality dirged out the principles of restraint. I put a hundred pound to win. Half the pay packet. I didn't feel the vivacious thrill. I thought of the kicker the pre-tax amount was. I didn't look at odds or rider . . . or form. My father knew all there was conceivable to know about racing. He never collected a shilling. "You have to study form . . . know the stats." He'd be martyred with yankee's doubles, trebles, cross trebles, and I wondered why he couldn't select one horse . . . one plain winner. I knew better than to share that thought with him.

I stopped outside to let the race occur. Pat, the bus conductor, followed me. I hadn't seen him since Christmas Day. He was chasing a cure then. Didn't look much like he'd found it.

"How are you doing, Pat?"

"Ary, Dillon, I'm smoking like a mad thing again . . . did you back anything."

"Yeah, I did Carlo's Choice . . ."

"That thing isn't worth a shite . . . I hope you didn't put much on him . . ."

"No . . . no."

I smoked half a cigarette . . . and he galloped through three. You couldn't accuse him of enjoying them. The grimaces were testimony of that. An aroma of stale booze enshrouded him. The word reek fits best. To add ridicule to the blatancy, he had chewed mints . . . a lotta mints.

"How are the buses these days?" I asked.

"Aw, Dillon, I'm off sick, the oul chest has bin acting up something fierce. How would you be fixed for a few quid. I can let you have it next Friday."

I gave him a five spot and we said no more about it. He lit another cigarette and smoked off.

Ho-kay . . . go get that result. Carlo's Choice won. At seventeen to one. The Bookie asked me to drop in the next morning and he'd have it "presentable." . . . I didn't know how to react to a big win. My whole life had been lived under the "fall syndrome." Crap will fall . . . and regular . . . and on me. So you kept your head down and stored in slices of goodness quietly. If ya didn't go a bundle on a bit of pleasantry, the Gods didn't feel the need to chastise you later.

I learnt the first rule of gambling. Look like a loser. Get that serious expression. Yeah, this is serious business. My heart didn't buy a word of this and bellowed and palpitated to its own celebration. Greece, I could go to Julie's Greece. If she was going to live there, I could take my holiday to coincide. I didn't know how delighted she could be. But I felt it would go well . . . right!

Not exactly.

I went to my flat to collect Julie's spare key. We had a reciprocal arrangement on this. I bought a bottle of that ouzo she was always raving about. Let's get this Greek show on the natived road.

I rang first . . . no reply. I'd leave the ouzo in her kitchen and that would knock a stir from her. It wouldn't. Nor would anything else . . . ever again. She was in bed and she sure looked like she was only sleeping. The empty Seconal bottle was minding the empty vodka. Lethal buddies. Both helped prop up the white envelope . . . "Young Dillon" was written there.

The power of T.V. I felt for a pulse. No. Carlo was nowhere to be found. Nor did I ever clap an eye on him again. I called an ambulance and got the taxi rank to contact her father. I took the envelope and without any hesitation . . . the ouzo.

The following evening I had a coffee with Mr. Brady. He looked like I felt . . . spaced.

"Was there a note or anything?" he asked.

"No," I said. I was thinking of how I'd lent her that Mailer book two years before. Was that where she'd picked up on the Seconal. Guilt by any other name. The power of dubious literature.

That morning I'd collected my winning. Well over £1500.

"Mr. Brady, I want you to take this, it's towards the cost of the funeral. Please let me do this . . ."

He gave me a slow look. Then he took the envelope.

"I think I know why it is you went to all them funerals."

"Do you?"

"Nobody went to your father's . . . not even yerself . . . it's as if you decided funerals in future would have at least one mourner. Would that be right?"

"'Tis close enough."

. . . and it was.

"You won't be at . . . at J . . . U . . . L . . . at this funeral . . . will you?"

"No sir."

. . . and I wasn't.

A big turn-out by all accounts . . .

Later that night . . . I had a mug of ouzo . . . foul stuff . . . like a wino's pernod. But mebbe it grew on you; I'd be finding out . . . soon. Julie's envelope contained only these lines, nowt else . . .

dear eddie
   . . . this legacy will explain everything and shed light on nothing.
"leave you
the leavings of
an inarticulated thanks
– will you
the echoes of the lives
as yet un-writ
term you
the keeper of my conciliatory heart
that heart
as mortgage held"

Was it on meself or did this ouzo grow on you . . . more of it . . .

***

Characters Concluding

O'Malley's case was heard. He was fined five hundred pounds. The muttering beneath his breath of the traditional form "ya bollix" may have contributed to the six months hard labour he also received . . . to be served in Mountjoy Prison. Which is a far enough shout from Kilburn High Road.

Carlo, the dog, never turned up. I like to think he found himself another Julie. But that's unlikely. She was kinda rare . . .

"Bad Weather" continues to hold his fixed opinion on climatic conditions.

Ted dropped his earring and has become vocal and tiresome in local politics. A bright future seems certain.

Robbie has begun to follow the funerals.

Raoul got run-over.

The three thugs are thugging.

Rooney, the tea-trolley maestro, got a stroke. He is now the recipient of dead tea and deader biscuits.

Marisa got engaged to Ted. She's involved in the arts and reads poetry at Race Meetings, or is it the other way round?

Nurse Allison Brown is dating a fading security guard . . . she seems happy.

The Funerals are still running . . . on the usual daily basis . . . or so I hear.

The winos . . . there's a new batch on the Square . . . but leaderless, insofar as I can tell.

Pat, the bus conductor, is being dried-out in the local hospital. He continues to smoke.

Gurteen is attempting to convert "Eileen" Nestor's Pub into-late nite disco. He still manages to put in some part-time psychopathing.

Mr. Darcy (Marisa's father) started drinking and is a regular fixture (if not attraction) of the early morning houses.

Mrs. Darcy got religion.

And *Julie's father* . . . well . . . he's staying sober.

"Funeral III"

"of
            the
                        wino"
Blame it on . . .
an intuition
I hadn't heard
and
certainly
would night on certainly
believe
a life
upon the streets

At least for long
I'd not survive
the sabotage in hope

for far too long
I'd lived
one drink

68

above despair
the turning to
the Kings Arms Public
House
A hearse
Before
I watched a wino
place
his hand above his
heart

I'd know
a cap
if he had owned
would slow . . . and
very slow remove
shake-so
the shakes . . . dis-
regarding

. . . "A silence in Respect" . . .
the cortege pass . . . press-on . . . to
press
his hand . . . the day across
this moment new
passed nigh beyond
the oldest explanation
a hand towards
expectations
not renewed

the coffin doesn't pass
the rich hotels
that cater to
the very rich . . . exclusively
their hands
towards the exhortations
aren't shaped.

***

The

End . . .

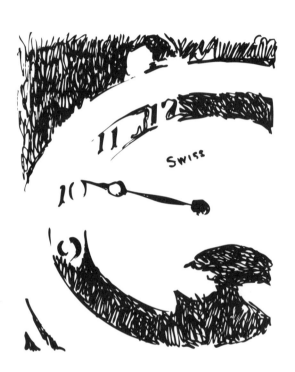

MARTYRS

"**b**e-cups . . . that's what I call them."

"Excuse me?"

"That's my little pet name for them. You think that's chauvinistic I suppose."

Beck didn't suppose anything . . . save the man was an ejit. The rumble of the tube train could be heard. People milled forward. The man moved right up to Beck, continued,

"Hey . . . hey, sonny, I'm talking to you . . . too much to expect a reply . . . is it? Too snooty to answer a person?"

A faint but persistent hiccup was indeed evident. Beck turned, said,

"Faint ones are a symptom of AIDS."

"What . . . Are you serious?"

"I don't know. I mean . . . personally I don't know. But according to *The Lancet* . . ."

Beck let him digest that . . . the train was fast approaching. He reckoned he'd the man nigh full primed. Another little push . . .

"*The Lancet* is . . ."

"I know what the flaming thing is. Christ on a bicycle . . . they'd know . . . I mean . . . they're the experts . . ."

"Gotcha," thought Beck and, "now." He let his expression darken and just before he hopped the train, said, "It's the masculine ones . . . the he-chaps . . . they're the ones to do you in."

As realisation hit the man's face, Beck was losing himself in the crowd . . . he muttered, "Suck on that."

Stephen Beck was 38 years old. To quote James Ellroy,

"38 and going on dead."

If he had to quote a writer, make it a crime one . . . and a particularly manic type. Keep them guessing. When people retorted,

"Ah, you read crime novelists."

He said,

"No."

He was 5'10" in height, losing what brown hair he'd had and stockily built. Brown eyes redeemed a mouth that longed to remain turned down. His nose looked broken and badly repaired. A sinus problem didn't add to its appeal. His teeth were white, even and gleaming. Usually in a glass.

Once watching Tony Bennett, he felt a surge of identification.

"Nothing about either of us is real."

Beck was a college graduate. In sociology. This equipped him, he believed, to juggle balls on street corners. What he did was run a market stall.

Tell folks you were in marketing and they launched into stocks and options banter.

"Which area of marketing, Stephen?"

"Where the Walworth Road meets East Lane. A statistic up from the Elephant and Castle."

They thought he was droll . . . if somewhat tedious. His mother on first hearing the news shrieked,

"For this you went to college . . . ?"

"Mother, I spent twenty years in Education. I reckon another twenty to undo the damage."

Beck had made some major fuck-ups. No argument.

An ex-wife, an ex-child and no excuses. His daughter, four years old, was the light of his existence. But it seemed he saw her less and less. Perversely he reckoned this increased his love . . . and it wasn't a redeeming love. It tortured him. He'd removed her photo from his wallet and scorched her further from his heart.

Lately, he'd placed a Dictionary of The Saints next to Elmore Leonard. He'd search through it, for the Martyrs, wanted to know how they screwed up initially and then recovered all in or by the final burning act. A death scenario he wasn't planning, but the general plan lay in there somewhere.

Take Kerry. A virgin she'd said . . . O.K. Then she'd blown, rode, teased, tied and used him through every variation. Midway she'd said,

"Don't come yet!"

"Excuse me?"

He wasn't claiming to be some expert but had he missed something along the way. But come on . . . was it the sort of quote virgins uttered – Surely . . . the coming was generally held to be of some surprising significance. Enough women had faked it with him for him to know the result.

Later, he'd had to ask . . .

"Am . . . I thought you said you were . . . am . . ."

"A virgin?"

"Am . . . yes."

"Technically I am."

"Technically!"

"Oh sure, I've had dozens of men – dozens."

A neon sign lit above his head. It screamed AIDS.

"No man has ever penetrated my heart."

. . . And goodnight Kerry.

***

The success of the family was Martin. He was almost beyond cliché . . . tall, handsome, smart, capable. You met Martin. You reached for superlatives. Worse, he was a nice guy. In the old sense of that label. He'd lend you money without a lecture and in his company you felt of worth.

He was three years younger than Stephen and they'd always been close. In the early '80s, he made mountains of money in property. A darling of the Gods. But, as usual, they turned vicious, sent "Black Monday" and Martin came crashing down. First financially, then all the others too. He hit the booze and then the booze lashed back. With ferocity. Dark clouds had never entered Martin's view. Now it seemed as if a permanent winter had bought his soul.

With no option to sell.

The spiral fizzled out at the Maudsly Hospital. Martin was now already ten months a patient there. Only Stephen was welcome.

He'd said,

"So, Stevie, did you know I tried A.A.?"

"No . . . any good?"

"Well now Stevie, I'm here, in the lock-up ward . . . What do you think, eh . . . am I a success story?"

"Are you going to tell me about it or not?"

Truth was, Stephen wasn't even vaguely interested. Martin sensed this and thus continued,

"They said it was easy. All you had to do was go to meetings and . . ."

"And?"

"Change your whole freaking life."

"Sounds a piece of cake."

"They're all C.I.A."

Uh . . . uh, thought Stephen . . . paranoid delusion, spooks everywhere. Wistful smiles from Martin.

"Don't frown like that, Stevie . . . it highlights yer baldness.

"C.I.A. . . . . it's a little A.A. humour."

"Oh yeah."

"Yeah . . .

Catholic
Irish
Alcoholic
. . . gettit?"

Yea, Stephen got it all right. What he didn't get was where it was particularly humorous. Perhaps you had to be there. But would you want to be?

Martin was warming to his theme. Stephen's sourness helped. A sidebar of Martin's illness was "No more Mr. Nice Guy."

"They're a weird outfit these same A.A's. A young girl told the most horrendous story."

"Her name wasn't Kerry was it?"

"What . . ."

"Nothing, you were saying?"

"Yea right. So this girl who is NOT CALLED KERRY does her horror number and you know what they did?"

"I have no idea."

"They laughed . . . shower of BASTARDS. Anyway, this guy cornered me after the meeting. A holy roller. Piety was leaking outa him. He was Welsh, with that singsong voice. I misheard him and thought he was trying to flog me something. Yo . . . boys, I said, I got family in the market . . . in the actual market place.

". . . O.K., so I was being literal but he got real shirty and pushed off. Only later I realised he was saying 'Higher Power.'"

Beck was lost.

"I'm lost, Martin, I don't catch the gist."

"For fucksakes, Steve-o, wake up and smell the coffee. I thought he said 'Hire Purchase.'"

Martin's voice had risen.

"You used to be so sharp . . . you're not paying attention, is that it. The mental case is boring the arse off you . . . is that it?"

Stephen tried to interrupt. Martin was a decibel from roaring and ranted further.

"The old mad house humour not up to yer high standards . . . ? Oh God, I'm shouting . . . Whoa, hey, can't have that. Keep the lunatic tranquil."

"Martin . . . Ple-ASE, don't say that."

"Well it's true, I mean look around you . . . this ain't the Golf Club. It's the Bobby Hatch

> A Home for the Chronically
> Wired
> for the dipstick dysfunctional."

A nurse came running.

"Time to leave Mr. Beck . . ."

"Yeah," said Martin, quieter now, "Run from the loony," and then in a whisper,

> ". . . Sorry Steve-o
> . . . sorry
> I'm sorry."

***

Steve fumbled his way to the bus stop. A bus came almost immediately. Dropping into a seat, a woman opposite him said,

"You're in luck love, this is the first bus for ages."

"No."

"I beg your pardon."

"Not in luck, what I'm in is bits."

The woman settled herself and her whole posture suggested "Chat." With a sinking feeling, he knew intuitively she'd share her surgical experience.

"Ah for fucksakes," he groaned, and leapt from the platform at Camberwell. He heard her exclaim,

"Well, I never!"

There's a mean pub on the Green, it has a reputation for violence.

"Good," thought Stephen and slammed in.

"Yo" . . . from the barman. "Here comes the Cisco Kid!"

Stephen did the smart thing, ignored it. The barman was short, bald and despite a beer gut, enclosed in an ultra tight waistcoat.

Stephen said,

"Gordons . . . yeah, Gordons if you've got it."

He wanted to add,

"And if you can spell it."

But, priorities, drink first, insults later.

Miffed, the barman said,

"Would sir require lemon?"

"Yea, float one of those suckers in there."

Large gulp and the glass was empty. Stephen felt it hit his stomach like bad news. Exactly what he'd planned.

The barman tapped his own bald head.

"When did your thatch leg it?"

"Excuse me?"

"It's not a difficult question, when did you go bald?"

Each time was like a fresh shock – somehow. Stephen hoped it was like the flu . . . unpleasant but of limited duration. He never believed truly HE was bald. Receding maybe, strong forehead . . . OK even, Godhelpus, stripped temples . . . these could be borne. But bald, so blunt and final.

Stephen had no answer to give so he didn't even try.

That the pub had a rep for violence was no surprise. People probably stood in line to pump the crap out of the barman.

"Let me have another Gordons, better make it a double . . . and have one yourself."

"Thank you kindly . . . don't mind if I do . . . the old stomach's playing up . . . perhaps a hint of brandy & port for settlement purposes."

They smiled.

"Cheers."

"Good health . . . and hair."

"So . . . no work today?"

Stephen sighed, said,

"It's raining!"

"This prevents you working? Good grief, I hate to be the one to break this to you, seeing how we just met, but you're living in the wrong country. To coin a bon mot," (he pursed his lips), "but England is not renowned for its dryness . . . thus in fact . . . The Burberry . . . "

Surely, Stephen thought, one brandy couldn't alone be responsible for this verbal onslaught. The bastard must have been nipping all morning.

"The markets. I have a stall."

". . . and no cover, thus climatic conditions have stalled operations."

"Touché," said Stephen, and all of a sudden he was tired of the guy.

Draining the gin, he made to leave. The barman performed what can only be described as a pirouette.

"You'll come back and see us real soon . . . you hear?"

Stephen muttered,

"Not in this lifetime, pal."

***

Stephen had a council flat near the Oval cricket ground. "An area coming back," according to a quality Sunday paper. "Where had it been?" he wondered.

In an old building, the flat was basic. One bedroom, living room, bathroom, kitchen. Each room appeared smaller than the next, damper than December. The living room had one armchair, one sofa. All of one wall was lined with books. A beaten record player, still functional, propped the books. Teems of records overspilt the carpet. One large bay window had a sizable hole. Depending on his mood, he attributed it to either the Pakistan fast bowler or a 12 gauge.

Times too, he half believed it. Why not, might it indeed have been thus. He took the Saint's Dictionary in his lap, the Penguin edition. The soft fold of the book was comfort of itself. Bend it, and in time . . . it slipped back to itself. Unlike Martin.

Was there a Martin the Martyr? He found this entry:

"MARTIN THE FIRST"

A pope no less, in 655. He fell foul of the Byzantine Emperor, Constans II. A nasty piece of work. For 47 days, Martin refused water to wash and was racked by dysentery. What food he received was enough to make him vomit. He died in the Crimea and was then deemed a martyr.

Stephen pondered this. Things weren't quite so rough at The Maudsly. He'd have to check out the food, but didn't imagine dysentery was a major problem. Still, in S.E. London, you couldn't be too careful.

On a flick through the start of the book, he was startled by an entry. Yea, under B. . . there it was, Bee.

"Nun, Refugee from Ireland."

Beck's mother was Irish and her full name was Elizabeth Mary Beck née Olionnor. She'd always been called Bee.

"As I was industrious . . . always working."

Stephen had never known her to do a hand's turn. From Galway, the hometown of James Joyce's wife.

"Oh, I knew Nora Barnacle. A plain girl."

Impossible as this must have been, she clung to it and felt it gave her an insight into the writer.

"If he'd found a pretty girl, he wouldn't have bothered with all that smut."

A tall woman with striking eyes, she gave the impression of intelligence. What she was . . . was sick. A cunning mixed with manipulation was cloaked in sweetness. You'd nearly thank her for making you feel bad. Stephen's most recent encounter with her had not gone well.

He'd gone round to her home off Clapham Common. Her welcome was close to manic.

"Stephen, darling . . . how wonderful. What a beautiful surprise."

"Bit over the top, Mother . . . eh?"

She was wearing a bright pink track suit, her hair was currently fiery red. The impression was of a thunderball, blazing . . . And coming right at you.

"Unchained Melody" was blaring in the background. She saw herself as a child of the sixties which was as true as the Nora Barnacle yarn.

"Sit down darling . . . you must have smelled the tea."

"Coffee, Mother . . . I don't drink tea . . . Remember . . . it's Martin, he drinks tea."

"How is Martin, poor Lamb?"

"Mad."

"Oh dear, at what?"

"Clinically mad."

"Yes, well, I'll get the tea."

Stephen fell into the armchair. Such times he wished he smoked. His mother chain-smoked Silk Cut Mild and he'd inject heroin before he'd follow.

"Now isn't this cosy."

A large tray was placed between them. China cups, scones and a mammoth teapot.

Stephen had a malicious thought, said,

"Let's let you be mother and pour."

Waste of time. She'd skipped past such remarks all her life . . . Stored them . . . sure, and paid back, but later.

"Milk?" she asked.

"That's tea . . . is it?"

"Yes, you asked for tea . . . odd, I thought you were a coffee drinker."

He gulped the tea.

"Jesus . . . Mother, what is that . . . dried seaweed?"

"Chamomile?"

"Couldn't you just get Lipton's or something?"

"You'll develop a taste for it."

"But why would I want to?"

"Health, Stephen, treat the body well and the mind will follow. It's not too late to save your hair."

. . . Paid back.

Wearily, he took a shot.

"This . . . this from a smoker . . . no . . . a chain smoker."

"Tut, Stephen, sticks and stones! There's something I wish to ask you."

"So ask."

"How would you like to call me B.B.?"

"What?"

I feel the time has come to deformalize our relationship. 'Mother' sounds so . . . so cold, distant even. I think this might bring us closer."

"Like buddies you mean?"

"Oh yes, Stephen, you've got it exactly. You are that clever. You could have gone so far, like Martin."

"I've just been to where Martin went. I didn't like it much."

"You like it then . . . B.B.?"

"Sounds like an airgun."

"You kidster, Stevie . . . Think how if we were in a restaurant, how it would sound to the waiter."

"You'd want the waiter to call you B.B. too?"

"NO, silly . . . he'd hear you address me as B.B. and . . ."

"And what exactly. He'd tell the boys in the kitchen, there's a bald guy calling his oul wan B.B."

"I hate to rush you, Stephen, but then I'm expecting an important call."

They had an awkward moment at the door. A hug was out of the question.

"Then you'll call me B.B.?"

He looked at his shoes . . . then slowly met her eyes.

"Not if I live to be a hundred."

***

Stephen replayed the talk with his mother on his marriage plans. At first she said nothing. Then,

"You know Stephen, I have quite a healthy nest egg put by."

"That's good, Mother. Nice to sleep easy at night."

"Well, I've been thinking. A young man ought to have his own pad . . . a bachelor pad . . . in a nice area."

"Pad . . . Jesus wept . . . Have you been mixing with beatniks or something? Jack Kerouac will never be dead."

"Really Stephen, you talk so strange. Anyway, where was I?"

"You were thinking . . . As Sundance said to Butch, 'Keep thinking Butch, it's what you're good at.' As I recall the Mexican army was just about to punch their tickets."

"Do stop interrupting . . . What I had in mind was £25,000 to secure down payment on a good single man's apartment."

"Ah, right, this . . . this inducement is open only to a continuing bachelor."

"Tut tut, Stephen, as if I'd bribe my own son. Really, the very idea of it . . . it's just that were you to marry at this moment in time, I'd be unable to disturb the nest egg."

Stephen knew exactly how to respond. How you'd tell someone you behaved. Naturally, you leapt to your feet . . . spluttering . . . bristling with indignation. He was especially fond of the bristle. The old splutter wasn't too bad either. You cried,

"How dare you attempt to bribe me . . . the effrontery to think for a minute I could be bought. This is the woman I love. I'll thank you never to mention her name again. The cheque hasn't been written, etc . . . However, if you didn't intend telling anyone."

Stephen rose, looked squarely at his mother and said,

"When might I have this money?"

Three weeks later, he and Nina were married. Mrs. Beck, Senior, was not among those in attendance. Peter Ustinov said that parents were the bones on which children sharpen their teeth. Stephen would dearly have loved to introduce his mother to him. See what he'd write then.

***

NINA

Stephen met her his first year at college. Just over 5 foot, she had the English pretty face that disintegrates into plainness. Inclined to plumpness, she lived from diet to tortured diet. Her quietness attracted him. She had a sporadic humour that time would sharpen.

Mrs. Beck disliked her instantly and showed it. Nina studied English Lit. and did a further year's training as a Teacher of English as a Foreign Language. On graduation, Stephen proposed and she said "No." She wanted to travel, and Stephen . . . he said,

"I want to stall."

"You've stalled enough, Steve, time to get moving."

"I'm serious Nina . . . I want to run a market stall."

"Whatever else you might be Steve, alas, serious isn't one of them."

Mrs. Beck was delighted.

"You're well rid of that wan. Mark my words, she'll end up working for the poor in Calcutta."

"She's a teacher for God's sake."

"Wait and see. The likes of that wan ease their guilt by highlighting everyone else's."

"Mother, that might even be profound were it not so vicious. As it is, it's plain vicious."

"And Nina is a professional depressive. She works at it . . ."

Stephen got his stall and then the years blended into casual encounters, the pub and banality.

The night of his 33rd birthday, he invited some of the market traders for a drink. On the other side of five vodkas, the good side, he said aloud,

"Fuck, how did I get to 33? I turned my head for an instant when I was 19 . . . and bang . . . I'm over 30 . . . from nowhere."

"Your language hasn't improved."

First he didn't recognise her . . . she had glasses, the plumpness was gone. A leanness now and her hair cut short.

"So," she asked, "did you miss me?"

"What do you think."

"I think you might buy me a drink."

He did, and six months later, they married. The twenty-five grand he lodged in a new account. Martin was best man. A rich one. He'd asked,

"Do you love her?"

"No."

"At all?"

"I'm not even sure I like her."

"Well Steve-o, I hate to be obvious, but why did you decide to marry?"

"She's pregnant."

"Steve . . . this is the '80s, buddy. No one does the decent thing. You fuck off, it's almost mandatory."

"I like to be awkward."

"From your lips to God's ear."

"I don't think God listens a whole lot anymore, Martin."

"Let's hope he isn't today."

The baby came, a girl, and turned Stephen's world. He expected he'd like the child . . . well, it was natural. He intended to provide for her. But he never expected to be involved. The day of her birth, they handed the baby to him. He had the appropriate responses prepared,

"Oh gee . . . wow . . . I'm amazed."

And then?

And then what you did was go to the pub and get legless. "Wet the baby's head," total strangers bought you buckets of it. He liked that scenario.

Ideally, you'd have contact with the baby when she was four and cute and most of all . . . behaved. All the leaky parts you left to the mother. Guys don't know about that stuff.

From the moment he held her, looked at her, he was taken. His heart felt kicked. The pub was forgotten. In the weeks after, he was the one to wash, feed, change and comfort. Nina went back to work, his stall went to the dogs. A love beyond him had altered the world. For 6 months, he lived in her tiny shadow.

Almost the caricature of the doting father. If a stranger asked him the time, he'd show her photo first. His local pub had her framed next to Lady Di. That he was tiptoeing on the lunacy of obsession fazed him not at all.

"You love that child too much."

"How can you love too much?" he asked . . . I wish I'd had that problem myself!

He bought a video to check out the range of children's cartoons and found he loved *Lady and the Tramp*. The day she'd watch with him was a source of joy in purity. Even *Sesame Street* had become unmissable.

When he was checking through brochures for schools, Nina sat before him.

"What are you doing Stephen?"

"Schools. I want to be sure they're the best."

"That's nice . . . Do you think the market stall will pay for them? What? You'll sell a few extra Korean watches and pay for a term, is that it . . . is that the master plan? Bearing in mind you haven't tended the stall for six months. 'If I might plan a little,' that's bloody rich, in fact . . . it's priceless."

Nina, this may be the best time of all to tell you. I have money. A whole bundle of it, and I think you'll appreciate the irony.

He told her . . . Then added,

"£25,000, are you delighted?"

"You're a piece of work Stephen, a real one off. You thought I'd be pleased . . . you . . . you fuckin' moron . . . As if I'd touch a penny of that . . . or let my daughter be smeared with it."

"Our daughter . . . Jesus Nina, come on . . . Money has no conscience, it doesn't care."

"I care . . . I bloody care, how dare you sell me?"

"What?"

"You like surprises . . . well, here's one for you. I got the job in Brussels and I leave in a week."

"Brussels, what job, you never said."

"No Stephen, you never listened . . ."

"But the baby, how will you be able to leave her?"

"I don't intend to."

"What, you think I'll go to Brussels?"

"I don't want you to come."

Slowly he began to comprehend what was happening.

"You're leaving me?"

"That's right . . . you'll miss me, is that it? You haven't touched me since the baby came."

He floundered, felt it all slide . . . in desperation tried . . .

"The market, that's it, isn't it? Don't worry, I'll do something else . . . use my degree."

"Worry . . . I'm not worried Stephen. I now know the market is where you belong. You can feel superior and still have street cred . . . 'Oh, I could do anything I wanted' – wise-up. You've risen to the level of your arrogant incompetence. Poverty is still a romantic notion for you. Well not for me. I was raised with it, the smell and feel of it . . . no toilet, six in a bed, third-hand clothes. You're worse than a loser Stephen . . . You just never showed up."

Stunned, he was silent. Nina had never spoken this much in all the time he'd known her. He wanted to say "my Mother was right about you." Looking at her face, he felt she might stab him if he did. Instead he said,

"I'll fight you . . . I won't let you take the baby . . . I'll use the money to get lawyers."

"You won't do shit, Stephen."

The curse was like a slap.

"You've never fought for a thing in your life. I don't doubt you think you want to, but you just don't know how . . ."

"Believe you me, I do and I will."

"You'll do nothing."

She was right. That evening she left for her mother's. Stephen sat in the same chair, the school brochures before him. From time to time, he'd lift one, give a soft murmur, and lay it gently back on the table. As gently, as carefully as if it was a baby. When the hall door banged, he remembered the stage direction at the end of Ibsen's *The Doll's House*. Remembered and felt forlorn.

When he was sure they were gone, he threw back his head and let loose a howl of anguish . . . Then he whispered,

"My Mother . . . my Mother . . . was . . . my . . ."

Unknown to himself, he'd begun to shred the brochures.

By the time darkness fell, his chair was littered with scraps of glossy paper. From a distance, the street light hit the shiny paper and suggested a picture of almost cosiness.

Soft cries, such as a baby makes, punctuated the silence.

***

When he'd come to trail the Martyrs in later years, it wouldn't occur to him to check "Nina." Eventually he would, and find no trace; saint, martyr or even blessed. A grim satisfaction followed.

During his years at college, Stephen had one close friend. A priest who had to take sociology courses as part of the new Church expansionist outlook. Fr. Jim was a mature student. Ten years older than the other students, he cultivated the professed Irishness so beloved by the B.B.C. A native of Dublin, he was over 6 foot, built to endure with a wild head of greying curls. Stephen met him as they near collided to the door of a lecture. Jim was carrying a large heavy stick. Stephen stepped back to allow him to enter first.

"Manners, Good Lord . . . what a rarity."

Jim was in civvies so his calling wasn't apparent.

"That cudgel you're carrying would improve anybody's manners."

"That's not a cudgel, yah ignoramus. You've no Irish connections, me boyo, or you'd know that's a hurley."

"A wot?"

"It's used in the game of hurling . . . and before you display further ignorance, hurling is a cross between hockey and murder. That wood is ash . . ."

"Ash and you shall be answered."

"That's very poor, are you sure you're on the right course, with wit as putrid as that, you should be in political science. Come to think of it . . . you have the look of a socialist . . . or is that socialite . . ."

"You don't half talk do you. I'm Stephen . . . Stephen Beck."

"Pleased to meet you, Stephen Beck. I'm Jim Nealy . . . in fact, I'm Father Jim Nealy . . . what do you think of that?"

"To tell the truth, I'm more impressed with the hurley."

"Wise man . . . let's go in and get educated . . . O.K.? Mebbe later we'll get a drink. You do drink, don't you?"

"Does the Pope dictate?"

" . . . Less of that, boyo . . . you don't know me yet."

***

Two days after Nina's departure, Stephen moved from the flat. He gathered up all the booze they had. Quite a selection.

> Scotch
> Crème de Menthe
> Rosé wines
> Port
> Pernod
> Guinness
> and even four of a lethal number called Arak.

He poured all into the blender, a wedding present, and let it rip. The he took the baby's bottles and filled six of them with this cocktail from hell.

They were lined up next to the armchair. Next, he prepared the music. A mix of

> Emmylou Harris
> Sex Pistols
> The Messiah
> And Jose Carreras.

He set the control to repeated play. Finally, he put on a battered pair of 501's and a Lakers sweatshirt. And in his bare feet, he gingerly in the chair.

"Let us now begin," he muttered, and chuzzled a swallow of the first bottle. The Sex Pistols began to roar as it hit his stomach. As "Anarchy in the U.K." stormed, he felt the bombshell hit.

"Oh, for the love of God," he screamed, as the urge to vomit began. "Stay, ya bad bastard."

It did. As the bottles emptied, he hollered out of key, out of tune, but mainly out of his head. The music kept pace.

At one point he believed the door opened and left it thus, sinking back into the chair. If an armchair had been sometimes described as the neurotic's workshop, then his seat was a monument to flagellation.

He felt finally a hand slapping his face, and fought against the climb to consciousness. The slaps continued.

"Stop frigging that," he roared and looked up into the face of Fr. Jim. His hand, trembling, reached up to touch his friend's face.

"Are you real?"

"To the bane of Protestants everywhere, that I am."

Stephen began to cry and the priest put his arm round and began to rock him. He said,

"Sure, why wouldn't you bawl. Anyone who had to listen to that racket of music need never do another day's penance."

Later, he persuaded Stephen to shower and change clothes. As he began to tidy up, he smelled the baby's bottle.

"Lord God, I can only pray you weren't feeding this to the child."

"No . . . it was me."

"And did you never hear of glasses? Sit down there and I'll make you some hot broth."

He didn't inquire as to Nina or what had happened. Such is friendship.

Stephen said,

"Are you wondering what happened?"

"No, if you need to tell me, you probably will."

"Because I'm conditioned to tell a priest, is it?"

"Ah, don't turn nasty, I'm your friend whether you tell me or not, and no matter what you tell me."

"I never understood why you're my friend."

"Me neither."

"She's gone . . . and the baby, too."

A wave of despair rocked him, and he bit his clenched fist to suppress a howl of anguish hammering at his heart. Jim moved to him and gave him a hug like he'd never experienced. They were locked thus when a voice from the doorway said,

"Well, I never . . . have ye people no shame, or is an open door an essential part of the kick?"

Mrs. Beck, resplendent in a bright green track suit, green trainers and a distinctly yellow tinge to her hair. Her hand held the inevitable cigarette.

Jim leapt back. Stephen said,

"Mother, this is Father Jim."

"A priest . . . worse. I've heard stories of course, but one never expects to have it shoved in one's face . . . and one's own son."

"Shut up Mother, just shut the fuck up . . . What's all this 'one' business? You're Irish for Godsakes . . . not some Tory outrider."

Jim made to leave. Unfortunately, so did Mrs. Beck.

Stephen said,

"Maybe you'd better go, Jim. Mother's about to pull her concerned parent number. It won't stop her smoking, but it's nearly always hysterical."

Jim left quietly, promising to call later. Mrs. Beck began to rock and waul; this was the Irish wailing and lamenting. Even without a hangover, it's rough.

***

Gradually, Stephen had returned to the world. The following four years were merely significant for their insignificance. His daughter's photo disappeared from the pub, replaced for a time by Arthur Scargill. But he, too, had a sell-by date and Elvis now alone remained. Some icons are built for endurance. Stephen moved to the flat near the Oval and Martin went down the toilet.

The market stall resumed and he made a steady income. Electrical goods of all descriptions and watches. If pressed for a quality rating on these, he'd have said, "Shiny." Shone they did but briefly. Surprisingly few people complained and he was doing all right. For some, it is written, comes a horseman, for Stephen it came November. To paraphrase Scott Fitzgerald, "it was always that month in the darkness of his soul."

November 5th
He lost his daughter.
Martin's breakdown.
His Mother's birthday.
And
The stall was crowded.

A line of Korean lighters called Tippos were moving fast. The sun was actually shining and Stephen felt, if not contentment, at least a respite from nothingness.

A man stood directly before him. "I shall require your attention."

"Not like that old son."

"I beg your pardon?"

"The sunglasses, Squire. I'm not talking to a set of black frames. I know my Paul Newman cinema. Next, two Tippos, a wise investment – need a bag?"

The man didn't budge, said something Stephen only vaguely caught, something about bats.

"No bats here old son, least not till the sun goes down."

"Could you move out of the way, I have a business to run . . ."

"Your business is exactly why I'm here. V-A-T . . . I should have to see your returns."

"What, now?"

What he thought was, "Oh shit," and debated legging it.

The man read him exactly.

"Let's do this quietly, shall we . . . No playing silly beggars, eh, there's a good chap."

Stephen stared at him.

"Silly beggars! I can't believe you actually said that . . . this isn't *Coronation Street*, nobody talks like that!"

"Wotcha say me ole cock we nip down the old Bush & Bull . . . drink a few old toddys . . ."

" . . . Do us a bleeding favour."

Which was probably the wrong way to deal with officialdom. His stall was impounded and he'd be notified of a court appearance. The sun continued to shine on the other traders. Rodney, the oldest trader, came to commiserate.

"Bad break son, want me to come to court with you?"

"Thanks Rod, yeah, that would be good."

"How's Martin, is he still something in the city?"

"Well . . . not in the city."

"And yer old Mum, how's she then?"

"Still smoking."

"Ah Stevie, you only get the one . . . Ought to watch out for yer old Mum, know what I mean?"

"Believe you me, I know exactly what you mean."

As they hauled his livelihood away, he managed to palm one of a new line of watches. The irony of stealing from himself was not entirely lost on him. He did what you'd do after such an event.

Drink.

The pub near Waterloo was packed. Train robbers and florists.

Much the same thing these days. Service was fast and furious. No food available. Not a place for dabblers. You went there to get micky-arsed. Darts, pool, etc. were never mentioned. Look for a soft drink and you'll be whistlin' Dixie for it. No decoration or photos. A sole mammoth poster behind the bar proclaimed,

"Elvis has left the building."

Stephen hurriedly got on the other side of several large scotches. The glow began in the pit of his stomach and climbed delicately up behind his eyeballs. Such times he almost had a sense of fellowship so that even his mother couldn't have upset him.

He checked his new watch. It was either midnight or noon . . . and remained thus.

"Uh . . . uh," he thought.

Russian made, not bad to look at. Just as well as it didn't appear it had a whole lot else to recommend it.

"Pay V.A.T.?"

On these . . . oh yeah sure. The man next to him was humming quietly. It had the vaguest relation to Colonel Bogey, he had the cut of a docker.

The drink was cruising in Stephen's system, and he thought,

"Such men are the salt of the earth, made England what she was."

He asked,

"Do you have the time please?"

The man slow turned and asked,

"What's that on yer wrist?"

Stephen thought-switched, "A bad bastard . . . and a big one."

"What's it look like, it's stopped."

"What make is it?"

Stephen felt fury obliterate his bonhomie.

"Jeez, what is this, a quiz . . . I ask you the time, you hit back with fifty questions. It's Swiss."

Huge guffaw from the man.

"Swiss . . . Christ son, where have you been, the Swiss lost interest . . . they're totally into chocolate . . . Look."

And here he shoved a meaty wrist under Beck's nose, resplendent with an instrument fit to launch rockets, he continued,

"Tells the time all over the world."

"Wonderful . . . Congratulations. Does it by any chance give an idea of the time in S.E. London? Remember where I came into this conversation?"

"Hey, don't get sniffy with me my lad, I've a son your age."

The scotch bellowed thru Stephen. "You can take him," it urged. He listened to it and said,

"Do you think if you gave him a call, he might know the fuckin' time?"

"Time! Time is it, laddy . . . maybe time you learnt some manners."

But whatever he was drinking veered off him in another direction. Mellowness suddenly lit his face.

"What would you think I do, laddie . . . Go on, take yer best shot."

Stephen debated a right hook to the jaw . . . but said, "The docks . . . you're a loader, are you?"

High indignation lit the man's face. He shot two ploughs of hands into the air. Stephen near ducked.

"Docker . . . these are artist's hands, laddie. I knew Salvador Dali. I've suffered like he did. Gala made a pass at me once . . . Yo, barman, bring us a bunch of drinks." The barman did.

Stephen wondered who Gala was. "Who was Gala then?"

The man slurped some major alcohol.

"Gala was his Belle Dame . . . and not an ounce of mercy in the bitch, not a friggin' drop. When I met her, she was having live-cell injections. Course she wrote the book on plastic surgery. Alas, all of it became unglued, (so to speak) – and,"

he gave a manic laugh,

"– She was like a walking exploded boil."

"Jaysus," said Stephen, who could see her.

"Dali abandoned her. I took my work away from him then. He spent seven years, begging for death, lying alone in a black room . . . and drip fed . . ."

Stephen slipped quietly from his stool and stole out. The man was booming.

"Augustus John, now there was a Titan . . . And women, he'd ride yer mother."

"Don't think so," muttered Stephen.

The fresh air walloped him and he gasped.

"Cripes, I'm well pissed."

A wino waylaid him.

"Penny for the guy."

"Here, give him a watch, it's Russian so he can do his bit for Glasnost."

As Stephen crossed Waterloo Bridge, he glanced back. The wino hadn't moved. He was shaking the watch then holding it to his ear. Seconds later, he was chasing a pedestrian in an attempt to flog it.

"A nation of shopkeepers," belched Stephen.

Back on the Oval, Stephen looked long into the bathroom mirror.

"Is it on meself or do I look less bald?"

This was a regular occurrence, he'd drink way, way past target and believe his hair was returning. Alcohol as a hair restorative was a secret hope. Some saw elephants, he saw follicles. Come sleep, come baldness anew.

***

Two days later, he took his dictionary to the table.

This, too, was a Penguin edition.

"MARTYR."

1) One who is put to death for a cause, esp. a religion.

2) Victim of constant (self-inflicted) suffering.

Time to visit Martin.

A nurse said to him, "After you visit Martin, might I have a word."

Her badge read, "Emma O'Brien."

A little over five foot two, she had soft auburn hair to her shoulders. Stark blue eyes were huge in her head. A button nose highlit a mouth that was built to turn down. Her face and personality had other plans. A slight Irish lilt gave a gentleness to whatever she said.

He was staring.

She said, "So, see something you like, fella?"

"Wot . . . oh right . . . am . . . I'm a sucker for anyone in uniform."

"I'd say you got the sucker bit right . . ."

***

Martin was dressed in black, a jet-black track suit. White trainers had smudged as black as he could make them. A book lay open in his lap. Stephen started to speak but was shushed as Martin began to read,

"As he paces in
cramped circles, over and

over the movement
of his powerful soft strides
is like a ritual
dance around a
centre
in which
a mighty will
stands paralysed."

"Know that?"

"I don't."

"It's Rilke. 'The Panther'. I found it in their library here. Pretty depressive dude all round, but he's in the right place. You're thinking I'm in black for the poem. Right."

"Actually I was thinking I'd murder for a cup of tea."

"Oh, we'll get you that . . . I'm in mourning for the person people hoped I'd be."

"I didn't hope you'd be anybody else."

"What else can you say. Who cares though, who the fuck cares what you think."

This fair obliterated conversation for a time. Martin said,

"I got a 'Get Well' card from Mother. Do you want to see it?"

"Am, not just now, maybe later."

"She addressed it to Martin Bic . . . does she think I'm a biro now?"

"It's so the postman won't know you . . . or her."

"What, do we know him? Anyway, she signed it B.B. What do you know about that?"

"It's a long story and a pathetic one."

Martin leapt to his feet.

"Nurse O'Brien, oh Nurse, two teas please."

Stephen began to protest but was cut off.

"You want the fucking tea or don't you?"

Nurse O'Brien brought two mugs. One had a logo for Rambo, the other read, "I'm your honey." Stephen took that. She asked,

"So lads, any biscuits or jam fancies for ye?"

They declined. Stephen drank, it was strong and kicked. Martin flicked his wrist and turned his mug over on his legs. The hot tea caused a rapid small cloud to rise. He smiled.

"They expect this sort of behaviour. Now you know why I wore black."

Stephen felt like rage personified, he bit on the edge of the mug for control. An urge to flake Martin to an inch of his petulant hide was overwhelming.

"Do you ever think of Dad?" asked Martin.

Mr. Beck had left when they were toddlers. Nothing had been heard of him since. Mrs. Beck had been linked to a man named Stan for fifteen years, but that's a later story.

"No . . . no, I don't."

"I miss him, Steve. I never knew him and I miss him. Daresay I say, isn't that madness."

"I don't . . . miss him . . . that is . . . he's a non-runner, an early withdrawal. He barely made it to the starting post, as it was. But I guess he's the English streak in me . . . You know I drop litter on the street, then I sneak back and put it in a bin."

Martin laughed, a real sound.

"Well, Steve, we'll keep a bed for you here."

"Thanks!"

"I don't think you'll find a more English Englishman than T. E. Lawrence."

"Lawrence of Arabia?"

"Yea . . . same guy. I like to think Dad is in the desert, looking at vast expanses of nothing and those amazing skies."

"Sure, full of scud missiles and other air-to-ground beauties."

"Last week I tired to read 'The Seven Pillars of Wisdom,' drives you mental, but one piece, I learnt it for you. Want to hear it?"

Stephen didn't, God knew he didn't.

"A little later, yea, I'm still digesting Rilke."

Martin stood, cleared his throat, and began,

> "'All men dream but not equally,
> Those who dream by night
> in the dusty recesses of their minds
> wake up in the day
> to find that it was vanity.'"

Stephen was unsure whether the recitation was concluded. It wasn't.

> "'But the dreamers of the day
> are dangerous men
> for they may act
> their dreams with open eyes,
> to make it possible.'"

"So, Stevie baby, how do you like them apples?"

"Is there a point to this?"

"There will be, oh you can count on that."

Martin stood up.

"Will you go now, I'm tired of you."

"What . . . oh, O.K. . . . is there anything I can get you?"

"Yea, actually there is . . . a Walkman, I'd like to blot out the shrieks in here. You sell them, don't you?"

. . . 't think it opportune to mention his V.A.T. trouble. He said,

. . . to . . . any tapes you'd like?"

Martin gave a look of pure cunning.

"Oh, Steve, I've my own tapes. I've been listening to them for a long, long time."

"Well, if you're sure. I'll say goodbye then."

"Say anything the fuck you like, just the fuck go."

Nurse O'Brien put five fingers in the air. He guessed she'd see him in five minutes or at five . . . in four hours time. He spotted a hardback chair and sat. A man came right up to him. He wore a puke green track suit and had glasses on a gold chain around his neck. These he lifted and used to look crossly at Stephen . . . who was thinking he'd like a share in the manufacturers of track suits.

"You're sitting in my chair."

"What . . . oh sorry, there wasn't a name on it."

"Well, get off it."

"Jeez O.K. . . . they need to increase your medication pal."

The man pulled a spotless white hankie from his pants and brushed the chair vigorously. Stephen wanted to put a shoe in his ass, but reckoned the poor bastard couldn't help it.

Nurse O'Brien appeared, with a navy mac over her uniform.

"Time to join me for my coffee break, Mr. Beck?"

"Sure . . . yes, I do. That guy in the grey track suit?"

"Dr. O'Connor."

"You're kidding . . . Jeez, well, I tell you, book him a bed . . . He's already got a chair."

"He's a marvel."

"He's friggin whacko is what he is."

"Now, now, Mr. Beck."

"Call me Stephen, will you."

"I could do that, yes . . . There's a small café just on Denmark Hill, they do a nice pot of tea."

Stephen groaned, and she looked at him. Understanding kicked in and she smiled.

"However, the pub does a healthy soup."

He thought, "she has definite potential."

This pub was aimed at the leisure classes, which accounted for its emptiness. A barmaid took their order, soup, roll and a large scotch. When the order came, the barmaid asked enough to ransom a small sultan. Stephen walloped the scotch. Emma looked on the verge of uttering,

"You needed that."

He said,

"I needed that . . . so Nurse . . . or Sister, was there a specific topic?"

"Please call me Emma . . . I wanted to know if your Martin has a mother . . . I mean . . . do ye . . . I think that's what I mean."

"What, you think we found him under a bush. Yes . . . we have a mother. Do you?"

"Oh dear . . . yes, I worded that badly. On Martin's form, under parents, he put *dead*."

The barmaid reappeared.

"Anything else?"

Stephen glared.

"What, you rushed off your feet or something? Yea, another large scotch . . . Emma, anything?"

"No, thank you."

"Our parents are alive, well sort of. Good ole Dad is M.I.A., and dear ole Mom . . . well, she's something else."

"A dysfunctional unit?"

"Is that the same as fucked? Yea, that's us all right."

Emma made to rise and said,

"Oscar Wilde would have loved you Stephen. He said,

'One begins by loving one's parents,
After a while, one judges them,
Rarely, if ever, does one forgive them.'"

"Wilde hadn't yet met my mother . . . not that she wouldn't claim she knew all belonging to him. When does a nurse get time to read him?"

"I ain't always a nurse."

Stephen didn't know what he felt for her; he did feel he didn't want her to go. He said,

"Don't go."

"And watch you drink, is it. Thanks, I've seen men drink, and I've seen mean men drink . . . I think you know which class you fit . . . I'll say goodbye then . . . Oh, and thanks for the soup, no doubt I'll find it sustaining."

And she was gone.

He drained the second whiskey and noticed she'd touched nothing. The buttered roll sat like an insult. On his way out, the barmaid shouted,

"Hurry back!"

***

Stephen stood for half an hour at the bus stop. The fast whiskies had rained off and down lashed further rain. A man offered to share his umbrella. Stephen was nearly too cranky, but he said, "O.K., thanks." The man was tall and too well dressed for bus travel. A wool suit that whispered, "a little cash." Hand-crafted shoes that were made to taunt English weather. Pale silk shirt and a tie knotted in what used to be termed, "Windsor." Before ties and the Royals went neck and neck down the toilet. A subtle hint of scent suggested, "ye olde Barber Shoppe."

"Car's in the shop," he said.

"The wife's got mine," answered Stephen. And didn't add, "plus my child."

He smiled in the way polite liars do. A flaw was then revealed in the man's impeccable appearance.

Rotten teeth, notorious to the point of horror.

"You've no work today?" he asked.

Still no hint of a bus. Stephen guessed he'd have to answer.

"No, compassionate leave."

"Ah, good man. Might one inquire as to the nature of your calling?"

"The army."

"Bingo . . . By golly, I knew it, despite your lack of hair, I recognised the bearing. I was with the Enniskillens myself. And you . . .?

"Fusiliers," said Stephen, not caring a toss as to how blatant his yarns appeared.

"Capital . . . splendid outfit. I'm not in current employment myself."

Stephen figured some interest as to why this was should be expressed.

"Why?"

"I'm glad you asked me that. The day they took Terry Waite hostage, I downed tools. Just walked right out."

"From where?"

"Well, the B.B.C. naturally. Didn't I say I'm a technician . . . and a rather good one?"

"Jeez, I hate to break this to you, but you can take up your tools again . . . the hostages have been released."

The man gave a loud, cynical laugh. "Oh, *those* hostages have."

"What . . . do you mean there are more?"

Now Stephen received a pitying look.

"There are always hostages . . . but the kernel of my protest, the very essence, the raison d'être of my gesture is, 'I shall never return as long as there's even the hint . . . even a smidgen of a suggestion that hostages can be taken.'"

. . . And still no bus. Stephen reckoned he was in that deep, he might as well find the bottom line. There always was. He asked,

"The D.H.S.S. . . . how did they respond to your, am . . . 'crusade'?"

"Nazis . . . not a schetzkel."

A bus came. The man stood back and gallantly waved Stephen aboard.

"I don't take public transport. I can't be seen to be weakening."

Stephen was still shaking his head as he offered a pound coin to the driver.

"No change mate."

"What . . . well, just give me a ticket. Keep the change, all right?"

"No can do mate, against regulations."

Stephen appealed to the crowded bus.

"Anybody got spare change?"

"Get a job," roared someone.

The driver re-opened the door.

"You're not allowed to beg on public transport, mate, against regulations."

Whatever Gods there are lightened up or got bored. Stephen found a vein of change in the lining of his jacket. After he got the ticket, he said to the driver,

"You're wasted in this job pal, they're crying out for the likes of you in the D.H.S.S."

***

Stephen rose on December 1st with a resolution to seriously alter his life. He'd return to literature and read one quality book a week. He spoke aloud, "Well, O.K. . . . a month, let's not go totally ape-shit . . . and I'll only drink on weekends. I'll join a computer dating agency and not worry about my hair."

He made scrambled eggs, a large tea and began to read a book by Lotus de Bernieres. This was selected because of its dedication,

> "To all those who are persecuted
> for daring to think for
> themselves."

Between bites of egg, he said,
"Sounds a winner!"
Stephen was relishing a character in the book who had elevated masochism to such a level, "that he learned to smoke in his sleep."
The phone rang. Stephen was still in throes of amusement as he said breezily,
"Hello?"
"Stephen Beck?"
"None other."
"This is Nurse O'Brien. I'm afraid there's been an incident here at the hospital."
"A what . . .? Good Lord, is it Martin, is he all right . . .? hello . . ."
She could be heard taking a deep breath.
"I don't really think I should go into it over the phone. Could you come to the hospital?"
"For Gods sake, is he dead, did he hang himself? Do I bring sweets or condolences? Tell me."
"No, he's not dead. Please come. I must go,"
. . . and she rang off.
The thought of his little girl zoomed into his head and he called her name like a lamentation.
"Suzy . . . little Suzy."
He could feel the warmth of her tiny hand and looked down. Looked down, half in dread that he might see her tiny fingers. What he saw was the fork with a dilapidated shot of scrambled eggs still clinging. Flung it across the room and said,
"I always hated fuckin' eggs."
The phone rang.
Snapping it, he shouted,
"Hello."
"Stephen, no need to shout, it's B.B."

"For Jaysus-sake, Mother . . . What?"

"Got out of the wrong side of bed, did we?"

"Was there something you wanted, Mother?"

"I've had some news about Nina."

"Nina . . .! What have you got to do with her?"

"I can't go into it on the phone."

"Jeez-louise, you don't know a Nurse O'Brien, do you?"

"What . . .? When can you come over?"

"Tonight, Martin's in some kind of trouble."

"Plu-eeze, Stephen, don't mention that boy to me, he's a heart scald. I sent him a 'Get Well' card and he never replied, the little pup."

"'Get Well' card! Mother, it's not the friggin measles, he's in a mental hospital. Look, I'll see you tonight . . ." and he banged the phone down. Give her a sore ear for a bit.

Then he remembered the Walkman for Martin. "Ker-ist," he thought, "I'd better stop off at the market." He rang a mini-cab and told them he'd be outside the Oval tube station.

The station thronged with winos and panhandlers.

A guy was roaring at the height of his lungs,

"Buy the *Big Issue* . . . Buy . . ."

It seemed to Stephen it must be like a bad night in Beirut. The cab came. A Pakistani driver whose geography was as bad as his English, got hopelessly confused by the roundabout at the Elephant and Castle, and twice ended up heading for the Oval.

Stephen said,

"Yo, buddy . . . let's pack this in. I'll walk. I'd like to get to the market before next Sunday. How much?"

"Fifteen pounds, friend."

Stephen gave him four pound coins, and said,

"Leave it out, Buddy, O.K. . . . I'm a Londoner and not a fuckin' tourist, O.K. . . . just don't start. You might consider a new career with British Rail."

His mood deteriorated as he saw the crowds on E. Street. Time was burning in his head. Rodney, the market perennial, came out of the caff.

"Steve, what's the story?"

"Rodney, am I glad to see you or wot. I have to get hold of a Walkman . . . for Martin, he's . . . well, you know he's away."

"No worries, son, give me five minutes."

Back he came, with the latest Japanese model.

"Yo, Stevey, this is state of the art. It does everything, in fact . . . treat it right and it will even walk the dog for yah."

"Smashin . . . what's the damage?"

"Tell you what, I might be able to put a bit of work your way, and there might be a drink innit for the both of us. Take it as a sub. Alrite."

"Yea, wonderful."

"So give us a bell towards the end of the week."

A wino bumped into Stephen and he nearly dropped the Walkman.

"Sorry Sur . . . so sorry."

Stephen noticed the man had a full head of hair. Tangles, dirty, but definitely luxuriant . . . He realised he'd never seen a bald wino. Had he discovered a cure, albeit a rough one. "Lose everything, but save your hair."

He spotted a No. 12 bus and managed to leap on to the platform. Anxiety or speculation as to Martin's condition hadn't had time to torment him. Rushing into the hospital, he asked at reception for Nurse O'Brien. A teenager, a girl with spiked blond hair, was waiting in admission. She had her head in her hands and was moaning quietly. A small bag with "ADIDAS" logo was beside her Doc Martens, the scuffed laced up boots were tapping rapidly.

Nurse O'Brien appeared.

"Dr. O'Connor will see you now, Mr. Beck."

"Mister . . . what happened to Stephen?"

"Really, Mr. Beck, I thought it would be more important to know what's happened to Martin."

Thus reprimanded, Stephen was led into an office. The doctor was behind a desk, reading a file. One chair, hard-backed, in front. This was the doctor who ordered Stephen from a chair on the last visit. He didn't look up. Stephen said,

"Will I just park it anywhere?"

Dr. O'Connor looked up . . . he had half-framed glasses which he straightened and peered through.

"Ah, the brother."

Stephen thought, "Uh . . . uh."

"Your brother . . ." Here he picked up the file, checked something with his finger, snapped the file shut, and continued, "Your brother, Martin, got hold of two forks from the refectory, and somehow used them . . . to . . ."

He hesitated. Stephen knew he was supposed to say something here, but all he could think of was the Les Dawson line, "POOR, you want to talk poverty? Till I was 16, I thought cutlery was jewelry."

He didn't say this and waited. The doctor said,

"He used these to puncture his eardrums . . . Rather seriously I'm afraid."

"Jesus Christ . . . what!"

"He's under sedation now, of course, but it would appear that the severity of the . . . action . . . will mean, he's going to be permanently deaf."

The room spun. Stephen could see the doctor, his mouth forming words, but for an instant, he too, was deaf. In that moment, something died in him. He felt a huge kick of pain and then it finished. Dazed, he felt reality return.

"Mr. Beck . . . Mr. Beck, are you all right?" The doctor was standing over him, shaking his shoulders.

"Get your hand off me."

"Mr. Beck, I realise it's a bit of a shock, but practicalities must be discussed."

"So . . . let's discuss them."

"Well, we can't really keep Martin here, the risk of further incidents."

"Private . . . get him in a private place."

"There are excellent facilities, but a bit costly."

"Do it then, I'm good for it."

Stephen stood up. The doctor extended his hand,

"I'll be in touch."

Outside, at reception, Stephen saw the teenager still waiting. He said,

"Here, have a Walkman."

She took the machine and looked at it closely.

"Where's the batteries?"

"In it."

"Got any tapes?"

Stephen didn't answer, and headed for the exit. Nurse O'Brien came running, catching him at the door.

"Mr. Beck, where are you rushing to?"

"Fuck off."

Outside, he thought, "Martin's got himself a permanent Walkman." The sounds of the world were now forever blocked out. A nightmarish thought then hit, "What if the sounds in his head, in his new silence, were worse than the world's, . . . what then?" Stephen clenched his fists and swore quietly, he swore he'd function on a harder level for pure maintenance . . . his and Martin's.

There were no through trains to Morden, he got off at Kennington. The lift out of order. The spiral staircase is the steepest climb in London. Rumours are that Chris Bonnington trained for Everest there. Totally knackered, Stephen emerged to a deserted station, save for one lone Santa who blocked his path. Gasping, Stephen asked,

"Bit early for it . . . isn't it?"

"Penny for the guy?"

The smell of drink was ferocious.

"Afraid you've got your festivals mixed fellah."

Santa swung at him. Stephen side-stepped, then moved in and kicked him in the balls. Santa dropped to his knees and Stephen leaned in close.

"They told us . . . Martin & me . . . As kids like, that Santa had no cobblers. Another myth gone . . . eh? But there's something for the guy," and head-butted him.

A couple looked in . . . decided not to take the tube. The man muttered,

"Muggin' Santa now."

He went home, lay on his bed and waited for the time to visit his mother. Waited and grieved.

He couldn't . . . and indeed, never had, grieved more for a lover lost than he did for Martin. If he couldn't ever now speak to him, then he was as if he were dead to him. When Fr. Jim's Mother had died, he'd quoted a poem of James Joyce. Stephen couldn't remember all of it but he could hear the solemn, measured tones of Jim as he said the lines. Now Stephen repeated what he could remember, and repeated them softly, over and over . . .

"She Weeps Over Rahoon"

"Rain on Rahoon falls softly, softly falling
where my dead lover lies
sad is his voice that calls me sadly calling
at grey moonrise"

He knew he'd spend the rest of his life calling to Martin. He knew, too, that his voice would never reach him.

Then the anger began to seep to his heart, and he felt if he could hug that cold rage, he could function and continue. Thus he began to mutter,

"Someone's to blame, it's got to be some fucker's fault, and by Christ, some bastard will pay. The tab will be paid."

***

It was evening when he stirred. Amazement hit him as he realised he hadn't gone on the piss. A change indeed had fastened to him, part hate, part madness, he knew, and said,

"Whatever gets you through."

He thought of his Mother and his upbringing. She had never neglected them as regards food, clothing and the essentials. But she had wielded a subtle campaign of belittlement and undermining. It wasn't a coldness in her, but an insidious spite. Fr. Jim had said,

"It's not
'Forgive them
for they know not what they do,'
Because, alas,
They do know."

He'd gone on to say that

"You can search for all the motivation in the world
and make every allowance but every now and then,
a person appears who's just a nasty piece of work."

"Amen to that, " said Stephen.

Stan, her "companion," was a constant visitor to the house. Like a shadow, you knew he was there but you didn't notice. A gruff man from Yorkshire, he had elevated the concept of unobtrusiveness to a fine art. Stan's face looked like someone had flung a pan of grease into it. Not only had it stuck, it had set. Stephen reckoned there was a factory up there that produced "Stans." They were solid and silent and said things like,

"I'm a no frills man,
I tell it as it is lad,
Yorkshire pud and two veg, that's yer staple,
Canno go wrong then lad."

If you misplaced your current "Stan" model, they'd slip you a new Stan by return, and you'd never tell the difference.

In the years when Stephen cared, he'd once asked him, "Don't you ever get excited, Stan? I mean, are you ever, 'Really starving,' could you really wallop in a few a cold ones . . .?"

Stan said,

"Moderation in all things, lad."

Yes, yea.

Stephen had searched through literature to find the meaning . . . if not of life, then perhaps . . . Stan. In Henry James, he'd read,

> "I never read a good English novel without
> drawing a long breath of relief that we are not part
> and parcel of that dark, dense, British social fabric."

Ironically, Henry James had said to his brother,

> "I revolt from their dreary deathly want of intellectual
> grace, moral spontaneity."

Stephen made coffee. A mug of black, strong instant. He put in two sugars and racked his mind as to what might give coherence to his thoughts. Anything, rather than the thought that he'd never say anything to Martin again.

Jim had introduced him to Schopenhauer and he searched the bookcase for him. Behind his Ruth Rendell's, yea . . . still there.

He took a large gulp of coffee . . . felt it burn his tongue, and exclaimed,

"Jaysus, that's sweet . . . I'm giving up sugar, but not today."

He read aloud in the hope that volume would bring clarification.

> "Suicide was thought as one of the options open.
> It wasn't.
> It was the end of all options."

Stephen was nodding his head and gulping coffee.

"Yea, O.K. . . . Schopy . . . I'm with you so far . . ."

> "Suicide may be regarded as an experiment. A question which man
> puts to nature trying to force her to an answer. It is a clumsy experiment

to make, for it involves the destruction of the very consciousness which puts the question and awaits the answer. While we live, there is always the possibility, the certainty of change."

He read the last lines louder, several times. Then he made more coffee, powdered heaped spoons of sugar, said,

"Mother gives the lie to them lines."

He was about to put the book down when a few lines caught his eye,

"Hello. . . ? I don't remember this bit."

"When a man has reached a condition in which he believed that a thing must happen, when he does not wish it. And that which he wishes to happen can never be. This is really the state called desperation."

"Now you're fucking talking," he roared, drained the coffee and got washed and dressed.

He caught the Northern line to Clapham, the Morden train.

The carriage was empty save for one old black man who appeared to have silver tips on his shoes. As soon as the doors closed, he got up and began to tap dance . . . tap, tap, tap, tap.

Stephen shouted,

"Hey . . . Hey, cut that out!"

. . . tap tap tap, tap.

And the man said, without looking at Stephen,

"What's it to do with you Man? Ain't hurting you . . . why I should heed wotcha say, Man."

Stephen stood.

. . . tap tap tap tap.

"Cos if you don't, I'll fuckin tap dance all over yer head."

The man sat.

An uneasy silence followed.

When Stephen got off at Clapham South, he looked back at the carriage. The man was dancing and he had his middle finger rigid in the air. Stephen suppressed a grim smile.

Stephen felt the cold December night pinch at his cheeks. He turned at the Rose and Crown after Clapham Common. The pub seemed full of pre Christmas warmth. "Come in," it beckoned.

He moved on to his Mother's house. She had an intercom recently installed. He ignored that and went down a quiet street at the back of her building and looked up. Her small balcony threw light invitingly.

"As if a person of welcome lived there," he said.

A quick flick of the back door, and he was in.

She threw open the door.

"What kept you?"

This evening she was sporting what the mail order ads call "A soft velour leisure suit," in a dashing pink. Her hair was now jet black with a flash of silver. Cigarette smoke caressed her.

"Christ, Mother, you're in the pink."

He moved to open the doors to the balcony as the smell of nicotine was ferocious. A tray of drink was perched on a small table.

"I will, thank you Mother," and he poured a large gin. Mrs. Beck faced him.

"Nina is in Khartoum, and Suzy . . . and Suzy is in the care of a man named André in Paris."

"What . . . Good God, how do you know that?"

"I hired a private detective, a friend of Stan's . . . it's my Christmas present to you."

"What, you're giving me a detective . . . sure beats socks and aftershave."

"Really, Stephen, don't be facetious . . . I should think you'd thank your Mama. All my boys are so unfeeling."

"Two, Mother, you have two. Did you get a detective for Martin, he'd like one."

"Plu . . . eeze . . . don't mention that boy, there's no talking to him."

"Ain't that the truth, no never, no more."

Mrs. Beck moved to pour a drink. Crème de Menthe – she was visibly angry.

"Don't you care that that . . . whore has left the child with some whore-master in Paris?"

"Don't call her that!"

"Oh I'm sorry Steve-o, how shall I put it . . . your wife is, 'a care worker' with the deprived of Sudan. She's staying at a place called . . . the Acropolis Hotel. What are you going to do?"

Stephen drained the gin and walked out to the balcony. He didn't know.

"I dunno."

Mrs. Beck marched up behind him and said,

"When she was in the hospital, I took one look at the baby and knew you weren't the father. She had the nerve to call me a . . . a walking disease . . . me!"

Stephen felt as if a knife was slow twisting in his stomach. An urge to throw up was near over-powering.

"Do you hear me, Stephen . . . do you hear what I said . . . she foisted some man's bastard on you."

Stephen turned, his left hand grabbed the top of her suit, the right gripped her hip. He moved one step, two, like the old waltz, then hoist . . .

hold . . .

. . . said, "fuck you B.B."

and flung her over the balcony.

She never cried out. A sound like a sack of spuds hitting the ground reached him. He stepped back into the room. Took his glass, rinsed, dried and put it on the tray. The gin, Crème de Menthe he uncapped and poured down the toilet. As he did, he saw a packet on the bath. It read,

"Midnight Black Hair Colour."

The Crème de Menthe bottle he left on the floor, the gin he stood on the balcony edge, looked at his watch.

8:10

Stan would come at 9 on the dot and use his key. Stephen let himself out and didn't meet anybody. By 8:40, he was getting off the train at the Oval . . . he headed for The Cricketers.

***

The barman had a name tag. "Jeff." Long, thin and bald. He spotted Stephen instantly as the unacknowledged fellowship of baldness dictates. Tighter than Masons. Stephen took a vacant stool and said,

"Yo Jeff, a large gin and Crème de Menthe."

"Not in the same glass, I trust."

"Good old London town, everyone's a comedian, a touch of 'dancing on the *Titanic*,' eh. No . . . the Crème de Menthe is for my old Mum, a pre-dinner aperitif."

"Her birthday, is it?"

"Yea . . . she's going over the top tonight. Give us a shout when she comes in . . . can't miss her, she's got jet black hair with a silver streak!"

"Bit of a girl, is she then?"

"Oh, she's a one, all right, have something yourself." Jeff set the glasses on the bar. Stephen took a hefty belt . . . and muttered,

"Mother's ruin."

The green liquor stood sentry as Stephen loaded down a chain of gins. He 'n' Jeff were getting as matey as magpies and as drunk as farts. Stephen was thinking of Oscar Wilde.

"We always kill the thing we love."

And reckoned he'd never felt a day's love for her . . . ever . . .

When Jeff roared,

"Stevie . . . hey, Steve, yer old Mum's at the door!"

Heart pounding, Stephen turned. A slap on the back from a jubilant Jeff,

"Just kidding, buddy! . . . Gotcha, yea."

Stephen was too weak to reply. A chill began to slide down his spine. What if it had been . . . he visibly shook himself. Such a route was a one way ticket to Martinsville. A very drunk Jeff was leaning over the counter,

"So, Stevie, wots the story, bud, where's the old bird, haven't done away with her . . . have you . . . eh . . ."

Stephen put his hand on Jeff's arm and looked right in his eyes.

"How would it be, Jeff, if I broke your arm . . . eh, Buddy how would that be? . . . so get the fuck outa my face . . ."

Jeff fell back.

"No offence . . . just a bit of fun . . ."

The fright had jolted Stephen into a wild sobriety. A powerful sexual urge swept him. He went into a phone box and sure enough, the wall was littered with personal ads.

> "Buxom 20 year old gives massage.
> All tastes catered for. Open till late."

He rang and was given an address on Kennington Park Road.

The walk down increased his desire. A block of flats. He walked to the 2nd floor and rang 2B. A middle-aged woman with dark blond hair opened the door.

"I'm here to see Tania."

"That's me, darlin' . . . come in."

The flat was spotless, as if no one lived there. Stephen said,

"You've aged since our call."

"Wotcha want darlin, it's late . . . I'm not into yer kinky scene,

    – no violence

    – no golden showers

    – no bondage"

"You wouldn't have a bit of tea or toast?"

"Ain't a caff, darlin, wotcha want?"

"Am . . . just the straight thing . . . the am . . . basic act."

"Set yer back twenty-five and five for the towel and French letter."

"You're going to write to me?"

"A condom, darlin . . . So you want to play or wot?"

Stephen gave her 3 tenners. She went into another room and then called him. His desire wasn't abating, it was downright fleeing. When he entered the room, she was dressed in suspenders and nothing else. Her "buxom" breasts were long past interest. A pot belly near finished him. She pointed to a sink.

"Give yer willy a wash and put this on."

She handed him a small packet. He filled the sink and removed his pants.

"Hurry it up, darlin, I'm hot for you."

He had to get her help in opening the packet, the condom highlit his lack of passion.

She appeared unfazed and lay back.

"Give it to me, big boy, you stallion."

"Am . . . I wonder if we could mebbe dispense with the conversation."

"Wotever you like, darlin, your time and money."

He lay on top of her and she turned her head to the side.

"No kissing."

Stephen jumped up . . .

"Ah fuckkit . . . This is ridiculous." He thought Martin would enjoy this story and that triggered a wave of despair.

He sat and hung his head between his legs. He heard her dressing.

"Never mind, darlin, happens to the best of 'em."

She patted his bald head affectionately and left the room. A few minutes later, she reappeared with steaming mugs of tea and toast. They ate and drank in silence. Stephen dressed and made to leave.

"You come back when you're more in the mood, darlin, there's a lamb."

Back home, he thought about thirty quid for a slice of toast. He lay on his bed and was sound asleep in minutes. The phone ringing failed to rouse him.

***

Stephen woke at nine. The events of the night flooded in. He didn't feel guilt, remorse, anxiety or even regret. A sour taste in his mouth was routed by toothpaste and he wondered if his lack of feeling was delayed shock. He strongly suspected it wasn't. At college, he noted his namesake, Julian Beck, who'd said,

> "We are a feelingless people. If we could really feel, the pain would be so great that we would stop all the suffering."

He showered and exclaimed, "Dammit, I feel like whistling."

So he did. A mangled version of Colonel Bogy as he supped tea . . . with loud noises. He ran through his list of martyrs.

> If Martin was a martyr to silence and Stan to mediocrity
> then he'd have to assign his
> Mother the mantle of unconsciousness.

"But not any more," he said.

A loud banging on the door. Two men in dark overcoats. He hoped it wasn't the V.A.T. crowd.

"Are you Stephen Francis Beck?"

"I am."

The man produced warrant cards and asked if they might come in.

Stephen said,

"It's a fair cop. I haven't a T.V. licence."

The men looked at each other.

"I'm sorry to have to inform you, Sir, that your Mother has met with an accident."

"What . . . is she hurt . . . or is she in hospital?"

"Perhaps you'd like to sit down Sir . . . Baker, go and brew some tea, there's a good chap. I'm afraid your Mother is dead, Sir. It appears she fell from her balcony."

Stephen began to whimper,

"Oh Mom, Mom . . . oh, God . . ."

"When did you last have contact with her, Sir?"

"Yesterday. I phoned her with some rather disturbing news."

"About your brother, was it Sir? We know about that. She took it badly, did she?"

"He was her whole life . . . oh, God."

He didn't want to overdo the whimpering and it was beginning to grate on his nerves. He decided to go for the distracted look and say nothing.

The other man brought the tea. Stephen didn't touch it.

"It seems, Sir, she may have been drinking and leant too far over the balcony. I'm terribly sorry, Sir. Is there anything we can do?"

He wanted to say, "Forget the T.V. licence" but opted for the stiff upper lip scenario.

The man produced a slip of paper.

"This is the address of the hospital . . . I've taken the liberty of putting an undertaker's number there, and they'll arrange everything."

"Thank you . . . thank you, you've been so kind."

After they left, he washed their mugs and said,

"As easy as that, well I never!"

A thought rooted him to the spot. What if they performed an autopsy? All that would reveal was a few sips of Crème de Menthe. How then explain the empty gin and liquor?

"Don't," he thought . . . don't try. Be as baffled as them. He'd seen too many *Columbo* re-runs where the suspect provided all sorts of motives and rationales.

If his crime reading had provided anything, it was that an innocent man usually didn't have an alibi.

Still, it worried him. The big cop . . . he was the one.

The next few days were a blur to Stephen. A stream of sympathetic calls and he fought hard to avoid the booze. Fr. Jim came and arranged everything. Stephen adopted the role of shell-shocked son and let him. The funeral was big.

Mrs. Beck had a wide circle. Rodney and the street traders came, and Jim did the service.

Stan, suitably morose, asked if he might call on Stephen that evening – "A matter of some urgency."

Stephen had one long-stemmed red rose which he lay on the coffin. He heard a murmur from the crowd and knew he'd played a blinder. Mrs. Beck was allergic to flowers . . . people too, but she hid that.

The mourners did the mourning things. Stephen felt, "Good riddance." A small grey man in a small grey suit touched his arm,

"So sorry to intrude, I'm Simon Alton, your dear Mother's Solicitor. Might you call on me tomorrow?"

Stephen would.

Rodney had arranged the function after. A blond lady in her early 20s hooked on Rodney's arm. She had a pale, beautiful face and her short black mini was like a magnet. Stephen reckoned it was Rodney's daughter as Rod was the outlaw side of fifty.

"This is Vikki, the Missus."

"What?"

"Yea, Steve, every bugger says that. What did she see in an old lag like me . . . eh."

Vikki gave a tiny smile. As the function ended, she said something to Stephen. Not hearing what she'd said, he said,

"Thank you. I'll miss her dearly."

She dug her nails in his arm, and near hissed,

"I'm going to 'ave you, and soon."

Stephen muttered.

"In the midst of death, there is life, and if me stirrings are anything to go by . . . a lotta life. Thank you Lord. I owe you a big one, big guy."

***

The following morning, Stephen called on the solicitor. Coffee was served and Simon Alton began,

"Do you have any idea of your Mother's worth, Mr. Beck?"

Stephen had known her worth a long time, but perhaps it was inappropriate to share this early.

"Please call me Stephen. No, I don't."

"Right . . . am . . . Stephen, she owned the flat in Clapham and it's of substantial value. Your Father made many shrewd investments in her name, and she added to them over the years . . . She has included Stanley Rice in her will, he receives five hundred pounds."

"What . . . I thought you said she was loaded . . . I mean comfortable."

"Ah . . . well, Stephen, she didn't trust men, her view of them was somewhat . . . shall we say, tarnished?"

"Good word . . . I like that . . . shall we cut to the chase."

"She felt Martin had made his own fortune, and . . ."

"Yea."

"The bulk of the estate goes to you."

"Jay-sus . . . you're kidding."

"I'll have the exact figures for you in a few days, but, suffice to say . . . you are an extremely wealthy young man." Stephen wanted to yell, "Yipee!" but kept a deadpan face and said,

"I see."

"Might I be so bold as to propose a number of schemes to ensure the continued prosperity?"

"No."

"I'm sorry . . . perhaps you misunderstood me, my guidance . . ."

"I said, N – O"

"Might I know why?"

"I don't know you and I don't want to, I'll handle my own affairs."

"This is most irregular."

"That too."

Outside he said,

"Rich . . . I'm fuckin wealthy . . . oh, yes."

He rang Stan and arranged to meet him at the Rose and Crown in Clapham. Nearing lunch time the pub was beginning to fill. Stephen ordered two large vodkas and tonics – V.A.T.s – and found a quiet corner.

Stan arrived, he was dressed in a duffel coat and though not clutching a cloth cap, Stephen felt it couldn't be too far away.

"Afternoon, Stan."

"Good afternoon, Stephen."

He smelled the vodka and didn't touch it, said,

"A little early for the hard stuff . . . my usual tipple is half a mild. Moderation in . . ."

"Ah, don't be such a prick."

Stan's face remained impassive. He said,

"You are aware . . . well, yes, you know your dear Mother and I had an arrangment of many years duration . . . I feel she would have liked me to reside in the Clapham flat. We shared many memories there."

"Naw . . . never happen old son."

"I'm sorry . . . I . . ."

"Don't be sorry, Stan, just give me the keys you have and then, basically, on yer bike."

Stan swallowed the vodka.

Stephen said,

"Your shout Stan . . . get 'em in . . . they're large ones . . . there's a good chap."

Stan did.

They settled again and Stan said,

"I appreciate you're under a lot of stress, and perhaps later . . ."

"Cut the shit, Stan . . . eh, let me ask you . . . did you go to see Martin?"

"Well no . . . I didn't think it appropriate."

Stephen drained the vodka, stood, and said,

"Righty ho . . . have yer gear out by the end of the week . . ."

Stan grabbed his arm.

"I know, lad, we mightn't have been close, but I felt I was there in the background for you boys. Your Mother would be very . . . distressed . . . I mean . . ."

"Hey, take yer hand off . . . my Mother is all through with feelings . . . and you . . . Stanley . . . You go fuck yerself . . . O.K. . . . Is that plain enough, is that 'no frills' message clear?"

He shook his arm free and outside he looked at the Common, and said,

"Nice day for it . . ."

As he waited for the tube, he thought about Martin, how he loved Scott Fitzgerald. The lines he repeated like a prayer,

"the horror has now come like a storm
what if this night prefigures the night after death

What if all thereafter was an eternal quivering on the
edge of an abyss
with everything base and vicious in oneself
urging one forward
and the baseness and viciousness
of the world just ahead no choice no road
no hope
Only the endless repetition of the sordid
And the semi-tragic"

"Jay-sus," he thought . . . "if that was going round in yer head, you'd mebbe have to deafen yerself or take to the big drink."

He ran the lines again in his head and thought,

"Yea. Words to live by, right enough."

***

En route to the tube, he had to pass the Catholic Church. He thought he might placate the Gods; he'd been battling heavy against them, and it didn't do to piss them off.

In he went.

The set of vodkas were singing in his head and he inhaled the smell of incense deeply. He stopped at the various shrines and poured money into each one. The Saints in statue weren't recognisable to him, looked a little like the Osmonds he reckoned. A sort of Brady Bunch in piety.

He'd been hoping for a good grisly martyr, but they all seemed in the peak of porcelain health. As if they'd had massive doses of Valium. Each time he lit a bunch of candles, Fr. Jim had said,

"A candle is a prayer in action."

Stephen had been schooled in Catholicism by his Mother, but had long since lapsed. The weary rituals of course were branded in his head, and he derived a melancholy comfort from them. Mrs. Beck, of course, knew all about religion and almost nothing about humanity.

To wind up Jim, he'd quote Graham Greene.

"The Church knows all the rules, but it doesn't know what goes on in a single human heart."

He'd read that only a Catholic Irishman, loaded with learning and cunning and soaked in the liturgy of the Church, could have produced the incredible mixture as Joyce did in *Ulysses*.

The he saw the statue of The Virgin Mary, all blues and whites. He moved right up close; someone had wrapped bright green Rosary beads around the clasped hands. Like handcuffs. The green crystals caught the light from the candles, and, with the vodka, gave him a dizzy feeling.

He looked up into her face. The alabaster eyes were closed. A replay of his Mother going over the balcony danced in his mind.

The Virgin's eyes opened.

Blue . . . the deepest blue . . . bored into his brain . . . and then they closed.

He started to back down the aisle. A whimpering sound reached him and he was afraid to look round. Then he realised it was himself . . . and galloped to the door. Heart pounding, he swore,

"Never . . . never, as long as I live and breathe, will I tell another soul about that . . . and I'll rebuild Tara . . . As God is my witness."

***

"So," Father Jim said, "Her eyes opened, then what did you do?'

"What did I do . . . I got the fuck outa there . . . that's what I did. Wouldn't you?"

"What do you think now, Stephen?"

"I dunno what to think, that's why I'm telling you. It's the business you're in."

Jim had come round to Stephen's flat after a frantic nigh hysterical call. They were drinking coffee. A plate of almond slices on a saucer. Jim reached over, selected the biggest one, and took a heartening chunk.

"Well, I don't wish to minimise the validity of your experience, but you admit you'd been drinking . . . and, after all the grief, the stress of your Mother's death."

"Jaysus, Jim . . . the validity of my experience . . . what's this, sociology one? Talk English for fucksake . . . I'm telling you. Her eyes opened. I thought this sort of thing was common. I mean in Ireland, they practically appear on talk shows."

Jim smiled and took another almond slice.

"What, Jim . . . did you skip breakfast or what?"

"Steve, miracles or supernatural events tend to happen to people who need convincing, they need demonstrable evidence."

"Or a good fuckin fright!"

"Steve, could you stop swearing. It's a bit overdone . . . O.K."

"Let me ask you something, Jim. If I confide in you . . . are you bound to secrecy?"

"If it's in the nature of confession . . . naturally . . . but if it's a tip for a horse, I'd feel honour bound to divulge it to Ladbrokes."

"Right . . . this is a confession . . . back there a bit . . . you mentioned my grief and stress over Mother."

"But of course, what son wouldn't be . . . When my own Mum . . ."

Stephen interrupted him, he couldn't stomach the sound of Jim laying into a third almond slice, which he showed all the signs of doing.

"Ah, Jaysus, Jim . . . Can we skip the homily about your Mother . . . eh . . . I've had a long day."

Stephen felt an overpowering need to rattle Jim, to shock him out of his smugness . . . and to stop him filling his face. He stood and snatched the plate with the remaining slices.

"I'd say we've had enough of them, Jim . . . eh, practice a bit of self denial or something."

"H-m-m, they were delicious, a touch more coffee wouldn't go astray."

"I killed her!"

"What? . . . C'mon, Stevie, it was just a statue."

"Not her . . . my Mother . . . I murdered her . . . so now . . ."

Jim shook his head, picking crumbs from his trousers.

"We all think that, Stephen, if only we'd been better sons . . . if only . . ."

"Yo . . . hold the fuckin phones here, buddy. I threw her over the balcony, and what's more, I'm only sorry I didn't do it years ago."

Jim stood up.

"Steve, my friend . . . you've been under tremendous pressure, with Martin, your poor Mother, God bless her . . . I think you should talk to someone."

"What . . . Are you deaf, you thick bastard, I'm talking to you."

"Of course you are . . . And that's good. A very positive sign, but it might be advisable to talk to a man of professional standing."

"I don't believe this, you dumb shite . . . Jaysus wept . . . maybe Martin and I could get a cut rate for a family thing."

Jim moved and put a hand on Stephen's shoulder.

"I'm serious, lad, you need help."

"Ah, bollocks . . . go . . . just go."

Jim went to the door . . . and said, "I'll pray for you."

"Gimme a break, Padre!"

A rage engulfed him. He picked up the phone and rang Rodney.

"This is Vikki . . . Rodney's not home right now . . . Would you like to come over . . . and . . . and wait?"

He would.

Rodney's house was in Balham. Where the muggers made housecalls. A nondescript one up building on the outside. Vikki answered the ring instantly. She was wearing a thin halter top, micro mini and the old fuck-me-fast heels.

The house inside was laden with antiques, electronic gear of every make, and deep, thick carpets.

Vikki said,

"Would you like a drink? I'm sorry, I've forgotten your name."

"Jim . . . call me Jim," said Stephen.

He grabbed her shoulder and slammed her against the wall. His hand pushed under her skirt and he tore the knickers aside. He reached for his zip, and as he plunged into her, said,

"Try remembering this."

He came immediately and withdrew . . . his heart pounding. Vikki adjusted her few clothes.

"'Ad a good time did you . . . eh?"

"Well, honey . . . I tell you, it hit the spot."

"Not mine it didn't."

She moved to a huge wooden world globe. It came apart to reveal a bar. He considered quoting Andy Warhol, "Sex is the biggest nothing of all time."

"Vodka?"

"Lovely . . . no ice but a wee smidge of tonic." He decided to pass on Warhol.

Stephen stretched on a recliner.

"I tell you, Vikki, a man could get used to this."

"Don't get too comfortable Jimmy . . . Rodney will be back soon and he's not going to be pleased. Oh no, he's not going to be pleased one little bit."

Stephen sat up. . . "I don't follow you honey, what's going to upset him?"

Warning bells went off in his head.

Vikki clinked ice in her glass. It matched the ice in her voice.

"You're his mate, ain't cha . . . when he hears you forced yerself on me . . . Well, Rodney's an 'ARD man . . . been inside, you know. Know wot I mean?"

Stephen knew exactly what she meant. He took a long swallow of the vodka, stood . . . smiled warmly at her and asked,

"Got a balcony . . . do ya?"

***

PART II

"There is no trap
So deadly as the trap
You set for yourself."
Raymond Chandler.
The Long Goodbye

The heat of Khartoum had walloped him like a fist.

A hard vicious assault. Three days in, he felt the temperature was still climbing . . . and the walls, he was close to climbing those.

Prior to departure, he'd gone to Jermyn Street, to "A gentleman's outfitter for the Tropics." Four lightweight suits later, he bored a sizeable hole in one of the major investments. April in London, he'd frozen in the cab to Heathrow.

His visa was of ten days duration. He'd reckoned that was ample time to find Nina. His guide book recommended The Acropolis Hotel as being cheap and laden with character. Cheap it wasn't.

Full of shady characters . . . yes.

He hadn't got the swing of the money yet. Whatever transactions he did seemed to cost a bucket of the Sudanese pounds. Smelt; there was a definite odour from the notes and they were filthy. Like newspaper print, they left black marks on his fingers. He'd been advised of the thriving Black Market, but hadn't found it.

Arak, yea he'd found that. The local booze, and he'd drunk gallons. It kicked back like a psychopathic mule and gave him the kind of diarrhoea he was truly alarmed by . . .

Huge patches of perspiration dotted his suits; they already looked like something Oxfam would see and say, "Ah no . . . the third world's not that desperate."

The way he felt now, he wished he'd simply sent the suits on the trip.

Rivers of sweat ran across his bald head and down into his eyes.

"Jay-sus," he said, "no one has this much water in them." If it continued he didn't think he'd have it much longer.

He'd reckoned spring was a shrewd time to head to Sudan. Khartoum, even the name had a majesty. No one had told him that April is the start of the habood system. Huge storms of dust howling in from the desert and covering everything. It had a sound like terror, a thin wailing that surrounded him.

Ten days, he'd no idea how he'd last and he still hadn't found Nina. The telephone system didn't work and no one had heard of her at the hotel. The care workers he'd met did know her and provided him with two phone numbers. Everyone he spoke to, he gave them his name and phone number. Finally, he'd given various Sudanese the equivalent of the budget for a minor country and they'd promised to find her.

Trying to spot her anywhere was a joke. The women all wore the black chador. These black silk cloaks were from head to ankle. Like huge flocks of grounded jackdaws or malicious nuns. He found them vaguely sinister and had no intention of approaching them.

So he drank the arak, fled to the toilet and counted the minutes. He was told of the huge famine in the Sudan and was near starvation himself.

There were massive shortages of bread, flour and water. He'd brought a packet of Rich Tea biscuits from London . . . on a whim . . . and was sparing them now like a lifeline. According to his guide book, there were at least forty types of mosquito in Khartoum and he'd no reason to doubt the claim. He'd been bitten by at least 36 branches of the things.

Chloroquine was the assured and established remedy but he suspected it was attracting them. A large spacious room had been free, and he'd been delighted to see it had an overhead fan. Visions of the movie *Casablanca* had unfolded.

It didn't work.

He'd paid a porter to install two floor fans which blew blissful streams of air.

Till the power cuts.

On inquiring when the power might be resumed, he'd heard,

"Insha Allah."

Back to the guide book which told him this meant, "God willing." God hadn't willed it for the past 48 hours.

He was sitting in his Marks and Spencer's Y-fronts, chugging Arak and dreaming of E Street Market. Oh, to be cold and miserable. A battalion of mosquitoes were stinging him.

A knock at the door.

"Jay-sus," he said on opening it, "The friggin Grim Reaper in person."

A black spectre shimmered there.

"Oh, do get a grip, Stephen."

The hood was thrown back to reveal Nina.

He nearly hugged her.

"Come in," he gasped, "Come in!"

She glanced inside the room.

"Actually, I'd rather not. Why have you got it like a furnace?"

"I've got some Rich Tea."

He had, in fact, three.

"Get dressed, we'll go to my place."

He donned one of the suits and wiped away a yard of sweat with the sleeve.

"Where did you get that suit?"

"Oxfam."

"Yes, well . . . they saw you coming."

Her place was a cool, airy bungalow on the outskirts of the city. They'd driven there in her small Datsun . . . air conditioned. Divans were scattered haphazardly. Clay pots and posters on the wall. He sank into a divan, said, "I might never leave here."

"Khartoum?"

"No, this room."

She made sweet tea which he found enormously refreshing. Then removed her chador. She wore jeans and a white T-shirt with the logo, "SOLEDAD."

"Why are you here, Stephen?"

"To see you . . . to find out about Suzy."

"A letter would have been cheaper. How did you find me?"

He smiled and looked around. A bungalow was the last thing he'd anticipated, the only place he could push her out was the door.

"Well, Nina . . . it wasn't easy. Since my family were martyred, you and Suzy are all I've got."

"Your Mother . . . and Martin . . . what . . . are they, are they all right?"

"Dead, a car accident . . . together."

It silenced her.

"So Nina, you're caring for the masses here . . . who's caring for Suzy?"

"How dare you . . . she's been cared for. I see her every two months."

"Oh wow, that will do it."

Nina stood up.

"Stephen, I don't know what mad scheme you're planning or what you hoped to accomplish. I want no part of it. I'll drive you back to your hotel, and if you want my advice . . . you'll go back to London. This is no place for you."

Stephen drained the tea.

The drive back was silent. A choking dust storm had risen, and as he got out of the car . . . whatever she said was snatched away. In the lobby of the hotel, a thin, dark Arab wearing the tight western clothes approached him.

"Al Labibi . . . a word in private."

"Why not?"

"I am Abdul, you are not comfortable here, my friend, I arrange for you to stay at the Sahara. Much clean, much cool."

"But it's booked out."

"Meet here, nine o'clock. I arrange all . . . Salaam a leccum."

And this, according to his guidebook, was "Peace be with you."

Abdul was the business. Not only did he effect a smooth hotel change, but showed the way to food, the black market services. Even Stephen's suits perked up and were whisked away for cleaning. The second night at the Sahara, a relaxed Stephen was in a generous mood.

"So, Abdul, you've got to let me pay for all your help."

They were drinking Amstel beer, a cold Dutch drink with a sizeable kick.

"No effendi . . . is for friend . . . no . . . maybe you can help Abdul, too."

"Sure, if I can."

"For what you work?"

"For whom . . .? is it . . ."

"I work for the Government."

"For English Government?"

"Yes."

"Ah Stefan, effendi . . . Habibi, can you make for me papers to go to England?"

"Am . . ."

"You have sad trouble here, my friend, Abdul know . . . not so happy. Meeting with infidel woman . . ."

Stephen told him about Nina . . . about his lost child.

"Ah is no good, bad womans – yes."

"Yea, you got that right buddy. I don't know what to do."

They drank and considered how far they might proceed. Echoes in the Sudan darkness. Abdul decided.

"Stefan . . . if womans go poof . . . ," (and he snapped his fingers), "is trouble finished?"

"What . . . yea . . . Am . . . but that's not possible . . . is it?"

"Ha . . . is Sudan my friend, life is nothing. Thousands die every week in famine. For money . . . ALL is possible . . . one can go," and he slapped his hands together – "BANG!"

Stephen took a long swig of beer. "How much . . . am . . ."

"Five hundred U.S. dollar . . . and friend help yes . . . for life's in England . . . is good yes. I go England."

They decided Stephen should give 250 U.S. "dollar" now and he'd make arrangements for Abdul's entry to England. "In a pig's eye," is what he thought.

The rest of the money on completion of the transaction. Stephen didn't think there was much chance of old Abdul doing a thing, but just maybe . . . and was willing to risk 250 dollars on the "maybe."

"I send you English Language paper with accident report . . . yes."

"Yea . . . you do that, me oul china."

"Is no problem, my friend."

"Insha Allah," said Stephen.

Abdul went to Khartoum airport with him. As they said goodbye, Abdul hung his head.

"Yo . . . Abdul, lighten up Buddy. Soon you'll be in London, sampling the delights of the D.H.S.S."

"My friend . . . always have I the visions . . . I see things . . . I see when the bad things to come."

"Like a racing tipster . . . yeah."

"For you, my friend . . . when the darkness is visible on your hands," (he held out his hands, palms upturned), "then, my friend . . . I am afraid the darkness will destroy your soul."

Sounds like William Styron, the darkness visible . . . Don't worry about me ole mate, I'll keep me hands to me arse.

***

It was April 20th on his return to London. At Heathrow, he went straight to the cafeteria and had double egg, double chips, five sausages, black pudding, a hint of fried tomato, toast, and the booster pot of tea. It nearly killed him . . . As he belched, he said

"Luverly."

It cost the equivalent of a middle class mortgage.

He headed on auto pilot for the Oval, then remembered, "hold the phone, stop the lights . . . I don't live there anymore!"

The new flat was in Holland Park. With a monthly rent that would have fixed an epidemic of accidents in Khartoum. His major requirement had been a balcony.

"For the view?" asked the estate agent.

"Yea, something like that."

He'd salvaged his photo of little Suzy, and had it enlarged to cover one entire wall. Another was transposed to a keyring. The trauma in his life had begun, he believed, when she'd been taken from him. Get her back and all would be well. Money could buy anything. If needs be, he'd go to Paris and see this "André" chappie who was minding her. The French could be had for cash and a Clint Eastwood video.

He swore.

"I will have her back . . . nowt else matters."

The prospect of casually mentioning "my daughter" at every opportunity made him night dizzy with delight.

Entering the flat, he said to her likeness,

"Soon Suzy . . . you'll be with yer Dad . . . people will say . . . Ah yes, the Holland Park Stephen Becks."

Picked up his new phone, called the off licence.

Yes . . . they'd be pleased to deliver some crates of Amstel beer . . . within the hour . . . certainly . . . "Thank you, Mr. Beck." The suits he placed in a black bin liner for Oxfam. A letter from his new solicitor and accountants assured him the V.A.T. had been fully paid.

How were his finances . . . very healthy . . . oh, thank God.

Rang Martin's private nursing home and he was doing well. Might they expect a visit from Stephen?

. . . They might not.

The next few weeks, he lounged around Hyde Park. Sometimes he ate chips from newspapers and muttered Suzy's name like an incantation. He had decorators prepare her room.

The nights were for clubbing. A stretch of women became available. Flick a peep of American Express Gold Card, and it was better than a load of hair . . . almost.

He liked to have them on the balcony. It gave a rush that the bedroom couldn't match. He'd run them out fast in the morning with the explanation,

"I'm expecting my daughter any minute!"

On the 19th of June, a letter from Khartoum. The envelope was as dirty as their money. Despite gingerly handling it, it left black tracks on his hands.

By now, he'd installed a wicker lounger on the balcony. Filling a glass tankard with Amstel, he stretched out and opened the letter.

A small press cutting.

"Khartoum today, a 32 year old English care worker, Nina Horton, was fatal-ly injured in a three car collision on General Gordon Boulevard. Tragically, Miss Horton's young daughter, Susan, was also fatally injured. It is believed the little girl was on a week's vacation. Other fatalities included a tax inspector and a porter from nearby Acropolis Hotel."

"Miss . . ." roared Stephen, "What this Miss Horton shit, she's Mrs. Beck . . . of the Holland Park Becks. . . "

The tankard slipped from his fingers as the rest of the piece sank in.

"Oh you stupid fuckin bastard . . . You cretinous murderous fooker . . . AR . . . GL . . . AR . . . GUH . . ."

The howl he emitted could be heard clear down to Notting Hill. He grabbed the rim of the balcony and began to hammer his head against it, shrieking,

"MARTYRS . . ."

SHADES OF GRACE

"**S**o!" he said to her, "You've decided to grow the moustache."

Dalton didn't whisper this. Ford, at the far end of the bar, heard him clearly. Dalton continued, "Not everyone can carry off a 'tash, but you've got the bones for it."

Sheila, his audience, looked as anyone would expect: mortified. Ford had known her for a while and the slight suggestion of hair on her upper lip was her daily crucifixion.

"There isn't an hour I don't think about it," she said. "If people aren't staring, I think they're being polite. If they are staring, well. . . you can work out how that feels."

Ford didn't know if he'd noticed in the beginning. The first time he met her she said, "So you're thinking, 'Who's the hairy chick?'"

He wasn't, was he? The shame-all was she had a pretty face. Not gorgeous or heart-pounding but in there. She'd been Dalton's girlfriend for three years. Put him on the other side of six drinks and out came the moustache. The crunch was he was gorgeous according to every woman Ford had ever asked. He'd stopped asking. Dalton was of medium build with a pot belly. "A lotta good cash to round that out," he said. His hair was in galloping recession and he had nail-you-to-the-wall eyes. The nose. Here lay the mystery. One of those snub noses that are appealing on tousle-haired kids. Cute, as the Americans say. On a grown man it should look ridiculous. Women loved it, back in the times when Ford had asked.

He'd been Ford's friend for ten years. "For sins of a past life," muttered Ford. Very heavy sins. Ford was currently a social worker. At thirty-six years of age he'd been in many occupations. Most of those he would no longer admit to. At one low point, an English language teacher. Worse, English as a foreign language and he certainly found it to be that. The final revenge of a lone Irishman on the English according to Dalton. Ford knew he was in deep trouble when he began to speak like students. "How you say", he remembered with deep shame. Twelve years he'd been in London and social working for the previous two. Prior to that he'd been open to suggestions and still was.

On Clapham Common today a wino had waylaid him. Ford had seen him coming and began the discreet weaving. This usually put him beyond the wino by the vital beginning of the plea. He misjudged it or perhaps the wino weaved better. Face to face.

"Please, *sur*," in that tone between servility and surliness.

"I've no change," snapped Ford, hating himself.

"I'm not begging," and this in a grievously offended voice.

The wino pushed a greeting card under his nose. It was a book token for almost fifteen pounds.

"Are you a reading man?" he asked.

"Bring it to the book shop for a refund," said Ford.

"They'll only give books," he said. "You can't drink bloody books."

Ford certainly agreed with this. He gave the wino his loose change and fled. He hated that the winos were Irish, another point for the English to cave. How many years of English language teaching would cancel that?

He stopped at The Rose and Crown. The barmaid was blowsy and many sheets to the wind. He got a large gin and her full lit smile. He should have had what she was having. Pity enwrapped him. As an antidote he played "Run Around Sue" in his head – he'd found it on a juke box in Camden Town a few weeks back. A punk rocker glared and immediately after selected "The Men Behind the Wire." In passing Ford he hissed, "Get real, granddad." True to tell, Ford's hair was thinning rapidly. How did you fatten hair? Now he kept his music internal and his hair on despair. A man nearing seventy sat carefully down near Ford. He had a full rich head of hair. Fat in fact, seethed Ford. The man peered intently at a five pound note which he ironed flat, then caressed and even smelled it. A sigh then.

"Excuse me, son?" he asked.

Ford moved nearer and the old man held up the fiver.

"It's not a ten, is it?"

"No – no, it's a five."

"Ar – agh."

Ford felt like a murderer. Should he have lied? And then what? All horrible complications would surely follow. Pity leaked further. Ford rose for a refill.

"Can I get you a drink," he offered.

"Ger off, I'm too old for pooftahs," he roared.

Ford went straight out the door and came here. Just in time to hear Dalton's statement and end a pitied day.

At work Ford had begun in a wild flush of enthusiasm. Full of fellowship and ideals, he reckoned on putting the "h" back in "humanity" in London's South East. Above his desk he hung Balzac's "Nothing prepares you for the heartless cruelty of people." A young black seeing it had asked, "The man from Brixton?"

His first client was a young Scottish girl, Angela, whose boyfriend beat her regularly.

"He's a good 'un though," she said. "He works and he doesn't drink."

"Rare qualities indeed," said Ford, "he just works on you."

Early in February she had appeared with both eyes blackened. Ford had suggested very strategic things to her. As she left she smiled at Ford as if he understood nothing and said, "He does it to show his love."

"Let me know what he does for Valentine's Day", Ford said.

He had initially believed the tone he needed for social work was a light ironical one. This he adopted till a West Indian punched him in the mouth roaring, "Don't get ironical with me sahib."

On first arriving in London, Ford had made the big mistake of handling fruit at a vegetable stall. The owner came screaming and spitting bile and aggravation.

"*Never* handle the fruit."

Since then Ford had seen countless other fruit vendors achieve instant psychosis as some hapless foreigner touched their product.

He felt there should be a large billboard on the White Cliffs of Dover proclaiming

"Don't touch their fruit."

Ford was big on control. Uneasiness gripped him when any area of his life slithered away. Yet he frequently drank heavily, thus forfeiting any personal direction. A lot of things got away from him then. Control definitely headed the pack. As the other faculties blurred, it leaped to win the stampede. Riddle him that.

Movies were his passion. Like Joseph Stalin, he had a penchant for the old American gangster stories. When men were men, and women were glad of it. He'd been to see *Ordinary People* and Judd Hirsch as the psychiatrist says, "I'm not big on control." This soured that for Ford. He even read Judith Guest's novel to see if that line was there. Oh sweet control! At such times Vikki spoke in his head. Ford once said "I love her because she loves me." Not the worst reason, he thought as he'd thought so many times before. Without bitterness, and sometimes even without regret, he didn't love anyone now. Not that heart-stopping, dizzying obsession that quakes your whole world. You didn't know whether to sing or puke. Once – oh yes. But a long time ago. "It wouldn't come again," he said aloud. Moreover, he didn't believe he had anymore what it took to rise to such heights. Such a level of one-dimensional obsession.

Ford didn't figure it required youth as much as energy, and he was all out of energy. "God help us," he added. This was an Irish benediction or condemnation, depending on your circumstances. Emotionally, Ford's words were woesome and he sometimes realized it. Vikki would say "Sweetheart, if you'd listen to Leonard Cohen sing 'Dance Me To the End of Love' you'd be grand." Maybe a lot of things, but he didn't feel then or now that grand was one of them. Grand really applied to hotels or weather. He didn't think you'd go far on grand emotions, not in South East London anyway.

***

On his fourth pint after work that Friday, Ford began to loosen up. Social work, jeez it was anything but social. His director, named Neville Whitlow, said a thousand times daily, "We can only try, children." A pompous ass. Ford found him pretty trying. Children! For beggars sake! That a grown man would address his staff as that. Ford seethed anew.

Neville was from Suffolk and this explained a lot. "There were two types of Neville down there," said Dalton on one of his rare visits. The Neville who stays put and the one who leaves. To be exactly identical in London. The director made the mistake of attempting to talk sensibly to Dalton.

"Are you a social worker, perchance, a socialite, mate?"

"Do you mean socialist?"

"Watch my lips, mate: now real S-L-O-W – socialite."

That was that.

To calm himself, Ford dismissed all thoughts of work.

He liked to muse on great book titles. A few were outstanding. *By Grand Central Station I Sat Down and Wept.* Sure you'd have to grab that. He'd yet to meet a woman who didn't love that title. In fact he'd yet to meet a woman. *My Brilliant Career*. Another cracker. Was she kidding, you thought. Irony. Right! Lay that ole irony down with a trowel and book awards yet mentioned. For his own book he'd title *In Santorini I Greek Mis-spelt Your Name*. Get the yuppies and the sour-ass romantics. The greek-o-philes would nod knowingly and shell out. *Powerhouse Sex*. In truth to tell, he'd sell it thus. Big red letters on a black jacket. Nowt else. Full of plunging and ravaging with buttocks heaving and bosoms hopping. Big buckets of sweat and grunting. 'She felt his manhood throb' type passages. Ford's own favorite was "love weapon" pronounced with a slight slur. "She unsheathed his love weapon." Not the easiest line to mutter with a straight face. Let's get down to fierce basics, thought Ford. The hero would be named Ramrod. Then Ford's mood darkened as the jukebox played Willie Nelson's "Loving Her Was Easier". Next would come ole Waylon Jennings. Ah, stab my unprotected heart. Tis a while since he'd felt anything throbbing at all.

Heading for the subway at The Elephant and Castle, he had that fragile feeling where you walk very, very carefully. Like a drunk, in fact. "Who, me?" Never, Neville! "When you're tired of London, you're tired of life." Whoever wrote that, had never traveled on the Northern line. The elevator was out of order. Well knackered from the stairs, Ford leaned on the platform pillar. Two skinheads were rough-housing. As the train approached Ford whispered, "Play well children," and hiccuped merrily. The skinheads suddenly raced towards him, and one shot him a kick in the groin.

"Score one for Milwall," he roared.

The Doc Marten had a steel toe, and Ford dropped like a felled tree. The train pulled off as Ford lay whimpering.

"I throb," he thought. His love weapon crushed.

***

Then there was what Ford termed Dalton's political conversation. Dalton claimed to have met an ex-Prime Minister on a train. If bodyguards were present, they had achieved an invisible profile. Dalton approached the man and he was receptive, even friendly. Perhaps he feared public indifference more than political danger. He spoke at length and Dalton managed an almost fine pretence of interest. Eventually, Dalton proposed a drink and borrowed a twenty from the man.

"Bit short on the readies, wife in the hospital, etc."

"So," asked Ford, "did you buy him the drink?"

"Of course. A ginger ale, mind. He had an image to portray. I didn't rejoin him. Lord no, but I said I'd get the money to him when the country got back on its feet. I left him to his ginger ale alone as I reckoned he'd a future behind him and might welcome some introspection if not downright reflection."

This way as unlikely a yarn as Ford had ever heard, even from the likes of Dalton. Dalton's credo was simple, based loosely on Henry Thoreau's: "Beware of any enterprise that requires new clothes."

"Look," he said to Ford, "everything is about dealing. God doesn't give you any class. OK, then maybe deal with the devil for a bit of style."

He pronounced devil as divil and not always intentionally.

"Is this a true story?"

"Whaddya mean?"

"Well, there are some flaws in there."

"What, what friggin flaws? You don't believe I subbed the money?"

"Oh not, that's all too believable. It's the ex-Prime Minister on a train bit." Ford paused, considered, then risked, "Had a season ticket, did he?"

Dalton was livid. "You scummy bastard! He's a man of the people, why wouldn't he take trains? Anyroad, what do you care if it's true, you enjoyed the story or what?"

"Yes."

"So, where's the problem? Picking up some integrity in the social work field, are we? Time was, Ford, you'd just enjoy a story. Now you need references. Jeez man, why do you care? Leave the caring to the Nevilles."

"Listen, Dalton, I love the story but I do care."

"It's that I kind of need it to be true."

"Ah, for crying out loud! You ludrimawn, you're W-E-I-R-D. Gottit? You remind me of that biblical fellah – what's his name? Jot?"

"Job."

"Yea, that's the guy. Always whinin' to heaven, 'Oh oh oh, why me, Lord?'" The Lord looked down and said, "Cos you really piss me off."

Ford laughed loudly, but Dalton wasn't placated.

"You keep laughing, son, it's what you do best. The end is nigh, and nigher than you think."

Dalton gulped down the dregs of his whiskey. Standing up, he looked Ford full in the face and said, "How yah fixed for a tenner?"

The briefest conversation.

***

Ford boarded the No. 12 at Notting Hill Gate. Not a riot in sight. The upper deck was packed but he managed to squeeze a space in front of two very well dressed women. In their fifties, he noted without interest. As the bus turned at Marble Arch he gradually filtered their conversation. He tried these days to shut out others' talk. Vikki had once accused him of being but an eavesdropper on life. "Fit that into a C.V.," he'd replied.

One woman said, "Well, I said to him, 'Trevor, you may certainly suit yourself, but I'm not wearing a bra.'"

"Gosh, I'll bet that set the cat among the old pigeons. What!"

I'd have told him I hadn't worn an knickers there either, Ford thought. Louis MacNeice was among Ford's favorite poets. Not least because he loved trains. Ford could sit and read *Autumn Journal* and know a measure of peace. He'd like to carve in granite MacNeice's description of the Irish:

> *"They stagger round the world with a stammer*
> *and a brogue and a faggot of useless memories"*

Paul Theroux too, those magical travel books, he was brilliantly crabby. You'd like to sit down with the guy and discuss serious irritation. His novel, *My Secret Life*, appeared to Ford to have been gouged from his very soul.

Ford liked the English, often despite themselves. That low key approach was mighty appealing. At their best they looked like they'd settle for a good thick rope. Absolute delight was expressed as *super*. "How was it for you, dear?" "Super."

The old stiff upper dick was Dalton's analysis. Thus we come to Bill. He didn't fit the stereotype. A cockney, he'd been referred to a social worker through the courts. Bill liked to drink. A lot. "Clients," Neville called them. Bill and Ford became friends. Last Christmas, Ford had given him Paul Theroux's impressions of the English, *The Kingdom By the Sea*.

"So, Bill, how did you like the book?"

"Wanker!"

As to whether this meant Ford of Theroux wasn't clear. They drank together, and recently Ford had fallen down a lot. Some insane part of him hoped Bill hadn't noticed. That lying prone was, perhaps, an odd way to behave in pubs, but not anything serious. So you had a few, and fell over, big deal. If Bill fell over a lot, would he mind?

As a social worker, he might inject a cautionary word. Very cautionary. Bill was six feet three and tipping two hundred pounds. No, nothing heavy or, God forbid, even mildly castigating.

Bill had asked Ford to meet him in Camden Town, an Irish suburb. They settled in the snug, and went to work on some Guinness. Ford got the next shout and, apparently as an afterthought, ordered a couple of scotches. Bill frowned.

"The Guinness tastes a bit sour?" asked Ford.

"Not the Guinness."

In such a situation you either shut up or asked, "Not me, I hope." The latter never paid dividends.

"Not me, I hope."

"You got that right, son."

Whoops! This was heading for the toilet.

"What, what's the matter?"

"Do you worry about your drinking?"

"No."

"Ever?"

"No."

"Maybe you should."

How big was big, so . . . OK, Bill was huge and so was his mouth.

"Bill, would you like to get right to it? This is like forty questions and I hate all the answers."

"Ford, I like you. You're weird for an Irishman, you're quiet and funny but I worry for you. Take me, I'm a big drinker. I drink and I do other things. Now, you. You drink and you drink and you fall over every time I see you."

Ford was raging. A deep surge of bile threatened to blast upwards.

"Well, Bill, where I grew up you suspected people who didn't drink. Some of the old Hollywood actresses said, 'Never trust a man who doesn't drink.' They could trust me. I kept hearing about role reversal on TV. Is that what we've got here? You're the social worker and I'm the big guy with the market stall, oh yea, and a drink problem, right?"

Bill tried to interrupt. He'd never heard Ford say so much. Neither had Ford. The look on Ford's face was chilling.

"Shut-up! You want honesty, then shut the hell up."

"I have a drink problem, it's my problem. You have a problem with that, it's your *bloody problem*. But, see, already your talk has helped. See these drinks – see! Who the hell needs them!

He was far too Irish to sweep them to the floor. He stood and swept out.

***

Ford liked to read about Paris in the Thirties, all the heavy-weights floating around dripping literature. The lost generation, how unutterably romantic. It tickled him to think that in fact a garage mechanic had coined the phrase. Gertrude Stein claimed it like the slick old bat she was. Personally, Ford felt he belonged to "the faded generation." "Wow, how did you get those dreams so faded?" "Stone wash . . . then hung them out to dry."

He read about Paris now to block out the scene in Camden Town. It didn't work. Whether Hemingway wrote one true sentence or Alice B. Tok told the truth in her woeful biography, who cared?

Crossing to his one cupboard, he rummaged there. Out came a bottle of Pernod, unopened, the seal intact. A present from Vikki after one of her Parisian jaunts. "Open that on a special occasion," she said. Her eyes had been as soft then as if the whole world had benefited from a belt or two of Pernod. He put Waylon Jennings on the turntable. The bottle he placed on the table before him. Hands clasped, as if in prayer, he sat watching it. Waylon sang.

Hemingway said in *A Moveable Feast* that at his happiest time with Hedley, they'd been in an oak cabin surrounded by wood. They hadn't touched or knocked on it, and how Hemingway rued that omission! Ford was damned if he'd touch wood either. The question was straightforward: "Was this, or was it not, the special occasion?"

Come Thursday night, Ford replayed his scene with a client at work. A middle aged travel agent was developing a taste for drink. Pressure from his wife led him to seek help or, as she said, "She'd travel." The initial interview had gone like this. Tom, the travel agent, was extremely nervy.

"Do you worry about your drinking?" Ford asked.

"No!"

"Ever?"

"No."

"Maybe you should," said Ford with the air of solemn experience.

He fixed Camden Town squarely in his sights, then continued.

"Tom – May I call you Tom? OK, Tommy. I like you, you're offbeat for a travel agent. You're quiet and, probably, funny. I worry for you, Lots of people drink, am I right, Tommy? Just nod your head. They drink and do other things. But you Tommy, you drink and you drink, and you fall down."

"I beg your pardon? I never fell down in my life," Tommy blubbered. "Never!"

"Ah Tommy, you look like a faller to me. No, no, no, Tommy, just nod. It's best at the beginning if you don't interrupt."

To Ford's amazement, Tommy took all of this for the mandatory two hours. Ford would have walloped the living daylights out of himself. Especially the "Tommy" touch. Phew! Perhaps travel agents were immune to abuse.

Afterwards, in Neville's office he'd been introduced to Tom's wife. A harridan, as the dramatists said.

"Thomas has gone outside to the motor," she said, eyeballing Ford.

"That's nice," said Ford. He was damned if he'd say on word about the interview. He stared right back and thought, "Yea, motormouth!"

After she'd left, Neville went into a long spiel about apples in the bud and other timely metaphors, down home Suffolk wisdom by the kilo. "Any impressions to share, old chap?"

"Yea, don't put all your eggs in one basket."

"Excuse me?"

"It's no wonder he drinks."

All of this would fill Neville's report. Ford didn't really see a huge future for himself in this field. Whoops! Depression's knocking on wood.

***

Ford scanned the evening paper. One eye on the bar. An American student was browbeating the bartender.

"Lemme tell yah, buddy, the English don't know shit for sports."

Ford didn't think the bartender was likely to be his friend. The American had a sweatshirt proclaiming "Cleveland 11." Ford hadn't really heard a whole lot about the first. He loved to hear them mangle and do absolute gymnastics with English. They had some choice expressions, apart from Muttah, which they prefixed to every conceivable kind of sexual activity and then flung the lot at you. He never ceased to wonder at "shit for brains". What construction, and this was an insult! Their predilection for the mammary gland was truly breathtaking. Ford smiled at his own pun. See, it's contagious, he thought.

"This country sucks," said Cleveland.

The barman was now most definitely not his buddy. Of all the names for news-papers, Ford liked this best, *The Cleveland Plain Dealer*. A man's paper, you felt. No floss, just the news, nothing fake or fancy. Calls 'em as we get 'em. Jack Webb would have bought it in his *Dragnet* fashion. He returned to his own paper. The Dow Jones index was down again. Ford knew two things about it. It went up. It went down. Pure simplicity!

Yet, you said in a reasonably crestfallen tone to somebody, "The Dow is down!"

Bingo, next time around, they were asking for financial advice. Worse, you were tempted to give it. He looked at the TV. Oh, gloried-be, *The Rockford Files*. Better than *The Sweeney* repeats. Forget the drink. Run home, re-heat the chili and relish. Bliss indeed! What mortal could ask for more (maybe *Barney Miller*). His cup runneth over. As he prepared to depart, he heard what sounded like a very vindictive rain out there. The lash-you-into-the-face type. The notion arose: was he over emphasising the joy of the evening ahead . . . just a tad overstating.

The barman roared. "All right you, I've had it, time to sling your 'ook." He leaped the bar and showed Cleveland to the door. Plain enough! Sling your hook. The English had a few beauts of their own.

***

Phew, Ford was sure glad it was Saturday. No putting the world to social rights today. He uttered a silent prayer that Tom the travel agent wasn't like death warmed over. With that wife, he speculated on how it could be otherwise. The phone shrieked putting the heart cross-ways in him. It had that shrill insistent yak which went "answer me and answer me fast." Implicit in that was the sly promise "but you'll be sorry." Most times Ford answered the phone, he regretted it. "Here goes," and reflexively his fingers crossed.

"Yea."

"Ford?" Dalton roared. He had the Irish habit of bellowing at phones. Loudness abetted comprehension.

"And good morning to you."

"Ford, have you been drinking already? Or is there a woman there? Hey, put a knot in it."

"More of it," said Ford.

"Listen, you know what a dip is, do you?"

"Anything to do with the Dow Jones?"

"What? Dow who . . . are you pissed?"

"No . . . And no, I dunno what a dip is, should I?"

"It's what the English call a pickpocket, you know, a Jimmy light-fingers."

"O.K."

"Well Ford, I got dipped . . . over sixty notes. What do you think of that?"

Ford didn't think much of it one way or the other. All he knew was, it would cost him. In fact he felt he was about to experience exactly what it was to be dipped by phone. Right now he wasn't in to the mood for Dalton.

"So, Ford . . . Ford, are you there? Hello?"

"Yea."

"I wonder if maybe you could let me have seventy-five?"

"Seventy-five!"

"Just kidding. Lighten up Ford. Seventy will do grand."

"I'll be in The Kings Arms around eight. O.K.?"

"What am I supposed to do till then?"

"You're always telling me you'd have been a gifted actor, that you missed your vocation."

"Jeez, so what?"

"So, act outraged," and Ford put down the phone.

***

Then there was Grace. A lovely name for a woman, and a lovely lady she was. You could put music to this. Ford wished he had. On one bright and shiny day he won on the horses. He'd noticed a horse called "Vikki's Way" was entered at Redcar. On a whim and a prayer, he put a tenner to win . . . and it did. He'd gone into Ladbrokes in Piccadilly Circus. The horse paid nine-to-one, minus tax. Ford was stunned. He had a fist of tenners. Something special to remember. He did a wee jig on the street.

Fortnum and Mason caught his eye. Why the hell not? A high English tea . . . cream buns and crumpet . . . ah! He really wanted a drink but he could do that later and seriously. In he went. The staff intimidated him, and it was crowded. On the verge of fleeing, he spied a table with one person. "Go on, it's a day for gambling," he urged. This was a fine looking woman here. Too late to gallop.

"Excuse me. Er – might I sit . . . Is the table free?"

She looked up. Blue, blue eyes and my, oh my, a face close to beauty. Around thirty. In there!

"Is it free? Now, mm . . . There is a vacant place, but I'd hazard a guess and say it's far from free. Not here!"

Wouldn't you know it? A comedian. What a wit! He sat anyway. Ford was very uncomfortable. So much that he ordered coffee and felt a distinct freeze. From nowhere a devil-may-care mood took hold, laced lightly with rage. A caff, that's all. For all the snotty trappings, it was just a caff. But the treatment wasn't quite over.

"And how would sir wish his coffee?"

You could cut glass with the smirk. Ford looked up. God! He'd be brawling in a minute. The woman sat and watched Ford. Enough already!

"I'll tell you what. Why don't you bring it in a cup, then if I feel maybe I'd like a bucket later, I'll get back to you. The coffee came quietly. Ford didn't think the attitude improved a whole lot but he sure felt better. Way, way better.

"You're losing your hair," she said.

Follow that! Ford couldn't. For starters it was true. Boy was it true? Every morning the mirror taunted, "Hey, you got so bald, where did all your hair go?" He had sandy, loose hair. A whole lot looser these days. Gloried be, some mornings there seemed to be more hair on the brush than on his head. A wig would never be a solution. His mother said a thousand times, "See a man with a wig, you see an ejit."

Pithy but effective. You hoped for a high forehead and the kindness of strangers. Not today. Was she all in it, he wondered. I mean, would you say to a person, "Hi, how come you're so bald?" or " I see you're missing a few teeth there, missus." Come on!

She had a hoity-toity voice with an underlay of America.

Ferocious combination. Ford looked at his coffee: could they find smaller cups?

"Don't sulk, you've a strong face," she said.

There isn't a man in the world who wouldn't swap a strong face for a head of hair. Ford ran a series of snappy rejoinders all of which sounded flat. Oh tonight, he'd have a veritable trove of crisp replies. He said, "You're all in it, are yah? Firing on all cylinders I mean?"

She looked startled, then smiled.

"You're Irish?"

Following this lady's thought process was very unnerving. She continued, "I couldn't understand a person coming here . . . for coffee."

"Well, I didn't think they'd give me Guinness."

"I don't think they're fond of me as it is." She laughed again. "I'm Grace," she said.

Ford considered, then went for the brogue.

"And tis graced I am myself to meet thee." Not bad. Not great, but he was new to this.

"Are you American?" he asked.

"Hey, very sharp. I though my Fortnum and Mason accent was foolproof. I'm from Wisconsin, and for a while there I had a limey husband."

"Lousy?"

"Yeah, that too. No, Limey. Like English. Cecil. Cecil's my husband," she smiled deeply here. "Hey, I like saying that. Back home, you call a guy Cecil, you better reach for a weapon . . . and be carrying something a little more lethal than an attitude. But he's a story that needs at least three bourbons for lubrication."

Ford considered. How dangerous could someone called Cecil be? Realistically, how much?

"What's your name?" she asked. "I mean, if you're buying me a drink, it helps. I'm not saying it's essential, but I'm curious."

"Ford."

"That's it, Ford? Blunt and macho. Well, no shit. Don't fool with this dude. Ever read Ford Madox Ford?"

"*The Good Soldier*?"

"Way to go, course you Irish have some sort of lock on writers, am I right?"

Did this require an answer? Ford didn't think so.

"Let me pay for this," Ford suggested, and she agreed. After he paid he stood with a vague smile, looking at the bill.

"Something wrong, Ford?"

"No." He was thinking this place has brought the "dip" to a professional level. They walked up Charing Cross Road past 84, and Grace said she'd sure like to have met Helen Hanff. Grace knew a small pub off New Oxford Street and they went there.

The barman said, "Hi, Grace," and Ford thought, "Oh yea?"

"How do you feel about sour mash?" she asked.

"Is that like sour grapes, or bitter spuds?"

"Droll, Ford. Let's drink Stateside liquor. They got 'em all here."

"Hey, Tommy, you want to bring us some sour mash and make them big suckers. On the rocks."

Tommy wanted to, and did. He was in his fifties with a lopsided leer. He showed his teeth a lot, which was a mystery. The teeth were not so much stained by tobacco as blitzed. Lashings of Old Spice didn't disguise the fact that Tommy had sampled some sour mash himself, and not long ago. Judging by his smile, maybe he'd drank the Old Spice.

"You're a doll," Grace said.

The barman didn't strike Ford as such unless The Brothers Grimm had designed some.

"You know why I like this place, Ford?"

"The ambience?"

"Good word, been reading Improve Your Word Power, in the *Reader's Digest*, I'd say."

She walloped back the drink so Ford did the same and nearly went through the wall.

"Arr . . . gh!" he cried.

"Old Kentucky Mule Kick," she said. "Tommy, get your ass in gear. I like this place 'cos they got a juke box. Wanna play?"

"Any Waylon Jennings?" he asked, still dazed by from the bitterness of the sour mash. Sour, it was the pure bitterness of Lucifer.

She looked at Ford as more mule-kickers arrived. She said, "Lemme guess, it's the wailing you like?"

"Well, Grace, I like the melancholy. Us Irish are happiest with a full blast of sadness. Music to hang yourself by basically."

"You and Sylvia Plath, both, be my guest."

Later, the bar began to fill, and Ford would have said something but his tongue felt shredded. The mule had indeed kicked. Grace began to stand up. Ford couldn't bear the thought of her departure. She moved her face right next to his.

"Here we go," he thought, "the old peck on the cheek and sayonara." His heart was broken.

"So, Ford," she said, "you wanna get laid or what?"

***

"How was it for you," Ford asked. He blew a nigh perfect smoke ring rising to the gods. If he felt any better they might have to certify him.

"Well . . . You're a cryer, I'll give you that."

Ford felt gut kicked. Who needed sour mash? She added, "I liked it, don't get me wrong, but it wasn't special. You wouldn't want me to lie . . . You're not that kind of guy."

I am, he roared silently, I am. Jeez! Lie to me and *lie big*. Who wanted honesty? He wanted to be a stud. Ford always felt that when someone said "I respect your honesty," you should check the silverware. He could see his epitaph:

"A man of integrity but a lousy lay."

Oh my God!

Grace turned to him and said, "So, you want to try again?" He did.

***

Ford knew the difference between a gift and mere talent. He had a talent for drawing. His sketches won him prizes at school. But gifted, no. You could develop a talent but you couldn't work towards a gift. You were or you weren't and he wasn't. Vikki had given him a lavish copy of Beardsley's work and he almost never looked at it. "Look and weep," he knew. Somerset Maugham had said, "The greatest curse must be to have the compulsion to write, and no talent." Ford shuddered on reading that. Substitute "sketch" for "write."

Feeling a time of inspiration around them, Ford had a mental picture of Addie Bundren on the back of a wagon. He could see the red clay of the Mississippi . . . and sketched it . . . over and over till he felt he caught Faulkner's vision . . . and obsession. It hung in his living room. With visitors to his flat, Ford appreciated the difference fully twixt talent and the jackpot. They'd say, "Nice sketch. Hey, I love your sofa, where'd you get it?" If he were gifted, they'd say, "Wow, what a sketch!" No mention of the bloody sofa.

Grace had looked at the sketch for what seemed like a long time. Ford, in anticipation actually fell on the sofa.

Finally she said, "Read any Faulkner?"

He loved her then. It was the best moment of all that they'd had. Ford was blessed just then because he knew the moment for what it was. Knew and understood and was grateful near to weeping.

***

Grace was in his life for three months. They drank sour mash, wailed with Waylon and made love a lot. Ford was never sure if he became a better lover. Certainly he became a more frequent one. Grace hadn't told him the deal on her husband. She wasn't a lady to urge "Tell me now."

Grace wouldn't live with him. That was O.K., he felt almost good enough to sketch again. Then that Friday she arranged to meet him at Finches on the Fulham Road. She arrived late and, uncharacteristically, bothered.

"Let's drink gin," she said.

Ford had already started on scotch, but hell, he was flexible.

She looked pale but it made her look lovelier to Ford.

"I hate this pub," she said, "almost as much as I hate gin."

"You aren't pregnant . . . or anything," Ford ventured. As to whether he disguised the hope in his voice, he'd never know for sure.

"No such bloody luck," she said. "Cecil has returned to London. He's been Stateside these past months . . . or do you think I invited him?"

"I dunno, Grace."

"Judas Priest! That's from *Hill Street Blues* . . . You couldn't invent Cecil. He's moving permanently to New York and . . . I'm the wife, so . . ."

"You're going to New York"

"Bingo! God, this gin is awful."

"Have something else."

"What! And feel better? I wanna get drunk, not happy."

"It's over between us then," said Ford. Stating the obvious was all he could muster.

"Tell you the truth Ford, I don't think we can bring you."

He could have smiled. I mean, a bit of levity was fairly vital here. But he didn't and it wasn't something he felt he'd regret.

"Say something Ford, any god-damn thing."

"Good-bye?"

"Ford, I like you a whole lot, for reasons you'd never even realize. But . . . Bottom line time: Cecil is rich and I like being rich. I like it a lot! Your mentor, Scott Fitz, 'The rich are different from you and me.' Well, babe, I'm with them. I like the difference."

"Daisy had the sound of money in her voice," Ford muttered. The gin was making him sick. Worse, maudlin.

"That kind of stuff Ford. You won ninety pounds on a horse and thought you were loaded. I'm talking gold credit cards and Gucci toothbrushes."

"Toothbrushes!" thought Ford. "She's hoppin' on my heart and talking toothbrushes!" He said, "I was rich that day I met you."

"Jeez, don't get poetic on me Ford. Not when I'm swiggin' gin. We had a good time, kiddo. Hell, a great time, but, I mean, was it love?"

She paused, then said, "I always wanted to ask you something . . ."

"Better ask now while I'm in such a carefree phase," he said.

"Vikki – did you love her?"

Ford walloped a measure of gin and wondered if the truth mattered. He'd once heard Sean Connery say on TV, "Tell the truth and then it's their problem." Worth a shot.

"I loved her because she loved me."

Grace was silent. She didn't order any more to drink and Ford didn't think he'd ever order another gin. He said, to break the silence, "Did I ever tell you that the very meaning of the word 'Grace' is 'a free gift'?"

She liked that. He didn't even have to look at her to know how pleased she was. She prepared to leave and handed him a bag with Tower Records splurged on it. A record, per chance?

"It's Waylon," she said.

"Who else?"

"You keep sketching, Ford, O.K.?" She turned to go.

"Grace."

"Yes?"

"You be careful out there . . . And that's from *Hill Street Blues*."

He thought, "God mind you well" as she walked out. Not that he would have said that. But oh, how he meant it. She won't look back, he bet, and this at least Ford got right.

The barman said, "You all right?"

"Yea . . . Thanks."

"Anything else?"

"Got any sour mash?"

Ford felt he should stay a bit after her departure. Like about a week. In the while, the pain subsided and he knew he had some decisions to reach. He decided to start smoking again and what else? Right. Buy Marlboro. Pity he hadn't a zippo.

It was time to leave when he asked a guy where the best place to buy hand-tooled cowboy boots was. He frequently considered sketching what it was he'd left behind there. Close his eyes and he could see it. The bar counter, a mess of glasses and the Tower Records bag. What eased the vision was the half empty box of Marlboro standing upright. Red, white and vivid against the gaudy yellow. As yet he hadn't bought a zippo. The cowboy boots he put down to a passing whim. No more than that. Nothing but a passing fancy.

***

The very next day Ford caught a snatch of conversation he was to rate among his absolute favourites. This would top his collection. Hungover! He was knocking on heaven's door. The phantom orchestras were full tilt boogie in his head. A cure . . . He'd have to have something before he appeared at work. Purely medicinal. The early morning houses at Smithfield. Have to be.

The pub was jammed with market traders. Maybe he'd turn his life completely round and party in the mornings. These people looked robust and . . . Good-lord! Alive! Back home, early pubs had the silence and sanctity of church, till later when the cures kicked home.

A large vodka with tonic. Oh God, was he seriously going to drink this? Weren't there people in the greater London area who leaped to the day and said, "I'm going to have a fry-up for breakfast. Runny eggs, fat sausages . . ." A jolt of nausea straightened him. O.K., here goes. With both hands trembling he got the glass to his mouth. Tilt the head preferably and slide the sucker down. He did and it did. A-a-rg . . . God on a bicycle! Ah, it's down . . . No, here it's back . . . No, oh please. And miraculously it settled. He saw lights and heard tongues. Buckets of sweat blinded him and ran down his arms. This was fun? He hadn't had such pleasure since those root canal sessions. The world changed, the Promised Land arrived. His heart ceased its mad fandango, the sweat evaporated and, was it possible, he felt pretty good. Might even have him another one of them vodkas, skip the tonic, bit gassy for his palate.

Thus a merry Ford heard a woman say to some guy – they were sitting to his left and he daren't risk a sudden turn. This new found health was too precious to squander on curiosity. She was saying, "Oh yea, I know all about you little guys. Come for just a little drink. Then, honestly, just a little sex," she paused and Ford could hear the sheer exasperation.

"Then there's a little baby and *guess what*? You're a little hard to find."

Ford wanted to howl. Howling was not a good idea despite the vodka whispering, "No, no, go on. It's O.K. Howling's good. Go on, howl a bit." He knew what happened to guys who howled in pubs. Next stop, the House of Confusion and white T-shirts . . . with straps. Wasn't he a social worker! God, work! To quote Grace, he better haul ass. See, see how mellow he was, he could think, "Grace". O.K. Odd, though, he didn't much want to howl now. He in fact hauled ass, albeit carefully.

***

Before quitting time at work, Neville said, "A word before you depart."

"Whoops," thought Ford, "on your bike time."

His final client of the day was a young, black girl. Ford found himself staring for just that too long moment.

"Is something wrong?" she asked.

"No . . . No, well, you've a gorgeous face."

She looked startled, then nearly pleased and settled on sad.

A diagnosis had found her to be an H.I.V. carrier. Unaffected herself, she carried the killer now. Ford was completely lost. He gave her the name of an Aids counsellor and some meaningless patter.

"Can I come to see you too?" she asked.

"Why," he thought, and said, "of course."

She was called Isobel and, this being South East London, she was know as Belle. Ford knew for whom the bell was tolling and hated himself for the flippancy. He didn't know what else to think. He said, "I'll see you soon." Ah, the wisdom of the ages.

Neville put a folder aside and said, "I need your help and – er – guidance."

"Sure," said a stunned Ford.

"The local authority insist we recruit a field worker, someone with street credibility."

"In other words, they don't need academic qualifications."

"Exactly. You've delved to the core of the situation. Social work has a very poor public image just now, so we need to get to the people."

"Before the people get to us," Ford mused.

"Any ideas?"

Ford hadn't. "I haven't," he said.

"Well, okey-dokey, let me put this scenario before you. How about your chum Mr. Dalton?"

Ford nearly fell off the chair. Chum!

"Dalton?" he croaked.

"I feel he may perhaps be that rough diamond we need."

"Well," said Ford, "they don't come much rougher."

"Excellent. Might I prevail upon you to broach the subject with him and for him to drop in for an informal chat?"

"Watch your wallet," thought Ford.

After he left Neville, he felt again as if he'd just been immersed in *The Guardian*. He didn't think he'd file these conversations amongst the gems, rough diamonds notwithstanding.

***

The "interview" took place in a congenial setting. The pub. Dalton was on a roll. He'd won on the horses and had a lady lined up for later.

"A goer," he said.

"Do I know her?"

"Not in the biblical sense, I hope."

"Where's Sheila these days?"

"Ah, that wan. She's gone into herself. I think she's gone vegetarian and is growing things, like a beard."

What could you possibly say to that? Defend her and Dalton would be on you like a rate.

Ford had already paid for two rounds and looked like he'd be going for a third. He said, "I thought you were flush. Where's the winnings?"

"I don't collect till tomorrow, but I'm glad you mentioned money. Could you slip me a fast fifteen?"

"Dalton, have you any notion of all you owe me?"

"Oh, I do indeed. A tally is being kept. The book has you noted."

"Mentioned in dispatches, am I"

"I tell you, Ford, you've changed and not for the better. You're always worrying about little things. Since Vikki ran off on yah, you've become a slight pain in the ass."

You had to hand it to Dalton, he didn't come "cap in hand," First he asked you for the cash, then he called you an asshole. Not your average people pleaser. In fact, something of a rough diamond. Ford thought he better get to it.

"How do you feel about social work?"

"Sick."

"No, seriously, Neville wants you to join the team."

"Join the team? What friggin' team? That's not a team, it's a show of gob-shites. God preserve me from teams, especially the caring ones."

He managed to make caring sound more offensive than his usual obscenities.

"You don't want to be a social worker?"

"Read my lips: I'd rather wank a snake."

"Delicately put. Jeez, you've been reading The Guardian again. Time you got a real job Ford, you're starting to sound English."

This was the cardinal sin. The Irish would forgive their own most things, apart from success and "aping" the English. You could even get a Yank accent and they'd say you had "no sense", only soft in the head. Become anglicised and you got otracised. Absolutely. Dead man walking.

"But I'll drop in on old Neville. That's too good to miss."

"You're not going to *touch* him!"

"God almighty, I have to work there."

"See what I mean, Ford? You need to lighten up."

"Any sign of that fifteen?"

Ford gave him ten and Dalton got up to leave.

"I've to go. Your wan will be drooling by now. Do you ever hear from Gracie?"

This pleased Ford hugely. The very mention of Grace's name left him with the afterglow. That Dalton thought to ask filled him with contentment. Dalton drained his glass and borrowed a cigarette from the barman. Inhaling deeply he looked at Ford before he left and said, "I'll tell you one thing. That Grace . . . She was probably the best fuck I've had in a long time."

The Chinese say if you're plotting revenge, you better dig two graves. Sure, said Ford, as long as one of them is deep and dirty. Quite what he meant by this wasn't altogether certain but it did two things. It sounded mean and it sounded angry. He was hitting all the points on those.

***

Back at his flat he drank steadily. He nursed the hurt carefully and delicately. A pure hatred burned. The more he drank, the colder he felt. A gesture, he thought, I need a melodramatic action to seal the feeling. Yes, yes, of course. He stood and staggered a little. Rummaging in the table drawer he found the scissors. The sketch came easily from the wall and left a wide, blank mark, like mourning. The frame proved difficult and he couldn't align the release catch. Furious, he put it down on the floor and brought his right shoe crashing down on the glass and hurt the heel of his foot. The crack was like a pistol shot and set his heart hammering. He dragged the sketch from the frame and still it resisted. The glass nicked his fingers and blood jumped across the table. "Damn you!" he roared and felt hot, bitter tears of frustration. The sketch was free. Without looking directly upon it,

140

he began to hack and cut haphazardly. Pieces jerked and fell like wedding rice. Wedding rice! "Oh God," he shouted. "Isn't that just bloody priceless?"

Exhausted by rage, he sat back on the much noticed sofa. Wiping the sweat from his face had left streaks of blood there. The cuts on his hand began to throb faintly and he whimpered at intervals. "I'm the sitting wounded," he said. Looking like some demented red Indian, he threw back his head and howled in clear and continuous anguish. All around him lay little vignettes of the Mississippi.

BOOK II

The steps toward Ford's revenge began with his marriage. Just how this would damage Grace and Dalton, he wasn't completely clear about. Like Indiana Jones, he felt he'd make it up as he went along.

At work Neville had said, "A mo please?"

Ford loathed many things, and shortening "moment" might top the list.

Neville continued, "I'm having a little drinks soiree on Thursday evening. My sis, Amanda, is up from the homestead. I'd like you to meet her."

Soiree, sis, homestead! The words bounced on Ford's head. A compulsion to fracture Neville's jaw was nigh overpowering. No frills, just wallop him and roar, "Talk bloody English, will ya?"

What he said was, "I'll be there."

Graham Greene had died. Ford felt pathetic fallacy was pulling a fast one. He thought of all the joy those books had given him. A bitter joy in truth, like the sketch. The quote of Greene's on religion surfaced:

"The church knows all the rules, but it doesn't know what goes on in a single human heart."

"Ain't that the truth," Ford sighed.

He dressed carefully for Tuesday. A Van Heusen shirt he'd found at Oxfam. The tiny red mark on the collar was ketchup, he hoped. The knot of his tie was the Windsor. "How awfully appropriate," he said. Permanent crease slacks that somehow had shortened. Maybe a burglar broke into homes and shortened trousers. A vicious type indeed. The slacks were grey, so Ford decided to risk all and go for the blazer. This was his legacy from the teaching days. Chalk had attached itself to the sleeves and neither prayer nor hope would move it.

Finally, he put on a stout pair of brogues he'd forgotten about. These were a formidable sight. Age had endowed them with a stiffness beyond description. "Ah God, the pain," he said as the brogues began to crush his toes. "For pity-sake, I'm crucified." Perhaps the pain would lend clarity to his thinking.

As he dressed he'd steadily drunk vodka from a mug. The mug had Snoopy emblazoned on the outside. Snoopy had the shit-eating cheerfulness that only a true sadist could have devised. The vodka was Poland's finest and slid down quickly. Like intimidation, it hit you later.

Ford bent to examine his appearance in the wardrobe's half mirror. Was it on himself or were the trousers shortening further? The brogues looked great and felt O.K. if you didn't move. Ideal they'd be if you could bring them separately. "Here's me shoes, the rest is coming."

A vodka giggle escaped him. Giggle! Ford couldn't believe it. Worse, he enjoyed it. The label on the bottle was in Polish so he wondered why he was trying to read it. A small symbol might have been a hundred degrees. Either this was good to drink in the tropics or it was mega proof. If the latter was true, well then, "Way to go."

Grace moved into his head. After making love, he'd looked deep into her eyes, her expression was hard to decipher. Ford had said, "I miss two people when I'm not with you."

"Oh yea?"

"I miss you and I miss the person you make me feel I am."

"Schmuck," said Grace.

Perhaps Polish in origin, mused Ford.

Neville had a flat in Kensington Church Street. Ford changed to the Circle Line, and the tube carriage was full of loud teenagers. He noticed the boys' earrings were fancier than the girls. "Fancy that," he thought, and suppressed a giggle. As he got off at Notting Hill, one of the girls yelled, "Hey Mister, yer pants is at half mast."

Reams of dog abuse followed him till the door slid closed. A light perspiration popped along his forehead. A slow anxious drizzle drifted down his back. The shoes crucified him. If he walked stoop-fashion, maybe the pants would meet the shoes. Neville threw open the door.

"Ford! Bienvenue! Mi casa es su casa."

Was it too late to run? It was. Neville pulled him inside. About twenty people were there. Like Neville, they wore jeans, T-shirts, and trainers. Not a tie in sight, windsored knots or otherwise. And, oh, never did trainers look such a height of comfort. The central heating was at full pitch and Ford felt gallons form beneath his shirt. In French, Neville asked Ford what he'd like to drink.

"For pity-sake, Neville, what are you saying?"

Neville beamed, which was not a pretty sight.

"What's your poison, amigo?"

"Something lethal, I think."

"Ah, that Ford humour! Your wish is my command."

Introductions were made. A flurry of Clives, Normans, a Keith, and a stash of Cecilys, Beverleys and Sarahs. Ford slumped in an armchair. Sweat rolled down his face. A measure of his desperation was his wish for Dalton's presence. Not his company, just his attitude. A girl sat on the chair next to him. He looked at her without interest. Small, but finely finished. Auburn hair to her shoulders, brown eyes, small button nose and a strong mouth. Jeans and a T-shirt, naturally. He'd have mugged her for the trainers.

"You're perspiring, she said."

What, he thought. Is there a neon sign above me that reads, "here sits he who sweats, gather all ye who wish to witness true perspiration."

"Fuck off," he said.

This made them both jump. The violence of the obscenity hung like a threat.

"So you're Ford! I'm Amanda, Neville's sister."

"That figures," said Ford.

"Will I get you a drink?"

"Yea, something to prolong depression."

He watched her move. Nice ass, he thought, and stifled the Americanism. Grace ruled, but far-from-O.K. Amanda returned and gave him a long glass.

"Chin Chin," she said.

"Christ!" said Ford.

He took a reckless swallow. Gin. Good. And then . . . Good grief! He spoke, "I'm sorry about the – er – the f . . ., you know."

She answered in a passable Irish brogue, "Ah, there's many would welcome a decent f . . ."

He nearly choked and in a rapid gin-change turn, he became philosophical.

"You hear people say, I f . . . her or him . . . rather than I made love and that's because that's exactly what they do. It's aggression, not love."

He looked closely at his glass. What on earth was in these to make him talk like that? Amand gave him a radiant smile.

"And you, Ford? What exactly is it you do?"

"Well," he said, "mainly I do the very best I can."

Over the next few weeks he did his best with Amanda. She was living with Neville till a flat could be found. Ford took her out almost every night to cinemas, theatres, restaurants. With her he drank little, and touched her even less. Each night he went home alone and drank with serious intent. All the music to hang yourself to was played. Linda Ronstadt's "Heart Like a Wheel," Willy and "Blue Eyes Crying in the Rain," The Furey Brothers with "Leaving Nancy."

No matter how much booze he put away, he couldn't play Waylon. He cried and drank. Mainly, though, he nurtured his plan for Dalton. The intensity of his hate stunned him. The bile his mind produced was to rock him to his very core. He knew it was eroding a vein of goodness he'd always had. Knew and was satisfied.

One wet Friday evening, he returned her earlier than usual to Neville's. He was anxious to get off to his booze and plans. Necessarily in that order.

"Come up for coffee," she said.

"Not tonight, thanks."

"Or any night," she paused. "Ford, this is not really a request. See it more as an imperial prerogative."

"Phew-ow!" he said.

Amanda fussed with coffee filters, and a light Mozart played. Ford fumed. The coffee aroma was wonderful though not quite as magical as escape. Ford sat in a hard-back chair. The sofa he ignored.

"Rather safe there," she said.

"Better safe than sorry", he answered and, oh, how he wished he hadn't.

"You're not gay, are you?"

"Well, I've been happier."

"Then it must be me. Am I so repellent?"

Oh God, he thought, tears next. And he was right. He reviewed his options. Drink the coffee, go to her, or weep himself. The third appealed most. He went to her. A flurry of wet kisses and awkward clinches led to them making love on the floor. The act was noteworthy for its haste rather than its passion.

"That was wonderful," she said.

"Do you have any cigarettes?" he asked.

Ford had the horrible clarity that she was the type who'd lounge round in one of his shirts. All leg and innuendo. A stale box of cigarettes were found.

"Wow!" said Ford, "that tastes good." It did too.

"I didn't know you smoked. But then I didn't know you'd be such a magnificent lover either."

Ford had to look at her. Was she winding him up? He'd avoided looking into her eyes all during the love-making. No, she seemed serious. Worse, somewhat dewy-eyed. The only eyes Ford looked into were on the wrong side of the Atlantic. Grace. A chill touched his heart as he wondered if Amanda would now love him. Love could ruin the total plan.

"I think I love you," she said.

"Better get an ashtray," he said.

He knew he might well have a coronary if she called him anything affectionate.

"You have a shower, darling, and I'll brew some fresh coffee."

Like a man condemned, he slouched to the bathroom. He was scalding beneath the spray when he heard her come in. Oh, God in Heaven, why hadn't he locked the door as easily as he'd bolted his heart?

"There's a dressing gown for you here, darling."

What! Were they already fifty years together? In jig-time she'd be finishing his sentences . . . and his plans.

Muttering, he toweled himself dry. Through the steam, he looked in the mirror. Even less hair when wet. Such adjectives as tousled, wind swept wouldn't be a feature anymore. The horror of receding, thinning, and let's face it, *bald*! Sign of virility eh . . . *plu* . . . *ee* . . . *ze*, as Gracie would say. The old, bald stallion perchance. That's it, he swore, no more mirrors.

The dressing gown was of red silk. Cold, oh wow-ee. On the right hand breast was written, "Neville". To remind himself was it? Did Neville lounge about in it and periodically glance down saying, "I know who I am, what about you, Mister?" Emerging from the bathroom, Ford felt ninety and all of them hard years.

Amanda was strewn on the couch, his Van Heusen shirt unbuttoned to reveal cleavage.

"Hey, big boy," she said.

Ford liked her. He'd have been content to have her on the fringes of his life. Like Chinese food, you'd be glad of it periodically, but it wasn't essential. The haunting question from one of William Trevor's books: "Yes, but was she amazing?" No. How he wished she were. She'd all sorts of good qualities but, alas, no edge. If Ford knew anything, he knew that bad drop was a staple to his life. Now Grace, dare he say, was amazing. Amazing and in America.

An early conversation with Amanda had set the tone. A literary bomb if not in fact a literal one.

"Who's your favorite writer?"

The only answer to this was Stephen King. That and throwing up.

"I dunno," he said.

"I must return to the Russians," she said.

Ford should have hit the hills then. Were the Russians like a return ticket that never expired? They hung about with a smug expression saying, "We know you'll be back." Amanda meandered on about romantic poets and the new realism. Ford just meandered.

***

A marriage date was set. Ford convinced himself that it was vital to his plan.

Neville said, "Tying the old knot wot? Sis is overjoyed."

"My own cup runneth over," said Ford.

The ceremony was muted. It took place at Kensington High Street Registry Office. Ford didn't inform his family. To marry an Englishwoman . . . Phew! Parnell wasn't that long dead. But a Registry Office? The fires of hell would burn long and gleeful. Dalton had been delighted.

"She's loaded, that one," he said. "Lotsa cash and connections. You landed on your feet, lad."

"I like her."

"Jaysus, who wouldn't? She's not bad looking, either. Big tits."

Saturday prior to the wedding was the stag night. Ford's plan came off the back the burner. He'd arranged to meet "the boys" in Pinches in Notting Hill. He rang Belle and invited her for a drink. She arrived in white. This set her dark skin shining.

"You look lovely," said Ford.

"It's a long time since I felt it," she replied.

Her eyes had a sadness that Ford didn't want to think about. Heads spun when he brought her into the bar. Ford left her talking to Neville and went to order. Dalton was on him.

"Ford, this is stag night. No women."

"She's not staying. Only a quick drink."

"Are you screwin' her?"

"God, Dalton, you're some animal."

"She's some animal is what you mean. Jeez, look at the body on her. I could do with some black meat."

Ford gulped down a neat whiskey. His resolve faltered. Choice time! But a bottle of sour mash on display sealed his fate.

He said slowly, "Well, the reason I brought her was she wants to meet you."
"You're coddin'!"
"No, but don't let on, O.K.?"
"Jaysus, I'll be up that like a rat in a drain."
"How poetic," said Ford.

A chain of whiskies later and Ford saw Dalton and Belle slip away. Something in his very heart withered. Neville was slapping him on the back, and Ford felt it was only to be expected. The evening finished with cabaret in Soho. Despite all his efforts, Ford didn't pass out. All his life he'd remember the stripper planting a scarlet wet kiss on his mouth. It tasted more like nicotine and despair. It doesn't come more bitter than that.

Back home they used the word "bronach" which fitted the hangover perfectly. It's a mood of sadness and melancholy, liberally mixed. The Irish had the lock on sadness. Sure weren't the very best of times underwritten by melancholia? They'd have taught Byron a thing or two. But he went to Greece and a fatal rendezvous with a mosquito. No mosquitoes in Ireland and very few flies on them either. So "bronach" it was. Sick too, but after a quart of scotch, who wasn't? The CIA ruled. Catholic, Irish, Alcoholic.

Ford recalled Neville hugging him and muttering, "We're a family!"

No wonder he was ill. T'was far from hugs Ford was reared. He grew up in a neighbourhood where the only touching going on was for money. You kept your hands to yourself. Put them on another human being, you'd lose them from the elbow. People there weren't big on affection. No doubt there was love in his family. He knew that, bit you didn't outwardly show it. The odd time the family were gathered for a meal it wasn't likely you'd hear, "I love you, Mother, pass the sugar." You didn't ask how someone was feeling; it was more, "How are you fixed?" Cash was the emotional currency. If you cared, you'd put your money where your hug was. As for feelings, well, you felt one of two things. "Mighty" as when the drink flowed, or "death-warmed-over" like in pay-back-time. All the songs were sad, and sadness was the great comfort. Dignity and self-esteem sounded like the names of race horses.

Ford knew his marriage to an Englishwoman put him beyond the pale. "Notions", they'd say; ideas above your station. Amanda had insisted he'd wear a wedding ring. "Yes," he thought, "and fix it firmly through my nose."

***

"To have and to hold . . ." Ford felt he'd been holding his own.

Now the plan was afoot, he'd be needing all the native cunning of his race. Amanda wore a plain white dress, her hair in ringlets. Ford wore the blazer, the shortening pants and his mind in bits. Balzac wrote, "Nothing prepares you for the heartless cruelty of people," and Ford added, "But maybe a marriage could be the salvation yet." Not that he believed it for a moment.

They went to Tenerife for a week's honeymoon. Ford was mortified. He felt their bright, shiny rings were screaming for notice. "Hey, hey, look it her, we're newlyweds."

The plane was crammed with yahoos. Any hooligan could afford a plane ticket, and it seems most had. The Brits at play, if not in The Fields of The Lord, the certainly on a Boeing 747. No sooner did they take off than the duty free was indeed liberated. Drunken roars of "Una Paloma Blanca" rent the air.

Ford knew all the airplane superstitions. If you heard the pilot whistling, don't board the plane. Was it on himself or were the hostesses all whistling? As a child Ford was taught that homosexuals couldn't whistle. Mind you, at that time in Ireland, they hadn't much to whistle about. On any given day on Ford's street, you'd hear all the young lads whistling for dear life. He remembered Lauren Bacall saying to Bogart, "You know how to whistle, just put your lips together and blow." Which was probably all you'd need to know.

Amanda said, "Ti amo."

"I think, sweetheart, that's Italian."

"Oh dear. Well in any language, I love you."

Ford thought of ten rude answers. What he did though was put his lips together and . . . blow.

They stayed in the South of Tenerife. "Playa Los Americanos", it was called.

The Americans, quite wisely, went to Greece.

Amanda brought her cassette player and throughout the week she played Julio Iglesias and Jose Feliciano. Jose Feliciano! Ford thought he'd gone down the toilet with Cat Stevens. He'd left all his whining music in London. Amanda got sun scorched the first day and had to stay indoors with the shades drawn. This also kept love making to a minimum. Ford sat in bars and had long drinks in long glasses.

The sound of Tenerife for him was the clink of ice and Brit voices. Numerous Doris and Bills engaged him in conversation.

"Hot, isn't it?" they began.

"Raining in England," Ford said.

"Are you holidaying alone?"

"No, no, the little woman is resting."

Ford varied the little woman's activities to shopping, sailing, and sightseeing. The urge to say "irritating" was ferocious. He liked the Spanish mornings. He liked them a lot. Order that kick Spanish coffee with the dark brandy as an apprentice. Mix them, drink and feel your heart leap to rainbows. Put a few of those away and adrenaline was king. One such morning he'd lingered till noon.

"I think I love you Amanda," said the brandy. "Race back to the hotel and tell her," urged the caffeine. And race he did. Amanda was lying in the cool darkened room. A light, short T-shirt was all she wore. A besotted Ford was in full gallop.

Near to the moment of bliss Amanda said, "Are you nearly finished?"

Love died a-howling. This episode and Amanda's sunburn kept them silent for the remainder. On the flight back she said, "I'm prepared to give you another chance."

Ford said nowt.

***

They decided to live at Ford's flat until bigger accommodation presented itself. Ford returned to work feeling he'd gained less a wife than a lodger and not a particularly welcome one. Bernard Shaw had written that marriage provides the maximum of temptation with the maximum of opportunity. Ford was now more than ever convinced that Shaw was an old fart. Lovemaking was not resumed. A polite iciness ruled.

"How was your day, dear?"

"Busy. And yours?"

"Ditto. Shepherds pie be all right?"

"Lovely."

Dalton disappeared. He'd not been seen since the night of the stag party. Neville, anxious to recruit him, made enquiries daily. Neville, in truth, appeared anxious anyway. He kept shooting furtive looks at Ford.

"Is something the matter?" Ford asked.

"Well . . . no – er – Any word of our prospective colleague?"

"He's been sighted at Archway, in Kentish Town and . . . even in Kerry."

"Any substance perchance to these sightings?"

"Well, those who lent him money sure hope so."

"I wonder if I might lure you for a drink this evening?"

"I'm lurable," said Ford.

They went to the Sun 'n' Splendour at the top of Portobello. Yuppies lined the bar, contempt lined their faces. What Ford wished to know was who lined their wallets?

"What's your poison, amigo?" asked Neville.

"Southern Comfort, neat."

"Ah, an American institution!"

"Take yer comfort when you can."

"You had an American girl, yes?"

"Just a passing fancy."

"Well, it leads nicely to what I wish to discuss."

Neville was drinking gin and lemon. Slim-line lemon. He also got two bags of plain crisps and a large roasted peanuts. He poured the nuts into the crisps bag and began to horse them. Loud gnashing noises assaulted Ford. The Southern Comfort was little comfort against that. Ford walloped his and ordered the same again, without the snacks. Neville took the lemon from his glass and sucked it with fervent concentration.

"Jaysus," said Ford.

"It cleans the teeth."

"And clears the pub," thought Ford.

"I'd like to discuss sex," said Neville. Ford night choked.

"If you feel you must," he said.

"This is a little delicate, I'm not sure how to proceed."

With extreme caution, thought Ford, so he said, "Tell it to me plain."

"Our family . . . the – er – Billings . . ."

"I know who you are."

"The deuced thing is, we're not big on sex, it's a sort of family heirloom. We don't rate it as among our priorities."

"Some bloody heirloom! The family jewels not too valuable, eh?"

"Please Ford, this is most difficult."

"For you and me both, mate."

"You may be aware that Amanda is a tad shy in this – er – area."

"Shy!"

"She's most upset about the whole business."

"You're joking me, right?"

"Thus, I must implore you to be patient."

"Well, damn the banging of that I ever heard, why didn't you give me the nod *before* the wedding?" shouted Ford.

"A chap doesn't like to presume."

"For God's sake! Jeez!"

"There's one other item . . ."

"What? What other heirloom have ye?"

"I'm gay."

"Oh, the Lord save us!"

A stunned silence settled over them. Many drinks were bought and lashed. Neither knew how or where to pick up the treads of the conversation. Finally, Neville made a show of looking at his watch.

"Dear, oh dear, is that the hour? I must fly. An appointment I've overlooked."

The lie danced between them. Ford said nothing. Neville stood, considered something, and thought better not. When he reached the door, Ford shouted, "Hey, amigo?"

"Yes?"

"Can you whistle?"

***

Despite the yuppies, the pub was near enough to Portobello to draw the remnants of the hippies. What marked these apart was that they were old. Very old. And sad. They'd given peace a chance for just too long a decade. Social Security had rotted the concept of love and their teeth. Scraggles of them still moved through Notting Hill with lice in their hair if not flowers.

One such half baked specimen sat beside Ford. He'd got the regulation Afghan waist-jacket. A vicious launderette had inflicted awful torture on it. A million tainted silver bangles moved on his wrists. A pint of cider was half drained. He was fifty if a day. What blond hair remained was long and unkempt. A nod to Ford. Beside him Ford felt nigh full head of hair. The man's leather sandals tapped.

"Got any smokes, man?"

"Ford gave him a Marlboro. He snapped the filter off and extracted a kitchen size box of matches from his jacket. A huge whoosh accompanied the strike. He near strangled the cigarette with his first pull.

A massive cough followed, "Argh . . . ugh . . ."

Ford said nothing.

"Wanna buy a T-shirt, man?"

"Not just now, thanks."

He produced a long-from-white T-shirt with the logo "John Lives". A particularly cruel looking Beatle peered forth.

"The Walrus, man," he said.

"Indeed," said Ford.

"Where were you when John died, man?"

Ford didn't like to point out the discrepancy between the logo and this question.

"I'm in a bad frame of mind," he said.

"I can dig it man, yea, that's cool. Know where I was?"

"Offhand, I'd have to say no."

"With Yoko, man."

"You jest."

"Just kidding, man. See where your karma's at . . ."

"I get good vibes from you, man."

"Which," thought Ford, "is better than getting cash from me."

"Wanna know where I really was? I was with Yoko, in spirit, of course."

Ford had absolutely no interest in where this guy had been then, or since, so he said, "I'm fascinated."

"In a South American jail. Yea. You probably saw Midnight Express? That's Hollywood, man. The real thing was unreal."

Unreal was what Ford felt best fitted.

"I got framed, man. For a drugs thing. Every morning, man, at nine, they came in and trashed us."

"How awful," said Ford.

"Yea, man. Awful! And awesome. See, they sometimes didn't show at nine. And you'd be waiting, expectant like. If you can't depend on a thrashin', it messes with your head, know what I'm saying?"

Ford would have thrashed for a drink. But he didn't want to buy the guy a drink. Mean, sure, but this guy had mean eyes.

He stood up and the guy jumped.

"What? You're going?"

"Dear, oh dear, is that the hour, I must fly. An appointment I'd overlooked."

He made the Neville show of looking at his watch.

"Got any loose bread, man? A ten spot's good."

"You don't need bread, man," said Ford.

"I'm not getting you?"

"Yea. Nor money either. John said, 'All you need is love.'"

***

150

Back home, Ford, the very worst for Southern Comfort, made a fumbled embrace for Amanda. He had landed one hand on her breast and was planting a wet smooch on her neck. This made a loud "sluch" impossible to ignore. If embarrassment had a voice, it might be spoken thus. She said, "I don't think this is on, fellah, wot?"

"Right. Er – Got a tad carried away, us being married and all."

"Perhaps some time when you're sober, darling."

"That would be lovely," said Ford. And, he thought, "yea, that and shepherd pie."

Ford went to the fridge. Drink had created the massive artificial appetite that sex might have slaked. A dubious half chicken looked back at him. "Come home to roost," thought Ford. He covered it lavishly with mayo and ladled shovels of coleslaw after. A mug of sweet tea to round up this gourmet fantasy. He was tearing thru this when Amanda looked in. Ford and the chicken waited.

"That's really quite disgusting," she said.

"Yea, but 'tis tasty. Come back here. I'm no family heirloom."

But she'd gone. Ford looked at the demolished sad chicken and caressed it with one finger. "Ah, you're my only friend and look how I treat you." He sadly continued to chew and thought it faintly tasted of carbolic. A fierce thirst rose and he lashed down the sweet tea. "Oh jaysus," he said.

Sleep snuck up on him and he laid his head down beside the dinner. One arm cradled the chicken and small sounds of desolation leaked from his mouth. To an observer it might have even looked as if the chicken was singing to him, and, in his dreams, perhaps it was.

At work the next day Neville adopted a civil tone. Courtesy on ice. This suited Ford who was as ill as he'd ever been. The police arrived about midday. In plain clothes, they had that politeness that slaps your face.

"You are Thomas A. Ford, of 11 Cockram Street?"

"Yes, I am."

"Were you acquainted with one Isobelle Banks?"

"Were?"

"Please answer the question, sir."

"Yes . . . I am . . . I was. God, is she alright? She was one of our clients."

"I'm sorry to inform you, sir, that the lady appears to have taken her own life."

"Appears? Is there a chance maybe . . ."

"No sire, it's her. Any light you can shed on her state of mind?"

"State of Grace," thought Ford. A spasm rushed through his system and he threw up in the waste basket. This had a label attached which read:

Social Services
Property of Wolberhampton Community
Care
DO NOT REMOVE.

He'd never noticed it before and wondered if the coppers would mention it. Sweat then tried to blind him. Madness in its purity somersaulted through his mind.

"Are you alright, sir?"

"Chicken . . . Arch. The bloody chicken is back."

The two policemen exchanged a look and withdrew. Ford fumbled for a pencil. On the blotter, he began to sketch a large menagerie of fowl. He worked quickly and rumbling pounded his stomach.

When he'd finished, he wrote across the top, "Foul Play."

Neville gathered the staff for a homily. A drained Ford cadged a cigarette from the receptionist.

Neville began, "People, I've collected you *en masse* to speak of our current sadness. Our profession receives a bad press. We are the unsung soldiers in this urban land war. Isobella turned to us when all doors were barred. Let us not dwell on the tragedy but believe we gave her solace in the months before. For all the Isobellas out there, I say, "We are here for you. We dare to care. Our great Wordsworth might have known our plight when he wrote:

> 'Let us not grieve for what
> we have lost
> but rather find strength
> in what remains behind
> let us remember in splendour
> in the grass.'"

"Whoops," thought Ford on these final words as Neville's eyes locked with his. Sun 'n' Splendour danced between them.

"Thus," concluded Neville, "I reiterate, let us dare to care and care to dare."

"What does he mean?" whispered the receptionist.

"That we're wankers," said Ford.

The receptionist was a small, blond girl from Aberdeen. Warm blue eyes, pert nose and a mouth built to smile. She had a threatening weight problem. This currently gave her an air of voluptuousness, and large breasts enhanced the image. If she wasn't quite the American mammary vision, she was within shouting distance. Her name was Alison. Alison Dunbar. Like many Scots, she had a low tolerance for subtlety. Ford staggered outside. Leaning his forehead against the wall, he thanked the coolness. Alison followed him and said,

"All in all, just another brick in the was."

"Pink Floyd?"

"Yes, do you like them?"

"I hate them."

"Well, there's no *maybe* in that."

"Con men!"

"A bit strong, Tom."

"Ford, call me Ford."

"A wee bit sorry for yourself, are you?"

"No, but that Neville. What an egomaniac!"

"I've never been sure, Ford, what ego is?"

"Where he goes, e-goes."

Alison accompanied Ford to the inquest. A verdict of death by misadventure was recorded. "Misadventure," fumed Ford, like some excursion that had to be cancelled due to rain. A large black woman sat in the front row and sobbed loudly.

"Mrs Banks," whispered Alison.

"Banks?"

"Isobelle's mother."

"Oh God!"

Afterwards, on the pavement, the woman stood and great heaves of grief hit her body in waves. Ford felt it would be best all around to let her be. Grief was a private thing.

"Excuse me," he said.

Big mascara streaks ran down the woman's fat cheeks. Thru the tears, Ford could see the warmest eyes he'd ever beheld.

"I hate to intrude, Mrs Banks . . . but . . . am . . . I'm so sorry."

"Who you be, boy?"

"Oh, yes . . . right. I'm Ford . . . Thomas Ford, I . . . am . . . was . . . er . . . Bella's counselor. No . . . her friend . . ."

Ford felt his full name sounded like he'd invented a motor car. Not a particularly exciting make either. The woman threw her arms round him. Ford thought she'd attacked him and let out a small "Argh!" The hug nigh suffocated him.

"A good mon . . . You be a good mon. Bella say you be white kindness . . . A true heart you be, Bella say."

She released him and began to rummage in her huge, black handbag. A white crystal rosary beads was pulled out. "They be Bella's, boy . . . I give them to you."

She wrapped the beads round Ford's hands and without another word, she turned and walked away. A shaking Ford looked at the beads on his hands. "Handcuffs," he said. He knew with absolute conviction that the sentence she had passed on him was without any prospect of parole . . . Ever. He knew and was damned.

Ford went to the off-license. He ordered two bottles of Kentucky Sour Mash. The proprietor was a burly Sikh. He looked at Ford's credit card as if it were rabid. A call was made to check the credit rating.

"This card's no good," he said.

"I beg your pardon?"

"Run out, it's no good."

He produced a large brass scissors. Ford thought he meant to stab him. A loud clip and the two pieces of plastic fell on the counter.

"Jeez, you didn't have to do that," whined Ford.

"It's no good. Run out."

"Cripes, you already said that. Do you have to tell the world"

Alison had enough cash to pay for a bottle of Scotch. The Sour Mash was put back on the shelf, like longing itself.

"C'mon, Ford," said Alison.

He looked at the two bottles out of reach and very out of pocket.

"What's with those bottles anyway?" she asked.

"Shades of Grace," he said.

Alison had a single bed sitter in Earl's Court. A single bed, a single window, and more loneliness than Leonard Cohen ever san about. It was spotless, and the vision of her cleaning this neat cell just about finished him.

"Let's have hot toddies," she said.

"And music," he whispered.

An old Stones album was selected. As "You Can't Always Get What You Want" began, Ford built some lethal drinks. Two spoons of sugar, big slurps of scotch, boiling water. Stir. "You can't always git what you wan," nasaled Jagger. Ford and Alison provided backup vocals.

"Wish we had cloves," she said.

"Cloven feet."

She didn't have a big music section so they played the Stones again. And again. Ford slid his hand under her skirt and she smiled. He gently rolled down her tights and knickers and she lay back. A massive hammering began in his chest as he mounted her. Light perspiration dotted his forehead as he began to move in her.

"Just come," she said. And he did.

Crammed together in the single bed, Alison cradled his head on her breasts. Soft cooing noises began in her throat as she started to sing, "Momma's gonna buy you a mocking bird." Her fingers gently caressed his face, and tears formed in his eyes. Her hand froze as his tears trickled and then washed over her fingers. Grief howled in him as her fingers wiped at his eyes. She continued to sing to him in her soft Scottish burr, and he slipped away to sleep.

***

He skipped work the next day and crept home. Alison had kissed him and said, "I'm here for you."

He let himself into his flat with a heavy heart. Amanda was sipping coffee, an impressive volume lay open on her lap. The Russians, no doubt.

"What sort of hour do you call this?"

"Morning?"

"Don't adopt that tone with me, Mister Ford!"

"Ary, take a tunning leap for yerself."

"I beg your pardon!"

"Lep – a leap. You bend yer aristocratic legs, you hold yer whist, then you jump as if a large flea was up yer ass."

While her face digested the shock, he continued, "And on consideration, *darling,*

I'd say in your case, a major flea."

He turned on his heel and walked out. You had to hand it to them Stones, they got the juices flowing.

Neville fired him.

At work the following day, Alison whispered to him, "I think you're for the high jump."

"Or leap," he said.

At coffee break, he was summoned. Neville had dressed for the occasion. A dark worsted suit and dark navy shirt. The school tie was un-windsored. He was all business, fixing papers and glancing at memos, ignoring Ford. Five minutes elapsed. He looked up from his desk.

"Ah, Ford, there you are."

"I like the suit."

"I have some bad news to convey."

"Well, you have the clothes to prove it."

"Ahem . . . Alas, I regret you haven't proved to be the fettle for which I had hoped."

"Fettle?"

"If I might continue, the business of Isobella, your conduct was not wholly professional. I'm not casting aspersions on your compassion. Your talents may lie in another discipline."

"You'd know about discipline, wouldn't you, Neville?"

"I'm not saying it's entirely fair, but I must now give you a month's notice. I will, of course, provide a reference."

"Well, Neville, you'd like to change the world, am I right?"

"One tries."

"Thing is . . . you're not even capable of changing your mind. Stick your reference up yer tight ass. I'm outta here. You know why you're firing me?"

Neville stood, all flustered dignity. "That's quite enough, Mr. Ford."

Ford yanked the still shiny wedding band from his finger and bounced it on the desk.

"Give that to your literary sister, amigo. Tell her it's a family heirloom."

It didn't take long to clear his desk. The phone rang. His cockney friend Bill said, "So Ford, aren't you talking to me any more?"

"Oh, I'm talking to you, Bill, I'm just not talking to you very much."

He put the phone down . . . and Bill. The staff stood awkwardly a moment and, as he prepared to leave, they all sat and busied themselves. "A sitting ovation," he thought.

At his flat, he could hear the sad piano of Gershwin. Amanda was spray foaming the carpet.

"Don't put your feet there," she said.

He planted both feet where she's indicated.

"Sit down," he said.

"I'm far too busy for nonsense this morning, Mister, so allow me to continue."

Ford rummaged through his work files for five minutes and didn't look up.

"Ah, Amanda, there you are."

"I beg your pardon?"

"I have some bad news to convey."

"Have you been drinking?"

"Ahem . . . Alas, I regret you haven't proved to be the fettle for which I had hoped."

"Have you lost your senses? Fettle?"

"If I might continue, the business of the chicken, your conduct was not entirely professional. I'm not casting aspersions on your compassion. Your talents may lie in another discipline."

Amanda just looked at him and he continued. "I'm not saying it's entirely fair, but I must now give you a moment's notice. I will of course provide a reference."

"Are you telling me I have to leave our home?"

"That's quite enough, Mrs Ford."

He went to the kitchen and began to make coffee. Amanda stood amid the spray-foam. She didn't remove her ring, shiny as it was.

As Ford sat, he listed all the reasons he shouldn't go to the pub:

1. Daytime drinking
2. No job
3. Self-pity
4. Money
5. Hangovers

This list was good and he liked it a lot. Jumping up quickly he knew he'd have to run if he was to beat the lunch-time crowd.

Amanda said, "Athol Fuggard. I must make a sincere effort to read him."

***

Ford didn't really think a South African was the comfort she needed right now. They weren't noted for it. The White Lion was a new pub for him. It was empty save for a few pensioners munching crisps and bickering over pension rights. Or was it the other way round? A big man behind the bar was cleaning glasses. His dominant feature was a riot of pure wavy, white hair. A broken nose took away from a tough, turn-down mouth. Beer had swollen his gut but a force came from him. The forearms were huge. He looked at Ford with neutral, blue eyes. The radio was playing loudly.

"Radio bother you?"

"No, sir, I like the wireless."

"Sir, is it? Don't hear much manners these days. Irish are yah? Wireless. Haven't heard that much either."

"Yes, sir."

"My mother was from Mayo. The bad bitch."

"The county? Or your . . . er – ?"

The man smiled, "Not from Mayo, are you?"

"No, sir."

"Good lad, what can I get you?"

"A pint of Guinness."

As he prepared the drink in the Irish fashion, Barbara Streisand came over the radio. "Send In the Clowns." Ford mad a supreme offer to block out the lyrics but he heard it. Clearly and loaded, "I've come to feel about you what it is you felt about me." That past tense. It gutted him every single time. He thought too how it is the dead are forever confined to a single tense . . . And further thought he wished he didn't. He ordered another pint and said, "Something for yourself?"

"Aye, I'll charge you for a coffee. I'm Jack."

"Ford."

They shook hands self-consciously. Jack put a coffee on the counter and from beneath produced a bottle of Courvoisier Four Star. He dolloped a large measure into the cup. A healthy sip was taken.

"Ah, Jaysus, I'm lit!"

All lit up, thought Ford.

"Do you like music, son?"

"The whine kind."

"Come again."

"Music you can whine to."

"Gotcha! The Irish connection. Not so much what you can sing to as cry along with."

He then moved up and down doing bar things. A hive of activity punctuated by coffee pit stops. Ford had so wanted to tell Grace about "The Way We Were". Streisand plays a radical student who falls in love with Redford's young writer character. A passionate love follows, then break-up. The movie's end, Redford's now a successful commercial writer without belief. He's emerging from a hotel with a bimbo on his arm. Streisand bumps into him. A look. Full of loss and might-have-beens. She puts her gloved hand on his face and her palm rests on his cheek. Then they separate. The moment to tell Grace this just never presented itself. Wasn't too likely he'd get to tell her now. The awful thing was the very sound of her name was a kick. He loved and loathed it. What's in a name, he'd thought, and back bounced the answer, "All you know of heaven and hell." A vicious truth.

Jack settled for a moment and lit a Gauloise.

"I've never been to France, but every time I smoke one of these babes I reckon I'll go tomorrow. What do you make of that?"

"Well, I dunno. I smoke Marlboros sometimes, but I've no desire to sit tough on a horse."

"Gotcha! Makes you wonder what Silk Cutters dream about."

Ford didn't wonder and cared not at all. Amanda touted the Silk Cut argument and that basically was that. Jack sighed, "I'm well bollixed, you know."

Did he mean well endowed? An advertisement perhaps. Or was he simply knackered? No reply was conceivable.

"What line of work are you in, Ford?"

"Looking."

"Gotcha! What's the previous?"

"Well, I thought I'd social work till an opening occurred as a waiter." Jack liked that.

"You're alright. What do you know about cocktails?"

"They're expensive?"

"That too. Know how to make them?"

"I know how to drink them."

"Sure, you're half way there. That's the hard part. What about ghetto blasters?"

"What about them? I don't know how to make them. I hate them."

"Right answer. So, want to be a barman?"

"Here?"

"Yes, Five nights a week, mornings free."

"Are you serious?"

"Sure am."

"Okay, then. Thank you."

"A few questions. Are you honest?"

"Mostly."

"Married?"

"Not any more."

"A nod to the wise old son. Don't let on about that to Stella, my missus. She's big on marriage."

Ford thought about this and felt Jack's own extremely irritating reply as appropriate. Cheeky perhaps, to use it, but there you go. He said, "Gotcha!"

"Gotcha! It's cash in hand, we'll not get confused with P45s and all of that."

A man breezed in, semi-respectable. He ordered a large gin and asked, "How far is the tube station?"

"About one and a half muggings from here. Alternatively you could try for the bus which is but one rape down the block."

Jack seemed well pleased and did a spin shine on the optics.

The man produced a pink two-pill packet, slit the edge and dropped them into the gin. They sank, dead weight. Ford stared.

"Aspirin," said the man.

"Headache, have you?"

"No, no, I never get headaches. I drop a few of them suckers in everything I drink. Bingo! I've never had an illness in my life."

"Save the serious one in your head," thought Ford.

The man drained the gin. The pills sat unmoved at the bottom, like bank managers. "'Fraid I threw something of a wobbly this morning," he said.

"Is that like throwing a Frisbee?"

"Tantrum, actually. Doris. That's my good lady. She told me my white shirts were all in the wash. Well, I mean . . . Really! So I gave her 'what's for.' A tad over the top, on reflection."

Ford shut him out. Grace took centre stage anew. She said to him once, "You're kind."

"Thank you."

"Problem is . . . kind of what?"

He smiled as he heard her accent. Sometimes, a huskiness ruled and that gave him literal goosebumps. Could you love a voice? Yea, and all the rest too. Weariness swamped him and he bid goodbye to Jack. The aspirin man was still on about white shirts.

As he left, Emmylou Harris on the wireless burned him with the line "And the hardest part is knowing I'll survive." He recalled the Chinese curse, "May you live in interesting times." What could you say? Phew-oh, perhaps, and add to that what it was he felt most all the time now, a sadness of infinity.

When he got home, he thought first he'd been burgled. The place was stripped. Even the carpets were gone. He considered checking if any trousers were shorter. Amanda had gone alright and took anything that moved. She'd left him one of everything: one cup, one knife, one towel, one massive resentment.

As the movers had obviously been in a ferocious hurry, care had not been their motto. Heaps of debris lay on the now bare wooden floors. He quite liked the sound of his boots in the emptiness. "I can hear me coming," he said. The few skinny bones of the sad chicken were in the bathroom. Had it tried for a last shower? A postcard near the upturned mattress caught his eye. It was from Boston and had been posted weeks ago. So, how come he'd never seen it? It read:

> "Hi Ford,
> We've moved to Boston. New York left me unmoved. Guess what fella,
> I miss you. Doing any wailing? I think I am. Back one for me.
> Grace."

Gutted! Oh God in Heaven, it was like being shot. Gut shot, and twice. How long had the card been here? How was he to feel? How did this mean she felt? How . . . Howling. Wouldn't you know? The Kenny Loggin's song began to unwind and slow play in his head:

> "You say please come to Boston for the Springtime,
> You're staying there with friends,
> I can sell my paintings on the sidewalk
> By a café, where you hope to be working soon."

Ah, Jaysus! Gimme a break here. Dollop on shovels of slush. Worse. The version playing was by Tammy Wynette. If God selected the discs from the celestial jukebox, He was in some manic frame of mind.

***

His career as a barman began, and he was good. A flair for figures helped him with change and, if in doubt, he undercharged. No one questions that. The cocktails he just laced with spirits base, and if they lacked the finer points they delivered a mighty wallop. The demand for these grenades increased. The big factor was his politeness, an art long lost in London. Shop assistants took courses in surliness. His attitude freaked them completely, and even assholes got the treatment. Jack was delighted.

"You're a good un."

"Thanks."

He then produced a baseball bat and swung it slowly. The swish cut a low mean music.

"You hear that?" he asked.

"Hard to ignore."

"You hear that, Ford, it's already too late. Do you know what I'm saying? I call it 'my edge'."

"Your customer relations act, so to speak?"

"Exactly."

In fact, the bat had only to be produced and trouble changed its mind. Jack's wife was almost a caricature of "The Guvnor's Missus". A breezy blonde, she wore the mandatory half sovereign rings. Ugly yokes that matched her moods. Cheap and loud. She liked the power and was forever demanding glasses be re-polished, floors scrubbed, the brass fixtures full shines. Everybody was called "darling." Not from affection, but sheer bloody mindedness. When she called, you did well to count your change. Vodka with bitter lemon was her staple diet, and the bar hummed with litany, "Put a little vodka in that, darling." In looks she wasn't unlike the said Tammy Wynette but a somewhat beat up version. That she modeled herself on Tammy was a cruel blow to country music. Lest you hadn't spotted the vague likeness, she had all the lady's albums and played them. A lot. Her all time favorite was d-i-v-o-r-c-e – "My d-i-v-o-r-c-e came thru today and me and little J-o-e are going a-w-a-y . . ."

She'd enunciate each letter along with the bold Miss Wynette. The Boston song wasn't in her repertoire, else Ford might well have quit. Or brought "the edge" to bear. After a bathe, or two, of vodka, a slight hint of Tennessee drawl crept into her speech. Fair enough, except it clashed with the South East vowels. The customers were nightly bid.

"Ya'll take care now, and ya'll come back and see us real soon."

From badness, Ford introduced her to Kentucky Sour Mash. The mule kicked, and she kicked right along. He felt there wasn't a whole lot the matter with Stella that a solid shoe in the ass wouldn't fix. Staggering from the cellar with the crates of bitter lemon one evening, waiting for Ford was a swaying Stella.

"Y'all wanna feel the merchandise, honey?"

This said in the dialect of S.E.11 was quite alarming.

"Not just now, ma'am," said Ford in a very poor Elvis parody.

"Gimme a kiss, darling."

And she groped for him. The crates of bitter lemon didn't smooth the embrace. A sucking sound ensued as she planted a big one to the left of his nose.

"Oh Jaysus," he said, Elvis forgotten.

She reached for his fly and expertly got her hand inside. The rings chilled his scrotum.

"Who's this, then?" she asked.

"Shake hands with the devil," he groaned.

He had her on the floor. The crates of lemon mocked him bitter as he pounded into her. As he zipped up and prepared to lift the crates, a slur in Tennessee drawl said, "Y'all come back and visit soon, hear?"

CONCLUSION

A year passed thus. Ford became a faster barman and infrequently banged Stella. Speed helped here also. Twixt the Grace longings and the Stella couplings, he began to love Alison. Their relationship built, and it was the music in his life.

He could talk about Grace, a vague voice wondered if a little too much. Naw, Ally didn't mind. What he adored was the songs she soft-sang. After making love, she'd lilt some lullaby from a long ago place. Once he'd called her Grace but was fairly certain he got away with it. Yea, she hadn't heard.

Amanda had divorced him in nigh jig time. It wasn't contested. In fact, it was close to him not even hearing it. Neville had friends who rushed it through. Ford felt a divorce was evidence you'd been here. Not too successfully perhaps, but it dented the anonymity.

Jack was paying him well, and all sorts of side benefits brought cash. People were as likely to give half a dozen free shirts as a slap in the mouth. The shirts last longer. Thus he began to plan the "Ceremony of the Rings." The Irish wedding ring has a heart clasped by two hands, topped but a crown. Icing on the cake. It originated in The Claddagh in Galway. In Ireland it was known as the Claddagh or Heart in Hand ring. Plainly titled. Due to the English never having heard of Claddagh and not being able to pronounce it, they called it the Irish wedding ring. The heart was worn inwards if you were spoken for. Outwards if you'd like to be spoken to – you were hunting. Ford wanted to buy two. The plan was a candle-lit room, haunting music and he'd produce the rings. No words need be spoken. They'd slip the rings on and then slip into something more comfortable, like each other. Hours of warmth from this scenario. After a particularly sweaty wrestle with Stella, he'd mind-play the ceremony and believe it cleansed him.

***

A hand-written note arrived from Neville late that February. It was addressed to "Mr Ford" and read:

Mr Ford,
It is imperative you contact me.
Neville R. Biggins, B.S.C.

Ford phoned him and was put through.

"Ah, Mr Ford."

"I got your imperative."

"Yes, well, the matter is of some delicacy and perhaps we could meet for an aperitif."

"A drink, you mean?"

"Yes, quite. Would 6:30 on Thursday at Finchs be convenient?"

"I'll be there."

And he was. Neville had the executioners suit, the dark worsted number.

"A drink, Mr Ford?"

"Got one, thanks."

Neville ordered a large schooner of dry sherry. Sipped it, fixed the crease in his pants and forehead and began.

"I trust we can be civilized about this?"

"Trust is an earned thing, Nev, and in my book, you're all outta credit."

"Be that as it may. Er – Amanda has produced a child."

"What? Jeez! Produced! Like suddenly flashed from her handbag?"

"A girl-child. Healthy and strong."

"Good grief! Girl-child? You sound like something from Kipling. Who's the father?"

"I feared you'd be disgusting, but really, that's low even for you, Mr Ford."

"I'm sorry. Truly, I apologise. It's a shock. I didn't mean that. O.K. sorry."

"Yes, well, watch your mouth. I'm a tolerant man, but there are limits and I'm trained in the self-defence arts. The child was named Annabel-Lee."

"You're coddin'! Like in the Edgar Allen Poe poem?"

"It was my mother's name."

"When can I see her?"

"That's the crux. Amanda says . . . She says you'll never, *never* see her. Those are her exact words."

"You can't! Jeez, c'mon Neville! You can't do that."

"Can. Already have. And will continue."

"You're some bollix. God, don't do this."

Neville drained his sherry. A grim smile danced on and off.

"*Never*, Mr Ford. As far as you're concerned, you are without issue. Now, I must visit the bathroom. Our business is concluded. I don't expect our paths to cross again. I bid you adieu."

The smile had grown full to an actual smirk. Imaginary crumbs were brushed from a crease and he marched briskly to the toilet. Ford's heart hammered like a wild thing. Red spots hummed in the very air. As he lifted the glass, his hand shook. Standing slowly, he followed Neville. The toilet was well kept, shining sink and mirrors. Neville was relieving himself, his back to Ford. Turning the cold tap, Ford mopped his face, the reflection showed a face in granite shock. The water was tepid but the coldness forming in his gut was ice in purity. Neville turned. A look of disinterest.

"Is there any point in pleading, Neville? I will . . . I'll beg, grovel, whatever. Do they need money? I have money. I have, honestly."

"Keep your money, Mr Ford. Use it for alcohol or some other Irish activities."

The first blow smashed Neville's nose and threw him back against the urinals. Ford bent, put his knee in his chest and slowly, methodically, began to, open palmed, slap the bleeding face.

"You fuck! I'm going to kill you!"

Slap. Pause. Slap. Back. A silence crept above the roof of the toilet, broken only by the sharp rhythm of the beating.

***

Neville lived, and Ford was arrested. They took him to Jeb Avenue, home of the brave, if not the free.

Brixton Prison. A grim place for remand prisoners Ford had grown up with black and white prison movies. You did hard time or "rolled over." Roll too your own tobacco and let no one fuck with you. In any sense.

The more current American movies were of the Clint Eastwood mentality. Hang tough. You picked out the meanest "muttah fuckah" in the yard and beat him to a pulp. Rather a surprise for that individual, thought Ford. Each new arrival had to stomp the man. Then no one messed with you. You had "tutto respecto." Lest a chap plunge a shiv in your back, you narrowed your eyes a lot.

The reality was totally different. He did two days there and what it was . . . was boring. Long tedious days and overcrowded. Like being in a permanent football crowd. A skinny thug tried to head-butt him but his heart wasn't into it. The smell was the worst. A mix of cabbage and stale urine.

A guy offered Ford a prison tattoo. The notion of Grace on his arm amused him. Perhaps "Millwall" on the other. What he said was "Give me a break. Piss off." Hangin' semi-tough.

***

Jack went to Court with and for him. The charge of grievous bodily harm was reduced to drunken assault. Ford was bound over for two years.

"Thanks, Jack, you helped a lot," Ford said outside the Court.

"Gotcha! Your reputation will be more effective than my 'edge' for boozies."

"Seriously, though, I could have gone to prison."

"Ah, I've been inside myself. Half of London would like to wallop a social worker."

"And the other half?"

"They are the social workers."
The Sun wrote a small article on the affair with the heading;

"Social Services Director Mauled by Former Colleague"

"Neville Biggins, BSC, was accosted and assaulted by a disgruntled colleague in the toilet of a public house. Thomas Ford, an Irishman, was said by a confidential source, to have gone berserk and threatened to blow up the Dept. of Social Services. The Judge called Ford (36) a public menace. The case continues."

The story underneath exposed a major rock star's obsession with his dead dog. Ford kept the clipping. Maybe send it to Boston and see what shook loose.

***

Back to work and to Alison. Her Scottish background understood all about the police and pub brawls. The ceremony of the rings moved closer. A week after the court case, Ford went to his bank. He asked for "new accounts." An assistant manager summoned him. Ford sat at the small desk. The nameplate read "A. Richards." As opposed to A. Wanker, mused Ford. A. Richards was about thirty, in there. Neville would have liked the suit. Brown wool with a discreet stripe. Bald on top, A. Richards had seriously swept hair from the side to cover this. It didn't. Thick glasses hid his eyes and the adjective prissy leapt to mind for his mouth. The desk said, "this is a busy man."

"Mr . . ." he looked at his notes, "Ford."
"You already have an account with us?"
"I'd like to open one for my daughter."
"Splendid. A savings account, I'd suggest. Her name, please?"
"Annabell-Lee Ford." His throat choked as he slowly said this.
A wee man kicked his heart, and hard.
"The mother?"
"I don't want to open an account for her."
A. Richards gave a professional laugh. An unpleasant sound.
"Of course. But I'll need her name."
"Why?"
"For our records. Very important, Mr Ford, for next of kin, etc. Not that I'm not certain you'll outlive us all."
He was beginning to seriously irritate Ford. Perhaps *The Sun* clipping would soften his cough.
"Amanda Biggins."
"Biggins. Is that Amanda Biggins hyphen Ford?"
"We're divorced. D-i-v-o-r-c-e, like in Tammy Wynette. Jeez, it's hard to give money to you crowd."

"How will the money be paid in, Mr Ford?"

"Carefully. Quarter of my weekly salary."

"Capital. Jolly good. A few days to process the paperwork and your book will be sent out. Good day to you, sir."

Ford didn't move.

"There was something else?"

"A question. Do you like your work?"

"Rather. One does one's best."

Ford stood up and leaned across the desk. He looked into what was visible of the eyes of A. Richards and said, "One felt you'd say that."

He bought a small cardboard box and adhesive labels. Alison had typed the name for him: "Annabell-Lee Ford, c/o Neville Biggins, 29 Kensington Church Street." She didn't comment. Carefully he wrapped the white rosary beads in crepe paper and put it in the box. A surge of grief begged for release. Sellotaping the box, he applied the label. A hand tremor caused this to appear crooked. "Like yer inlaws," he said. Gently sliding the package into the post box, he muttered the words from Belle's mother, "Who you be boy?" Indeed!

Outside the Post Office, an apprentice thug held a rottweiler on a thin leash. The dog's jaws leaked spittle. The thug, though, appeared to have the edge in madness if the eyes were any indication. Both wore spiked collars. You sensed that neither had yet achieved the full potential in thuggery, but were getting there. He wore a red T-shirt which proclaimed "Shit Happens". "And sooner than you ever imagined," said Ford. Though the slogan might not achieve the wisdom of the ages, it was current and it had a ring to it. "Would suit Neville, match up with his dark worsted."

***

Ford was cleaning the bar. The only customer was an old Irish lady drinking a milk stout. Everyone said, "She has a heart of gold." In other words, a nobody. The door swung and Dalton walked in. A very different model. The swagger was gone. Weight hadn't so much fallen from him as fled. His usual furtive look had become one of total desperation. Ford hadn't seen him for well over a year.

"It's yerself," he said.

"Yea . . . Give us a big drink."

No hugs of reunion here. A double whiskey was put before him. Draining it, he looked round and saw the old lady.

"Who's the oul biddy?"

"She's got a heart of gold."

"I'll bet, sewn in the drawers, I'd say. You're a hard man to find, Ford. What have you been up to?"

"Well, let's see, I got fired, married, divorced, arrested and convicted."

If any of this was a surprise to Dalton, he didn't show it. He said, "And did you rest on Sundays? That Neville sacked you, did he? The bad bastard. Want him fixed?"

"Fixed?"

"Yea. A ton will buy a full beating and he won't be squealing to no one."

"Naw. Thanks all the same. What's your story?"

Belle hovered in the air between them. Another double was poured and put away.

"Remember that black wan. I slipped her a mickey finn. And later, I slipped a little Irish into her. Know wot I mean?"

"Jaysus!"

"Yea. Well, a while ago, I musta caught some bug. I'm cold all the time and feverish. My throat muscles keep locking. Christ, it's terrible. I've had tests done and I'll hear next week. What do you think?"

"Sounds rough. I'm sure they have something for it."

What he thought next was, "Yea, a coffin." He looked at Dalton and felt hatred like a shroud envelop him.

Dalton said, "I need a fair bit of cash. I'll get it back to you, don't worry. But it's like, I'm in a hurry."

"Upstairs, the end room. There's the till takings from last night. We're forever being turned over here, so no worries. There's only me here at the moment so you're safe. Just be quiet and quick."

"Jeez, you're a life saver, Ford. What did I always say? You're one of the very best."

"I'm well graced, so to speak."

"What?"

"Nothing. Better do it before the Guvnor arrives. He's a tough one."

"Ah, all them crowd are wankers. The day they worry me, I'll pack it in. Catch ya later."

Those were the last words Ford heard from him. After Dalton slipped up the stairs, he lifted the phone.

"Jack, I don't know if I'm imagining it or not but I think I heard someone on the landing. I was in the cellar for a few minutes. Will I come up?"

"No, son. Leave it to me."

A ferocious racket erupted, and then Dalton was carried by the seat of his pants down the stairs. Jack had the bat in his other hand. Across the bar and flung into the street.

Jack said quietly, "If I see you again, I'll kill you," and he shut the door.

"Well done, Ford."

Ford had read how the use of brutality itself brutalises. What he felt might be even worse – self righteous and justified.

***

The Ceremony of the Rings!

The day had come. He read his horoscope and it promised "Momentous events to those who care." Sounded not unlike Neville. A lot of Uranus entering cusps of Capricorn, which was highly suggestive if not downright lewd.

"Lewdness is good," he said.

He withdrew a wedge of cash from the bank. It sat in his pocket like reassurance. Then the jewelers. A gaggle of schoolgirls were, as usual, outside. Shrieking and pointing, the window display brought them to fever pitch. A well dressed man asked him for Guy's Hospital. Ford went to pains to tell him, and the man said,
"Might I trouble you for the price of a meal?"

"Ya chancer. Hoppit!"

"Wooftah! You bald wooftah."

A little shaken, Ford purchased two Irish wedding rings and spent more than he'd planned. "Thin end of the wedge," he lamented. Next, two bottles of Chivas Regal and back to the bank for further funds. The same teller said, "Have you considered the benefits of a credit card?"

"Have you considered the merits of minding your own bloody business?"

Well pleased, if poorer, he next purchased a dozen long-stemmed roses. The price rocked him.

"Bit steep," he said.

"A rose is forever," said the dreamy sales assistant.

"Jeez, it would need to be."

He called Alison and arranged for her to arrive at eight. A call to "Gourmet Services" and a hot, sealed dinner was scheduled for home delivery at seven thirty. The Chivas Regal was opened and he poured himself a big one. "Ain't Life Grand" was the song he hummed.

Fair damage was done to the first bottle when Alison arrived. She'd had her hair done. A tight, black miniskirt set Ford's pulse zooming. The roses pleased her immensely. The gourmet meal hadn't arrived so he began to kiss her neck. His hand slid under her skirt, and in jig time he was astride her.

As he came, the blood pounded in his ears and he said, "Oh my God! Oh! Argh! I love you. Oh . . . Grace, I love you."

That he loved her now wasn't open to even the slightest doubt. He'd bought two extra large, white T-shirts and they sat in the afterglow. The T-shirts read "We're a couple of Scouts." He'd managed to blank out the "u" and Alison was delighted. Ford took her hand and began to slide the ring on her finger . . . It didn't fit, not any finger . . . His own fit. Too tight, and he knew only prayer and soap would next detach it. It squeezed like amputation.

"Will you, Alison Dunbar, marry me?" he asked.

"No," she said.

Elvis was singing in the background, "I jest can't help believing, when she slips her hand in my hand, and it feels so small and helpless . . ."

And was it pure sadism, or was The King deliberately emphasizing, "This time the girl is gonna stay"?

Maybe she hadn't heard right.

"I'm asking you to marry me!"

"I know that, and NO, I won't."

"You can't be serious. I love you."

"You love Grace! You call me that all the time. In fact, you just did."

"A name! A bloody name. You're turning me down over a friggin' name."

"That name. Yes. And . . . I don't love you."

"You don't love me! You've been stringing me along. I can't believe it. You . . . hussy!"

Alison gave a mighty laugh from deep within her.

"Hussy! Well, where on earth did you find that?"

Ford struggled to his feet. "Out! Get outta my house . . . my life."

Alison took her time dressing. Ford rushed through a series of drinks, all ball busters.

"Alison, what did we just have here, eh?"

"What we had was lovely."

She opened the door and a man in a white jumpsuit said, "Gourmet deliveries."

"In there," she said as she departed.

The food was deposited on the coffee table. Alison's ring sparkled beside it. In a daze, Ford pushed a bundle of notes at the man who counted it carefully. He stood waiting.

"What? Is there a problem?"

"No tip?"

"No friggin wonder. Here, d'ya like roses? Give them to your girlfriend."

The gourmet took them and left muttering darkly about lunatics. With a ferocious sweep of his arm, Ford took all the food from the table. He kicked the cartons for good measure. In a paraphrase of the old saying, he thought:

"To lose one woman is accidental
To lose a second is tragic
But to lose a third . . . It was downright criminal."

"What in heavens name is wrong with them?" he roared.

Grace had told him once, "Never talk to a woman about another woman." And he'd asked, " Even if she asks you?" "Especially not then." "Wow", he thought. Why hadn't I heeded it? Advice always seemed particularly wise after you'd ignored it.

He was sitting in the bar with Jack after closing time. They were sipping beer with whiskey chasers.

"Hits the spot," said Jack.

"Yea."

It was a week since Alison's departure. The ring stubbornly refused to budge. It clung. Like gossip. Hurt too. The loss of her had shocked him. A hole seemed to sit in his gut. Jack said, "This business suits you."

"I like it."

"Ever think of getting your own pub? I'd recommend you to the Brewery."

"I dunno."

"Thing is, you'd have to be married."

"Oh!"

"What about young Alison? I thought you were serious there."

"Her? No. No, I blew her out. She started talking about love and stuff."

"Jump 'em and leave 'em, eh Ford?"

"Something like that."

"Well, have a think about it. See me and Stella . . . made for each other. She's never looked at another man since me. Want to know why?"

"Er – Okay, why?"

"Bed. I give her enough. She's not likely to stray, and that's the secret. Good humping."

Ford drained his glass. A mountain of tankards waited to be washed.

"Better get going on that lot."

"Naw, leave it. Lemme tell you how to satisfy a woman."

Ford's heart sank. The word that leapt to his lips was "wooftah".

On his free mornings, he began to frequent that bar off New Oxford Street. It was here she'd asked, "So Ford, wanna get laid or what?"

Tommy, the barman with the lopsided grin, was still there. He still smelt of Old Spice and old ruin. If he remembered Ford, he hid it well.

"Remember me, Tommy?"

"Can't say that I do, John."

"Actually, it's Ford."

"Whatever you say, John. You want a drink or conversation?"

"Sour Mash."

"Coming up."

Ford couldn't leave it alone.

"Remember Grace?"

"An American chick?"

"Yes, that's her."

"Listen, John, everyone remembers Grace."

"Oh! I see."

He didn't, and certainly didn't wish to pursue this. Over the next six months he got there about three mornings a week. Each time, Tommy called him John and acted as if he'd never seen him before. It wasn't even personal. He called everyone John.

Ford drank sour mash and brooded. Sometimes he played the jukebox. The old rock and rollers. Everly Brothers, Buddy Holly. Like that.

One morning he was startled to hear Tommy speak to a customer.

"The bloke over there. Looks half asleep. He's a sour mash drinker too."

He looked up . . . There she was. Those blue, blue eyes. Dressed in a grey sweatshirt and nigh faded blue jeans. These were tucked into soft leather boots. Her hair was now to her shoulders. The sweatshirt logo read "I'd rather be in Philadelphia." Ford knew W.C. Fields loathed that city. On his tombstone was such an inscription. She smiled and walked over.

"Bin waiting long?"

"Two years."

"Sorry I'm late then."

Silence. They eyed each other. He loved what he saw. She just saw.

"Are you back long?" he asked.

"Like six months, I guess."

"You didn't think to ring me?"

"Guess not."

Another silence. He wanted to throw his arms round her and plead love and adoration. But hurt too, he wanted to lash out and see pain. As the silence built, he got up and ordered a double round of sour mash.

"I thought of you the other week, Ford."

His heart leapt.

"The Quiet Man". We caught it on cable. I said to Cecil, "Hey, Cecil, I know a guy like that."

Cecil! Bloody Cecil. And he couldn't resist it. He had to know.

"The John Wayne character?"

"Hell, no. The little guy. The priest. Barry something or another."

"Fitzgerald. That was Barry Fitzgerald."

That was the trigger. He started to speak, and in a low monotone he told her of all the events since last he'd seen her. She was silent as the saga unfolded and at odd moments, signaled to Tommy for fresh drinks. Near exhaustion, Ford finished and swallowed the nearest drink.

"Jesus H. Ke-rist! Well, way to go, Ford."

"That's it, Grace? That's all you have to say, 'Way to go'?"

"Well, it's interesting, but I mean, it's not high drama, is it?"

Rage engulfed him.

"Well, I thought the Dalton bit would worry you?"

"Dalton! Why would that worry me? You mean the vicious little guy who panhandled?"

"Yea. The guy who fucked you."

Astonishment lit her face, and he knew it had never happened. Relief and rage battled for supremacy. Grace's face clouded and she leant over. For a kiss, he prayed.

"Just wait one ga-damn minute! I get it . . . He told you that and you . . . you dumb bastard! You believed him, didn't you? All the rest, your pathetic story. You did it for revenge. You poor, dumb shit-kicker. All your grand design . . . Based on an empty premise. You sorry schmuck . . . You *prize horse's ass!*'

She stood up. Panic grabbed him.

"Grace . . . Oh God! Grace, listen . . ."

"Take a hike, buddy. You're one sick son-of-a-bitch." And she was gone.

Gone, and he knew – forever. Horse's ass. Good Lord! What a term! Him?

He looked up to see an effeminate man at the bar. The guy moved his hand suggestively to his crotch. Slow turning, he pouted his lips and blew a kiss to Ford.

Perhaps there was such a thing as unisex violence, thought Ford and then he said, "Nothing . . . tis nothing but a passing fancy." He surveyed the carnage of empty glasses. Very cautiously and with full deliberation he began to whistle. And whistle as if he meant it.

SHERRY
AND OTHER STORIES

THEY'RE OUT THERE . . .
AND THEY'RE ACTIVE

"For today, don't react. To every situation, bring the gift of gentle response."

Charles wrote this carefully in his notebook, next to his shopping list. London had been dancing on his nerves and, short of moving, he'd run out of answers. Then this gem of lucidity.

He was fifty-two years of age and recently redundant. A tall man, his hair was grey and thinning. A fragile build made him most unsuited to urban strife.

Samuel Johnson had written, "When a man was tired of London, he was tired of life." Charles was tired of Johnson. He'd like to have Johnson with a bus pass . . . see how wise he cracked then.

Breakfast was one boiled egg, one slice of toast and one cup of tea. He knew that loneliness thrived on single items and, phew . . . he'd been lonely for such a long time. Colette had met another man ten years ago and they'd scarpered to Amsterdam. The chap was an artist and according to her . . . "FUN." God, that word was like a curse of woesome proportions. He washed the cup and steeled himself for the day. He didn't expect "fun" to be prominent.

He was third in the bus queue. A sizeable crowd fell in behind him. Top of the line was a cheerful black woman who seemed unfazed by the wait. The bus appeared, driver-only model. The line moved expectantly. The doors opened and the driver moved from his seat; he began to manoeuvre the outside mirror.

"Are you changing drivers?" the black woman asked.

"Hey . . . What does it look like I'm doing?"

"Fixing the mirror."

"Hooray, give her a chat show."

Finally, the driver moved back inside and the line began to enter. A man asked,

"Do you go over London Bridge?"

"Ask the fat lady, she's the one with the answers."

A silence fell on the group as they gauged the insult. Cowed, they filed to their seats. Charles couldn't find a gentle response and he didn't think silence covered it either. What he wanted was to slap the driver full in the mouth. He got off at Camberwell Green and resolved to put the incident behind him. "NAZIS," his mind roared.

"Give them a uniform and the Third Reich thrives."

Outside McDonald's a young wino asked,

"Got any change?"

"Am . . . afraid not . . . all my loose change went on the bus."

"I'll take notes! . . . and we accept major credit cards!"

Charles hurried on, the shouts of abuse bounced against his neck. He found the employment office and crossing his fingers went in. The receptionist was an impossibly young seventeen and reading a magazine. She didn't look up.

"Excuse me, Miss."

"Yea."

"I've an appointment with a Mr. Hamilton."

"Not here today."

"Oh dear, I'm supposed to see him at eleven."

"Well, he's not 'ere, is he . . . he's got flu . . ."

"I see . . . I see, shall I leave my name then?"

"Suit yerself."

He stormed out . . . BLAST . . . Blast and damnation, he muttered . . . bad-mannered trollop . . . probably a reader.

He glared at passers-by with black hatred in his heart.

"Tea . . .," he thought. ". . . a cup of English tranquility."

A café on the Walworth Road and he sat wearily. Ordered a large tea. The waitress was sixty and tired. Her hair matched the colour of the tea. Only a fool would risk the soup.

"Colour coordination," he thought.

A smudge of pink lipstick clung to the mug's rim. Charles wanted to fling it through the window. A man sat opposite and ordered toast with poached eggs. When it came, he removed his false teeth and slipped them into his pocket. He said,

"I hate eggs."

Charles sighed and wondered who'd planted the pink kiss on his forlorn mug. The man tapped him on the arm and said,

"Them Yanks . . . they've got all kinds of serial killers" (he pronounced it cereal) "and psychopaths. Here in London, we've got our own band."

"Oh really?" said Charles.

"I'm telling you, matey . . . they're out there . . . and they're active."

Charles began to tilt the mug and let the tea seep onto the table. He said, "Can't say I've noticed, old boy . . . no can't say that I have."

THEY DREAM OF ANGELS

He was a sad man. Even his clothes sang of sorrow. Old, too, she knew he'd not see seventy again. His face featured the look that said he wouldn't want to, even were it possible.

The coffee bar was full and Cora desperately wanted a seat. New shoes were crucifying the very blood in her toes. Her Mother used to say, "A lady always buys a size smaller." She wished her Mother were wearing them . . . see how lady-like she'd be.

Only the man's table was free of other occupants. People sense misery and avoid it. Woe was neon-lit above the man's head. On a busy day, who needed that. A full head of white hair topped his worn, lined face. Cora reckoned he'd smell of mustiness, old hangers and faded shirts. He'd probably have those hideous false teeth that startle in a face, like a shout.

Cora was thirty. Blonde and petite. At least her friends said that. "Petite" . . . it sounded like a delicate chocolate you'd hoard for a special day, or a fragrance you can never quite identify.

"May I sit?" she asked.

He looked up. Brown eyes, decked in some lost grief. Standing, he half bowed. It made him more forlorn.

"But of course."

Cora ordered cakes and coffee. The waitress brought a tray of pure temptation. The coffee had a rich smell, like energy. Cora didn't want to draw the old codger on herself but he was so thin.

"Join me in a cake," she offered.

He gave a beautiful smile, even his eyes were linked to it. The teeth might well have been his own, uneven but clean. All of him was clean as a whistle, as if he'd been shine-scrubbed for viewing.

"I'd dearly love to but alas . . . I've gone beyond delicacies!"

Cora thought she'd leave well enough alone.

"Miserable old goat," she thought . . . he'd probably have some yarn about a dead wife and sweet cakes . . . and yet. She said,

"Don't be silly, nobody's beyond a bit of sweetness."

The near wisdom of this hung between them. She selected an éclair, her absolute favourite. Cutting carefully, she saved the cream, which galloped to the side and popped a wedge.

"Ah bliss . . . ," she thought, "all of heaven" . . . and double bonus, felt the softness meet like joy against the roof of her mouth. A shot of coffee and she knew true contentment. He looked directly at her.

"When are you due?"

Astonished, she nearly forgot the cakes.

"How can you tell . . . do I show?"

"No, no . . . it's the bloom, you have . . . a radiance."

Her English mind searched for an English word to catch her reaction.

"CHUFFED" . . .

Yes . . . exactly that. A proper description.

"Have you children?" she asked.

"No. No, I don't. A woman once told me I wasn't responsible enough for such a grace."

Cora was appalled.

"Damn cheek . . . you don't believe that do you? . . . surely not?"

He thought about it.

"I hope not," he answered.

A silence fell. Cora finished the éclair. A second one was winking for her attention. She thought that might be greedy but oh . . . it looked lonely without its mate . . . weren't they better in pairs?

"Excuse me, dear, but I must to the Gents . . ."

When he returned, he didn't sit but stood straight as if he was going to recite. He said,

"My dear, please indulge the whim of an old man. I paid for your coffee . . . and TWO éclairs.

(They both smiled.)

"I'd be so pleased if you'd eat the partner remaining. I wish you and the baby a whole mountain of light. I always thought that babies dream . . . do you think they do?"

Cora didn't know.

"I dunno," she said, "what on earth could they dream about?"

"Exactly . . . that's it . . . I'd say they dream of angels."

After he'd gone, Cora sliced the second éclair and with deep relish, ate it. Was it possibly more delicious? A smudge of chocolate lit her upper lip. Even had she known, it's doubtful she'd have cared. A hint of a lullaby was coursing out from her heart. Gently and slowly, words of childhood began to trickle from her mouth. As she hummed, she wondered if she'd risk another coffee.

LIVER

"The cruelest lies are often told in silence."
R. L. Stevenson

Mary fretted.

When would be the best moment for the gift?

She didn't look fifty-five. Her face retained the fresh Irish expectantly. After thirty-five years of marriage she expected precious little. Up close her face showed the lines of disappointment. Not many got close, not anymore.

She'd retained most of her figure, not through vanity but disillusionment. A steady diet. Dark rinsed hair highlit blue eyes. A mouth built to smile . . . didn't, at least not often.

Charles was ten years older. Wiser, too, to hear him tell it. Tall, he used his height as a weapon, of sneak intimidation. Completely bald, he polished the pate with gusto. "VIRILITY" and he spelt it.

Wide grey eyes lulled you to interpretations of kindness. Till he spoke. A voice fuelled on contempt wiped the impression. Their thirty-fifth anniversary. He'd chosen the restaurant for its hauteur. Belittlement was the main course and ensured its success.

Dressed in dark blue pin-stripe, Charles surveyed the room with glee.

"Class," he said, "No yobbos."

Mary didn't answer. He was accustomed to an audience, not a participant.

"Snob-appeal," she thought.

His tie established his status as a Tory outrider.

A waiter appeared, greeting-less.

Charles commanded,

    – No starters.
    – Chicken Maryland for me.
    – the fish for my wife.
    – side order of
                sauté mushrooms
                jacket potatoes
                celery sticks
                broccoli and carrots.

"The chicken is fresh?"

"Yes sir."

"Good. A carafe of the house plonk . . . and mineral water for my wife. MALVERN . . . none of that French rubbish.

"Your face is unfamiliar to me."

"I'm new, sir."

"Well, chop chop, the food won't arrive of its own volition."

The waiter withdrew.

Mary was mortified, not a new experience but always raw. She longed to say something. Instead, she took the package from her bag and shyly placed it before him. Her heart was pounding. It was beautifully wrapped in black and gold paper. A tiny ribbon enhanced its appeal.

"What's this?"

"A little surprise for the occasion."

He frowned, and said, "I hope you haven't been playing silly buggers . . . wasting money again."

She flushed, and said, "Go on dear, open it now."

Sighing, he crudely tore it open. A thin gold watch fell on the table.

"I have a watch," he said.

Something rattled near her heart.

"But Charles, this is special, it's a dress watch . . . and . . . I had it inscribed."

He looked at the back. It read "TI AMOR."

"Spanish is it . . . of some significance I suppose?"

"Italian, dear . . . it's Italian . . . it says . . . well am . . . that I care about you."

"Stuff and nonsense . . . here put the damned thing away before the new chappie brings the grub. I declare, where you pick up those silly notions. AND, marked like that, it lowers the pre-sale value."

"It's not marked, it's inscribed."

"Same thing," he said, and pushed it at her.

She lifted it gently and let it rest a moment in her lap. Then she let it slip to the floor, using her right heel, she began to grind down.

The food arrived.

Charles set to . . . and drank noisily. He'd eaten half when he set down his fork and loudly summoned the waiter.

"Yes sir, is everything to your satisfaction . . . and madam?"

"New . . . you said."

"Y . . . es . . . sir."

"What does this look like to you . . . go on . . . have a good look."

"Chicken, sire . . . Chicken Maryland."

Mary's stomach churned.

"Well, pigs might fly, not only does it look like CHICKEN, it damned well tastes like it."

"I'm not sure I understand the problem sir."

"Remarkable . . . he doesn't understand, from one of the Grammar schools I shouldn't wonder. I ordered liver."

"I beg your pardon, sir?"

"LIVER . . . are you dense as well as deaf . . . what did I order dear?"

Mary couldn't answer.

"Cat got your tongue, woman? . . . TELL him what I ordered."

"I'm not sure, Charles . . . I wasn't paying attention."

"You weren't WHAT!" and he banged the table.

Mary reached over quickly and grabbed the remains of the chicken. With a small yelp, she flung it out across the restaurant. All eyes turned.

"See . . . ," she said, ". . . mebbe it's bacon . . . or some breed of bird. But liver, no, I don't think so darling . . . You're right as usual."

GOD WORE SHOES

Violence! Don't talk to me about bloody violence. Brady's roar shook the customer who had innocently commented on urban crime. Brady was nigh 6'5" in height and close on 200 pounds. Built to be a publican. At 50 years of age he radiated menace. Almost bald, this added to his aura of force. He had mean eyes and they meant exactly that. The nose was misshapen through nature and brawling. A generous mouth covered teeth dominated by a gold filling. The gold flashed frequently but merriment almost never.

Brady was obsessed by crime. He gave directions accordingly. "Want the nearest tube? . . . two muggings from here . . . the bus stop . . . a rape away." A farmed portrait of Ruth Ellis was enshrined at the centre of the bar. "See here," Brady would say, "now there's British justice for you." Nobody was sure if he meant this as approval or not. Alice, his wife, may have known but she'd fled some years ago. "The missis . . . oh I've her buried in the back," he'd say. Undoubtedly, such a fate awaited her if he were to catch up with her. But she'd run fast . . . and far.

Brady's pub was situated at the wrong exit of The Mile End road. "Bandit country," according to the locals. The clientele consisted almost exclusively of policemen. A stray drinker would be advised by Brady as to this and then cautioned . . .

"Watch your wallet."

As a youth, Brady had been a merchant seaman and at some point had been tattooed. The right arm predictably proclaimed "Mother." The left read "Watch Out." One was well advised to heed this. During his travels, Brady had acquired a long, wooden club. A narrow handle led to a thick, ugly baseball type body. It had been fashioned with oak for weight and bamboo for flexibility. When swung, it made a vicious "swish" which put the fear of eternity about. The customers were very familiar with it. At closing time, without fail, the club would appear with the same cry "Drink up or join the club . . . permanently." To policemen, of course, this was the height of comfort. The nightly "swish" was indeed Mother's milk to their blue heats. Beat your own, so to speak.

On a wet November morning, a young Irishman attempted to steal from Brady. He managed to get into the yard at the back of the pub and was in the act of forcing a shed door. Brady caught him there and went to work with the club. The "swish" almost drowned out the litany of "Oh Sweet God . . . oh for the love of God and His Saints." The he stopped. The words of entreaty hung on the air. Brady dropped the club, the wood rattled on the concrete yard. "God is it . . . ya thieving Mick . . . see those shoes . . . I worked for them . . . like everything else." So saying, Brady three times swung his shoe at the unconscious head. And three times you denied me! Brady made a few telephone calls and the youth was discreetly removed from the premises. Cleaning the club took longer and afterwards it was placed under the Ruth Ellis shrine. The staff kept clear of their boss as he began to drink with ferocity. All through the evening session, he continued to drink and felt "watched." From the corner of his eye, he'd sense a man's eyes on him. He'd snap round and no one was staring. Last orders rang early and Brady's surliness cleared the pub quickly. Along, he double-checked the door locks and windows. Moving to the centre of the bar, Brady felt he could watch the whole area. A fresh bottle of Scotch was open and the club rested on his knees. As the bottle diminished Brady's attention lulled.

A man stood inside the bar, his back to Brady, covering Ruth Ellis. The sudden sight of him snapped something in Brady's chest and a jolt of pain drew him upright. "Hey . . . who the bloody hell are you . . . want some of this . . . what . . . want to join the club fella?" As he lifted the club, a double jolt slammed his heart and he fell heavily on his back. The whiskey crashed to the floor. Brady tried to clasp the club but paralysis spread through him. He heard the man's footsteps as he began to approach. The shoes made an odd sound . . . like the lilt that pervades an Irish wake. As the man's shadow fell across Brady he roared "for the love of . . ." But blackness took away completion.

The pub didn't open the following morning. By evening a group of thirsty, rather than concerned, coppers forced the door. Inside they found the bar had been cleaned and polished. No Brady! Eventually, a chief inspector from Hackney ventured the three flights to Brady's bedroom. He found him in bed with the sheets up to his chin. The face was spit-clean and he looked as dead as he indeed was. More coppers came up and they drew the blankets back. Brady was clad in pyjamas with the sleeves rolled back to display the tattoos.

"Bugger's dead," they agreed. It was further agreed that Brady would wish them to have a few drinks. Shortly, a festive atmosphere prevailed and the drink flowed. A police cadet, fresh from Stepney Green, was assigned as barman. Cutting a lemon for the Chief Inspector's gins, his eye fell on the Ruth Ellis photo. "Hello . . . it's Marilyn Monroe . . . I'll be having that," and he quickly stuffed it beneath his tunic.

Upstairs, the door had been closed on Brady. For a while the sounds of merriment reached there but gradually the silence spread and settled. The club wasn't found behind the bar and nobody seemed interested in its whereabouts.

In the months to come, Brady was remembered but was seldom missed.

TWIST OF LEMON

"All you need is your own place . . . and a cat called Norman."

Jack was eavesdropping on two women seated behind him . . . Norman . . . why Norman?

The pub was full and he worried about the delay in getting served again . . . if . . . and when, Melanie arrived. Jack was forty-three years old, five foot eight with a slight stoop.

A pot belly was building but he felt powerless against its march out and onward.

He had brown thinning hair and daily distress at recession. Soft brown eyes were his redeeming feature. They almost compensated for his poor nose and poorer mouth. He was doing what he did best, worrying.

Melanie arrived, looking carefree and careless.

A petite blonde with blue eyes, she was dressed now in jail sentence outfit. Short black mini, black boots, white cling sweater and midi leather coat.

"God," he thought, "I worship her, I'll light candles to her."

"Hello," he thought, "I worship her, I'll light candles to her."

"Hello," he said.

"Oh hello."

She had the knack of always sounding as if she'd never met him.

"What will you have?"

"A vermouth

and perhaps . . . yes.

a lightly tossed salad . . . mm . . . m

Some French bread, check it's fresh

and

a twist of lemon in the drink."

His heart

s

a

n

k.

The barman was an animal and a very busy one. They'd already traded glares.

A tossed salad!

"Coming up," he said.

It took fifteen minutes before he got the barman's attention.

"We don't got no turned salad."

"Tossed, that's tossed salad."

"You winding me up Guv? . . . we got salad sandwiches and we got burgers . . . we got other customers too. So, you wanna get yer skates on or wot?"

"Am . . . fine, a salad sandwich then, a large scotch and a vermouth, please"

He couldn't, he just couldn't ask for the lemon twisted or otherwise. The order was slapped down with no change from the ten pound note. Jack offered it for some soul in purgatory and fought his way back to Melanie.

She'd let his seat go and was chatting to the occupant, a navvy. In donkey jacket and vicious work boots, a hard-ass. Jack sighed and put the sandwich down, like an offering. He tried to slip the vermouth next to it.

"WHAT'S THIS THEN?" she screeched . . . she and the navvy eyed the sandwich.

"It's all they'd left . . . am . . . darling."

The navvy sniggered at the endearment. Jack wished for a bundle of things.

a) She'd lower her voice.
b) He didn't feel the suicidal compulsion to call her affectionately.
c) He was in South America.

"That's all they had love . . . the am . . . the tossed salad wasn't available."

Jack took a lethal belt of the scotch, chocked and felt his face burn.

"Toss the sandwich more like," said the navvy.

Melanie removed the cellophane and delicately lifted the bread. Very dead lettuce hid slyly against the light. The navy roared,

"Lettuce pray for the recently departed."

Melanie pushed the sandwich away and glared at the vermouth.

"Didn't they have any lemon then?"

Jack finished his drink. He and Melanie had separated three months ago. This was to have been an attempt at reconciliation. Was it on himself or was it going down the toilet.

"Sweetheart," he croaked, "could we mebbe go some place else."

She stood and gave him an icy look.

"Go! . . . the only place I'm go-ing is back to work," and swept out before he could reply.

"Bye honey bunch," he whispered.

The loud voices of the crowd beat against his heart. A guffaw from the navvy as he headed away. Jack took the seat and quoted H. L. Mencken,

"Love is what makes a goddess out of an ordinary girl."

He wanted to cry
to cry out.

Instead, he lifted the sandwich and began to chew. A piece of limp lettuce floated to his lap.

"Not bad," he said . . . not bad at all. A single tear slipped down his cheek and splashed gently in the un-touched vermouth.

He sipped that and added,

"She's right you know, it definitely needs something, it needs a bitterness right enough . . . I'll call her later, she'd appreciate a call . . . I will, I'll do that . . . that's the best thing . . ."

DADDY

His daughter, wounded . . . stared at the soggy cornflakes. Pain writ full on her face. Tom sipped his tea and tried not to notice how old she looked. She was thirty-nine and had come home "for a few days."

That was three weeks ago.

If only he could grab her pain, he'd hug it to himself as he'd never hugged her. A teacher, she made him feel un-learnt.

"Did you ever hear of Tennessee Williams?"

He hadn't.

"Am . . . I'm not sure."

She smiled and quoted "'Happiness is insensitivity' . . . what do you think?"

He thought she made the tea too weak. But never, he'd never tell her. When Mary was alive, the girl seemed happy. After . . . well . . . things died in little places you'd never even been aware about. His own daughter had never used a term of parental address with him. No one else seemed to notice. One weak day, he'd said it to Mary and heard the faint whine in his own voice. Mary answered,

"Don't be an eejit."

The girl's sense of humour baffled him. At dinner yesterday she said, "Life's a bitch but I don't have to be one."

Her marriage had failed. What a description, he thought, as if you could re-take it like a driving test . . . and they sure didn't give any lessons for it, all those came after.

She'd only talked the one time about it; she'd begun "At the table, Rob leant over and punched me in the face."

Tom was frozen. Rage and hurt assaulted his very heart. He managed to ask, foolishly, "what did you do sweetheart?"

"Do? . . . I fell off the chair, that's what I did. But the food must have been good, he carried on eating."

Tom tried to unclench his fists without the bones cracking.

She continued, "Rob was very proud of a butcher's cleaver he'd got on the cheap.

"A big ugly-looking instrument. At four in the morning, he was snoring loudly. I rested the blade of the cleaver lightly on his Adam's apple . . . and I waited. The steel was cold as ice. His eyes opened and do you know . . . he said nothing. I had his full concentration. I guess a blade will do that, get your attention I mean."

Tom was horrified, he said,

"Did . . . did you do anything darling?"

A laugh she gave chilled him.

"I said . . . 'next time.'"

Tom thought he'd brew more tea . . . toast too, a fresh batch. As he buttered it she said,

"Will you butter a slice for me?"

"I will, honey bunch."

"When I was little, you always buttered Mummy's toast. I thought – when I marry, I'll marry a man who'd do that.

"What I did was . . . I met Rob . . . and the rest is . . . as they say . . . Grief or should that be brief?"

"You'll meet someone else love, you're young yet."

"You never did."

He chewed the toast and tried not to crunch it. She was the very beat of his heart. What else is there . . . he didn't know or want to know.

"I'm leaving today."

"Ah no . . . sweetheart . . . why?"

"Because I'm in your way . . . don't fret, it's not your fault.

"You're a solitary man but there's not a breath of loneliness about you. I always liked that."

After she'd packed, she came and pecked him on the cheek.

The kiss burned there like afterglow. She looked at him and said,

"Can I ask you something?"

"Anything darling," . . . God forgive him, he thought it was money."

"You never use my name . . . you call me darling sweetheart honey bunch. Anything but my name. I wonder why that is Daddy."

He was speechless. She smiled and said,

"Now don't you start worrying about that. You're not to make a big deal out of it. So you won't. Promise me . . . Daddy, will you promise me that?"

SĦERRY

"So . . ." he said, ". . . are you some kind of alcoholic or what?"

Amy nearly fell off the chair. This balding fat man with perspiration on his upper lip . . . how dare he! Before she could reply, he leaned under the table, pinched her knew and roared "Just kidding . . . lighten up Ann . . . or should I say . . . drink up," and he actually guffawed. Not a pleasant sound.

"Amy, it's Amy."

"What . . . are you sure . . . well of course you are. I could have sworn the form said Ann."

The form in question was supplied by The Zodiac Dating Service. For fifty guineas they found your "star mate" and guaranteed "future happiness." It was written in the stars. This was Amy's third star mate. The other two burned out in jig-time. The guineas tag was supposed to suggest class and old fashioned romance. Smelled of a con, thought Amy. This third and final star was named Oliver. Amy saw he'd been more than liberal in his vital statistics. He'd chopped a good fifteen years from his age and maybe two stone from his weight. Obviously he'd shrunk two inches since posting his form.

She'd been a touch free in her own vitals. Amy was 5'2", currently permed blonde, plump and forty-nine years old. Her form said thirty-nine, 5'4" and, she blushed at the thought of it. . . SVELTE. Not quite sure exactly what that meant, she hoped it suggested mystery and allure. A bad moment now as she wondered if it was some awful code for kinky. Would he want to tie her up and smear her with garlic . . . or was that treacle. She'd read somewhere about roses and maple syrup.

Amy was single. Funny she thought how that description seemed to diminished a woman. A single man had charm. The term "splinter" was a mental mugging (to her). It reeked of desperation. Over twenty years she'd achieved the position of Head of The Typing Pool with a large insurance company. These past few months she'd begun to lose it. Lack of companionship was her own verdict. "Drink," said the pool.

"O.K.," she said . . . and said aloud at the bus stop. Talking to herself on the streets was a whole new terror. It crept up gradually. So I take a few drinks . . . a few tots of gin at night. Mother's ruin, he Mother said. To balance her talking to herself she'd purchased a dog. A Yorkshire Terrier and terror she was. Sherry she called the pup and was stunned at her love for it.

The pup wreaked early havoc and chewed furniture or shoes with equal abandon. But the welcome . . . ah. Returning from work, Sherry went into paroxysms of delight at her key in the door. Amy was made to feel the very centre of another living creature's existence. Dizzy stuff. Perhaps she was, and it warmed a heart that cold had roughened for too many years. Amy's flat was almost in Notting Hill Gate. She told people she lived in Holland Park. Not that a soul seemed to care if she lived in Hackney.

She'd managed to ration the gin and didn't drink every evening. Well, not Sundays. Oliver! When she'd received details on him she felt lucky. Third time

188

blessed and all of that. An accountant . . . probably drove a Bentley and had a little weekend place. He'd be sensitive but strong. Not above whacking the thugs at Notting Hill, but saddened by the homeless too. A rugby player, he'd write concise sonnets in secret. With deep understanding, only Amy would ever see them.

Oliver Philips. It had solidity. Presenting Oliver, Amy and Sherry Philips . . . the family Philips. The Holland Park Philips. Yes! she thought . . . oh yes. She'd dressed carefully for the meeting. A dark navy two-piece and discreet shoes. Pearls she'd considered but thought . . . over-toried.

A silk scarf with a splash of red to show her flair. For what exactly she wasn't sure but she could wing it. She fixed her accent with the tiniest tot of gin . . . keep those vowels subdued. All hints of south of The River must be muted. South East London indeed . . . never heard of it. And now, this moron! "I'm an accountant, lass" was his opening "on account of there's brass in it, geddit . . . can you FIGURE it out."

Their date was set at a small grill and bar off the Charing Cross Road. Amy thought it boded well for her literary aspirations of Oliver.

"I picked this place, lass, cos I do the books here," he said. More accountancy wit followed. "Cook more than the books . . . eh!" Amy would never swear to it but, to her horror, he winked. She had begun with a small gin, then ordered a second as the Oliver humour disintegrated. That was when he'd made the alcoholic reference. The evening shambled downwards. Oliver continued a vein of bawdy innuendo. During dessert (a forlorn crème caramel with septic cream), he'd tried to ram his knees between her legs. With the coffee, he launched on a treatise about knockers and Amy stood up.

"Shut up," she said, "you stupid lecherous oaf." Oliver did. She swept out, somewhat regally she thought.

A taxi got her home and she felt her heart had been mangled.

The pup tore around in delight at her appearance. Amy kicked off her shoes and pored a murderous length of gin. Two slow tears crept down her cheeks and fell softly on the ritzy scarf. More tears gathered. The pup launched herself onto Amy's lap. A small, warm tongue began to lap at the tears. A bitty tail endeavoured to shake itself into a frenzy. Amy felt a glow of love at its purest.

"Oh Sherry," she said, "Sherry darlin'."

PRIEST, PART 1
APPARITIONS

Man, born of woman, is full of misery and has but a short time to live. Morgan read the words and felt them heavy in his mouth. "God," he thought, "but they're depressing."

He woke . . . the same dream.

Fr. Morgan to be exact. He was six foot and lean. An unruly mop of greying hair refused settlement. Blue eyes and a nose that looked broken. His mouth had a tendency to turn down. This was due to experience rather than temperament. At forty-two years of age, he felt every one of them.

His doctor had recently given him a full physical, even including measurements.

"You're six foot," he accused.

"I'm awfully sorry."

"But you can't be."

"Well, Doctor, I didn't come here proclaiming I was . . . in fact, I never mentioned height."

"Only one man was ever six foot."

"Don't tell me."

"Himself."

"Didn't I just ask you not to tell me . . . what did I ask you?"

"It's remarkable. How's the priesting?"

"Steady . . . that war scare always drums up business. People like to get their premiums paid."

"You're an unlikely priest."

How true that was. If he'd had a vocation, it was fast eroding. Now he saw it as a job and that was deep trouble.

"You think so?"

"The heart isn't in it. Ah, you do the priestly things but like an actor . . . and speaking of heart . . . how many cigarettes are you doing?"

"I'm trying to cut down."

"They'll cut *you* down, laddybuck."

"I'm having some problems sleeping, can you give me something?"

"Yes . . . advice . . . STOP SMOKING."

"Ah, no . . . no, I won't. I can go somewhere else."

"Who'd have you, Father?"

"Wait till your next confession, by jingo, you'll hop."

***

On the street he'd felt a powerful urge for a drink. But pubs were for citizens. He'd love nothing better than the freedom to pub crawl. He walked the short distance to his parish. On the outskirts of Clapham, his church was "a good appointment," and he was going to be the governor, as the locals said. The parish priest, a Fr. Malachy, seventy years old, had dropped dead after Sunday Mass. Malachy the miser. Never spend a penny when you could borrow two. Morgan was temporarily assigned his duties and a year later, he was still the boss.

As he turned the corner to the church, he was turning into nightmare such as his sleep had never conjured. He'd been with Malachy before the priest had said that Sunday Mass. The priest had turned to him and said,

"Some day, Morgan, you'll come to know a high holiness."

"You may be right."

"But first, I feel you may have to understand the 'Benediction.'"

"I do."

"No, you don't. In fact, you suffer from what Herbert Marcuse called true ignorance . . . contempt prior to investigation. Now for a layman, it's just a pity, but for a priest, it's downright tragic. Smirk all you like!"

Outside the Church, the housekeeper, Mrs. Fleming, was pacing. She looked frantic. A dumpy woman from Tipperary. She was over sixty and a worrier.

"Ah, Fr. Morgan . . . Thank God . . . oh, you won't believe what's happened."

"Now calm down, Mrs. Fleming, tell me nice and slowly."

"It's the altar, Father. They've . . . well, I can't describe it . . . come and see. Tis pure blasphemy and worse."

Morgan sighed and followed her.

The large crucifix usually suspended above the altar was inverted. A chill whispered at his heart. Along the aisle were strewn entrails from fowl or an animal. An appalling stink rose.

"Jesus, Mary and Joseph," he said.

"There's worse, Father . . . look . . . on the altar. I'll wait here."

It took all he had to approach. Scolding himself "I'm a modern man, this is just hooliganism," he went. The torso of a headless cat was laid there. White Rosary beads bound its back paws together. Nausea assailed him. Bile rushed to his throat as he looked at the beads. Given to him by his mother for his ordination. He had to grip the altar to keep from fainting.

"The police . . . call the police," he choked.

***

"How did they get the beads?" asked the policeman. A detective no less. No common bobby for church matters. He was a beefy man over fifty. The face looked squatted in . . . and for a long time. "I'm Brady," he'd said, "and mind, no jokes about 'The Bunch.'"

"I don't know how they got them. I keep them with my breviary upstairs. My mother gave them to me . . . she passed away five years ago."

"I'm sorry," said Brady.

Whether for the mother or the beads, he didn't specify. He had his men plod round the altar doing police things. They had the look of knowing more and, moreover, they'd be keeping it on a "need to know" basis. As usual, nobody needed to know.

Brady said,

"You have to wonder though."

"What on earth about?"

"The head . . . where's the head? Did you see *The Godfather*?"

"No . . . no, I did not see it . . . can we get on with this?"

"The head of a horse, they put it in a bloke's bed."

"Pl . . . uu . . . ze."

"Any enemies, Father?"

Morgan couldn't believe he was seriously asked this.

"Detective, I'm not altogether sure your attitude is quite the correct one."

Brady ignored this and soon after, he left. The cleaning up fell to Morgan as Mrs. Fleming had legged it. After cleaning the debris he took nearly two hours to re-align the Cross. An elderly parishioner watched him wrestle with it and chuckled.

"Ary, Father, I don't think there's room on it for the both of yer."

Morgan fled to his room. It used to be Malachy's. A large mahogany writing desk usually gave him fierce bursts of pride. Not today. The bed was just a wish short of being double, you climbed in you didn't ever want to emerge. An urge to check for the cat's head was nigh ferocious.

"Enough already," he muttered, "time to stop this paranoia."

He lit a cigarette and was drawing deep when the phone rang. It put his heart sideways.

"Hello."

"Fr. Morgan . . . am I speaking to Fr. Morgan?"

"Yes, you are . . . state your business."

Cold . . . formal . . . sure, but he was all through with pleasantries for this day . . . he'd left them at the altar.

"I'm Kate Delaney and . . ."

"The journalist?"

"Yes . . . you've heard of me?"

"The radical feminist . . . you wrote a series of articles called 'Men and other Garbage'."

"Guilty as charged . . ."

"What do you want?"

"The incidents at your Church, I'd like to talk about them."

"Would you now . . . Miss . . . or Mzzzz or what Mmm is current. Well, the integrity of woman isn't threatened so you can go claw some other tree."

"Claw . . . very apt, Fr. . . . Very catty, in fact. You're a feisty old devil, aren't you?"

"Good day to you, Ma'am," and he hung up.

There's a terrible power in this. You just shut them down. Feeling like a wicked child, he glared at the phone. It rang.

She pestered him through three more calls, and more to get away from the Church, he agreed to meet at Charing Cross. He looked forward to trimming her sails.

The rendezvous was at a small Italian coffee shop where The Strand meets Charing Cross. As he entered, a woman rose from a table.

"You're Fr. Morgan, I presume."

"And you're an awful nuisance."

She was tall, almost 5'10", and with a full figure. A navy blue suit showed the curves discreetly. Jet black hair fell to her shoulders. The eyes were dark brown and her nose was finely finished. Full lips revealed strong white teeth. The overall effect made him feel shabby. They sat.

"Would you like to eat something, Father."

"I'd like to get this over with."

"Testy!! . . ."

The waiter, a true Italian, was in heaven. A woman and a priest. Twin gods to be servile before.

"Buongiorno."

"For God's sake," said Morgan.

"S'cuzi?"

"Cappuccino . . . yes, two."

"Bene . . ."

Kate looked at the priest and said,

"You'd need to lighten up there, padre."

"Look . . . call me Morgan, it's my name, I'm not your father and I very much doubt you're Catholic. What am I to call you?"

"Kate, it's my name . . . and I am . . . or was Catholic."

"Worse, the lapsed ones are the worst. Neither fowl nor beast."

The waiter brought the coffees amid a flourish of flattery and servility not heard since Popes went to Ireland.

Kate took a sip, smiled, and said,

"It's my birthday."

"What age are you, or is that a huge chauvinist crime?"

"Forty."

"You don't look it."

"Well . . . Morgan, as Gloria Steinheim said, 'this is what forty looks like.'"

"That . . . another neurotic."

"Tut tut, I do believe you're attempting to wind me up. Relax . . . I won't bite, you know."

The waiter slid over and hovered.

"What . . . what is it?" asked Morgan.

"Telefono, Monsignor . . . you are the Padre Morgan?"

"Telephone . . . for me? . . . here, but it can't be."

Kate said,

"Did the caller give a name?"

"Ah, si . . . he said he be 'Father Malachy.'"

Blood drained from Morgan's face. Kate stood and said,

"I'll go . . . just wait here."

He couldn't have moved anyway. Icicles ran down his spine and he actually felt the hairs bristle at the neck base. He didn't think that was ever anything but a figure of speech.

Kate returned.

"The line was dead."

Her figure of speech nigh finished him off.

"What's going on, Morgan? . . . you look like you've seen a ghost."

"Or heard from one."

He resolved that, whatever else, he wouldn't tell her. No matter how strong the urge, she'd get nothing. Then he told her.

"You've got to be kidding."

"Look at me . . . do I look like I'm kidding . . . do I?"

"Valium . . . do you have any valium?"

"I wouldn't take those!"

"Not for you, for me. Jeez, I thought you guys had stuff for all emergencies."

"That's social workers, pills and patronisation."

"Whew. Rough . . . if I write this, they'll shoot me."

"Graham Greene, are you familiar with him?"

"You think he'd written it?"

"I was about to say that he remarked how priests and writers found success unavailable."

"Speak for yourself, fella. I'll get the check."

She had a car, a beat up Rover, and on seeing his expression, said,

"Pretty macho, eh?"

He was too spooked to wise-ass, thought he wanted to . . . instead he took the lift back to the Church. Her driving was strong and careful . . . like real Irish tea. Practised and sure. At the Church she said,

"Well be seeing each other, Father Morgan, you can count on that."

As she drove off, she thanked some God that the remark on the tip of her tongue had stayed there: "Cat got your tongue, then?"

Someone had the cat's head and the priest's attention. Attracted to him, too, she knew that from the moment she saw him. That he was a priest didn't make him untouchable . . . just difficult.

Entering the Church, the first thing he heard was whistling, and if he wasn't much mistaken, it had the air of "The Kerry Dances." Sister Benedventura. Her whistlin' was on a par with her shining. If it moved, polish and then spit shine. Malachy had said "she'd shine the head of a pin" . . . and God, he sure didn't want to think about him. What he wanted . . . and fast, was a big drink.

Sister Ben said,

"There's someone here for the post of secretary."

"Ary, God. Blast it . . . sorry, Ben . . . sorry . . . look, gimme five minutes and I'll see her in the Rectory."

"She's been waiting an hour already."

"Well, she won't mind a few more minutes. Give her tea or somethin' . . ."

"Tea."

"Yes . . . tea . . . or sherry . . . just stop giving me grief."

"Well, I'm sorry I spoke, your Reverence."

"Get on with it."

As he stopped off, he distinctly heard the whistle turn into to "Colonel Bogie." He felt like a prisoner of war himself and heavily tortured. In his room, he opened a bottle of Jameson. A deliberate choice. Reading Graham Greene, he'd learned a large glass of this looked like a very watered drink. In company, you could appear pious and get absolutely pissed. Such is the learning of literature. He poured a single . . . considered . . . then shrugged and built an Irish double. Clug . . . wait and wham-oh. Wallop! The eyes nigh jumped out of his head. A few seconds later, a sense of well-being flooded his system. He said aloud,

"Aw, Jaysus . . . isn't that only might. The Holy Name be glorified."

Chance another, better not . . . so he did regardless. An urge to sing nigh overwhelmed him. As he went to interview the woman, he glanced around the room and went . . . pss . . . pss . . . nice cat . . . pss . . . pss. Ah, wasn't life on an upsurge. Entering the Rectory, a slight jauntiness lit his step. A woman rose to her feet. Early thirties, blonde streaked hair and the face of an angel. She was about 5'2" and a figure that screamed to be hugged. The eyes were oval-shaped and intelligence-blazed. Her hand was extended.

"I'm Sera Blake."

"Sarah . . . is it?"

"S . . . E . . . R . . . A . . ."

"Ah, sorry, that's an unusual name."

"It's the one given to me, Father."

"Yes . . . yes, of course, quite lovely . . . am . . ." (He wanted to say how even lovelier she was.)

He took her hand and electricity burned. A jolt of passion nearly toppled him. She knew . . . a tiny smile hovered. Sweat broke on his forehead.

"The job is quite varied . . . apart from Church correspondence, there's personal letters, etc., I'd need you to take charge of."

She handed him her references.

"Very impressive, are you married, Mzz . . . Miss . . . am."

"No . . . please call me Sera."

"Grand . . . and let's dispense with the formalities. I'm Morgan . . . and when can you start?"

"Tomorrow . . . I never got married because the best ones are 'unavailable.'"

She gave him a look that Raymond Chandler said "you felt in your back pocket."

Lust tore throughout him and he felt the physical signs of this were soon to be mortifyingly obvious. Shame and Jameson burned his face.

"How is Malachy?" she asked.

Too stunned to answer, he gaped at her.

"I used to know him when I attended this parish years ago."

"Am . . . he's . . . no longer with us . . . I'm sorry to tell you he's deceased."

Sera prepared to leave. As she got to the door, she turned and said,

"I like to think they're always with us . . . don't you, Father?"

He sat down and lit a shaking cigarette. The nicotine burned like revelation. Alcohol whispered,

"No worries, son, nothing here that a few stiff belts won't fix . . . let's nip upstairs and finish that bottle . . . how much can be left in it."

He did.

The small hours of the morning he came to. Stretched on his bed, still dressed and a mega hangover waiting. Looking at his watch, he remembered Scott Fitzgerald's "It's 3:30 in the morning of our souls." Time of fear.

Thirst drove him out to the landing. Someone was at the top of the stairs.

"Hello," he ventured.

His mother turned and smiled.

The impact floored him and he fell to his knees. Whimpering, he forced himself to look. The landing was empty. Trembling he eased down the stairs, expecting a hand on his shoulder. The sheer screaming of his thirst got him to continue. He turned the lights on in the kitchen. A gallon of ice cold water he promised. Opening the fridge, the cat's head was grinning at him. A shriek made him worse and then he realized it was he who was making the woeful sound. Thirst forgotten, he fled back upstairs and bolted the door of his room.

Morning came, slow and heavy. A pack of cigarettes had brought his thirst to manic proportions. A scalding shower helped, and he drank from the bathroom tap. The shake in his hands made shaving a near massacre. Dressed in civvies he made his way tentatively to the kitchen. All was bustle and activity. Mrs. Fleming said,

"Tis yourself."

"Sort of," he thought.

A couple of altar boys were throwing toast, Sister Ben was shining the taps, and Mrs. Fleming moved back and forth from the fridge with ease.

"Nothing for me," he said, "just coffee . . . and black . . . no milk."

"But it's all ready, Father."

"What did I say . . . does everyone have a contrary opinion?"

"Oh well, please yourself. I'll leave it for the cats."

His stomach lurched.

"Hurry up with the coffee."

The Church bell rang and then the visitors. Mrs. Fleming went, muttering darkly about the starving millions in India. Morgan made a full mug of coffee. Toast sailed past his ear.

"Get out, for the love of God," he roared. The altar boys fled.

"Sister Ben . . . did you use the fridge this morning?"

"Is there something missing, Father?"

"Jaysus . . . sorry . . . sorry, could you just answer yes or no?"

"What's missing?"

He made a manic run for the fridge. Sister Ben shouted in alarm. Flinging open the door, he steeled himself. Nothing out of the ordinary. Just fridge things. He didn't know whether to laugh or cry. Mrs. Fleming returned.

"A visitor for you, Father."

"Who is it?"

"Oh, I don't think it's my place to ask."

Gulping down half the coffee, he considered putting her head in the fridge. A wino was waiting at reception.

Tall, over 6'2", he had a huge mop of white hair, black ragged beard, and sunglasses with red frames. A heavy grey overcoat came to his knees. The wino's tan covered large hands and his face.

"I'm Walter," he said, and offered his hand.

Morgan shook it.

"Bit early to be looking for money, isn't it?"

"I beg your pardon, vicar, I'm no beggar . . . ask for nothing from no man. None asked, none given, harsh but equitable."

"I'm a priest, this is a Catholic church, the other crowd are across the common."

"Are you sure? A policeman gave me directions. I've no idea how he jumped to a papist conclusion."

"Well, good day to you then, sir."

"A moment, priest . . . I've been toying with conversion. Anyway, I'm new to this borough and I like to present my credentials with the relevant authorities. Am I too late for breakfast penance?"

Morgan laughed. Something he thought he'd never do again. He took Walter through to the kitchen and instructed a sulking Mrs. Fleming to feed him. As he left, Walter said,

"I can see you're fond of a drop yourself. I'm definitely converting."

Morgan said a shaky mass and noticed a large crowd. Word of yesterday's events was circuited widely. As he took the wine from the altar boys he saw them exchange a knowing look. "God," he thought, "I'll be known as the dipso priest."

Sera was waiting in the small office. She wore a short black skirt, black blouse and black stockings. It made her hair shine like brilliantine.

"I'm all yours," she said.

Passion again engulfed him. He outlined the work and added,

"I've some personal letters later."

She crossed her legs and the sound the nylon was like a bomb.

"Your personals will receive my full attention."

Unable to reply, he excused himself. Fresh air, he reckoned . . . and a drink, but that would have to wait. A killer, but vital. As he turned the corner outside, he nigh collided with Kate Delaney.

"You macho brute," she said, and laughed.

"Sorry . . . sorry, I didn't expect to find you creeping round here. What do you want?"

"A small favour."

"What is it?"

"There's a drinks pity party this evening to launch a new charity and the sight of a priest will boost the funds."

"To go with you . . . is it?"

"Would that be so horrible?"

"Well, all righty. I will."

***

They sat on a church stone seat. Weak September light gave an impression of warmth. He resolved not to tell her about last night. Any sane person would ask had he been drinking. She'd think he'd had the D.T.s. A moment later, he told her the lot.

"And had you been drinking?"

"A bit."

"Sounds like the D.T.s"

Before he could reply, Sera appeared carrying a sheaf of papers. She looked brazen at Kate, to him she said,

"I'll need your signature, Father."

Kate smiled.

"Do introduce us, MORGAN."

He did.

A loaded tension settled. He felt as if he was six years old and couldn't think of a further word. The parishioner who'd watched him wrestle the Cross came by.

"Double dating, is it, Father? . . . Yah saucy rascal."

Sera told him she'd wait inside. He watched her walk with renewed feelings of guilt and lust.

"Watch out for her, Morgan."

"I beg your pardon?"

"As they say in Southeast London, 'she'll be 'aving you, that one.'"

"Don't be ridiculous, I'm a priest."

"And it must be said, a pretty naïve one. I'll pick you up at 7. Meanwhile, do keep it in your pants."

Flabbergasted, he watched her leave. What had happened to the world? In his youth, you'd never dare talk like that to a priest. Never . . . never were sex and the clergy linked, at least never verbally. An old word surfaced and he uttered it with grim satisfaction,

"Hussy."

Thing was, he wasn't altogether clear as to which of the women it applied. A blast of fatigue hit him and he resolved on a few hours kip that afternoon.

Once, reading Saul Alinsky, he'd underlined a line which he hadn't comprehended. It read,

"He who fears corruption fears life."

Where on earth this left him now was up for grabs.

He looked onto the vestry. An altar boy had a bottle of wine and was clugging like an old hand.

"Yah pup, yah," roared Morgan.

The boy fled, droppin' the wine. Morgan managed a brief, powerful kick to the boy's behind and heard him howl. Morgan said,

"I'll skin yah alive if I catch yah at that again."

The boy turned, defiance writ large on his face.

"My dad says you're an oul souse!"

It stopped Morgan cold . . . souse! . . . Where they find them.

***

Round three, he could postpone a nap no longer. Entering his room, his heart lurched anew, a body was outlined beneath the blankets.

"God in Heaven, what now?" he asked.

Tiptoeing over, he grabbed the top blanket and pulled. Walter leapt up, startled, and then leapt at Morgan. They wrestled for a furious moment before recognition lit the wino's eyes.

"The priest."

"Get off me . . . you reprobate . . . who the hell were you expecting?"

"Be fair, mate . . . I thought it was the old bill . . . the coppers, you know . . . the filth."

"You're wearing my pyjamas . . . how dare you."

"But don't you Catholics share all?"

"Not bloody likely."

"What about the Francis guy?"

"A Franciscan . . . a queer set of semi-hippies at the best of times."

"Are you going to call the rozzers?"

"Who?"

"The police, don't you speak any modern English or is it all Latin . . . eh?"

"Clear off before I do something drastic."

"I have a confession to make."

"Yea, well, Saturdays, from 9 to 12."

"I used your toothbrush."

Walter gathered his belongings and humming "Ave Maria" he left . . . in the pyjamas.

Morgan was too tired to clean up or change the sheets. He lay on the tousled bed and slept immediately.

In his dreams, Sera came and made sensual love to him. She brought him to a peak of passionate climax that hurled him gasping to consciousness.

"Good Lord," he gasped.

He lit a cigarette and the irony of this escaped him. How to face her. Surely his face would betray the contents of his dreams. A vague trace of perfume lingered in the room. Unless he was mistaken, it was patchouli oil. It hardly belonged to Walter. At the seminary, in the late '60s, the fragrance was associated with the hippies. It always appealed to him.

"Ary, I dunno what to think," he said.

A hot shower and shave banished all analysis. He selected a grey suit and just a hint of the dog collar. The look was sufficiently priestly without being pious. Just the thing for a charity event. Get their money with subliminals. Nothing pushy, but effective. He whistled a bar of "Ave Maria."

He remembered a passage from his reading. It went,

> Q: Why have you come my son?
> A: To seek truth
> To seek salvation
> But mainly to have a good laugh.

A copy of *Ulysses* was quarter read. Someday, he'd give it his full attention. The profile of Joyce he knew best was

> "Only a Catholic
> Irishman, loaded with daring
> And cunning
> And soaked in the liturgy
> Of the Church
> Could produce the incredible
> Mixture
> That is *Ulysses*."

Kate was waiting in the car, the engine of the Rover quietly humming. She was wearing a tan suit with a very short skirt. The skirt had risen very close to her hips. He didn't know where to look. She said,

"I finally identified it."

"What . . . whatever happened to hello?"

"That, too . . . when I met your little friend Sera. I knew I recognised something."

"So . . . is it a secret or do you want to tell me."

"Her scent, it's patchouli oil."

He fumbled for a cigarette.

"Please don't smoke in the car."

"Let me out so."

"Don't be childish, surely you can do without one for ten minutes."

He lit the cigarette. Kate opened the window. There wasn't a whole lot of further conversation on the journey.

On arrival she said,

"I do hope your behaviour will improve."

"Have you any children?"

"No."

"No wonder."

Her face looked slapped . . . and hard. He was too shaken to apologize. The expression on her face changed to one of indifference.

"Shall we go in, *Father.*"

They did.

For Morgan, the fund-raiser was not a success. The only beverage served was white wine and he drank far too much. Kate circulated widely and avoided him easily. Money was raised and spirits lowered. Morgan was cornered by a fervent man with a ponytail. In his thirties, he was very bald on top and he had the eyes of a zealot.

"You're the priest?"

"I am."

"I'm Jeff. Tell me about yourself."

"I don't think so."

"Are you a man of the people?"

"Well, I'm one of them."

"Semantics, verbal escapism."

Morgan looked a little more closely at him. What he'd have liked was to give the ponytail a good and hard yank. "Some more wine and I might," he thought.

Jeff persisted.

"Where do you stand on homosexuals?"

"Well clear."

"How facetious . . . do I detect a trace of an Irish accent?"

"You might."

"Would you like me to tell you the trouble with the Irish?"

"Listen, Jude, why you don't take a flying leap is what's the real trouble."

"It's Jeff, actually . . . I see you came with Kate . . . the old protective cover, eh! How would you like to slip off somewhere for the old mano el man."

To Morgan's astonishment, the guy winked. The wine was roaring in his head and he was a bit dizzy from the nicotine.

"Ary, fuck off," he said.

He headed for the door and ignored the polite greetings from various people. On the street, he looked in vain for a taxi. North of the river was about all he knew of his location. Bound to be a tube station and he trudged hopefully down the street. It was residential with front gardens. The lighting was poor and he began to fret. An urge to relieve himself built from deep within. Looking round furtively, he hopped energetically over a small gate. The garden had a large tree and he trotted over.

A low growl was the only warning before half a ton of Rottweiler attacked. It knocked him flat and then sunk its jaws in his thigh.

"Ah, Jesus, Mary and Joseph," he screamed.

Was it trying to sever his leg? He grabbed its huge head and with ferocity, sank his teeth into its neck. A howl of agony from the dog.

"How do you like it, you bastard?"

Releasing its grip, the animal backed away. A near-full insane Morgan roared,

"Want a piece of me, do you . . . you mangy cur, I'll tear the bloody bollocks off you, yah bloody mongrel."

Rising shakily to his feet, Morgan backed towards the fence. They watched each other warily . . . A truce understood. The priest looked down at his mangled thigh. A blast of pain near blacked him out. He was trying to light a cigarette when the Rover came by. Kate rolled down the window.

"Morgan, what on earth happened?"

"I was mugged."

"And the mugger tried to give you some sort of lethal blow job . . . better get you to the hospital."

Slumped in the front seat, he thought,

"I'm in a Rover and ten minutes ago I was nearly in a Rottweiler."

Hysteria blocked the agony.

Kate insisted on taking him to the hospital. An Irish nurse was on duty. She exclaimed, "By the holy, what sort of animal was at you at all, Father? Is nothing sacred?"

Morgan glared.

"Save me the leprechaun spiel, sister."

"And a mouth on him . . . we'll have to have a tetanus shot."

"What, all of us?"

"Aren't you the one . . . hold still . . . this won't hurt."

It did.

Kate drove him home. He felt bedraggled and old.

"I feel bedraggled and old, Kate."

"God knows, you look it."

At the Church, he got out then leant back in for a moment.

"Kate, what I said about the children, I didn't mean that."

"Yes, you did, but never mind, I like you anyway."

He watched her drive off and regretted the pain he'd caused. The ache in his thigh was throbbing. Some years before, he'd watched a young mother and her little boy. The boy was eating chocolate, he'd broke off a bit and said,

"Mummy, would you like a taste of my chocolate?"

The boy had then gazed as his mother ate the chocolate. A look of adoration twixt wonder. Morgan had felt then a sadness of infinity. Such tenderness he'd never experience. The same feeling swept him now. What he most longed to do was sit on the kerb and weep. To have someone put an arm round him and say,

"Like a piece of my chocolate?"

But as he wept, he wasn't altogether sure he'd ever stop.

"Do priests cry?" he asked. "Not in public," answered the dregs of the white wine.

Sera was sitting in the kitchen. A cup of tea sat beside a fruit plant and her papers.

"Bit late, isn't it?" he said.

"Oh, I'm nearly done. I just wanted to water the plant."

"What is it? . . . that fruit looks almost like strawberries."

"Yes, they do . . . don't they? Try one."

She broke off a piece and offered it to him. The fruit was a scarlet red, like her lips.

"Eve in the garden," he thought, but what he said was,

"Not right now, thanks, it's late. I'll be getting along."

"It's deceptive."

"I beg your pardon?"

"It looks sweet, luscious even, and you can't wait to sink your teeth in it . . . But it's tasteless."

A cold finger crept along his spine. Sera sank her even white teeth into the fruit and smiled.

"So few things are what they seem . . . are they, Father?"

Lust roared in his loins and the pain in his thigh only highlit that.

"Good night to you then."

He'd almost reached the door when he heard her whisper,

"You need not be bereft of chocolate or comfort . . . ever."

He kept going, perhaps he'd just imagined it.

"Yea, he muttered, "I'm highly wrought, that's all."

A bile taste in his mouth, he felt hairs in his teeth . . . using his fingers, he extracted the Rottweiler's strands.

"Ah, Jay-sus," he cried, "I've heard of the hair of the dog, but this is downright ridiculous."

The dreams again were Sera and sensual. He came to with a feeling of guilt and delight. Sunday, the day of rest, not if you were a priest. The face in the mirror would give winos a bad name. A night on the tiles, in fact he looked like he'd tried to eat them.

He hadn't prepared a sermon and reckoned he'd wing it. Who listened anyway? Could he remember a single sermon he'd ever heard? Not one . . . not even his own. Mrs. Fleming was busy with kitchen things, and he made a pot of strong black coffee. In last night's turmoil he'd forgotten to get cigarettes.

"Mrs. Fleming? You . . . you wouldn't know of any cigarettes hidden around?"

"I certainly would not . . . hmm, the very idea!"

References! . . . "yea," he promised . . . "I'm going to re-check those that Sera had provided." What he could recall had been excellent. Malachy had said to him once,

"Beware the person with a perfect past."

Mrs. Fleming began to sweep round him, then under his feet. It felt like McDonald's.

The lack of cigarettes frayed his nerves.

"For God's sake, will you let me have my coffee in peace."

"My, my . . . aren't we touchy this morning."

While he was at it he fumed,

"I'll check this biddy's references, too."

The Church was packed. As Morgan climbed the podium he recognized Kate,

Sera and Walter.

He began,

"Sin is like a Rottweiler, it fastens itself to your thigh . . . I mean soul. It leads us into dark gardens of the night. Yet the very heart of man yearns for a cigarette . . . sorry, for salvation."

The congregation shuffled nervously.

"We live in an age of AIDS and poll taxes. The cure for our afflictions lives in a bottle . . . I mean it doesn't live in a bottle."

Sweat ran along his forehead.

"Sex is the modern obsession. You cannot screw . . . I mean steal your way to salvation. He who lives by the dick . . . SWORD, shall die by the crowd . . . by the Sword."

Isolated bursts of laughter began.

"I tell you, he who laughs last didn't understand the joke. Is God the Tommy Cooper of today? To be switched off when we tire of his tricks. We are deceived by the appearance of things. What looks sweet and desirable is tasteless. Does God ask for references? When we despair, is He there with comfort and chocolate?"

People were muttering. A desperate Morgan knew he'd have to go Biblical. Snow them with the ring of authenticity. The less comprehensible, the more ominous.

"Verily I say to you . . . what is begun is begun. Jacob howled in the wilderness. The Lord God of Abraham smote the hordes of Babylon and the Citadel was built on sand. Hosannahs will be heard above the covenant and a mighty reckoning will occur. In vino veritas, secolo secularum. In Nomino Patre . . ."

The crowd tentatively took up the refrain. Morgan reckoned Millwall wouldn't spit on this lot of a Saturday afternoon.

He raced through the remainder of the mass and hoped the Bishop didn't get to hear of this. "A lack of nicotine, if only I'd got a few drags," he thought. In the vestry, he sent an altar boy for cigarettes.

"Hurry up," he said.

He wasn't facing that lot smokeless. No way.

Morgan locked himself away for the remainder of the day. He left the phone off the hook. Towards evening Mrs. Fleming came banging on the door.

"Go away," he said.

"I've left a tray here, you'll have to eat something."

"Clear off."

"Father Conor is back, he says he's coming up."

Conor was second in command. Just recently ordained, he had the gung-ho of the truly native. He looked like an Irish choirboy and hailed from the West of Ireland. Tall and stringy, he was wildly enthusiastic about everything. For the past month, he'd been on a course in "Urban Psychology." Morgan felt "Urban Terrorism" would have been more useful. It was said he had "the ear of the Bishop."

"Aye," thought Morgan, "and the heart of a snake."

Sure enough, a while later, he knocked and came in.

"Why did you knock?" asked Morgan.

"Oh, I think it's very important to knock before entering a room."

"But you came in anyway."

"Ah, Father Morgan, you're teasing me."

"Ary, catch yerself on, little girls get teased. I'm trying to get your attention."

"I hear you're not well."

"From your lips to the Bishop's ear."

"Isn't that to 'God's ear'?"

"Not in your case, laddybuck."

They eyed each other warily. Neither was keen on what he saw. Conor outlined the itinerary for the coming week and then came to the point.

"The Bishop will want a full report."

"And you're the one to do it."

"With your guidance, of course."

"Was there anything else, Conor?"

"The new secretary, Sera, she's a treasure. Well done!"

Morgan looked carefully at him. Was he winding him up?

"Are you winding me up?"

"Good Lord, no . . . I mean it . . . she knew Fr. Malachy."

"Yea, but before or after he died, that's what worries me."

Conor was taken aback. He'd never understood Morgan and knew only that the humour was never straightforward. This had to be a joke. So he laughed, albeit a trifle hollowly.

Morgan said,

"What's the joke, lad?"

"Am . . ."

"I dunno what ye find funny in the bogs of Mayo, but it's a different story here. Off with you now."

A confused Conor withdrew.

On a bus bound for Kennington, Mrs. Fleming was heading home. Thoughts of the roast in her bag kept her content. She "liberated" it from the Church and was well pleased. A priest greeted her heartily as he rose to leave the bus.

"Bless you, Ma'am."

It was a full five minutes before she realized who he was. Walter . . . the wino. In Fr. Morgan's best suit. A malicious smile began at the corner of her mouth.

***

The next week restored Morgan to near sanity. No incidents occurred in the Church, his dreams were quiet, and Sera worked with Conor. Kate rang once but he hadn't returned the call. He cut down on his cigarettes and the drink seemed less a necessity.

Morgan found himself whistling as he entered the Confessional for the Saturday morning session.

A list of petty sins nigh lulled him to sleep. He distributed light penance to all and word spread that a good deal was going and parishioners flocked for the cut-rate penance. Just before one, the door opened on the penitent's side and he slid back the grille.

"Bless me, Father, for I have sinned."

A woman's voice, but not familiar.

"How long since your last confession?"

"A very long time."

"God will forgive you, my child."

A chuckle from the darkness. A deep, almost masculine tone. The hairs at the base of his neck tingled. Then the woman's voice.

"I've been having sex with a man."

"In marriage, my child, that's perfectly normal."

"I'm not married."

"Well . . . have you plans to be wed later?"

"He's already married."

"I see."

"To the Church."

A wave of patchouli oil blasted through the grille. The deeper voice said, "And will his God forgive him? Answer me, priest . . ."

He was too stricken to look towards the voice. The penitent's door opened and the woman said,

"See you later, lover boy."

Morgan was hyperventilating . . . he pushed open the door and staggered out. Blindly he groped his way along to the open air. He heard two old ladies whispering, "He's drunk again . . . absolutely legless."

Trying to gather his senses, he gulped in huge breaths of air. A parishioner approached.

"Fr. Morgan, I just want to say what a fine man that new priest is."

"Well, Fr. Conor is a West of Ireland man, something in the water breeds fine clergy."

"And," he thought, "even finer madness."

"No . . . not the young whippersnapper, the more mature man . . . Wally . . . no, Walter . . . Fr. Walter."

"WALTER!"

"The very man, he has the common touch . . . and compassion . . . it pours from him. We might all take a page out of his book."

"I'll take more than that . . . I'll have a piece of his hide."

PRIEST, PART II
DEMONS

Morgan invited Kate to dinner. He felt woesome about his crack on her childlessness. He was going to feel worse.

Mrs. Fleming was approached for the meal preparation. She said,

"And is that all you think I have to do, prepare special meals for floosies?"

"Floosie? She's a respectable woman."

"Is she married?"

"Am . . . I'm not sure."

"Hah . . . I thought so!"

Morgan was seething. Not easy when you need a favour from the seethe dispenser.

"Forget it, Fleming . . . I'll make other arrangements."

"Suit yerself."

Sister Ben was next approached. A litre bottle of Lourdes Holy Water was all it took. He suggested something simple and she said,

"Rely on me, Father. I put the 'C' in clerical culinary."

He decided not to investigate that. Some statements are best left alone. A functions room at the back of the Church he thought would do nicely. Looking at the room, he said,

"This will do nicely."

When he invited Kate, she sounded surprised and pleased. She asked who was cooking.

"One of the sisters," he said.

"In the feminist or religious use?"

"Now, Kate, don't start. I'm trying to be nice."

"Some people are nice without trying."

"Yer fairly trying yerself . . . are you going to come or what?"

"Well, Morgan, I'll show up, whether I come or not is the great magazine debate."

It took a moment to sink in for him. His cheeks burned.

"I'm a priest," he gasped.

"Let's all attempt to bear that in mind," and she hung up.

***

Irish stew. Sister Ben had made enough for a small country.

"Would ye like consommé to start?" she asked.

"Con-fusion is more like," said a disappointed Morgan. He'd hoped for some dish he couldn't pronounce. Still, he was grateful it wasn't bacon and cabbage. Sister Ben gave him a run through where the various pots were simmering, and the fridge with red jelly in bowls. He gave her a small medal and said,

"There's a plenary indulgence attached."

"Can I return it if I'm not fully satisfied?"

"Sister, I'm not sure it's a matter for jocularity."

"I'd have preferred money."

"And what, tell me, would a nun do with money?"

"Buy lotto cards."

"That's gambling."

"It's popular, Father, that's what it is. Sister Mary won big . . ."

"Away with you, Sister, I won't listen to such worldliness."

Sister Ben stared at him. Rebellion etched her fine features. What she said, she said in Spanish,

"Vaya con dios."

Morgan, whose English was suspect, was suspicious even of Latin. His bread and butter so to speak.

"What's that?" he roared.

"'Tis Spanish."

"Hmmph, well, if you read anything besides *Woman's Own*, you'd know Dominick Dunne described it as the language of maids."

Sister Ben muttered and left.

Kate arrived with a bottle of scotch and two bottles of wine. She was dressed in a pale blue suit, the skirt was to her knees. Morgan felt relief and regret. She said,

"I was going to bring flowers but you'd go all mawkish, I think."

"Scotch is good. Will I pour?"

"As if you meant it."

The dinner table impressed her . . . and the smell of stew was comforting. After the soup, Morgan ladled mountains of stew on their plates. They ate in silence and drank the wine.

"More?" he asked.

"No . . . wow, that stew was delicious. Who made it?"

"I did," said Morgan.

"Well, it was excellent, I didn't think priests cooked."

"It's a long tradition, you never know when the culinary call might be needed."

She smiled. Morgan poured more wine and asked,

"Jelly?"

"I beg your pardon?"

"For dessert, there's red jelly."

"I'm sure there is but is it on myself or does it sound slightly suggestive."

They skipped the jelly. He made coffee and slipped a shot of scotch into the cups. If she noticed, she kept it to herself.

Kate was silent for a long time, then she began,

"I was married . . . Martin died three years ago and there isn't a day I don't miss him. He was an alcoholic and a nicer person even drunk than most are sober."

"Was it his heart?"

"No, it was suicide."

Morgan was horrified. Words of comfort wouldn't give themselves.

She continued,

"One bleak day, he obviously lost the battle with his demons and carbon monoxided himself in the garage. Not the Rover, his own one . . . a Datsun. Naturally, if you're going to commit hari-kiri, use a Japanese car."

"I'm so sorry."

She seemed not to hear him. Her look was far and far away.

"Is he damned forever then?"

Morgan didn't know so he said,

"I dunno, I think there's a special compassionate part of Heaven for such desperation. You used the word 'demons.'"

"What would you use?"

"Did he describe them?"

"Morgan, they don't come with identikits. The nature of them is their non-descriptiveness. If you could name them, mebbe you could fight back."

Morgan fetched the scotch. He was leaning over Kate to pour into her cup. The door opened. Sera stood there, the light behind her lit her hair like a halo. She said,

"Well, isn't this cosy?"

Morgan shot up . . . fumbled . . . and dropped the scotch.

"Ah, Jay-sus," he said, as the golden liquid spread across the floor.

"Join us," ventured Kate. Sera tossed her head, saying,

"Three's a crowd, I don't think the priest is yet ready for the *ménage a trois*."

Departing, she nigh took the door off its hinges.

"What on earth," gasped Morgan.

"That . . . is a woman scorned."

"Surely you don't think . . . I mean, you don't think she thought. Oh, God."

Kate smiled and said,

"A murderess is only an ordinary woman in a temper . . . and that, Morgan, is no ordinary woman."

Morgan began to clear up. Rattled by Sera, he resolved like Scarlett O'Hara to think about it tomorrow. Kate said it was late and she'd better get moving. He agreed and walked her to her car.

The Rover was parked at the rear. They found the tyres slashed and red paint had been lashed across the windscreen. They both hoped it was paint. They went inside for Morgan to call a taxi. Kate was pale. He made her a coffee and poured the remaining scotch into it. The dregs of the wine gave him some semblance of a drink, too. She said,

"Let's not even hazard a guess as to what happened. We can speculate tomorrow. Right now, I have to go home alone."

"Tell me about Martin."

"I found with him what it means to truly love. I put everything about him before my own wants and needs. I wanted to please him more than I wanted him to please me. For as long as I loved for myself, I felt frustrated loving him, for his loving me set me free. Do you understand?"

"No."

"Before Martin, I prided myself on my sensitivity. In fact, I was a touchy little bitch. I only knew what hurt me. Through him I learned that sensitivity is knowing what hurts others . . . so . . . gimme another shot of that lethal coffee."

Morgan had to raid the church supplies to find drink. A bottle of Napoleon Brandy was kept for the Bishop's visits. He took it. Two dynamite coffees were made. He said,

"Here's to the Bishop."

"May all his children be baptised."

"Jeez, Kate, keep your voice down. I'd better call you a taxi . . . to Streatham, is it?"

"That's home."

"Is it a safe area?"

"Well, Morgan, I dunno about safe, but the pitbulls travel in pairs."

He laughed and rang the taxi. Kate said,

"Gimme another of those suckers and I'll skip home."

"Aw, I think you've had enough, Kate."

A tad unsteady, Kate allowed him to guide her outside for the taxi. The driver got out to help her. He looked at Morgan, one eyebrow raised.

"Plied her with drinks, did you, Vicar?"

"I beg your pardon."

The driver smiled. "You know what they say, Vic, a bird in the hand is worth two in Shepherd's Bush."

"What are you suggesting? I have the number of your vehicle, I'll have you know."

The driver shrugged. As he put the car in gear, he rolled down the window and said,

"I have *your* number, Vic . . . yah randy old git . . . the *News of the World* pays for stories about the likes of you . . . give us a shout for the Christening."

With a squeal of tyres, he roared into the night. Morgan said,

"A black Protestant."

As Morgan re-entered the Church, he heard a loud voice.

"Great God, I would rather be a pagan suckled in a creed outworn so might I have glimpses that would make me less forlorn, have sight of Proteus rising from the sea or hear old Triton blow His wretched horn."

Walter was striding up and down the function room, slugging from the brandy.

"Walter! . . . what the hell are you doing?"

"Wordsworth, I'm quoting the lyrical poet himself."

"That's the Bishop's brandy."

"Ah render unto Caesar those things that belong to Caesar."

Morgan grabbed the bottle, saying,

"Sit down. I want a word with you."

Walter was dressed in blue dungarees and a fisherman's smock. Brand-new work boots peeped from below the pants. Heavy gel was keeping his hair straight back. He sat and Morgan said,

"What's your game? You've been masquerading as a priest . . . do you think this church is your house?"

Walter sighed and spoke as you would to a particularly dense child,

"Morgan, Morgan, Morgan . . . this is God's House and it's time you learned that. Is it not true that you are the one masquerading as a priest?"

"I don't believe this . . . are you stone mad?"

Walter hopped up and before an astonished Morgan, poured two large brandies.

"Join me in the fruit of the nectar."

He knocked back the brandy, clenched his teeth and went,

"Ar . . . ar . . . gh."

Then he examined the remnants of the meal.

"Was it the Gaelic dish? . . . any left or did you villains scoff the lot? I saw jelly in the fridge. My, oh my . . . I do love a sliver of jelly."

Morgan said,

"Looks like you put it in your hair . . . I'm going to ring the police for you, me lad."

Walter put up his hand.

"HALT . . . let me share my wisdom with you. Never mind you didn't share the stew. I bear you no malice. Are you conversant with Ralph Waldo Emerson?"

Morgan was lost, he didn't know how to rid himself of the man. He drank and said,

"Not recently."

"A facetious answer but I'll plough on," the man said. "There are three wants which can never be satisfied. That of the rich, who want something more. That of the sick, who want something different, and that of the traveler, who says, 'Anywhere but here.' What say you to that, Father?"

"I identify with the traveler."

"I wish to put myself forward as caretaker to this Church. I am both plumber and scholar."

Morgan felt he'd never be rid of him . . . if he was employed here, at least Morgan could keep some control. He said,

"I'll consider it, but you better behave yourself."

"You don't believe I'm a scholar, do you? I'm particularly a fait with Greek mythology. Have you heard of Ares, the God of Warfare?"

"Enough for one night, Walter. You can begin by locking up. I'm for the leaba."

"La . . . bah?"

"Leaba, it's Irish for bed. Goodnight to you."

"Morgan . . . reverse it, use your mind."

A weary Morgan climbed between the sheets . . .

"Reverse what," he thought.

Just before sleep overcame him, he thought and dismissed it,

SERA
   ARES

Malachy made a guest appearance in his dreams. He carried a slim volume of Longfellow's poems. Next to money, he'd liked few things with such intensity as this poetry. Malachy opened the book and read,

> "Such songs have power to quiet
> The restless pulse of care
> And come
> Like the BENEDICTION
> That follows
> After prayer."

As in all dreams, events were jangled and confused. Malachy was dressed in Walter's dungarees and spoke like the Bishop. Sera appeared and screamed at Malachy,
"What warehouse of the soul awaits you now?"
Morgan felt his shoulder grabbed and came awake to find Conor at his bedside. He said,
"Good God, Morgan, you were wailing like the Banshee . . . you woke the whole parish."
"Jaysus . . . where am I? . . . I'd a nightmare that Tobe Hooper would be afraid to film."
"Who?"
"Tobe Hooper . . . *The Texas Chainsaw Massacre* . . . do you know anything? . . . yah ignoramus. I suppose the bloody Bishop will hear of this."
A highly offended Conor shot back as he departed,
"At the volume you were roaring, I'd say he's already heard."
Morgan spent the day on conscious low profile. His face said, "Not available and that means you." A purposeful stride suggested industry and kept him moving. Late in the afternoon he took a stroll in the gardens.
Walter, in bright green overalls, was berating a middle-aged parishioner. The man, a shopkeeper, was a heavy contributor to church funds. Walter was saying,
"Listen, mate, the last time you got it up, the bow and arrow was a secret weapon."
On Morgan's arrival, the man beat a hasty retreat.
"Walter, what on earth were you saying to that poor devil . . . Good grief, what are you wearing?"
The overalls had stenciled in big black letters,

OFFICIAL CARETAKER, T. P.
Removals done at Competitive Rates.

"My uniform. You have to let people know what's what . . . Joe Public respects the uniform."
"What does the T.P. stand for?"
"I should have thought that obvious to a man of your hearing, Reverend. It's

'Trainee Priest'."

"You're testing me to the limit, bobo. Keep it up, and you'll rue the day you were born. What do you think this is, an employment incentive scheme? This is a bloody Church."

Walter tut-tutted.

"Tut-tut . . . less of the obscenities, your Worship . . . I have a query of ecclesiastical significance."

"Out with it."

"Who's Harold?"

"Harold?"

"Yea . . . I've been wrestling with the prayers your crowd use. One goes, 'Our father Harold is yer name . . .'"

Morgan took a deep breath.

"Get outa my sight, you lud-ri-mawn."

"I'm history . . . "

This was said in wise-ass American and would have guaranteed a shoe in the arse if he'd been moving any slower.

The late post brought a Thank You card from Kate. She quoted Margaret MacDonald,

> "To dream what one dreams is neither wise
> Nor foolish, successful nor unsuccessful
> No precautions can be taken
> Against it, except perhaps
> That of remaining
> Permanently awake."
>   XXX Kate

He stood and read the card a number of times. Then he said,

"If I understood this, I'd probably be greatly disturbed."

Then he tore it and dropped it in the waste paper basket. A little later, Sera retrieved the pieces and went in search of Sellotape. A grim smile touched her mouth but never reached her eyes.

Morgan met Sister Ben near the altar, she was polishing the brass rails and whistling, "Love Story."

"How's it going, Ben?"

"Your ladyship rang twice but I couldn't find you."

"Not to worry, I got her card."

Sister Ben stood, hands on her plump hips.

"She told me, Father Morgan cooks great stew."

"Am . . . oh dear, a slight misunderstanding."

"Mrs. Fleming will love to hear you're now a cook."

"Sister Ben . . . I trust you'll keep this under your . . . cowl."

"With my plenary indulgences, I suppose."

Morgan knew defeat . . . he reached for his wallet.

"And how much are those lotto cards?"

"Well, if you buy ten at one pound a time, you're bound to win. That's how Sister Mary scored big."

***

Another week of calm followed, Morgan again believed "All was well" and life had returned to dull routine. Was he ever in love with dullness now. Monday morning, the phone rang. The Bishop's secretary, he was to meet His Eminence at two that afternoon. Morgan asked,

"Is anything wrong?"

"No . . . no, just an informal chat."

Very bad, that was prelude to execution. He knew he was for the high jump. Conor . . . get hold of him.

Conor was instructing trainee/altar boys. They had the surly look so essential to urban life.

"Conor. A moment of your time . . ."

"Can it wait?"

"No, it can't, do you think I'd ask you now if it could wait . . . do you?"

The altar boys were delighted. The priests went to the kitchen. Morgan began to look for cups. He asked,

"Coffee?"

"Is there any de-caff?"

"For God's sake, man, have something real in yer life . . . jaysus . . . de-caff . . . Plu-eeze."

He made the strongest brew he could. Then ladled sugar on top. Conor grimaced on tasting it. Morgan began,

"The Bishop wants to see me . . . any clues you might provide?"

"I can't help you there, alas."

"I tell you, Conor, he's a vicious bastard."

"Morgan, one, that's a sin."

"Cop on to yerself. I think it was H. L. Mencken who said,

> 'It's a sin to believe evil
> of others, it is seldom
> a mistake.'"

"You're fond of the quotations."

"As long as the Bishop doesn't know I'm fonder of the drink."

"I'd better attend to the education of the altar boys."

"Do that, Conor. Here's another quotation for you . . . from the oul man himself."

"You mean the devil?"

"No, George Bernard Shaw, but he'd have been flattered at the comparison. He said, 'Education in the ways of the world was a series of humiliations.' Good luck to yah."

***

The Bishop's residence was secluded from the street. Muggers weren't likely to make house calls in this area. Inside, a battalion of nuns were polishing as if their lives depended on it. Fr. Coleman, the Bishop's secretary, kept Morgan waiting for half an hour. He looked round, not an ashtray to be seen. Just a sea of black shining nuns. He decided to risk a cigarette. The first drag was as sweet as temptation. Fr. Coleman glided over.

"Please don't smoke here."

"Where will I put it?"

"I'm sure I've no idea . . . please don't use the floor . . . it's being polished."

"Oh . . . I thought them nuns was searching for money."

The summons came. Behind a massive, black mahogany desk sat the Bishop. In his fifties, he was bald and spotless. Hooded eyes overlooked a grim mouth. If anything had ever amused him, he'd managed to put it behind him. The desk was bare save for one lone file. Nothing was said for a few minutes. Finally, he said,

"You're a smoker, Morgan."

To Morgan, it sounded like "joker" and he replied,

"I like a bit of a laugh, sure enough."

"You'll find very little mirth here."

As Morgan watched him, he began to fully appreciate the meaning of PRIG. The Bishop had long bony fingers. One of these tapped the file. No chair was offered. He said,

"These . . . 'occurrences' . . . Any explanation to offer me?"

"I haven't a clue."

"I think you've forgotten something, Father."

"Like what?"

"RESPECT . . . there is a proper form of address to your Bishop. I'll thank you to use it. Now, who's this Kate person . . . and what is the nature of your relationship?"

"She's a journalist . . . and she's a friend."

The Bishop opened the file, extracted the Sellotaped card. Perusing it, his nostrils twitched as if smelling something very unpleasant.

"The tone of this would suggest otherwise."

Morgan felt a rage begin.

"That's private . . . the bloody cheek of you . . . yer Grace."

Uncertainty flicked across his Grace's face.

"There have also been stories of your drinking. All in all, I regret to say that we'll have to take steps to replace you."

"Steps . . . steps by God" and Morgan stepped forward. He snatched the card from the Bishop's hands, roaring,

"Gimme that."

"Control yourself, Father. This isn't helping your case."

Morgan took a deep breath, reached for a cigarette. The Bishop jumped up.

"There'll be no smoking in here."

The cigarette was slowly lit and followed by a loud exhalation of breath. Morgan said,

"You think you can fire me . . . you've treated me like dirt. You jumped-up guttersnipe, I know a few strokes you pulled when you were over at Kennington. You fire me and I'll give the newspaper such a story that you won't be allowed to serve mass. I'll say you arranged the incidents at the church to drum up attendance. Now, how so you like them potatoes, your Worshipful?"

The Bishop was dumbfounded . . . He sat back down and said,

"You wouldn't dare . . . no one would believe it."

"But they'd print it . . . you go after me, laddybuck, and I'll bring you down into the sewer with me. You're nothing but a thug in robes. Don't ever threaten me again . . . here, hold this."

Morgan put the half-smoked cigarette on the file and walked out. The secretary was hovering near the door.

"Get an earful, did you . . . yah, Judas, if I ever see you near my parish, I'll break yer friggin' neck . . . now get out of my way."

The secretary jumped back and the nuns had stopped their shining. Pausing at the door, Morgan turned and said,

"Ladies, I bid ye adieu."

Giggles of delight rose from them as the secretary rushed to the Bishop. His eminence was caught having a fitful pull of the cigarette.

"Shut the door, you imbecile!"

The nuns hadn't felt such excitement since Sister Mary had the big win. This was almost as rewarding.

**

That evening Morgan had two stiff belts of Jameson. He had asked Sera to meet him when she'd finished her work. All he knew was he was getting rid of her. No evidence of wrongdoing existed, but he knew with certainty she was malevolence. A hammering in his heart he called nicotine. He could be afraid of her . . . could he?

A slip of a girl . . .

A light tap on the door.

"Come in," he said.

Sera was again in black. A dress above the knee and black tights. The blonde hair shone like expectation. He tried to remember what it was the Buddhists said on that . . .

> "Expectation
> Is one of the great sources
> Of suffering."

She never made any noise, he realised. As if she glided. Passion tried to rise in him again, but he was determined to suppress it. A slight smile hovered as always on her lips.

"Sit down, please. Would you like a drink?"

The rustle of nylon as she crossed her legs.

"I'd like whatever you have, Father."

He got another glass and poured her an Irish measure, i.e. generous. He started,

"I've no complaints about your work, and of course, I'll give you great references, but . . . you don't belong here . . . you'll get severance pay, of course."

Sera raised her glass, ran her tongue along the rim . . . and sipped.

"Strong," she said.

He didn't know if she meant the drink, what he'd said . . . or worse, him. He said lamely,

"I know it's a shock, but really, a nice lady like yerself, you don't want to waste yer life around a bunch of middle-aged clerics. There's a good girl, finish up yer drink, and I'll see you out."

He took a hefty swig of his drink. All in all, he felt it had gone quite well.

Much better really than he'd reckoned. Firmness, he thought . . . that's the key . . . but fair, too.

Sera's smile didn't change. A wave of patchouli oil slowly reached him. She said,

"I'm pregnant."

"You're what . . . !"

"With child."

"Do I know the father?"

"But of course . . . you're the father, Father."

Her eyes burned, the smile now spread more as a grimace. Morgan's head reeled, he said,

"Sure what nonsense is this, girl . . . I think you need some serious help."

"Treachery, thy name is man . . . you took your pleasure, priest, now is the time to take your name."

"Ah, for the love of God, come on . . . clear out of here . . . you're stone mad."

He reached out his hand to take her. Sera grabbed the hand and sunk her teeth into the fleshy part of the palm and chomped down. Visions of pit bulls danced before him and the pain shot to his brain.

"Ah, Jaysus," he gasped, and swung his other hand in a side arc. The blow slammed against the side of her head and knocked her to the floor. The bite had gone almost clean through. She sprang to her knees and spat.

"Priest . . . you belong to me . . . the Jezebel shall not seduce you from me . . . The Whore of Babylon will not be triumphant."

A string of obscenities, mixed with Latin, followed, the likes of which he'd never heard.

The door opened and Conor stood there. Walter followed behind in black overalls. Conor said,

"What in the name of God . . ."

Sera sprang at Morgan and tore her fingers down his face, missing his left eye by a fraction. The man grabbed her and tried to hold her. She broke free and ran to the door . . . turning, she said,

"And a fearful vengeance shall be visited upon ye all."

And she fled.

Three deep gouges were imprinted on the left side of Morgan's face. He said to Conor,

"Call a taxi. I'd better get to the hospital."

Walter said, " If that's the result of chastity, I may have to re-examine my options. Does this go on at The Church of England?"

At the hospital, the same Irish nurse was in attendance. She said,

"By the hokey, you have some effect on women, Father."

"Stay out of my face," he said.

"'Tis a bit late for that, by the looks of you . . . what you do at weekends I can't even begin to imagine."

Conor, still in shock, laid his arm on Morgan's shoulder. He said,

"In all me born days, I never saw such ferocity. That woman was like a demon."

Morgan groaned.

A fragile feeling clung to him over the next few days. Nothing was heard of Sera, but he lived in dread of an appearance. Conor said only,

"I know how much you like quotations, so maybe Leo F. Buscaglia is appropriate."

Morgan had never heard of him.

"I never heard of him. What had he to say for himself?"

"That when we cling to pain, we end up punishing ourselves."

"Oh, very deep, Conor . . . stick to limericks, they're more your line."

He rang Kate, and she arrived with a bottle of bourbon.

"Let's go American," she said.

"You betcha."

They talked about everything save Sera. The level of the bourbon sank. Kate asked if she might use the phone to call a cab.

"Use the one in the hall."

Morgan was feeling the drink, and as he reached to put the glass on the table, he staggered, knocking Kate's large handbag. It hit the floor and spilled open.

"Aw, shit," he said.

Getting down on his knees, he began to gather the various items. A small bottle caught his attention. The label read "Patchouli Oil."

"What? . . ."

He upturned the bag again and began to sift more carefully. A notebook. He flicked through. Halway along, the address of the coffee bar on the Strand. Where he'd first met Kate . . . and underneath was printed a name,

"Luigi d'Agostino."

"The bloody waiter . . . she already knew him!"

Another entry gave the date of Malachy's death. His mind was reeling . . . Click

. . . Click . . . Click, came the sound of her heels . . . he dived back to his chair, the contents rammed back into her bag. Messy, but what could he do . . . hope . . . a lot. Kate was smiling and asked,

"We've time for another bourbon?"

"Absolutely . . . look, Kate, I just need to go to my room for a second . . . help yourself."

As he left, she gave him a curious look. He bounded up the stairs, his heart in his mouth. The full impact of his discovery was nigh too much. A series of deep breaths didn't help.

A sound behind . . . Kate was at the door. She said,

"So you know, priest . . . don't you?"

"Why . . . what on earth for . . . Jaysus, I can't get a grasp of this."

Kate spoke, the voice from the confessional.

"The altar was easy . . . and true, the cat struggled . . . but your mother's beads were a tremendous help. A personal touch is so endearing. Kept it in the family. When Martin died, the Church, your fuckin' Church turned from him. Even in death, he was to be tormented. I thought I'd introduce the Church to some demons of their own. A suicide kills two people. I died with him. The church condemned us both."

"But Sera . . . what about her?"

Kate chuckled, it sounded like a straight line to the very nature of viciousness. She continued,

"Might one say, the luck of the devil, a pure coincidence. A trollop on heat. Your thinking was all below your waist. You petty dipso cleric. I spit on you from a height . . . and always. I'll be bear . . . to you."

Tossing her head, she gave a laugh like a shriek and turned back to the stairs. He ran after her and made a grab for her arm.

"Are you insane?" he shouted.

She pulled free and her heel caught on the top stair. The movement threw her body forward, and she crashed down . . . a horrendous cry as she fell. Morgan rushed down. Her neck was twisted to the side and her legs were broken beneath her body. He knelt and began to form the words of Benediction.

Her mouth moved.

"F . . . u . . . c . . . k you, priest . . . I'll be in your dreams . . . watch for me."

***

Over at the convent, celebrations were in full roar. Sister Ben had turned her final lotto card and screamed,

"Cripes . . . I've won . . . it's flaming torture . . . God forgive me cursing . . . yippee!"

Walter was on the other side. At the Church of England near Balham High Road. He was laying lavish praise on "The Book of Common Prayer" to a puzzled Vicar.

Conor was studying literature. He'd reckoned he'd found a gem in the following . . . from one of their own calling, too. A man of God . . . Thomas a Kempis. The quotation read:

> "We could enjoy much peace
> if we did not busy ourselves
> with what other people say and do,
> for this is no concern of ours."

"Even Morgan would appreciate that," he said.

ALL THE OLD SONGS AND NOTHING TO LOSE

BOOK I

"And all the old songs. And nothing to lose"
"The Emigrant Irish" by Eavan Boland.

"England's fucked!"

The thoughts burned neon in Danny's head. As the train moved off from Kennington, he watched the antics of two skinheads. They were sprawled across a range of seats and the train was crowded. Instead of chucking these two from the seats, people cowered away. In the English fashion, as if the two didn't exist. An Englishman's home might be his castle, he thought, but they'd given up all rights on the underground.

The skinheads couldn't have been more than 16 years old. But they were aged in bitterness. Nazi signs competed with the Union Jack in their display of tattoos. A series of grunts and obscenities dribbled from them. They'd keep.

At the oval, Danny had to fight to leave the train. A young black woman with a baby in a push-car cried,

"Excuse me . . . excuse me, I'm getting off." No one moved.

Danny grasped the end of the push-car and helped her on to the platform.

She gave him a frightened look.

"Such is London," he thought, "the Good Samaritan matches the police photo-fits." The Four Top's song, "Reach Out, I'll Be There," unraveled in his head.

He could go the distance so he said.

"The stairs are steep, why don't I help you."

She looked round, but no other offers were available.

"O.K.," she said.

They'd just gotten to the escalator when Danny was jostled and the skinheads raced past, a breath of badness lining their speed. One roared,

"Yo' nigger lover . . . give 'er a bit o' white, John . . . eh."

The girl appeared not to hear. You traveled on the Northern Line often enough, you developed a selective deafness. It was that or get a *walkman* . . . or a *magnum*.

Danny smiled.

"Do you like the four tops?"

"Who?"

"Motown, the hits machine . . ."

She looked blankly at him. He shrugged and said,

"Never no-mind."

The skinheads were baiting a guy who was attempting to sell *The Big Issue*.

"Geroff . . . buy *The Big Issue* . . . Yah prick . . . hey, gis a job man."

Danny walked straight to them, said,

"Excuse me?"

The skinheads, surprised, took a moment before the sneers set.

"Wotcha want, nigger-fooker?"

"I wonder if I could interest you chaps in some money." He hoped his plum accent would hold. They looked at each other.

"Yea, how much then?"

"A hundred pounds, how does that sound?"

"Each."

"Well . . . Oh dear, all right, a hundred each . . . you chaps drive a hard bargain." The two now leapt to suspicion.

"Hey, is this some gay-boy thing . . . you wanna play bumboys, is it . . . you get somefin' in your arse all right mate, yea, a fookin size 12 Doc Martin."

Loud guffaws engulfed them. Danny waited, he never expected this to be easy. Then he said,

"Good Lord, no, I'm doing a magazine on the youth of London. I'd like you two chaps on the cover."

"Yea' . . . wot's the magazine, then?"

"*Borough Life.*"

"Yea', well . . . when do you want to do it, then, like we got fings to do man."

Danny shot his hand out, he couldn't resist a leap out of them. His hand narrowly missed one of their faces.

"See St. Mark's Cathedral, over there? We'd like that as background. This evening at 7, where the benches are." Uneasiness passed between the, and before they could protest, he added a sweetener,

"I'll bring along a case of beer. You chaps aren't averse to a little drink, I hope."

"Yea' . . . get special brews."

"All right then, see you at 7."

As Danny walked briskly away, he felt a river of sweat cascade down his back. He muttered,

"Jesus."

The pain in his back hovered.

***

Danny . . . Danny Taylor was forty-six years old. He'd worked as a site foreman for the past fifteen. Two years ago, a fall had injured his back. An industrial tribunal had awarded him substantial damages, and he lived from that. The years on the sites had kept him fit, and his 5'10" height was free from flabbiness. Brown hair was graying fast. It didn't give him a distinguished look, it looked like brown hair graying. A slightly crooked nose gave a hard look to his face, and he didn't discourage it. Brown eyes with heavy laughter lines. Danny didn't believe laughter had much to do with them. His mouth was set mainly in a hard line but transformed completely when he smiled. A rare event.

Danny owned the ground floor of a house on Vassil Road. He kept it Spartan and functional. The sole luxury was music. One wall was lined with albums. He hadn't yet joined the C.D. revolution and felt a record belonged on a record player. Mainly, he just liked the feel of a disc and to handle the sleeve of a record. He made coffee and let the Moody Blues re-sing the seventies. A Scot on the building site said once,

"I came to London on a Sunday for a Moody Blues concert."

. . . And . . .

As "Knights in White Satin" kicked in, the face of Kathy tried for a foothold in his mind; he blanked it and sang.

"never reaching the end, just what the truth is, I can't say anymore"

He took down the metal aerosol container and checked the spray was loose and ready.

"Test time," he said.

In his small bathroom, he took a newly purchased sponge and set it in his bath. The sponge was shaped as a pink duck. Then he judged the distance . . .

"Get up close . . . O.K."

And he pressed the nozzle.

Later that evening, he dressed for the meeting. A worn faded track suit that, apart from being comfortable, gave him ease of movement. Dark trainers that gripped and weighed almost nothing. He put four cans of special brew in a hold-all, and then carefully laid the aerosol alongside. Taking a deep breath, he said aloud,

"Let's rock and roll."

After he left, a faint hiss still came from the bathroom. Shreds of the pink duck lay in the bath. Part of the enamel from the bath's side was fully dissolved as the last of the acid burned through. On the floor were the usual creams and cleansers. Nigh hidden among them was a full jar of Brylcreem, the old style formula. Glue like it sealed the hair when applied.

The end of March, and Danny had clocked up three events. He called them that as he refused to use the word, "Attack." Each event, he'd used the aerosol. A white chart hung in his bedroom, and in black script it read,

1. Two skinheads
2. One punk
3. Two teenage girls

The newspapers were slow to pick up the thread. But now they'd sensed a pattern, and the "events" got to page 2 on most of the tabloids. He hadn't made the quality papers yet, but he wasn't in any hurry. It was time for a new weapon, and he'd gone to High Street Kensington.

***

". . . we learnt more from a 3 minute record than we ever learnt at school."
Bruce Springsteen, "No Surrender"

As he strolled past Barkers, a line from Bruce Springsteen leapt in his mouth,

"We're casing the promised land."

You could night smell the money that lined the street. A young man asked him for "a few bob". Danny recognized the lilt of Dublin. Katie had the same accent. For her, maybe, he gave over a few pound coins. The man was astonished.
"Jaysus, thanks a lot."
"How do you like London?"
"Fuckin' brutal."
While perhaps not how Samuel Pepys would have put it . . . the accuracy couldn't be faulted.
Katie had introduced him to the poetry of Louis MacNeice, the lines from "Autumn Journal" about the Irish. Danny saw them lines as a sort of damning:

"they stagger round
the world
with a stutter and
a brogue
and a faggot of useless
memories."

A part return, he'd bullied her into listening to "All the Old Songs." When Darcy had come along, the little girl had lit his world with wonder. Once she said,
"Daddy, do you love me as much as songs?"
Whoa-hey.
Thoughts of Darcy hit his stomach like a poll tax. He forced a new feeling into place. Right here on Kensington High Street, Richie was driving and they'd stopped for a red light.

***

From nowhere a windscreen merchant appeared. Before you could protest, these guys had your windscreen covered in suds and then wiped it off. A spit and sod job. Richie rolled down the window.
"Hey . . . hey, you wanna ask or somefin' before you paste my screen with that gunge."
The guy smirked and said,
"Any contribution will help."
Danny leant over and said,
"Here's a contribution, learn some manners."

The guy turned his face and said,

"Who asked you, fuck face?"

Danny was out of the car, grabbed the guy's right arm and snapped it cleanly across his knee.

Richie gunned the engine and Danny piled into the back.

As they burned rubber, Richie asked,

"What the hell is wrong with you, Dan-yell, are you crazy? Jesus . . . what a thing to do, You broke that cat's arm."

"I wanted to break his legs, too."

"Chill out, Danny . . . Good grief, you're losing it, get a bloody grip."

Danny asked,

"What do you think of Philip Larking?"

"Yo . . . I dunno them National Hunt jockeys, I only follow the flat."

"You ignoramus, he's regarded as among Britain's finest poets."

"Hey, Danny, I'm a black man, remember. What I want to know about a white man's poems?"

A sulky silence settled as the car moved slow towards Marble Arch. Richie spoke.

"O.K. man . . . what we have to say, this Barking . . ."

"Larkin! He said that poetry was like trying to remember a tune you've forgotten."

"So, Daniel . . . are you writing poems, is this some confession, man?"

"Jeez, Ritchie, I dunno why I bother trying to talk to you. I'm showing you a piece of my soul here. My life feels like that . . . as if I'm trying to remember a tune that had all the right words, if I could just get the melody, I'd be all right."

"So, meanwhile, you break my arms, yea'? I dunno what that is man, but I don't think it's poetry."

And, indeed, theirs was an unlikely friendship. Five years before, Danny was managing a site in Croydon. One of the labourers called him,

"Dan . . . Danny, there's a darkie looking for a job, he's down in the office."

"Tell him we're not hiring."

"Jaysus . . . Danny, he's a big fooker, you tell him, you're the governor."

Big he certainly was. Over six foot and weighing in at about 15 stone. Not so much black as tinted.

Danny said,

"You're a big 'un."

"I'm not afraid of work, man, and I'm strong."

"Where were you before?"

The man looked around, then down at his feet and finally taking a deep breath said,

"I was in prison man, alright, and mos' like I go back there. But I met a woman, a real fox, and she on that straight and narrow. If I to keeps her, I gotta work. This kinda work, yea' man, I gotta be outa them doors . . . so man, I ain't askin' . . . I'm begging, and I ain't never, no sir, no time, ever begged in my life. But I got's to tell you, I only gonna beg once and this here is it."

Sweat had cruised down his face and he swiped at it.
Danny said,

"When can you start?"

And they took it from there.

***

Danny snapped out of his reverie. An American sports shop was next to Kensington Market. No sooner had he entered than an assistant was upon him. A lanky man in his twenties, he wore a Laker's T-shirt, baseball cap and aviator glasses. His American accent lapsed into Hackney at intervals.

"Yo, partner, and what can we do you for?"

"Excuse me?"

"Was there a particular item sir wanted to purchase?" Danny felt his teeth grit but resolved not to lose it; however, he had to know one thing.

"Firstly, I'm not your partner, O.K. . . . or your buddy, so let's drop the breezy tone. Secondly, are you American?" The man looked anxiously around. No help in sight. "I've spent a lotta time there, quality time."

"But you're not actually an American, so let's drop the phoney bit, eh. Now, I'd like to see a baseball bat . . . not metal or some new unbreakable plasticine. Just wood, can you do that?"

He could.

In no time, he brought back a long box and produced the required item. He then stood well away. Danny rested it in both hands and then took an easy, flowing swing. A quiet shoosh followed in the wake. The man said,

"State of the art, sir, and as a special promotion, we provide a Yankees cap in a colour of your choice." Danny stopped his swing.

"Do me a friggin favour, eh."

"You don't want the cap?"

"Just wrap the bat, alright."

As Dany left the shop, the radio in the shop kicked into life and Peter Sarstead came on,

"Where do you go to my lovely."

By the time Danny got to the tube, he hummed most of it and a gentle sadness lined his face. He gripped the bat tightly, like a prayer.

Back at his flat, he rang the largest of the tabloids and asked for the features editor. Finally a gruff voice came on,

"Baker here, what's the story?"

"Are you familiar with the L.V. attacks?"

"L.A., the riots, that's old news, fellah."

"L.V."

"What . . . what's that, luncheon vouchers or somefin', eh?"

"London Vigilante, do you want this story or not?"

"Oh, right . . . am, just let me get me a pen here. Now, your name is?"

"This is to tell you there'll be three more 'events' this month. The acid will be replaced by a new instrument."

"What . . . is this on the up and up? Are you the one . . . hey, I can make you famous fella, rich too . . ."

"Baker, is it . . . give it a rest, O.K. . . ."

"Look, fellah, you can trust me . . . really, I'll put this paper right behind you."

Danny laughed.

"Good grief, wot a horrible idea . . . all you need to know is that a small piece of London is being claimed back for ordinary people."

And he put the phone down.

His shirt was wet through from perspiration, he said aloud,

"Is that what I'm doing . . . is it, am I making a difference . . . am I?"

***

This event was to be the one in which he got stabbed. 'Event' was his father's word, and Danny wondered how he'd like the use to which it was put.

His recurring image of his father was scalded on his heart. The man leaping to his feet, struggling to pull his belt loose, roarin',

"I'm going to skin you alive."

Danny told people his father was a drinker.

He wasn't.

His nigh psychotic temper was simply – bad temper.

He liked to beat people, he loved to beat Danny. Time reaches out for all bullies. At 17, Danny's father pulled his belt loose and prepared to launch another event. Danny had moved straight to him, seized the belt and whispered,

"How would you like that wrapped round yer fuckin neck, you bastard."

"Ah son, it's been to make a man of ye . . . see, see now you're learning."

Danny had snapped the belt from his hand and flung it across the room.

***

If time brings forgiveness, then Danny reckoned the clock had a bit to go yet.

"Ya bastard," he muttered as he fitted the bat into a sports hold-all. He took the train to The Angel. A small park near the station was his target. As he waited for the train, he watched a small, aged oriental woman. She had the tiniest feet he'd ever seen, and they were shod in sparkling new white sneakers. Obviously fascinated by them, she made little jumps back and forth. He thought she'd probably been subjected to the binding of her feet as a child. Now she was relishing the freedom or . . .

"Or," he whispered, "maybe she just likes the fucking shoes."

The train came. A line of Flaubert burned in his head.

"I'm crammed with coffins, like an old cemetery."

March was nearing an end, and he could see a stretch in the evenings. Once, he'd have cared. Checking his watch, two minutes to seven, near mugging-hour. He sat in the small park and composed his victim's face. This was a mix of eagerness and a slightly lost look. It instantly had an effect as a middle-aged woman hurrying paused,

"Oh, you don't want to sit there, love, no, you don't want to do that."

"I'm waiting for someone."

"Well, my goodness, love, don't wait long. It's not safe here."

He wondered where was, and thanked her for her concern. Richie was expecting him at 10 for a drink. His woman had walked at Christmas and soon after, Richie did the same from his job. He was smoking a lot of dope.

"Nothing hard," he explained.

Danny liked the explanations for drugs these days.

"Designer" . . . or "Recreational." As if they were a nigh useful fashion accessory and definitely not hazardous. His favourite description was "soft drugs." Did they make you soft in the head, he wondered.

That too.

A nagging suspicion tugged at Danny that just maybe Richie was into dealing. He had to put this on the back burner. If such were so, didn't Richie qualify for an event? He shrugged it away.

Richie's most recent acquisition was "ICE." An amphetamine derivative that was popular in Japan. Just beginning to dent the market in Britain. According to the stories, it was used originally by the Kamikaze pilots. Danny thought that was a suitable metaphor all in itself, but as a selling point? Danny had asked him,

"So what does it do for you?"

"It makes you hyper tense, but like, you see with 100% perception. You don't eat, sleep. And it lingers for about three days."

Danny said,

"Bit like love, is it?"

In fact, the 'events' did much the same for Danny. Two youths, black and white, approached him. As if they materialized from the shadows. He hadn't seen them enter the park, and resolved to cut out these reveries . . . and muttered,

"Money-vampires. Predators from the pavement."

"Got the time, John?" they began.

And so did he.

Danny's daydreaming had nearly cost him his life. He never saw the third. Later, he'd ruefully parody T. S. Eliot,

"Who is the third
Who walks behind."

The knife went in on his left side, deep and ferocious.

***

He was never quite sure how he'd gotten away. The sound of the bat's swing and his own agonized grunts were the soundtrack. That and breaking bone.

A wedge of money persuaded the cab driver to take him to casualty, plus a mugging yarn.

They patched him up and he was sitting in reception after, waiting for a pain-killer prescription. A nurse stood over him.

"What happened to you, at all?"

Soft brogue.

He looked at her. Average height with dark, curly hair, blue eyes and a full mouth. Pretty in the Irish fashion. Her name tag read, N. Mulkerns.

"Is the 'N' for Nurse or Nosy?"

"Nora . . . what are you so touchy about?"

"Go away, Nora, peddle the Mother Theresa act down the wards."

She smiled and it transformed her. An average, pretty face came close to beauty. Not completely but in there.

"Aren't you the wicked one, you have a mighty fierce tongue on you."

He stood up and pain took a mighty wallop at him.

"Fuck," he said.

"What kind of language is that from a nice lookin' man? I'll get you a cup of tea, to sweeten your disposition."

She did.

"No bikkies, I'm afraid, economy cuts."

Danny took a swig of the tea, realized he was parched and drained it. A burning sensation like memories.

"Well now, you certainly enjoyed that."

Danny felt for his watch . . . gone in the event.

"What time is it?"

"Half past nine, I'm off duty at 10."

Danny looked closely at her, said,

"Why are you in my face, is this some follow up treatment or are you just trying to annoy the shit out of me, 'cos believe you me, you're succeeding."

She put her hand on her hip and replied,

"You think I'm a hussy, don't you, that I'm forward. But that's how things are today. It's a woman's prerogative to do the asking."

Danny reckoned she wasn't all in it.

"You're not all in it, are yah . . . O.K. let's go for a drink, just let me get my pills."

"In case you got lucky . . . is it . . . I'll get my coat."

Danny went to the phones and found the pub's number. After a delay, Richie came on the line.

"Richie, I can't make it."

"Who can, Daniel, but we have a little something to put pepper in the old pencil."

"What, is this drug humour, is that it?"

"Whoa, lighten up, Daniel . . . I'll see you tomorrow."

Nora was waiting. She'd put on a belted navy coat over her uniform. To Danny she looked like a policewoman, but he knew he was batting paranoid.

"So," she said.

"What?"

"Do you like my coat?"

"Are you serious, I don't know you five minutes, you ASK me do I like you're coat."

"It's not a difficult question."

"Look, I don't even know if I like you . . . do you want me to call a mini cab or wot?"

***

BOOK II

Nora had a car, a beat up mini in what was once bright red. She said,

"Don't look at it like that, it goes great, the appearance keeps it from being stolen."

"Promise me one thing . . . Nora, don't tell me it has a pet name and start outlining a history of loveable eccentricity. It's a car, and it goes? Right, let's go."

She drove fast but measured. Danny's wound throbbed and they stopped at a late open chemist. He had the prescription filled and got back into the car.

Nora smiled.

"I hope you didn't buy any of them condom things."

"Excuse me?"

"I never do it on a first date so you'll have jumped the gun . . . if you'll pardon my Freudian slip. Let's go to The Anchor. It's a quiet place."

They did.

They did.

The pub was near empty. They'd just sat down when the barman came over.

"Evening all. What's your poison?"

Nora ordered a medium sweet sherry and Danny asked for a double scotch. Nora said,

"No you won't . . . bring him a mineral water . . . you're not to mix alcohol with those pills."

Smirk from the barman. Nora said,

"Don't sulk, I'll treat you. What do I call you?"

"Danny."

"The pipes . . . the pipes are calling."

"That's very original . . . Nora, it's Nora, is it? I've never had that line before."

"That's my name. You say it like a caress, as if you were reciting a poem. I'd like you to drop the sarcasm though." The barman brought the drinks.

Nora said, "Sláunte."

Danny said nothing.

She took a sip of the sherry and said,

"If I'm not mistaken, Clapham . . . and the year . . . hmm . . . 92 . . . m . . . m. Are you married, Danny?"

"I was."

"Drove her away with your levity, did you?"

Danny drank the mineral water and knew he shouldn't reply.

All his instincts said to batten down.

"Well, Nora . . . interesting you should use the word 'drove.' My wife Katie . . . and our little girl, Darcy, were waiting for a bus at Camberwell Green. A joyrider ploughed into them. Cut Darcy in half . . . and she was only a tiny thing . . . killed Katie too. People said the joyrider couldn't have been more than 14, said he couldn't even see over the wheel. He legged it and they didn't catch him . . . not yet anyway."

Nora looked sick.

"Oh, God, Danny, I'm so dreadfully sorry . . . I mean I never . . . I wouldn't, oh sweet Jesus, me and my big mouth. Oh God!"

Danny excused himself, went to the bar. The barman slowly brought his smirk to the counter.

"A large scotch, please."

"Don't let her catch you, eh."

Danny said nothing, took the drink, and walloped it home.

It shook him. He said,

"Same again."

"If you want my advice, sir."

"I don't, what I want is the same again. Can you do that, eh?"

He could.

Danny brought the second drink to the table. Nora asked,

"Do you know Annie Lennox?"

"Why?"

"That's the song. Heaven's above, how did you know?"

"Whoa hey, hold the phones lady . . . before you get hyper on some ESP garbage or unspoken communication, I was only asking a question, alright . . . so let's calm down." Hurt washed her face and she took a sip of the sherry. Then she said quietly,

"I was only going to say there's a line in her song that goes, 'Why can't I learn to keep my big mouth shut.' Do . . . do you know it?"

"I only know old songs. I only like old songs."

They said little after that and Nora drove him to the Oval. As he was getting out, she gave him a slip of paper.

"That's my phone number, if you . . . well, anyway . . . you'll know yerself."

He said goodnight. Almost immediately, a man in his late 30's approached.

"Wanna score, got some quality stuff?"

"Yea' . . . got any speed?"

"My man, I got it all. More variety than Boots, and no prescription required."

They moved into a small lane, lined by railings. The man produced an envelope and began to spill coloured capsules into his palm.

"Let's see . . . speed-o . . . hmmm . . . downers, quals, dexies . . . ah, yea'."

And he dropped some. He bent down quickly and Danny grabbed his hair. With all his force, he slammed the man's face against the railings . . . once, twice . . . and a third, and then let the man slide to the ground. Danny bent and rummaged through his pockets, took a bundle of money and two more envelopes. As he walked away, he stopped and went back to lean over the groaning figure, said,

"My man, do you have the time?" and removed the man's watch, a heavy, silver Citizen. He liked the irony of that brand name.

As he headed home, he hummed The Commodores,

"You're once,
you're twice,
three times a lady."

Richie came by early, a smaller black man in tow. But anyone appeared small next to him. They both sported the reversed baseball caps. Danny felt hungover and his side ached. He went to make tea. Richie introduced his friend as Roy.

Elvis was extolling the "wonder of you," and Roy said,

"Got any rap?"

Danny said it was tea or nowt. He made a mountain of toast and plonked it all down on a small table. Roy bit into the toast, he was on his third slice when Richie slapped his shoulder.

"What the fuck wrong with yo' man . . . this be the man's breakfast . . . wotcha gonna do . . . and take dat cap off man, jeez . . . where you been?"

He snatched the cap from Roy's head.

"But ye be wearing yo' cap, Rich."

"Am I eating de toast, you see me eating de toast?"

Danny marveled anew at Richie's rapid register of accents. He'd throw in a toff amid a swelter of Jamaican. Richie turned to Danny.

"So, my man, what's shaking?"

"Not a lot, Richie . . . just doing it."

Roy took a tabloid from his jacket, unfolded it and held out the front page.

"Some bro' bin sticking it to the street people." The headline read,

"Vigilante strikes twice in
one evening.
Four seriously injured."

Danny put down his cup. Richie said,

"Dat de kind of crazy shit you likely to pull, eh, Danyell . . . you probably rooting for this dude."

"You think he's wrong?"

"I think he's fookin' crazy, that wot I be thinking and I think he be a fascist, too."

"Come on Richie, a fascist?"

"Yea, them Vigilantes, today they come for him, tomorrow they be coming for you . . . Them dangerous mut Danyell, you all listen to ole Rich here. I see them fascists in de prison, all tattoos and patriotism."

Danny looked at his watch, his Citizen watch. He was unfamiliar with its weight.

Roy's eyes shone.

"Nice piece of watch, bro'."

Richie had an odd expression, said,

"Man could be mugged for a piece like that."

Danny smiled.

"Oh, I don't think so, Richie, I don't think so at all."

"Roy, how about you start the car, seeing is yo' all had 'nouf toast, n'all."

Roy put his cap on, fixed it fussily in it's reverse position, said,

"That Elvis, sure can sing, yea . . . I'd like to hear him rap."

Richie stood, looked round as if he expected someone.

"Danny, I gots a problem, need to ask you a favour."

"O.K."

"I gots this package, I can't keeps it at my crib so . . ."

"Should I ask what's in it?"

"No . . . no, Danyell, bests be you don't."

"Let's have it, then."

Richie produced a brown paper sack, and gingerly handed it over. Danny took it with both hands, it was sealed with brown tape and weighed like a pound of sugar.

"I come by in a few days, take it offa yer hands, how that be?"

"That would be fine, Richie."

"O.K., my man, you take care now, huh," and he grabbed Danny in a bear hug. "You no beauty Dan-yell, but you alright."

"Excuse me."

"That an old song, that be your Boss, Bruce Springsteen, see, I be listening out for you, always."

After he'd gone, Danny did what he'd see in a hundred movies. He ripped open the bag, put his index finger in, tasted.

"Well, it doesn't taste like sugar," he said.

It had a bitter kick-back. Danny considered it for a moment then went to the toilet. He upturned the bag and watched the white powder spill into the bowl, then he flushed.

"Nobody will find it there," he said. He most hoped it belonged to Roy, he didn't like Roy at all.

***

Danny had to forgo his exercises as his side was too painful. A little worrying this, as he had to be in shape for the events. The lack of these exercises also allowed his memory to kick into gear.

From a blind corner came the words of "Honey". One of the great schmaltz records, everyone derided it as pure slush and yet it was a massive hit. Twice. It was on its first massive upswing when Danny met Katie and she'd hum it to them, half-in-earnest. Danny frequently called Darcy, "Honey II".

He wondered what Nora would make of it. A long time ago he'd thrown out the record, with the photos. Danny went to the West End. As he strolled through Leicester Square, he marveled at the amount of event candidates. A nigh feverish hunting ground this would be.

Entering the record shop, he was stunned at the poster for the current hit-makers. Who were these people, he'd never heard of any of them. So 'O.K.' he though. 'I'm out of touch. I'm over 40, but this was a complete alien world.' He moved to a counter.

"I'm looking for a honey," he said.

"Excuse me?"

"Honey, that's h-o-n-e-y!"

"Sorry, sir, this is a music store, there's a chemist two doors down. Or you might try our cafeteria on the third floor."

The girl turned away. Danny wanted to hit her.

"It's a song . . . from 1968 or so . . . by a guy called Bobby Goldboro."

She looked confused, then like a cartoon a bulb seemed to light above her head. A huge smile and she said,

"I get it, you're Bobby GoldsBERG, that's it . . . is this some 60's revival thing? You'll have to go to the basement, sir, for vintage stock."

She began to giggle, all of 17 years and he must seem older than Steptoe. He turned away, deep mortification burned his gut. Another sixties song, "A Deck of Cards" had a line he could use,

"I was that Soldier."

But what he was, was tired.

***

In McDonald's, he got a large, black coffee. They throw in a dab of hostility for free. Danny began to think about his mother. Perhaps Nora being Irish too, had let her loose in his head. Or maybe, he thought, it was just time to think a little about her.

A small, shy woman who loved to sing. Her favourite was, "Pal of My Cradle Days." She'd sing that in a loud, clear voice, and all shyness fell away.

"God gave us songs," she'd said, "because he didn't give us wings."

A shiver ran down his spine and he gulped at his drink. He thought it was Margaret Atwood who described coffee as "Jitters in a cup."

"Yea'", he thought, "that, too."

An employee was attempting to mop under his feet, persistently. The place was packed, yet the man hung at Danny's table like glue.

Danny touched his arm.

"Hey, could you give it a rest, mate, it's clean, OK . . . you've been at it for 10 minutes already. It's fine, OK?"

The man looked blankly at him and began to wipe the table.

"Hey, for fucksake, piss off, alright!"

The manager appeared, he looked no older than the assistant in the record shop. His name tag read, "Bob".

"Is there some problem here?"

Danny handed him his coffee carton.

"Be a good lad, Bob. Leap up there and get me another of them coffees. No milk mind, and . . . yea', I seem to have plenty of sugar. Yea, plenty of that."

To the amazement of all three, Bob did. Danny said to the astonished cleaner, "Aye, there's nowt as odd as folk."

His mother had caught Guillain-Barré syndrome. Danny often wondered about the usage of the word "caught." What, the person went out looking for it or something? "Ah, here's an interesting disease, gotta grab me some of that!"

Danny shook his head. When his father was told the news, he roared,

"Oh, naturally, nothing common for your mother, she'd have to get something that no one an pronounce. Sounds like a poxy French job, eh . . ."

As time went by, her breathing became more and more laboured. The disease eventually leads to death by suffocation. Danny had been with her till she died. He said to Kate once,

"Do you know what my Mother said the moment before she died?"

"What, Danny?"

"Nothing."

"Are you serious?"

"No, I'm making it up, what do you think, take a flying, friggin' guess!"

He was making it up. His Mother had taken his hand and whispered,

"Ah, Danny, I was always afraid in London, afraid of the streets, but not afraid now . . . well, only a little bit. I'm glad I don't have to get up for school in the morning, I'll be here where it's warm."

Her hand had slipped from his.

The third event fell into his lap. He'd planned on recuperation, let his body and mind heal. He was wary too, of becoming hooked on the adrenaline rush. Fear of arrest didn't bother him, he just didn't want it to happen yet. Rising to his seat, he said to the still lingering cleaner,

"I'm going to the toilet, will you be cleaning in there, or can you give me a head start?"

As he put his hand to the door of the toilet, it was pulled open suddenly. A middle-aged man stuck his head out and said,

"Go find another toilet, shit head, I'll be here for a while."

Danny took a quick glance round.

"O.K." he said, and pushed the door with all his might. He felt it slam the man and he followed through. The man had been propelled back against the wall, blood already pouring from his nose.

"What the fuck," he gasped.

Danny moved right in, kneed him in the crotch and caught him as he fell, dragged him to the toilet bowl, said,

"You got a dirty mouth mister, and we're gonna clean it out."

As Danny worked the flush he thought,

"That's twice today I've flushed the garbage."

He went to the basin and washed his hands. As he left, he met the cleaner, and said,

"It needs tidying up right enough."

***

There's a small, second-hand jewellers in a near-forgotten lane off Piccadilly Circus. The owner was a small, fidgety man of indeterminate age. As with most London retailers, he treated custom with blatant aggression. His radio was playing, and, to Danny's delight, Long John Baldy.

> "Let the heartaches begin
> I can't help it
> I can't win
> I've lost that girl for sure."

The owner gave Danny a sour look.

"What d'you want?"

"Civility would help."

"What, whatcha say?"

"I want to get a locket and chain, one that looks old."

"Antique, is it?"

"Did I say antique, did you hear me use the word antique . . . I said, 'That looks old'."

Danny found that a taste of psychosis brought manners to most shopkeepers. That it might also bring the police was a calculated risk.

The owner mellowed a bit.

"I have one that looks old, alright, needs a bit of polish. Could let you have it for thirty-five."

He produced a very worn locket. Danny opened it. The left frame had a very faded picture. Too hazy to distinguish, even the sex wasn't evident. It was perfect, he couldn't have designed better.

"It's not what I had in mind. I'll give you twenty."

"Twenty five and I'll polish it."

"Twenty two and I'll polish it myself."

The deal was made.

Outside, Danny took the two envelopes he'd lifted from the drug dealer and felt them. PILLS. He was about to sling them when an idea whispered to him, and he put them back in his pocket.

As he walked up Shaftsbury Avenue, the early edition of *The Evening Standard* was out. The billboards said,

> "Vigilante Fever
> hits London."

On the train he read of a series of "events" all over the city. What they called, "copycat" acts. He hadn't planned on this, but felt it could only be in his interest. A police spokesman described them as, "a dangerous and reckless trend." The police were pursuing a definite line of enquiry.

"Yea'," he muttered, "and pigs might fly."

He stopped at the off-license and bought a bottle of Crème de Menthe and a bottle of brandy.

He rang Nora and got her answering machine. All over the country, no one was home anymore. If they could now arrange for the answering machines to make calls, people need never use the phone at all. The message he left said he'd like to take her to dinner and if she'd like that, he'd be waiting at The Oval cricket ground at 7.

His flat was so Spartan that it didn't take much tidying. He put fresh sheets on the bed as he said,

"You never know, maybe I'll get lucky."

But he didn't care a whole lot one way or the other.

***

That evening he put on a pale blue shirt and knitted tie. A dark wool suit, and resisted the impulse to put a hankie in the top pocket. As he inspected himself in the mirror, he said,

"As I live and breathe, it's Chief Inspector Morse. Thames Valley CID."

He'd have hummed the signature tune if classical music was hummable. A faint twinge of excitement was building in his stomach, and he called it "wind."

He got to the Cricket Ground and saw her red car immediately. She opened the door and he got in.

"You look like Morse . . ."

"Whoa, hold the phones, doesn't anyone say 'hello' anymore."

"Hello," she said.

"Hello, yourself."

She was wearing a tight black mini dress with black tights. In the small confines of the car, it was hard not to stare.

"You can look," she said, "my legs aren't my worst feature."

"You can leave the car here, the restaurant is only a few minutes walk."

He walked on the outside and she gave a smile in radiance. He said,

"It's how I was reared."

"You don't need to explain matters, and rudeness . . . well, it's inexplicable."

A white teenage boy on a skateboard zoomed past them, turned and prepared for a second run. Danny pointed his finger.

"I wouldn't."

The kid looked at Danny's face and tore off in another direction. Nora had been startled and now looked into his eyes.

"Mother of God, you should have seen his face . . . and yours, you looked like you could kill him."

"I don't think I'd have gone that far . . . but still."

"Are you serious, you wouldn't have done anything surely?"

"I'd have broken his right leg."

"What . . . oh, you're smiling, I thought you meant it."

"So did he."

She linked his arm and it had a profound effect. If he knew of any gestures more endearing, he couldn't think of any. A wave of emotion fought with the murderous impulse he'd just experienced. She said,

"You're shaking."

"Ah, it's ah . . . brisk."

"I'll mind yah."

The restaurant was an infrequent haunt of Danny and Ritchie. Guido, the owner, greeted them warmly.

"Danyello . . . Senorina. Welcome."

He seated them at their table, lit the candle with a flourish.

"Ah," he sighed, "Amore." He produced a bottle and two glasses, poured out a pale liquid.

Nora was completely charmed and near taken away when Guido presented her with a rose, long-stemmed. He'd even managed a drop of water on the petals. He crooned, "Though not as fair as thee."

Nora said,

"A bit of a chancer that fella, I'd say."

"He's got the moves."

Guido brought a copy of the late Standard to the table. The front page was dominated by a photo fit of the Vigilante.

Guido exclaimed,

"See, Bellissimo, a true hero. I give him the freedom of my restaurant."

Nora looked at the photo fit, said,

"This could be half the men in London, or absolutely nobody."

Danny took a look.

"Bit like the Chancellor of the Exchequer who's been mugging the country himself."

"Guido reappeared, order pad in hand. Danny said,
"Let me order for us both."
She smiled, said,
"I do so like mastery."
He ordered thus:

> Clams Oreganata
> Linguini fruitti di mare
> Lasagne
> Meat dish pizziada
> Two bottles of Asti Spumanti

Guido was delighted and Nora was mystified.
"Will we be able to eat it, or is just to impress Guido . . . do you speak Italian?"
"Nora, there are days I can hardly speak English. No, I learnt that from the Godfather movies. Darcy used to love the names. You know how children love repetition. I'd say,

> Linguini
> Valpolicella
> Oreganata

and she'd squeal with delight. It got her to eat dinner, too."
Nora watched him closely during his story. He was in another place. She said,
"I was thinking of you today, and the horrendous grief you've suffered. I haven't read as much as you, but I do remember things. I once read,

> 'Grief can take care of itself
> But to have the true value of joy,
> You must have somebody to share with.'

I can't remember who said that."
Danny was about to say Mark Twain, but thought he'd let her have the moment. She continued,
"I dunno how you survived it."
"What makes you think I have?"
"Good heavens, no, I don't mean that, but you're functional and here and . . . well, doing things . . . you know?"
"I'm doing things, that's the truth."
Guido came with battalions of food. He spread plates like a man with a winning streak . . . stood back and shouted,
"Eat . . . eat . . . enjoy."
They did.

After, Guido brought zuppa. He'd laced them with lethal dollops of rum and Nora said,

"How can I drive after these?"

Danny said,

"You don't have to, you can come home with me and drink coffee."

"Oh, Danny, I don't think it's drinking coffee I'd be doing if I went."

He didn't know what to make of this, so he muttered,

"I don't know what to make of that."

"Pay the bill and let's find out."

They went to his flat. She looked round it and said,

"If a person's home makes a statement about them, this says nothing."

Before he could reply, she moved to him and kissed him ferociously. She said,

"Now, have me now on the floor before words spoil anything."

He did.

Later in bed, they lay entwined as Carol King sang of gentler moments. They played it continuously and didn't let their own words ruin the feeling. Before she slept, Nora said,

"A woman could pray for a man like you."

And he knew he could take that either way. His mother used to say,

"The oul prayer is great."

After Katie and Darcy were gone, he'd memorise whole passages of books and try to numb his mind. One passage he ran through now, the famous introduction by Professor Karl Averbach's lecture on Freud's "Future of an Illusion."

Averbach believed in coincidence as a determining factor in the development of strategies for social survival.

> Coincidence begets mysticism
> Which begets religion
> Which begets sin and retribution
> Which beget
> > Repression
> > Guilt
> > Psychosis

By giving significance to random events, we input a hidden logic which leads to the creation of a hidden power controlling our lives.

We then invent strategies to propitiate this hidden power. In other words . . . we pray.

Danny wondered how the police would react to this line of defense. He could hear their judgement,

"Whacko."

There was one prayer he felt should accompany the "events." It said,

"O Lord God of Abraham
keep me
alive and smart
The rest
I'll figure out for myself."

***

Carol King switched off and Danny tried his damnedest to follow suit; he was partially successful.

Danny rose early, prepared a breakfast tray. Tea, toast, two eggs, hard-boiled. He then got the locket he'd purchased in the West End and wrapped it in a napkin, which he placed beside the tea.

He woke her gently, her face lit in a smile.

"Is that tea . . . oh, thank God. I was afraid it would be coffee. I'd have to drink it and would be a walking bitch the rest of the day . . . and toast . . . I could eat a horse."

"Aren't you hung-over?"

"I'm a nurse, we get hungry, not hangovers."

And she put her hand to his face, kissed him easily.

She lifted the napkin and the locket fell from the tray.

"What's this?"

"It was my mother's, and . . . well, I'd like you to have it."

"But, Danny, I can't . . . your mother."

"She'd have wanted you to have it."

"Is this her . . . the photo . . ."

"Or the Chancellor . . . it's a bit faded."

"No . . . no, I can see you in her."

Danny thought that was fair enough. A sort of poetic justice.

"You're a good man, Danny. I'll take care of it . . . and you . . . if you'll let me."

He walked her to her car and promised to ring her for the weekend. The love making had done wonders for his body.

He felt as if he'd had an interior massage.

When he got back to the flat the phone was ringing. Richie.

"Yo, Dan-yell, what's shaking?"

"The usual."

"You got my package safe?"

"Where no one can reach it."

"Yo' the man, Danyell."

"So they say."

"I send Roy later to pick it up . . . that bro, he eat or drink anyfink . . . sorry 'bout the toast. I'll catch up soon my friend."

"O.K. Ritchie."

Danny took the envelopes he'd liberated from the dope dealer and spilt the contents on the table . . . a feast of pills. Next, he got a razor blade and a plain sheet of paper. Each capsule he slit and let the contents gather on the paper. He thought about Nora, her expression as she examined the locket. He thought of the lines from Flaubert,

> "I shall only tell the truth,
> but it will be horrible,
> cruel and bare."

Boney M were having a revival, and he hummed "The Rivers of Babylon" as he worked. When he'd finished, he poured the powder in a large, plastic beaker and added a drop of Crème de Menthe. Next, he put a heaped spoon of coffee and then two sugars . . . and began to stir. STIRRED WELL,

"Like the Greeks make," he said . . . and immediately came the "Beware of them bearing gifts."

"Yea," he said, "that too."

Finally, he added two fingers of brandy and put the lot in the fridge.

"Allow to cool," he whispered, "for a moment of resentment." Then he settled down to wait.

Roy came late evening. What appeared to be a frenzied tea cosy sat on his head. A pink track suit proclaimed, "Boyz N' Hood." The prerequisite high tops with the laces undone.

Danny completely unnerved him with a huge show of welcome.

"Roy, great to see you, come in . . . sit down."

He nearly said, "I missed you," and thought he'd better get a grip.

"Yo' got my package, man . . . I'm in a big hurry. Gots a man to see."

"Hey, buddy, you're Ritchie's friend, then that makes you MY FRIEND. You've got time for a quick drink."

A sly grin from Roy.

"Always got time to drink, man."

"You've heard of a Rob-Roy. It's a cocktail . . . well, lemme give you a dynamite drink they call F. Y. Roy."

"FROY . . . ?"

"Yea', that's near enough. Might taste a bit sweet to start."

"Oh. I likes 'em sweet . . . young, too."

Danny thought, "You're a funny man, Roy, real class sense of humour."

He handed Roy a mug, and with his own mug . . . toasted him.

"Cheery pip . . . down the hatch in one."

***

BOOK III

As Danny helped Roy behind the wheel of his car, he had to actually turn the ignition for him. The package was full forgotten.

"Wot . . . wot de name of my drink, man?"

Before Danny could answer, the engine turned over and they took off. He'd rehearsed telling Roy the name all day . . . now he said it quietly after the departing car.

"An F. Y. Roy . . . gettit, a fuck you . . . yea' . . . you drive careful now, you hear."

A weak spring sun was doing its best to break through. Danny thought he'd sit in the park and marvel that the sun would attempt to shine this late in the evening. He knew darkness could only be minutes away, and the dinner bell to sound for predators.

Barely had he sat than a young woman approached. She was dressed in what Time Out described as killer-bimbo power-gear. Micro-short mini, sheer stockings, and the vicious spike heels.

She smiled.

"Wanna get laid?"

Danny wondered anew why half of London was attempting to talk American.

"I've been laid."

"Not like I do it, Honey."

"No. You do it for money, right? I didn't have to pay for it."

She gave a loud laugh.

"Oh, you paid, Honey, in one way or another, you always pay."

"You might be right. Gotta go, but thanks for your input."

He considered ringing Nora, but felt he had had enough communication for one day.

***

Danny had overlooked an irony he would have relished.

The influx of American was something he constantly derided. Yet, he himself was an exponent of a uniquely American concept,

> The "Vigilante"
> and worse.
> as "folk hero."

He slept late the next day. Rising, he felt still the afterglow of Nora. It sparked a small light in his soul where the darkness had so reigned. Selecting Roy Orbison, he showered and shaved in near buoyant mood. Roy O' sang,

"A candy coloured clown they call the sandman
tip-toes to my room late at night,
just a faded whisper, then to tell me,
go to sleep, everything's all right."

He joined in the chorus,

"In dreams,
I walk with you . . ."

Opening the front door, he jumped back. Richie was standing there, silent and grim.

"Jesus Christ, Ritchie, you put the heart sideways in me. How long have you been standing there."

"Long enough. I could hear you singing to your records, be a happy morning for you, I figger."

"So, are you coming in or wot?"

"Yea', I comes in."

Agitation came in waves from Richie . . . and something else too . . . something Danny had never for from him, hostility.

"What's up, Richie, you want some tea or coffee?"

Only later did Danny realize that as Richie spoke, he'd dropped all the accents, not a hint of patois nor a flavour of Irish. Even the clipped British inflexion was absent. His voice was plain and cold.

"What time was Roy here?"

"In the evening, it was still bright, in fact, the weirdest thing . . . the sun tried to shine. Don't you want coffee or something?"

Roy Orbison was now "Running Scared."

"You want to turn that shit off Danny, I need you to hear me."

Danny considered it, but decided to let it slide.

"O.K."

"And Roy left here . . . with the package?"

"What the fuck is this, Richie . . . are you interrogating me . . . I turned off the music but don't get ahead of yourself? Yea, he had a drink . . . he was very hyper . . . as if he was something . . . and, yea, he left . . . with the friggin' parcel . . . wot you think, I flushed it down the toilet?"

They were facing each other, and violence hummed all round. Richie climbed down.

"Yea' . . . sorry, bro'. Roy hit the roundabout at the Elephant and Castle at over 90 miles an hour. The car was totaled and him too. I've been telling him, don't mess with that stuff. Thing is . . . that package, it been bought and paid for. I was like . . . a courier. You heard of The Yardies?"

"No."

"North London gangs, use shooters and no messing round. Scotland Yard was so concerned they set up a special task force just to deal with them."

"And did they . . . deal with them?"

"Shit, no, those fuckah's are beyond crazy. You see 'em, you run."

"What's this to do with you?"

"Their package, man, and they be wanting it soon . . . jeez."

Danny got two mugs and made coffee; he placed the brandy bottle on the table too. They sat down.

Richie took a large gulp of coffee, grimaced and grabbed the brandy bottle. He dolloped generous shares into both mugs. They drank in silence and let the brandy work its therapy of chemistry.

It kicked in. Danny began,

"You remember when Darcy and my Katie were killed?"

"Jeez, Danny, yea' . . . man, I never forget that . . . never."

"Well, I was thinking, the kid who was driving, he was probably on drugs."

"I dunno, Danny, mebbe . . . yeah, who know. Why?"

"Oh, I was just thinking that."

Richie got another major hit of the brandy. He shuddered.

"You know, Danny, I'm a big man . . . yea', ain't nothing I been scared of. But one thing, one thing does. You know what that is?"

"Those Yardies?"

"No, Danny. You. You scare me, man. Ain't no human being, alive or dead, I care mo' for, but I gotta tells you, man, you give off a chill. I dunno for sure wot you doing, man, but it's not righteous. I was always to you, 'take care', but I been thinking, it's me . . . me was gotta take care."

He stood up. Danny didn't. When he opened the door, he looked back, and Danny said,

"Take care, Richie."

***

During the night, Danny woke suddenly. Sweat was teaming down his body, the nightmares of his childhood. He cried out loud, and tears mingled with the perspiration.

Malcolm, his dad's name. All through his early years, the pleas of his mother,

"Malcolm, please."

But there was no pleasing Malcolm. During the last year of her illness, his mother could hardly speak, and her beloved singing was out of the question. Danny had bought her a songbird, he'd gone all the way to Knightsbridge to get a guaranteed songster.

It sang for her.

Ole Malcolm refused to acknowledge her illness. He expected business as usual. Laundry, meals and homage. Returning one evening, no meal was prepared.

"Danny will make you a sandwich," she said.

"Sandwich, wot poor people eat. I'll show you a fuckin' sandwich."

He'd grabbed the songbird from its cage and slapped two slices of bread round it.

The songbird, being of such a delicate nature, was dead when he put it back in the cage. Danny's mother had a year to endure still. Malcolm had whined,

"Ah, lass, I was only joking . . . eh, can't have been much of a canary if it can't take a bit o' handlin' . . . No mind, lass, we'll get you a dog soon . . . keep the boy company, too."

As Danny tried to settle back in bed, he muttered some lines of Edna St. Vincent Millay, followed by his father's words.

> ". . . summer sang in me once,
> it sings in me no more,
> eh . . . lass,
> never mind, lass."

***

The following evening, Nora came to his flat. She looked tired and said it was a long shift.

Danny said,

"I've cooked Irish Stew. I dunno how authentic it will be, but I piled in the meat and potatoes, so . . . ready to eat?"

"O.K."

"Hey. Lady, liven up. I don't think you've know me long enough to pull moody. You've had a bad day, everybody gets a bad day. Trick is, don't prolong it." Nora came to life, eyes blazing.

"Bad day, is it, how dare you presume to know my life. We had a woman in the hospital today, you know what she had . . . in this era of central heating and technical brilliance – hypothermia."

"Well, that's rough, I grant you."

"Oh, you do, do you, Mister, let me tell you how hypothermia is. The body tries fiercely to compensate for the drop below the normal 98.6 degrees."

"Nora, I don't think I want to hear this. O.K., lemme get the stew and . . ."

"You will hear it, the body starts to speed breathe and then to shiver and to try to make heat. Blood vessels in the arms and legs start to shut down. The brain can't get blood and the mind goes. This is the good bit, Danny, you're a coffee drinker, you'll appreciate this. Palpitations begin and the heart gets walloped with a massive assault . . . so don't tell me I've had a bad fuckin' day . . . O.K.?"

Then she began to cry, large tears rolled down her face and a quiet whimper started.

"I just want to be held. I don't want stew, just a hug, can you give that to me."

He could.

From that to the bedroom. After that, she asked him,

"What age are you?"

"42."

"You don't look it."

"Well, thank heaven for that."

"No, I mean you look older, I thought you were 50."

"Jesus, maybe I am."

***

In the kitchen, the stew sat cold and forgotten.

In Brixton, they began to break Richie's legs.

In the morning Danny made love to her in what he reckoned was a fairly impressive manner.

"See who's 50, now," he thought.

Well pleased, he settled back to await her flattery. But, apart from various little sighs, she didn't say anything.

"So, Sweetheart," he asked, "was that good for you, or what?"

"Hmm, let's just say it was English."

"Excuse me?"

"Now, don't go all offended, it was adequate, but you know, English."

"What the hell does that mean?"

He was out of the bed now.

"Ah, Danny, lighten up. The English do it as if they read the instructions, but with no passion."

"I don't believe this, I don't flaming believe this, you're some sort of global expert, are you . . . fucked most of the world, have you . . . God, you're incredible. That's the most bigoted remark I've ever heard."

"True though, and more's the pity."

To his utter amazement, she turned over and slept. He stormed to the kitchen, but no amount of banging drawers of slamming cutlery woke her. A thousand things raced through his mind, and aloud, he said,

"Go figger."

Danny dressed and went to the local shop. It amused him that above the door it read, "local shop." It didn't amuse him now. The rarity about it was, it was owned by an Englishman. A nation of shopkeepers were now multi-national.

"Morning, Bill."

"Morning, Dan."

In ten years, they'd never gone beyond this. Danny took the paper, milk, bread. Paid. As he was leaving he turned.

"Bill."

"Yes, Dan."

"Do I look old to you?"

"None of us getting any younger, Dan."

"Right, right, but would you describe me as old . . . say if you were talking to another customer?"

"I mind my own business, Dan, best way."

"Yea, but hypothetically speaking. I mean, I'm not going to quote you for Chrissakes."

"Can't says I'd rightly know, Dan, can't say I do. Leave the tittle tattle to the little woman, know what I mean."

"Well, would she . . . oh, forget it, eh . . . Nice talking to you, Bill. I may well go home and build a novel on this."

He'd shop somewhere else in the future he resolved, and thought.

"What a wanker."

***

There's a makeshift rubbish dump off the main road into Brixton. It's not official, but always busy. Most of Richie was thrown there, amid 7-Eleven and Diet Coke cans.

Danny was making toast and still ruminating on England and its citizens. He reckoned the reason he analysed it so much was the Irish blood in him that prevented full acceptance. No one he knew had even heard of Philip Larkin, the most English of poets.

But Larkin's father . . .

"Another one," muttered Danny.

Sydney Larkin, fascist. He kept a statue of Hilter on his mantelpiece. When you touched it, it gave the famous salute. Philip Larkin said of his family life that it filled him with

Black
surging
twitching
boiling
HATE.

Danny knew all about that. He thought that yet again he might use as his won defense, the dictum of Marx,

"the past weighs like a nightmare on the brain of the living."

"Yea' . . . let them chew on that, the bastards," he said.

He chewed on the toast and washed it down with scalding tea.

"Hits the spot right enough," he'd said when Nora appeared.

"Who are you talking to?"

"England."

"Ary, you're not all in it, is that toast for me?"

She leant over, kissed him on the neck, and helped herself to a slice. Danny turned the radio on, he felt fairly turned on himself.

The DJ was talking about RAGGA, the music of the angry black underclass. It began in Kingston, Jamaica, in the violence of the dance halls. White urban America was apprehensive about some of the lyrics, which appeared to glorify guns, gangs, homophobia, and a hatred of women.

Danny switched it off.

"You can't beat the old songs," he said. Nora looked concerned.

"I'm afraid of black people."

"Why?"

"I don't even know why . . . 'cos I'm white, I suppose."

"Believe you me honey, there's white folk out there you should be afraid of."

She picked up the paper and read the police were confident of an early arrest in the vigilante case.

"This poor devil, this vigilante, he needs help so he does."

Danny smiled.

"He seems to be doing all right on his own."

"Silly! I meant medical help, he's obviously off his head."

Danny got up and made fresh tea. He needed a moment before he could trust himself to reply.

"You're a psychologist now are you, or have you been reading Cosmopolitan?"

He heard her cup clatter on the table.

"You condescending little bastard, Danny, how dare you insult me like that. You sound as if you approve of this lunatic."

Danny sat.

"Look, ordinary people live in fear. Every time they go out on the streets they have to wonder if they'll be mugged, raped or attacked. While they're out there, they also worry that their homes are being ransacked. There's no let up."

"But it's the times we live in . . . all the unemployment."

"Ah, don't give me that. I'm talking to you about the way it is, not why it is . . . No, no, let me finish. Now imagine if it were possible to reverse things a little. If it were dangerous out there for them,

the muggers
thugs
the predators.

When yer average thug is combing his hair with his knife one evening . . . what if he was to worry about being attacked . . . eh, how would that be?"

"Ary, that's nonsense, Danny. Can I have a shower? I'm free today, would you like to spend it together?"

He wouldn't.

"Sorry, Nora, today's the day I go to the cemetery . . . to see . . . well, to visit Darcy and her Mum."

Nora had a lost expression for a moment, then took the risk.

"I could come with you, if you liked . . . that is, if you wanted me to . . . for the company, you know . . . am."

"I don't need company there, in fact, that's why I go there, for their company."

"Yes, well . . . O.K. . . . I'll just have a shower and get out of your hair. I won't be two seconds."

After she'd done that, she seemed not to quite know how to leave. She said,

"I'm not sure how to leave."

"That's no problem, Nora, I'll walk you to your car."

He did.

They didn't kiss, and he said he'd ring later. She had an expression of full sadness, and said,

"I better not hold my breath."

Danny resolved he'd think about it later. Right now he had to get ready. The Morse suit was trotted out again. En route to the cemetery, he bought six red roses and an ALF doll. Darcy was dead before ALF made it big on the children's favourites. But, for a long time, he had watched TV to gauge what she'd like. He didn't want her to miss anything, she'd already missed everything. The ALF was a small fortune and he'd have paid that twice over if he could once again see her smile.

"Jesus," he muttered.

As he entered the gates, it was one of those cold, brisk April days. Earlier rain had washed over the headstones, they gleamed and shimmered. A drinking school was gathered under a tree, bottles of V.P. and Jack being passed round. Danny wondered what he'd have done if they'd perched on his family's plot. He knew exactly what he'd have done, and tried to get a hold of his temper.

Looked at his Citizen watch . . . minutes before noon. The two headstones were midway in the place.

"Hello, Katie," he said, and laid the roses before her.

Then he placed ALF down and said,

"Honeybunch, this is ALF, he's a bit crazy like yer old Dad."

Time passed. He felt somebody behind him and he whirled around.

A priest in his early 30s was standing there. Tall, with a huge head of black hair. Some broken veins in his face told of his fondness for the bottle.

"I'm sorry, I didn't mean to startle you, but you've been standing there so long."

Danny checked the time, 3.30, and felt aches in his legs. He shook his head to end the trance he'd been under.

The priest moved a step closer.

"Loss is a hard burden."

"Yea . . . tell me about it."

"Well, God's hand seems heavy at times, but we mustn't lose hope."

Danny gave a tight smile.

"Well . . . how many of you exactly am I talking too."

The priest lost it momentarily, then rallied and tried anew.

"I'm Father Riordan, but most people call me Joe. A new era in the church, less formal."

Danny didn't call him Joe. He didn't say anything.

"Well, then, if I can be of any help, if you feel you need to talk."

"I've just talked to the ones I needed to talk to."

"Yes, there it is, they're in a better place."

"Hey, Padre, do us a bleeding favour, eh, give it a rest."

Danny strode past him and heard the Priest rush after him.

"Those things . . . am, the flowers and the . . . toy, they'll be lifted, you know! I mean, it's terrible, but it happens all the time."

Danny said without turning,

"Not while I'm here, they won't. When I'm gone, it doesn't matter."

He was glad of the ache in his legs, it kept him from dwelling on the devastation in his heart. Searching his mind for an old song, he couldn't find one and said,

"Sometimes, you just can't sing 'em."

***

Danny rang the newspaper when he got home. First he was put on hold, then a young voice,

"Can I help you?"

"No, I want to talk to Mr. Baker."

"Yea, you and the rest of the world. Ring back on Friday."

Danny smiled.

"Do you have a pen?"

"What, oh right."

"Write this carefully, as it will probably be your final piece for the paper.

'Mr. Baker, the Vigilante rang, and
I told him to ring back Friday.'

Have you got that or do you need time to spell vigilante."

"Don't hang up . . . O.K. . . . I'm putting you through right away."

A sound of muffled voices, banging receivers and vicious obscenities, then,

"This is Baker . . . hello."

"Mr. Baker, I wanted to give you major advance notice of a big event."

"And when might that be? I gotta tell you, pal, the story's near finished already."

"In three weeks, on May 1st."

"Not some sort of lost commie, are you? Look, why don't you meet me, give me an exclusive. We'll put some jizz back in this . . . people are bored already."

"Not of Royal fascination . . . eh, Baker?"

"Any chance of your being 'Squidgy' . . . I mean you don't have to be, just claim you are. We could work up a front page there. Di and the Vigilantes, now she moves papers."

"You've been told."

Danny went through his records, found Buddy Holly and turned him to full volume.

"I guess it doesn't matter anymore."

He sang along with Buddy. It was an old recording, but Danny reckoned those Crickets sounded fine, yea' . . . just fine.

That night a bone-exhausted Danny fell into bed. His father shot briefly into his head. He knew where the grave was, but he'd never been to visit, and, if there was an afterlife, where was his father now?

Aloud, Danny said,

"If there's any justice, and I fear there isn't any, he's, I hope, where he deserves to be."

And just before he slept, he muttered,

"Hot enough for you, is it?"

***

The Brandon Estate is notorious, even by South East London standards. Coming up the Kennington Park Road, it's merely obscured by the park, but you turn it, and it seems to jump in your face.

The police refuse to accept there is any area in London that's a "no-go" for them.

"This, after all, is not Northern Ireland."

Not yet.

Thus as they deny their refusal to enter any district, they add quietly,

"Except for Brandon, of course."

It's already huge reputation was solidified when poll tax collectors were literally strung up. They didn't die but they never returned either. Social workers refer to it as a "black hole" in the field of community care. Others simply call it, the black hole. Almost anything illegal is available there, and legend has it that even the hardened villains are apprehensive about using it as a hide-out.

The whole of the ground floors are a bazaar of drug dealing. The basements are a shooting gallery, for junkies and shooters. A tight-knit band of dealers move merchandise to and from the ground floor.

Richie was accepted there, though on a tentative basis. He'd brought Danny there on two occasions. Whether as protection or education, Danny hadn't asked. Colour is not an issue, as to your intentions, they better be vouched for.

Danny's years on the building sites had given him an eye for planning and lay-out.

All of the next morning, he laid out charts and designs of the estate. The detail of the concept was soothing to him, He almost felt like he was working again. What would have helped most was Richie's collaboration, but Richie knew he couldn't ask him. Richie's help would have been invaluable on every level (of the operation) but he'd have had to tell him what the "event" was.

"No," he said, "no, Richie's out."
He sang quietly as he worked,

"Old flames
can't hold a candle to you."

The risks would be enormous. He had no illusions on that. But he was determined on a simple plan, and, if he didn't pull it off, then he'd be a permanent resident on Brandon. Once, in his reading, he'd found a proposition in Part 4 of Spinoza's ethics. He'd copied it down. It had found its significance now, he thought.

"A free man
thinks of nothing less than death
and his wisdom
is a meditation
not of death
but of life."

Standing, he stretched, and ran the lines over again.
"Time to chill out, Richie . . . eh?"

***

The Buddhists believe you can measure "a man's wealth by what he can do without."
They'd have had an interesting concept in Frank Norton. He was a "getter." Not a go-getter as his parents might have wished. Whatever you could want that wasn't available legally, then, provided you had the cash, Frank would get it. He didn't ask questions save one,
"How much are you willing to pay?"
Years ago, he, Danny and Richie had had a few drinks together. Then they'd gone to see Wall Street. A scene in the movie has Marty Sheen say,
"I never judge a man by the size of his wallet." Frank had laughed out loud, and said,
"Fuckin' Hollywood, what do they know."
They'd gotten curry take aways and walked along by Waterloo.
Before they parted, Frank had touched Danny's arm, whispered,
"You ever want anything on the QT, you give Frank a bell, you know what I mean . . . nod to the wise, eh."
Danny knew alright.
Now he certainly needed some items and decided to test just how good Frank was. He phoned, and a cautious Frank agreed to meet him in the pub in a few hours.
En route, Danny decided to sit in the park and get his yarn ready for Frank.

Another fine April day, and all the park benches were taken by winos or pensioners. A young woman in a grey track suit had a bench to herself. She looked familiar, but he couldn't place her. He decided to go for it.

"Is this seat taken?"

"Well, what do you think?"

"What do I think, I think it's impossible to elicit a civil answer in this town."

"Solicit . . . is that what you said?"

He sat and remembered her. The hooker from the other evening, she of the killer-bimbo outfit.

"Mislaid the American accent, did ya?" She laughed and said,

"I know you, the guy who never pays for it, right?" Danny stretched out his legs and took a good look at her. Without her working gear, he estimated her age to be early 20's. Blonde, streaky hair, button nose, blue eyes, and a cupid mouth. Not pretty, but in there.

She returned his look.

"You're in fairly good shape for an older guy."

"Yea, but in shape for what. Have you a name?"

"Nikki . . . spelt NIKKI."

"Hey, I don't want it tattooed on my arm, just to throw it into the odd sentence. Aren't you a bit wary of strange men?"

"Honey, I can't afford that luxury."

"No, I mean . . . you should be more careful."

"You've got nice eyes."

"Ever see a photo of Ted Bundy?"

"Who?"

"Never mind. Look Nikki, I've got to go."

"Wanna have a drink with me, tonight?"

Danny was amazed. Whole blocks of time went by and it seemed as if he was invisible to women. Now they were all over him.

Before he could answer, she said in a world-weary tone,

"Forget it, wouldn't want to socialize with a working girl . . . right?"

"I'll have a drink with you."

"What . . . oh, great. I'll be in the Cricketers at eight . . . Is that good?"

"Remains to be seen . . . you be careful, Nikki."

She gave a look of pure devilment.

"Isn't that what condoms are for?"

***

Danny had arranged the meeting in The Mitre, a pub favoured by the building trade. He had to push his way through to the small booths at the back. Frank Norton was already there. A thin man, nearing sixty, he exuded a mix of energy and furtiveness. A sharp, thin face had pit lines, but the eyes showed deep intelligence when they smiled. His clothes suggested he'd just walked off the site. In fact, he hadn't worked on one for years. But he liked the image.

Two pints of bitter were already before him.

"So, Danny, bitter right?"

"Yea', that's fine."

They took sips, did the "Ah" business and exhaled. Frank said,

"Tastes like piss, eh?"

"Does a bit."

"Hear you did alright from your fall."

"I did."

"O.K., then, what can I get you?"

Danny looked round, nodded and began,

"I need two things,

   Merchandise
   and
   Information."

"The second one's likely to be expensive."

"I can pay; I need explosives and timers, five if possible, the smaller and more compact the better. Second, who runs Brandon Estate? Who's the man?"

"A Lebanese named Yusif, nasty piece of work. The five items will be costly. When do you need them?"

"As soon as."

"State of the art?"

"If possible."

Danny took a fat envelope from his pocket.

"Down payment."

Frank didn't open it, but quickly put it away and asked,

"'Nother pint?"

"No thanks."

Father drained his glass, leant over and said,

"They had me in the hospital a while back . . . no, not any-fink serious. A loony bin. It's a long story and not relevant now, but I learnt about psychopaths. Know about those?"

"London's full of them."

"They have no interest in other people's suffering, no conscience, no morals. You can't deal or reason with them. Once they get fixed on something, they follow it, regardless of anything or anyone."

"Well, Frank, fascinating as this is . . . is there a point to it?"

Frank stood up and said,

"You and me, Danny. They've a name for us now. I'll be in touch."

Danny wasn't offended, even surprised. He put it down to Frank's flair for the dramatic. If he got the items, he could name call till Doomsday. A builder recognized Danny and hand-signalled a drink. Danny shook his head. The man approached.

"Jesus, Dan, sorry to hear about yer mate. Can't says I liked him, but no man deserves that."

"What . . . who?"

"Yer mate, the big black 'un, someone butchered 'im, threw bits of 'im all over a Brixton tip. Didn't you know?"

Danny jumped up. Without a word, he elbowed his way to the street. Outside, he threw up and leant trembling against the side of the pub. Two women passed, tut-tutted, and said loudly,

"Should be ashamed of himself, arseholed before tea time."

Danny forced himself upright and muttered,

"O.K. . . . I'm O.K. . . . I've got them before, I won't think about this, I'll blank it . . . fuckit, I can do that . . . yea, I'll be O.K."

As he turned towards home, he whispered,

"Only the dead know Brixton, eh, Richie?"

He threw up again in his bathroom and force struggled for control.

"Toast," he said, "dry toast."

And it helped. Not a lot, but in the general direction.

Then he lay down and sleep or shock took him. It was six in the evening when he came to. Came to, and remembered.

"Read, come on Danny, you've read mountains . . . think on that, let the lines come for this."

The lines that returned were,

> "the fortress had fallen
> and we are pursued
> naked and terror-stricken
> through open country
> by an enemy who knows
> we will soon surrender
> seeing the sanctuary of slavery
> and the security of chains."

He forced himself up and roared,

"Never fuckin happen . . . not yet."

As he prepared for his date, he played the Stones, loud and pounding,

> "Gimme shelter."

Checked himself in the mirror, navy polo neck, faded to white jeans and well-worn brown midi leather coat. He looked sick, but thought,

"Can't be helped, and, any road, she's a hooker, she's used to sick people." He couldn't really decide on whether he looked like a refugee from the set of The Avengers or an off-duty dentist. Or both.

The Walker Brothers' were belting out "You've Lost That Loving Feeling" with those big voices.

All along the bar counter, people were joining in, it's one of those bigger songs you can't resist. Even the barman was adding,

"Gone
gone
gone
whoa . . . oh . . . oh . . ."

Nikki was dressed in a light powder-blue track suit. Her blond hair was falling on the collar, she looked nineteen.

"My mum used to have those guys on her wall."

"The Walker Brothers?"

"Yea', they're like the Chippendales with clothes." Danny was glad to see her, and realized he'd have been glad to see almost anybody, even Roy. He was bone tired of himself. He said, and couldn't disguise the disappointment,

"You didn't dress up."

"I dunno, to tell you the truth, I thought you'd know. They used to say, 'Wranglers and wrinkles don't match.'"

There were drinks in short glasses on the table. She indicated them.

"I bought you brandy, scotch and gin. I felt one was sure to be the business."

***

BOOK IV

Danny smiled, picked up the first glass, and said,

"Guess what, tonight they're all the biz."

After he'd lowered them, he continued,

"Times like this I wish I smoked."

"It's not too late."

"Darlin', it's too late for a whole batch of stuff."

Nikki seemed at a loss how to continue, so she asked,

"Didn't all your generation smoke?"

"My Dad did, and I've tried never to do a single thing like him. Not one bloody thing."

Nikki brightened.

"My Mum and Dad, they were crazy for each other, always smooching and cuddling. My Mum said they held hands in bed every night he was alive."

Danny was going to ask a question, but changed his mind. She caught it.

"You're thinking, so how come I'm a hooker? No big reason. I'm just a bit fucked in the head, always have been. What's your name?"

"Danny."

"Oh, I thought it might be Barry, I'd have liked a Barry . . . or Cliff even."

Danny wasn't sure he could apologise for his name. So he decided to try out the old chestnut.

"Well, it's like the song."

"Wot song?"

"Ol' Danny Boy."

"Never heard that . . . can you sing it?"

"Not just now, eh . . . same again . . . of everythin'?"

Nikki looked at the empty glasses and shook her head.

"Something sweet, do you think they have that green stuff . . . It's sticky."

"No, they don't."

"How do you know?"

"Trust me on this, Nikki, I won't be getting you that."

What he did get her was a snowball, and she liked that. A lot. She chewed the cherry they'd popped on the head.

He could have told her how his father, for the only time, was afraid as he died. Afraid, because it was one thing that wasn't his idea. Instead, he asked,

"Do you have any brothers, sisters?"

"One brother, Keif. He said to me,

'if you weren't my sister
but like a real woman,
I wouldn't touch you with
a barge pole.'"

"Sounds like a real prince, does old Keif. I'd like to meet him."

"He's in the army."

"Now why is that no surprise?"

"I said to him, 'Keif, if you were a man you would.'"

Danny liked it. He found he liked her. Not sexually, not yet. She leant closer and said,

"Will you be fuckin' me after?"

And he spluttered his drink.

"For crying out loud, girl, what a thing to ask."

"Well, isn't that wot men do to women?"

He wanted to say that sometimes they make love. But figured he had little right on this day to lecture on the human condition. Not this day when he'd fucked Richie permanently.

Nikki drank another snowball and then Danny said he'd walk her home. She lived in Cottington Lane, near Kennington Tube. Her flat was in a modern building complete with intercom and grilled windows.

"If you come up, I'll cook you something."

He did.

The flat was small, spotless, and decorated as if a studious teenager lived there. Fluffy cushions everywhere, Snoopy dolls and posters of European cities. Danny thought of how Darcy might have turned out.

"You look sad."

"I was thinking of a little girl."

"I can be that for you, of any fantasy you like. I know them all."

"You mentioned food?"

She made omelettes and placed two glasses of milk with them.

"We can have ice cream after. I got that American one that nobody can say."

They ate. Danny even drank the milk. It was surprisingly tasty and he cleaned his plate. She said,

"I read once, that around 1840, one in every 25 Londoners was a prostitute. They worked it out it was one for every 12 men."

What Danny thought was "so what?" but he said, "How interesting?"

She got up and came over beside him, sat and rested her head on his shoulder.

"Do you feel bad because I'm a prossy?"

"No, because I'm twice yer age darlin', and, believe me, I feel it."

"Come on," she said, and took his hand, "you don't have to do anything," and she led him to the bedroom.

They slept holding hands. A Snoopy duvet over them. Before she slept, Nikki said as she squeezed his hand.

"Like my Mum and Dad, I'm glad you're here, Barry."

***

And in all sorts of ways, Danny was glad too.

For the next four days, it was like a holiday for Danny. He returned to his flat to change, shower, and nothing else. The old songs were left unplayed. He spent the days with Nikki and they went to:

1. Kew Gardens
2. The Zoo
3. The Cinema (Twice)
4. Madame Tussauds

And in the evening they shared the bed. Sex didn't take place. He knew he was treating her like a daughter, to have the brief time with her he knew he'd never have with Darcy. Glad he was, too, to have the rest and healing. Some sort of restoration was vital if he was to attempt the Brandon event. But, most of all, he just enjoyed it. On the fifth morning he slipped out of bed early and wrote her a note. He propped it against a glass of orange juice. He put a thick wedge of bank notes in an envelope. He went to the sofa and from underneath, where he'd hidden it, he pulled an ALF doll. Under ALF's arm he lodged the envelope. The note read,

My Darling Nikki,

You're a wonderful girl. You're smart and funny and beautiful. I have to go away, but I want you to know I wish you were my daughter. I'd be proud if you were. This is ALF, he's a smart ass, but you probably know that already. Go into another line of work, you're too vital for this. Here's some cash to kick start. If I believed in God, I'd ask him to mind you well. I believe in you.

Barry.

Back at the flat, there was a note from Frank.

"The pub at 1.00
Bring plenty, Frank."

"So it begins," said Danny, and selected Led Zeppelin, "Stairway to Heaven." As the familiar rock began, he started to do his exercises.

***

Frank was dressed again in the building gear. If you touched him, clouds of white dust would rise. Danny wondered if he'd bags of it he applied at home. A somewhat pleasant scent emanated from him, so perhaps he used talc.

Danny bought the pints. A snot-nosed barman bounced his change on the counter. Frank smiled, said,

"You'd eat the likes of him for breakfast."

"Yea', but would I want to?"

"He's what my ol' fellah used to call a pup, a sort of apprentice thug. They manage somehow to have a swagger in their face. Not any easy accomplishment."

They moved to a table. Next to it, a young man in a tee shirt and jeans was playing a Nintendo game. A ferocious amount of noise came from both. The back of his tee shirt read,

"Sticks and stones
May break my bones
But only chains
Sexually excite me."

Frank raised an eyebrow, asked Danny,

"Do you want me to get him to hop it?"

"Naw, the noise will benefit us."

Frank had a large blue sports bag. He moved it near Danny's foot.

Then he took out a very ornate fountain pen and a scrap of paper. He scribbled a figure on it and pushed it over.

Danny looked and let out a low whistle.

"Steep."

"But Japanese. Pure simplicity. You attach the main, make sure you're well away and flick . . . it's good-night, Irene. The bag is thrown in free."

"Right, just give me a minute."

And Danny went to the toilet, locked himself in a booth. He took out three large envelopes and piled wads from two into the third. In the bank en route, he caused apoplexy in the bank manager. Danny considered for a moment, then put another batch into the third envelope.

Back at the table, he slid the huge envelope to Frank, said,

"There's a bit over the top, what you might call a sweetener."

Frank looked offended.

"I know how to keep my bin shut."

"I know you do, Frank, but let's say it's appreciation."

Frank sulked and Danny let him simmer. Then he shrugged, said,

"Fuckit, Danny, you're alright. I'm a bit touchy. O.K.?"

Frank went to the bar and got a couple of short ones.

"Guess I can afford to buy you a drink . . . eh, Dan?"

"Sure, cheers."

"About that guy at Brandon, the Yusif character? He's extremely valuable."

"I'll handle him."

"Word to the wise, me old son . . . he lost a hand . . . some say they chopped it in one of those sand nigger customs. Hand in the till, so to speak. Any road, act as if you haven't noticed it . . . O.K.?"

"Thanks for the tip, Frank."

Danny tried to pin down what he was getting from Frank, apart from the merchandise. Then he clicked and bent close to Frank.

"What's got the wind up you, Frank, eh . . . what are you afraid of?"

"Nothing, Danny . . . jez . . . honest . . . when you throw the switches, be sure you're well away . . . eh?"

Danny considered a moment then decided to ride a major bluff.

"Frank, I hope you're not contemplating playing both sides of the street. There's plenty of motivation in that envelope to keep stump, but I noticed you never mentioned Richie. No, no, don't start now. Let me give you a word to the wise. If I can do that to my best mate, think of what I might have in mind for a blabber-mouth. You catch my drift?"

Danny stood up and said,

"See yah, scouser."

Frank said nothing at all.

The next week, Danny increased his exercises, checked and re-checked the merchandise, and psyched himself for the next event.

Twice he left messages on Nora's machine, saying he'd get back to her. Then a letter arrived from her. He didn't read it for two days, nor did he read anything else except from "The Hound of Heaven" by Frank Thompson.

"I fled him, down the nights and days I fled him,
down the arches of the years I fled him,
down the labyrinthine ways of my own mind."

And aloud,

"For ah, we know not what each other says,
These things and I in sound I speak
In sound I speak
They speak by silences

And smitten to me by my knee
I am defenceless utterly
I slept, methinks and woke,
I stand amid the dust of the years
My mangled youth lies dead beneath the heap
My days gone up in smoke."

***

Nora's letter:

Danny boy,

*I don't know what to make of you. You live behind a wall. I dunno is it grief
or rage? Yet you gave me Mother's locket. So I think you care for me. I really
care for you. Am I being brazen in writing to you?*
*Ary, I don't care. I want to go home to Ireland. I'm not able for this heathen
place any more. I have an interview in Dublin on the 25th of May for a big
hospital there. I'd say I'd get it. I'm going to make a bit of a holiday of it and
not come back till the 28th of June. That's my birthday.*
*I'll put a Dublin phone number at the end where I'll be. Here's the big bit . . .
will you come over and we could hire a car and go to the West. It would be
lovely. I'll leave it to you. Take the chance. The pipes are calling now.*

Warmest love,
God mind you well,
Nora.

He put the letter down, then checked again. Yea', she'd put the phone number down. The radio had been playing, but only now did he let it filter through.

Nanci Griffith was singing, "Speed of The Sound of Loneliness."

For the first time he allowed himself to hear a new song. It touched him. When a pilgrim had traveled halfway cross the world to ask a wise man for the answer, he'd simply said,

"It changes."

Danny stretched and said,
"You got that right, fella."

***

Brandon. May 1st.

Danny had gone to the Edgware Road and in the Lebanese shops, he'd bought them a myriad of delicacies, sweetmeats, and candies. He'd have them gift-wrapped. Now he'd piled them into the sports bag. The explosives he'd also gift-wrapped, marking them by a red ribbon. They lay to the side of the bag. Next, he took wads of large, demonstrational notes and dispersed them through the packages.

"Keep it simple," he whispered.

Out came the leather coat, he put in the control console and felt the switch,

One
Two
Three
Four . . .

The fifth explosive he left at the flat.

He walked to the estate, took a deep breath, and turned in. No one was around as he entered. Then a shadow behind him, he turned to see a large white man, mid 30's, with a blond crew cut. Dressed in a plum track suit he looked like he was rarely away from lifting iron.

"Got business here?"

"I'm looking for Yusif, I'm a friend of Richie's."

"Let's see the bag."

Danny handed it over.

"What's this?"

"Lebanese delicacies and a down payment on some business."

"Richie . . . the black guy who's chop suey?"

"That's right."

The man handed the bag back.

"Wait here, don't go wandrin' off," and he gave a tight smile, "it is not safe."

Danny felt rivers of perspiration roll down his sides. The man returned.

"I'm Charley, follow me."

There were five doors on the floor. All were shabby and looked like they'd been hit with everything from boots to heads.

Danny had thought for one frozen moment about Katie. The only person who'd ever made him feel he was more than he was. Not that he'd wanted to be more, but it was a good feeling then.

"What in the world am I doing standing in a grimy hall with a bag of chocolate and explosives, trying to meet a reptile?"

He banished the thought and followed Charley.

The flat was like a set from the Arabian Nights, as conceived by Channel Four. Huge silk draperies lined the walls. There were no chairs, just large cushions and low divans. Four men were playing cards at a small table, they looked like what Richie met. Even sitting down, they looked like what Richie would have called, 'hard cases.' All gave Danny 'the look.'

A fifth man was stretched on a divan. No more than 5'6", he had sallow skin, jet black hair and protruding eyes. Like a vicious Marty Feldman. He was missing his right hand, and an empty sleeve hung by his side. He summoned Danny with his left.

"You knew Richard?"

His voice was low and cultured. Only a very faint accent was detectable.

"We were partners, but he got greedy, and alas . . . his 'retirement' has left me without a supplier."

"You bring gifts?"

Danny took out a pile of parcels, two red-ribboned among them.

"Perhaps, you'd be kind enough to open one or two, I am indisposed."

Danny opened three and each one he passed over.

Yusif smiled.

"You are familiar with my people?"

"Naw, just the Edgware Road."

"But resourceful, I like that, my friend. You planned ahead. This bodes well for any . . . joint venture. All these gifts . . . solely for me."

"Well, I thought I'd leave one at each of the other flats, as an introduction. To let your people know you have a new customer."

"You took a grave risk, my friend, it's a dangerous thing you've done."

"I'm a dangerous man."

Yusif gave him a long look then laughed.

"I believe you may be right . . . yes . . . what is it you wish to purchase?"

"As much dope as I can safely carry." Yusif held up his left hand.

"Wrong . . . you are in error my friend, I deal in dreams. I merely supply 'merchandise' to fuel the dreamers. Purely a service."

The men laughed. Danny felt his patience ebbing. He wanted to say, 'yer slimy little fuck.' He wasn't sure how long he could control his temper, so he took out a pile of notes.

"I brought this as a down payment . . . to demonstrate my sincerity and intent."

Yusif didn't take the money, but let it lie on the floor. "My friend, we'll have to check you out. Come back in one week and I'll let you know what I can supply . . . and the price. Take your money, it's a pittance."

Danny did so, and couldn't resist a shot.

"Don't touch the old cash yourself, eh . . . don't blame you, really, seeing's how you fared the last time you'd yer hand in the till."

Yusif's face froze as he did all activity in the room. Then he lifted his left hand and clicked his fingers.

Before Danny could react, two of the men grabbed him and pinned him to the floor. Yusif said,

"I feel we'll be able to do business, but you'll have to learn some respect. My own 'infirmity' is a daily reminder to me. I'm going to share a little of that knowledge with you. In the hills of Lebanon, we learnt a refinement of what terrorists call 'knee-capping.' Nothing so permanent. Indeed, our way is quite artistic. We shatter the cartilage, but not the kneecap. You won't be crippled, but you'll be in a great deal of pain . . . but mobile. You'll be able to . . . what's the English word? Hobble . . . yes . . . out of here."

One of the men put a small hammer in Yusif's hand. Danny tried to kick free and roared,

"For fuck's sake!"

And Yusif brought the hammer down with one ferocious swing. White hot agony ripped through Danny, and he let out a howl of pure dementia. Then he passed out.

He came to with Charley slapping his face.

"Time to move, Sunshine, can't lie about here all day, eh?"

Danny gritted his teeth, bit down against the pain. Charley helped him to stand. He could . . . and found that 'hobble' was indeed the appropriate word.

Yusif said,

"Take your bag, my friend. I thank you for the gifts. Feel free to distribute the others on your way out. I shall expect you in one week."

Danny said nothing. He managed to leave without falling. Charley watched as he left three red-ribboned parcels at three doors, and said,

"You'll need more than friggin little bundles with that mob."

Danny struggled to concentrate and said,

"Any chance you might help me to the main road so I can flag a cab?"

Charley behaved as Danny hoped.

"No friggin danger, mate, I got a game of cards to finish. You toddle off now. Come back and see us soon."

Danny slowly made his way off Brandon. Waves of nausea tried to engulf him. A red mist seemed to shimmer before his eyes. He reached the main road . . . whispered,

"Now, you fucks, here's an old song, 'Let's Dance', eh?" and moved his finger to the first switch . . . said,

"You put your right foot out,"
       – flick
"Your left foot in"
       – flick
"You do the hokey-pokey
       . . . and"

***

EPILOGUE

A train known as The Dart brings commuters into the center of Dublin. Early in June, the sun danced along the green, sleek carriages. The Irish revel in a bit of warmth.

Cries of,

"Glorious weather."
"Mighty day."
"Isn't it grand to be alive, and in yer health."

rebounded through the train.

Save one.

Here, three youths in the advanced stages of yahoo-ism were tormenting passengers with shouts and obscenities. When the train reached the city center, the three horse-played on to the platform, drooling beer and insults.

A man approached and said in a pronounced English accent,

"I say . . . I say, you chaps, might I interest you in making some money?"

A slight limp as he neared was barely noticeable.

THE TIME OF
SERENA-MAY

&

UPON THE THIRD
CROSS

A COLLECTION OF SHORT STORIES

UPON THE THIRD CROSS

"He'd have dropped his trousers in The West End for a Valium," Bridie said.
Tom nearly dropped his fork.

"Bridie . . . for God sakes . . . he was your husband."

"That's why I know him, he'd have become a bum boy for a fiver."

Tom looked closely at his sister. What was she now, thirty-nine? She looked it, he thought. About 5'3", she had blonde streaked hair. Streaked with desperation. Brown eyes, a large nose and a mouth that was built to smile. Always plump, she was leaping right into fat, no gentle slide there. Yet she still attracted men. Not the desirable type or even frequently. But sufficient to keep her in a state of anxiety. They were eating in a vegetarian bistro off the Kennington Park Road. A huge plate of salad sat untouched before her. She said,

"I got some decent shoplifting done this morning."

Tom put down his fork.

"For heaven's sake . . . is that meant to shock me . . . so okay, I'm downright . . . okay . . . now gimme a friggin break."

Bridie smiled.

"Oh, Thomas, I'll give you more than that. Look, look what I have here for you. Close your eyes first."

Tom didn't want to do that. What he wanted was to get to the bottom line. Dreadful it would be, it was always that.

"What the hell," he said, "go on so, I'll close them."

"Now!" she said with a nervous giggle.

A tartan sweater lay over his plate. He could see "The Scotch House" label. Talking two hundred nicker . . . he sighed . . . easy. He said,

"That's about two ton . . . in there, yea."

"No, Tom, it wasn't anything like that."

"You nicked it. I'm supposed to wear a hot sweater, is that it?"

"You're supposed to be grateful, sometimes you sound just like Gerry."

Gerry was her first husband.

Bridie's face darkened and she said,

"Well, if I go to prison, you can give me tips on how to survive."

He knew she instantly regretted it as she reached over to touch his hand. To have spent two years inside and he wondered himself if he had survived.

The waiter appeared with a jug of water. Tall, in his twenties, he had a blond fake punk hair style. An air of smug blondness enwrapt him.

"Is everything to Madam's satisfaction?"

Tom sat back, the "Madam" would cost him plenty.

Bridie held up her glass and asked,

"Are you married . . . what's yer name?"

"Sevy."

"Sevy! . . . that's a pretty name . . . and Sevy, are you married, is there a Mrs.

Sevy, a bunch of littles Sevies at home?"

"Ah, no, Madam, but I am on the lookout. One lives on hope."

"Well, go peddle it at some other table."

"I beg your pardon?"

"Fuck off, Sevy."

Tom was already rising and reaching for his wallet. This scene had an all too familiar ring. He paid at the cash register and heard Bridie shout:

"I saw Gerry this morning."

Tom kept moving. Outside, he shook his head and vowed never again. Gerry had been dead for over five years.

**

Much later, he remembered he'd left the tartan sweater behind. Chances were that Sevy would end up with it. Aloud Tom said,

"And who's to say, the bastard might well deserve it, he would certainly earn it."

He took a Morden train and sat between a black man and a man in a pin-striped suit. The black gave him a radiant smile and asked,

"How you doing, man?"

Tom figured he was drugs or religion. He was inclined to believe the latter was more dangerous in the long haul. It was hard to distinguish them. An old Roxy music song same to mind.

"Dancing in the City" and boy he thought, these days, they were certainly doing that. The man in a suit was listening to a Walkman. Tom would have heavy bet on a classical item but the sound leaking through sounded like noise.

"Must be the distortion," he thought, "or else noise is the distortion."

The black man said:

"Jesus is coming."

And he said it loudly.

Tom wasn't clear as to whether a reply was expected but felt on behalf of the carriage, he'd answer,

"I'll be here," he said.

No one indicated whether this had been appreciated and Tom got off at Clapham Common.

**

Laurel Street is just off Clapham Common, and Tom could actually see trees from his window. He rented the bottom half of a two storey house. The owner lived above but was rarely in residence. Tom had once seen a photo of Thomas Morton's monastic cell. The Spartan bareness appealed to him. After prison, he was even more careful to avoid clutter. Furniture and fittings were kept to a minimum.

Tom examined his face in the bathroom mirror. He was into the fourth day of growing a beard and looked like a vagrant. He had hoped for the *Miami Vice* effect but no . . . downright dirty. It itched ferociously and he headed for the razor . . . considered and reckoned he could live with it a tad further.

He was forty-six with grey brown hair. The temples weren't so much receeding as galloping. Brown eyes and a nose that had been broken. Deep lines were etched into his face. Such made Tom look haggard. Five-ten in height, he'd been described as thin in his twenties, slender in his thirties . . . and now, at forty-six decidedly ill.

Tom made coffee and went to the wardrobe in the bedroom. He extracted a bundle from beneath a pile of linen and took it over to the bed.

Unfolding the bundle, he slowly extracted a swan-off shotgun. The short blunt barrel was cleaned to a dull sheen. He tested the weight and held it up in his right arm. From the bundle he took a box of 12-bore cartridges. With a practised movement he broke the gun and fitted two shells.

Immediately the gun felt different and he whispered,

"Now we're talking."

He began to quietly sing, "If ever you should leave me." His voice was strong and even. Standing, he continued to sing and practised the swing and switch of the gun.

"It could only be . . ."

Lightly touching the triggers, he contemplated the damage possible at close range.

***

Robbie Colbert considered his surname. He said it aloud with what he hoped was a French accent.

"Col-bert . . . mm . . . Colbert . . ." yea better, deep breath, "Ah oui Monsieur Colbert."

He thought it would need a little work. It was the old gallic attitude he had to perfect. He believed he'd buckets of charm, but it was to blend that with a certain arrogance.

"Tricky," he said . . . "now sang fluid, as soon as I know exactly wot it means, I'm going to have me some of that."

He lit a gauloises with a battered Zippo and inhaled deeply.

"Fuck!" he gasped and stubbed it out. He reckoned he'd settle for the aroma and lit up a Silk Cut.

"Better yea . . ."

The phone rang.

He snatched it. Earlier, he'd told his secretary not to put through any calls, especially from his wife. It was his wife.

"You bastard!"

"Ah Liz, I was hoping you'd call, I was just thinking about you."

"You haven't signed the papers."

"They're right here in front of me, darling . . . and one or two points I'd like to

277

discuss."

"Listen you piece of shit, there's no discussion, either you sign those or I reveal the other business."

Sweat broke out on his brown, he couldn't quite contain his anger.

"Reveal to whom, are you going to set that ex-husband, the convict on me . . . is that it?"

"You better pray I don't."

And she banged the phone down.

Robbie was 5'8". Black hair was swept back in a flourish, mainly to cover a creeping bald patch. A bulky frame was leaping to fat and all his clothes were a tight fit. A handsome smooth face was ruined by a mean mouth. All of him now shook. He moved to his desk and rummaged in a top drawer, took out a clear plastic bag. As he looked at the white powder he briefly remembered his father.

There'd been a drink then named Dick Turpin. His father would say,

"Two bottles of this and you flaming think you are Dick Turpin."

The powder he laid out in lines and then folded a sheet of paper into a thin funnel. Bending down, he snorted five lines in a fast, jerky movement, stood straight and waited for the explosion.

It came. He roared,

"Ah, I can fucking see India!"

Mrs. Dalton, his secretary, came rushing in.

"What's happening . . . Mr. Colbert?"

"Col-bèrt, you cow, we're moving into Europe and stop putting calls through or I'll fire yer fat arse . . . do you hear me . . . where's my coffee?"

Mrs. Dalton retreated, thinking ruefully that "things go better with Coke" was way wide of the mark. She reckoned the only place that lunatic was going was down the toilet.

Robbie had offices in Canary Wharf. The rent was frightening and he hadn't paid it for six months. A prospective real estate deal with a South Korean was the living hope. The one big sweet deal to clear the books and plonk Robbie on easy street. The prospect of jail was a spur to the deal. He had begun eating poolgogi as an omen to South Korea.

The first time he'd done cocaine had been at a friend's flat. Robbie had been skeptical about its potency and was of the opinion that a double scotch was equally effective. His friend prided himself on a valuable Siamese cat which watched with contempt as Robbie loaded his nostrils. The flat was the fifth floor of a South Kensington residence.

Earlier brandies and the power of the cocaine propelled Robbie into a blackout. Next day, the friend rang to tell him he'd launched the cat from the window into the South Kensington night. Robbie felt sure this might be an amusing after-dinner anecdote but it hadn't become so yet. Liz's mention of "the other business" sliced through the cocaine high and he said aloud,

"God, I wouldn't have . . . it's too awful to contemplate."

***

Tom dreamt he was back in prison. Back at the long table for a breakfast of porridge, dry bread and watery tea. Being locked in for 18 hours a day and two showers a week. One hour of TV every seven days.

In the dream he missed the hour's exercise after breakfast and was straight into the morning lock up. He woke with a shout and though his head knew he was out, his heart walloped in his chest. An overpowering stench of boiled vegetables filled his nostrils and he shook his head to clear it. You left prison but it never left you. That, he reckoned, was the real sentence.

The long unbelievable hours of crushing boredom, accentuated by the sudden violence. Reading . . . he'd read so much his eyes hurt. Escape that way was only part escape. The heart hugged a pain that nothing would ever obliterate.

Married men did maybe the worst time. Thoughts of betrayal festered in a world that fed on paranoia. Tom had wanted to marry Liz before he met her. Small, dark, beautiful and appeared to worship him. Their daughter Kendra, was her miniature carbon copy. He'd said,

"Lucky twice over . . . lucky

lucky

lucky."

Then he got caught, got four years. Liz came unexpectedly on a wet Thursday. Their conversation was burned into his mind, like a bad prayer.

"I want a divorce, Tom."

"You can't be serious. Sweetheart, I'll be out in two years."

"You got four."

"It will work out at good behaviour at two years."

"That's too long, Tom, I'm sorry."

"Liz, for God's sake, I mean it's not as if you've met someone else."

"I have."

"Oh God."

"He's a good man, Tom, you'd like him . . . and he loves Kendra . . . it's not as if he's a stranger. I used to work for him."

"That Colbert fuck, you said he was a slimy bastard."

"He's doing really well, the property market is booming."

***

That was then. The bottom fell out of the game and Liz and Colbert's marriage.

Kendra was six now. Only in the past few months had Tom been able to see her. The girl seemed confused as to who he was and he felt the same, most of the time.

Tom was a thief. Early in life he discovered he'd a flair for it. The trick was to work alone, not get greedy and keep a low profile. Once, he'd broken all three rules and went to prison. The only mistakes he now believed were the ones you learnt nothing from. Two years behind bars to reflect on that.

He made coffee and checked to see how the beard was developing. Now he looked like a rested wino. But it changed his look all right. It gave a hard slant to his features and in London, how far wrong could that lead you.

One cold December morning in prison, he'd felt close to suicide. The building stifled you in summer, froze you in winter. The small church was a prospect of heat. A service had just concluded and the men were shuffling out. Clouds of their breath hung condensed in the air. Like false hope. A smell of incense was balm from the urine habitual stench. That mixed with bad cabbage.

Near the altar, someone had placed a home made version of Calvary cleverly constructed from nails, the three crosses had been buffed to a high sheen. Makeshift match figures to symbolise Christ and the person on His right had been dyed white. The third cross was vacant. Either the maker had lost interest or reckoned this figure didn't merit significance. Tom reached down and touched it. It was held down and he gave it a sharp tug. Palming it, he turned quickly.

Tom had thought about the thief to whom Christ said, "This day you shall be with me in paradise," and he thought, "Did that guy get lucky or what?" What started out as a pretty rough Friday sure turned around. But what of the other chappie. Where did he go? Even some crude prison artist hadn't reckoned his cross was worth filling.

"Time to go to work," he said.

He dressed in worn plain splattered jeans, heavy sweater with holes in the elbows and rain blotched heavy work boots. Looking in the mirror, a labourer looked back. Walking up and down, he adopted the macho strut beloved of the building sites and let out a low wolf whistle. Tried out a few of the well tested lines.

"Cor, look at the body on 'er . . . wotcher say darlin' . . . get a load of this sweetheart."

"Yea," he added, "that will do it."

***

On his release from prison, he'd hit a depression that was all enveloping. Access to Kendra was denied, money was short and he couldn't adapt to London. One tortured morning he'd woke with tears in his face and knew that crying in his sleep was serious distress. A half remembered line had surfaced in his head.

"When you can't stand it anymore, try kneeling."

He'd thought, "And what have I got to lose."

Bending his knees, he said,

"God, if you're about, this is a good time."

And nothing happened. For ten minutes he remained thus and heard only the beating of his heart. Various platitudes bleated in his mouth.

"The meek shall inherit the earth," and immediately he thought of what Paul Getty said,

"Yea but they won't have the mineral rights."

280

And Job crying in torment.

"Why do you test me so hard?" and The Lord answered,

"Cos you really piss me off."

Finally his knees began to ache and he looked upward, said,

"That's about what I figured."

Later that day he'd returned to thieving. He didn't bother God any further.

Tom worked the "holiday" flats. These were short term luxurious lettings advertised in the quality papers. Usually Arabs, but lately drug dealers were the tenants. He'd draw up a list of the very best ones advertised then ring the agency to see what was vacant. Continue to ring until the letting was made. Then he hit immediately. Dressed as a labourer, he was near invisible. Ten minutes was the maximum time he'd spend and took only cash, coins or gold. It astonished him that people believed they'd found clever hiding places. Dirty laundry was the most common. He wore surgical gloves and recently, in a soiled pair of socks, was two grand in a tight roll. The shotgun had come from a block in Kensington Church Street.

Depending on the hauls, Tom estimated he'd need only six "Runs" a year. Too, there was the pipe dream of one major jackpot. What he'd do then, he wasn't sure. The adrenalin rush, the sheer fix of the job would be hard to kick.

As he headed toward the tube, a small fat black woman galloped beside him. In a sing-song voice she gasped,

"Jesus wants you, only Jesus saves."

He wondered why it was that short fat black ladies were particularly prone to lunacy. Almost every High Street had one and he contemplated if the councils provided them. Almost as prevalent as muggers, they appeared to work longer hours. He said to her,

"He saves, does He? . . . for what, a rainy day . . . is it?"

She gave him a worried look and began to back away. He moved after her.

"No, come on, don't be modest, give me the credit plan."

He learnt the only thing crazies feared was craziness. Put an even more psychotic face right into theirs and they legged it. Which is exactly what this lady did. Tom remembered a similar lunatic who'd been spraying his message on the walls of the tube.

"God might help you to travel
but you have to call the airport."

Tom had thought then, there are two kinds of people.

One – those who can read the writing on the wall.

Two – those who put it there.

He thought much the same thing now.

His father had died during Tom's first year in prison. He'd been escorted out for the funeral. The warder said,

"You get out to plant the ole boy."

Handcuffed.

As they slapped the cuffs on him, he said,

"Bit fuckin' strong, eh?? I mean . . . how dangerous am I, for heaven's sake?"

The warder said,

"Shut yer mouth."

He did.

It had been a freezing cold day. A drizzling rain soaked them. The mourners were few. Bridie was then in one of her periodic drying out clinics. After they'd planted his dad, a man had approached Tom and handed him a frayed, battered envelope. A previous name had been scratched out and his father scribbled hastily below,

"Your father's effects"

"Bit scarce on the envelope, were ye. A shortage in the friggin' stationery, is it?"

The effects were pitiful, one worn wedding ring. A strapless watch and a page of a jotter, neatly folded. It had "Thomas" written on it in his dad's neat simple hand. On Tom's release from prison, the first thing he'd done was hand these to a wino. The wino had roared,

"This watch's stopped!"

The letter read:

> *My Dear Thomas,*
>
> *I'll be dead when you read this. You have been a fierce disappointment to me. Poor Bridie was always away with the fairies but I expected more of you. I know it was hard on you that your mother was taken from us early. But I did my best.*
>
> *I can't believe how you've repaid my efforts. The shame of you in prison. It would have killed your mother.*

Tom had paused here, sighed deeply and read on,

> *The mortification of your life hasn't helped my health. It's no use pretending otherwise. I don't know what will become of you. It's not too late to change. Go to confession and mebbe have a private chat with the chaplain. Ask him how you can make amends. Tell the authorities your plan to toe the line. God mind you, God knows I tried. I'll leave you my ring but you'll probably sell it.*
> *Your heart broken father,*
> *Thomas senior*

For a long time, Tom had sat motionless and finally muttered, "Tell the authorities is it . . . I'll tell them shit, you can bank on that."

Shredding the letter, he'd dropped the pieces in his slop bucket.

***

Tom had watched the black woman gallop off towards the oval and whispered, "But is it cricket?" and gone thieving.

The job had gone surprisingly easily and he'd been in and out in fifteen minutes. Such ease was deadly to caution. He knew you could think it would always be so. And . . . he broke his own rules.

The wardrobe contained 6 Giorgio Armani suits and he'd taken two plus a small leather Bible he'd found in the bookcase. Always check the books, people distributed notes of large denominations amid the pages. This time, he found 500 dollars in *The Day of the Jackal* and thought, "some books just keep making money." In the toilet cistern, he found four hundred pounds.

Later, he flicked through the Bible and paused at the crucifixion.

> *The criminal who hung upon the third cross hurled insults at Jesus.*
> *"Aren't you the Christ? Save yourself and us."*
> *But the other criminal rebuked him.*
> *"Don't you fear God?" he said, "since you are under the same sentence.*
> *We are punished justly for we are getting what our deeds deserve. But*
> *this man has done no wrong."*
> *Then he said,*
> *"Jesus, remember me when you come into your kingdom."*
> *Jesus answered,*
> *"I tell you the truth, today you will be with me in paradise."*

Tom smiled. His father would have loved the "good thief." Tom reckoned the guy was just hedging his bets. Now the other criminal, he'd have liked to know about him. What Christians saw as taunts and insults. Tom reckoned was pure desperation, he'd have liked to know his name.

Tom slept that evening. In prison he'd learnt to sleep at a moment's notice. Any given day was shriek-full of noise,

> the slamming of cells
> rattling of keys
> cries and yahoo's
> the resonance of rage
> and
> the echo of desperation

You learnt to tune out or you got some kind of noose and let yer heels dance their final fandango.

He learnt.

A warden asked him once,

"What will you do when you get out?"

He'd taken a long time to discover that you get out but you're never released. It got into your soul and a past there was forever imprisoned. He'd heard the Eagles song, "Hotel California" and reckoned they'd got it right with the lines,

> "You can check out anytime you want,
> but you can never leave."

Rising, he showered and rubbed gel into the increasing stubble. Making strong coffee, he put on a plain white shirt and decided to try on an Armani. The suit was a little big but the general loose cut disguised that. Rejecting a tie, he closed the top button of the shirt. Shaping up before the mirror, he thought if he'd less hair he could pass for Phil Collins and said,

"But would you want to?"

And grabbing the hair brush, he held it like a microphone, did a rapid shimmer, bent his knees and sang,

"Don't be cruel."

How it would seem to anyone else, he couldn't guess, but he thought he sounded pretty good. Drinking the coffee, he felt a burst of adrenaline. Once, he'd mistaken that artificial buzz for hope.

Not anymore. Now it was only caffeine. Janis Ian had sung

> "Measure out your life in coffee-spoons."

As the job had gone well, he decided to celebrate. A meal and a hooker. Satisfy all the appetites. He decided to head for High Street Kensington. The tube was full and he had to stand.

"Give them a chance to admire the suit," he thought.

He was feeling good, not great or euphoric, but ticking over. A young woman boarded at Victoria with a small boy. The child was carelessly beautiful. As if the gods finished him with a flourish. Blond tussled hair, blue eyes and a hesitant smile. The woman carried Harrods bags and wore effortless expensive clothes. Designer sunglasses crouched in her hair, in wait for all contingencies. A man offered his seat and she took it without thanks. Without preamble she began to tongue-lash the boy. A stream of vile whining complaint. The boy, his face glowing red with shame, glanced around.

"Don't look away when I'm talking to you," she said.

And

Arm outstretched, she began to give him long sweeping blows to his head. People looked anxiously away. She was in mid-swing when Tom seized her wrist.

"Mind yer own business," she spat, "he's my child." Tom bent down and looked her full in the face, and said,

"You mindless bitch, hit him one more time and I'll break your fucking nose."

She sank back in her seat. Tom leant into her face.

"I know where you live, you take it out on the child later, I'll know."

"You don't know me."

"You tramp, I've known you all my life."

He released her wrist and moved back to the door. The boy's eyes shone, in wonder and fear. Tom thought, "What the fuck, the kid will probably grow up to become Ted Bundy."

A parable from childhood church days returned.

The parable.

A man is jogging on the beach. The tide has washed up hundreds of starfish and they're marooned above the tide mark. Another man is slowly and methodically throwing the creatures back into the sea. The jogger approaches and says,

"Bit of a futile exercise, eh, what difference can it make?"

The man pauses mid-throw, looks at the starfish in his hand, answers,

"Makes a difference to this one."

Tom sighed and whispered,

"The wisdom of the fucking ages."

And got out at High Street Kensington. He didn't look back.

At a spaghetti house, he ordered a bottle of Asti Spumanti. The waiter served with a splash of indifference that was close to catatonia. As he paid, the manager asked,

"Was the meal to Sir's satisfaction?"

"It was hot, I'll give you that."

Sometimes, that was the best it might be.

***

In a telephone kiosk, he scanned the cards plastered to the booth. A whole range of sexual offers. He rang what seemed like the least offensive one,

> "Busty American lady gives relief and fantasy.
> Ring Lisa."

The address was within walking distance and he headed there.

An intercom buzzed him through the third floor. A woman in her late twenties was peeking out the door.

"Lisa?"

"That's me, honey. Y'all come right in."

"Actually, there's only me."

"Ya kidder, honey. I do surely like a man with a sense of humour."

She had a Dolly Parton wig, more makeup than Boots, and . . . as advertised . . . very large boobs. A flimsy pink wrap-around was . . . wrapped around. Her accent was a mix of Texas and London Bridge.

"A drink, darlin'?"

"Scotch would be good."

She gave him a heavily watered one and he took a slug.

. . . very large boobs. A flimsy pink wrap-around was . . . wrapped around. Her accent was a mix of Texas and London Bridge.

"A drink, darlin'?"

"Scotch would be good."

She gave him a heavily watered one and he took a slug.

"Y'all know what you'd like, darlin'? Y'all want me to dress up or dress you up or tie me down or . . ."

"Hey, Lisa . . . hold the phones, okay. I just want the basic business. Stop calling me honey or darlin', alright."

"Well, okey-dokey, hon . . .! That's seventy-five in advance. I didn't charge you for the drink . . . Y'all want Lisa to freshen you up?"

"No, one glass of water is my absolute limit. Can we get a condom?"

She lay back on a sofa and began to moan.

"Give it to me big boy, oh you're really hung . . . no kissing on the mouth and touching the hair . . . come on, yah big stallion."

"Lisa . . . hey . . . yo, Lisa, drop the dialogue for pity sake . . . just shut the fuck up already."

She did. He did the basic business and got out of there in jig time. He made a note of the building and reckoned he might return in a working capacity . . . after all, he'd money invested there.

***

Folie
à
Deux

"The Rake's Progress."

Fried up a batch of eggs, washed them down with scalding tea and headed for the local mini-market. Bought the papers, edible chews for Rusty and on consideration, half a pint of Vodka. Back home, he rifled through notes on literature he'd begun to keep. Notes on Abbott's *In The Belly of the Beast.*

The literary elite had come together to gain Abbots release from prison. The first night out, he stabbed a waiter to death and the elite galloped for the hills.

"Oh dear, we got that wrong . . . sorry."

Next up was Jean Genet.

Tom was particularly interested that Genet's stealing was linked to the other obsessions he had . . . betrayal. Genet liked to present himself as

"the golden thug"

Thief
Convict
Homosexual.

Tom's research in the prison library had revealed a somewhat tarnished thug. Four years Genet had spent inside. Later, he seemed to specialise in the betrayal of friends and the desertion of lovers.

Tom made fresh tea and thought that for him, prison was the reference point in his life. Everything new came back to that. He didn't dwell on "what might have been". The thing now was to stay out, at any cost.

The day of his release, as he'd waited in the office for the paperwork to be processed, a radio was playing,

"Haberna" from Carmen.

As if lucidity had been bestowed on him, he'd mouthed the lyrics,

> L'oiseau que tu croyais surprendre
> Battit de l'aile et s'envola
> L'amour est loin tu peux l'attendre
> Tu ne l'attends plu, il est là
> Tout autour de toi vite, vite

A taste for opera had sparked then, but he'd never have told a soul of that. It occurred to him now that he'd play his favourite pieces for Rusty. Dogs loved what you loved, and they didn't criticize.

"Top that," he said and heard the doorbell.

"The dog hates me," was Bridie's opening gambit.

"Only the dog?" asked Tom.

She stormed in hauling what looked like half a ton of Alsatian. The dog perked up on seeing Tom and his tail began to wag furiously.

"Jesus, is that opera? . . . don't you have any Bob Dylan?"

Tom released Rusty from the leash, fought off his licks of love, and let him out to his garden.

"Bridie, nobody listens to Bob Dylan, not even Joan Baez listens to Bob Dylan . . . would you like tea?"

"Ah, Tom, I need a pick-me-up . . . you wouldn't believe what's been happening. Gerry called yesterday."

Against his better judgment, he gave her a medium vodka and put his hand on her shoulder.

"Bridie, you've got to stop this craziness. Gerry's dead . . . alright. You start up this lunacy again, they'll put you away. Do you hear me?"

She nodded and tears began to slide down her face, into the glass. It seemed to Tom they made a soft pling. Her mascara ran and she began to resemble Alice Cooper.

"I'm so afraid, Tom, I'm so afraid of being left on my own."

"Hey . . . come on, I'll mind you . . . okay, you, me and Rusty, we'll open a guest house in Brighton."

"I like Brighton, we went to see *The Exorcist* on my honeymoon there."

Tom went to the garden and fed the chews to Rusty. The dog gazed at him with loving admiration. Henry James it was . . . he thought it was him who said if you wanted to know about spirituality, look into the eyes of a dog. Someone else said that religion was for people who were afraid of hell. Spirituality was for those who'd been there.

"What d'ya say, Rust, wanna go to the park and chase muggers? Yea . . . I thought you might."

When Tom went back inside, Bridie had composed herself. The vodka hadn't hurt the process.

"Do you ever miss Kendra . . ."

"Take a wild fuckin' guess, Bridie, eh."

"I'm sorry Tom, I wish I'd had a child, no one would ever have taken her off me . . . the bastards."

He thought she was little more than a child herself but he couldn't resist the sarcasm.

"What did you think, Bridie . . . that I could have brought her along to jail but decided not to? Is that it . . . you think I had some fuckin' choices then?"

She hung her head. He wanted to shake her and shout,

"Wake up, smell the coffee."

But instead he put his arms round her and stroked her hair.

"I might marry a Yank," she said.

Tom released her, went to the bookcase and picked out Nancy Mitford's *The Pursuit of Love*.

"Do you still like her?"

"Oh, Tom, yes . . . Remember you used to read her for me. Will you read something now . . ."

He flicked through, found what he'd hoped and read in a clipped colonial tone,

> "One is always rather pleased when there is one America less in the world and I'm sure God will send them to a different place from one."

He paused for the punch line . . .

> "from one and Lord Byron."

He'd held the book upright so that Bridie couldn't see he was actually reading from tacked-on notes and not the text. The remark was from Mitford's essays and letters.

"*The Pursuit of Love* was dedicated to a French officer. She based Fabrice on him. They'd had an affair during the war. The officer had seen seen it as an amusing diversion and that's all. To Mitford, it was the grand passion, so much so that she even moved to France. For 30 years, she hung on as a pathetic admirer. One morning, she read in the newspaper that he'd married into the French aristocracy and she died soon after."

He closed the door and told her none of this.

"Was Nancy Mitford happy, Tom, did things work out for her?"

"She was. They did . . . Yo, Rusty, WALKIES!"

Before taking Rusty, he plugged in the iron, set up the board and laid the newspapers on it. Carefully, he ironed the paper.

"Tom, you're ironing the newspapers? I knew you were neat, but good Lord."

"It's to dry the ink. I hate to read a newspaper and end up with my hands covered in black. Plus, you get a crisp solid read."

He gave Bridie another hug and promised to be in touch. What he thought was she was touched in the head. The insane are revered in Pakistan as being marked by God. How he could apply this kernel of information to his own dilemma was a complete mystery.

The walk with Rusty was exhilarating. Released from the lead on Clapham Common, the dog near took flight returning home. Tom noticed a new billboard near the tube station. It was for the Diabetic Association and showed a mother holding her baby. In one hand she held a syringe. The caption read,

"Every day of life, this mother has to hurt the baby she loves."

A faintness hit him and he felt his knees go. Rusty gazed at him with concern. He put his hands against a wall and force-kicked himself back to strength.

Kendra was diabetic. For her first year, he'd given her the insulin shots and she cried every time. It had torn the heart from him then, it did the same now. Feeling steadier, he made his way home, the dog eyed him carefully.

Back home, he got the vodka bottle and drank deep . . . it burned and roared down his throat. But it took near instant effect, he walloped another blast and sat down. The scene would replay now . . . now or in his dreams. He didn't fight it.

It was a year ago. Liz had rung, warm and friendly. She asked if he wished to re-establish his links with Kendra. He'd taken Liz out to dinner and she'd been coy then flirtatious. They'd gone back to his place. No sooner in the door than she'd clung to him, whispering,

"Make love to me, darling, do it now."

He did.

Afterwards, they were entwined on the couch and Liz, nigh drunk with after-glow asked,

"Was it good for you, sweetheart?"

"Well, Liz, it was about how I expected."

She'd pulled away, stunned and finally said,

"What exactly is that supposed to mean, Thomas?"

"It means you get to feel what I felt the day you came to me in prison . . . you get to feel fucked."

She'd risen and gone to the bathroom. Emerging, she said in a clear cold voice,

"The man your daughter calls daddy, he's been showing her a little of what you just now so elegantly described."

And she'd stormed out. It took some minutes for the total implication to hit him. He took after her but she'd gone. He knew now he might well have killed her then.

Shortly after, he'd found the shotgun on one of his jobs. He'd once heard that a person gets two chances to partake in the very glory of God. Once in teenage years and secondly, in the mid 40s. He'd reckoned he could have left the gun there. Each time he polished and oiled the weapon, he was glad he'd taken it,

Kendra's birthday was due shortly and he felt that day would be appropriate.

As he relived this now, tears coursed down his face and sobs broke from him. The dog lay at his feet and whimpered. They stayed thus until a long time after the light had gone.

Periodically, the man's hand strayed to the dog's head and rubbed him behind the ears.

***

On the other side of London, a little girl tossed and turned in her sleep. Her mother stood in the doorway, dragged viciously on a cigarette and thought evil and brutal thoughts.

The smoke hung above her head like a shroud of morning mist. An angle of the darkness was like an omen of destruction.

***

Come morning, Tom moved from the chair and did an inventory.
"What have I got Rusty, eh well lets see

1. An attitude.
2. A broken cross.
3. Nearly a beard.

And I've got you Rusty, that's good, that's really good, so how about I feed you.

As he watched the dog eat, for reasons linked to things he couldn't articulate, he quoted a line from a book by a young Indian writer, Ferdie Kanga,

"In Bombay there lives a rumour that walks in disguise as a fact."

***

Terry and Bill were in the breakage business. Human breakage. They were known as "the bone breakers". Both in their late 40s, they could pass for twins. Describe one, you described both.

Potbellied
Balding
Medium height

Merry twinkling eyes
Broken noses
Cockney accents.

They weren't cockneys. From Romford they'd gravitated to the East end and adopted the usual history. Like so many minor villains, they claimed to have known the Krays. It was a mandatory requirement.

"Yea, sure, knew ole Reg, salt of the earth, loved his old Mum he did."

In the "Rent-a-Hug" industry, they were prominent. Recently, they'd hired out to the drug market and come in contact with Robert Colbert.

They were having a drink with him in a quiet pub in Docklands. Robert's nose was nearly permanently running. A tell tale sign of the chronic coke abuser. He swiped at it and said,

"Can't seem to shake this cold."

The boys exchanged looks, Terry said,

"Oughta get yerself some of them lemsips, son, they'll see you right, watcher think Bill, them lemsips help him?"

"Oh yea, be right as rain tomorrow, me old Dad swears by 'em."

Robert ordered a fresh round of drinks and said,

"I'm putting the finishing touches to a deal and if it comes through, there'll be plenty of gravy in it for you boys."

"Gravy . . ." said Terry.

"Thing is, I've got a slight problem. My missus, she's threatening her . . . her ex-husband on me."

"Big bloke is he?"

"Ard he is."

"Oh he thinks he's tough just because he's been inside."

"Well Mr. C, how about if Bill and I go round and have a bit of a chin wag with him, how would that be?"

"Yea, Mr C . . . give him a word to the wise."

Robert beamed, took out an envelope and laid it on the table. He said,

"Capital, it just so happens I have his place of residence at hand and a little something for you boys. A drink in it for you."

Terry took the envelope, looked inside, looked at Bill, raised one eyebrow. He said,

"Very generous Mr C, very white of you. We'll drop round on (he looked in the envelope again) . . . young Tom this very afternoon. You've nowt planned, Bill do you . . . free are you?".

Bill gave a huge smile.

"No Terry, all free this after as it happens."

A worried look crossed Robert's face.

"Am . . . nothing too physical boys, just so as he gets message."

"No need to fret Mr C, we'll just have a bit of a chin wag, have a nice cup of tea 'n' all. Eh Bill, wotcher think."

"Yea, a nice cup of tea . . . maybe a couple of biccies eh."
Robert drained his drink, sniffed and got up to leave.
"I can expect a progress report then."
"Yea."
After he left, one or both said, "Wanker."

***

Robbie rang the Korean and hyped on Coke, he felt he had the deal almost clinched. A few more weeks and he'd kiss them all goodbye. He was fuelling the coke with chain cups of hot black espresso. The adrenalin suggested he ring Liz, his estranged wife. She answered on the first ring.

"Liz, listen sweetheart, just to let you know the cheque is in the mail (he thought, and pigs might friggin' fly)."

"It better be."

"Now now darlin, that sounds suspiciously like a threat."

"You can bank on it, you won't like Tom, oh no . . . you won't like Tom at all."

"What? The convict, oh honeybunch, I don't think we need worry about him. Some colleagues of mine are due to have a little chat with our boy."

"Those cockney cowboys, the two fat assholes you hang out with. He'll eat them for breakfast."

"We'll see, shall we sweetheart . . . how is Kendra?"

The phone slammed down.

Robbie smiled and said,

"And nice talking to you."

He felt his time had come. All the loose strands were about to be nailed down. A little celebration was in order.

Robbie opened his top drawer and took out a walkman. Ran his fingers through the cassettes and selected Neil Young. A gun catalogue lay under the tapes. He loaded up Neil Young, turned the volume to maximum and began to look through the catalogue.

The coke in tandem with the music nearly lifted him out of his seat. He could feel the beat to the core of his soul and stabbed at the air with his right fist.

"Ale-rite real fuckin A! Jeez, those old hippies got it right."

Harvest Moon.

Right . . . yea.

The first gun in the catalogue, a .38 Arminius Titan Revolver attracted him instantly. Next up, a Colt Python got equal attention, he flipped back to see who supplied these babies. An address in Waco, Texas. The irony went right over his head.

Mrs. Dalton's face suddenly appeared at desk level. Arms waving to get his attention. He reluctantly removed the earphones.

"Better be good Dalton, I'm very busy here, this is a top priority tape here."

"Really Mr. Colbert, could you try lowering your voice. You could be heard down the street with your roaring . . . what on earth is a harvest moon?"

"Don't get shitty with me Dalton. Remember who pays the wages."

"Actually Mr. Colbert you haven't paid me . . ."

"Can it Dalton, was there something of special urgency?"

A man appeared behind her, dressed in a dark suit and carrying a briefcase.

"This gentleman insisted on seeing you. I said you were busy but alas he could hear your . . . singing."

Robbie stood up, all business now.

"Off you go Dalton, I'll handle this . . . and you are, sir?"

"Naylor . . . I'm the bailiff."

Robbie momentarily lost it then rallied.

"All the more easy for you to nail 'em eh?"

"Very humorous I'm sure Mr. Colbert, first time I ever heard that little pun. Very first time. You've landed yourself in some serious financial waters."

"Which I'm just about to solve . . . no worries, everyone gets paid."

"And when might we expect this joyous event."

"Now see here Naylor, I'm not altogether sure I care for your tone. Might I remind you who pays the piper calls the proverbial . . . eh."

Naylor gave a deep sigh.

"In fact, you pay no-one . . . that's why I'm here . . . You do seem inordinately fond of a tune Mr. Colbert. In exactly one week, all properties and goods pertaining to you shall be seized. The jig is up . . . shall we say."

With that, he left, leaving a raging Robbie. He wondered if the "bone breakers" might be set on Naylor. Would a bailiff be missed?

"Not friggin likely" he guffawed, and delighted by his own resurgence quoted a line from Oscar Wilde,

> *Murder is always a mistake; one should never do anything that one can not talk about after dinner.*

He slapped the earphones on, debated another line or so of coke and shouted,

"Do it to me Neil . . . way to go buddy."

Outside, Mrs. Dalton covered her ears.

***

Liz tried three times to get Tom on the phone. The phone rang unanswered. She said, "Bloody man, never there when it's important!"

In Tom's flat as the phone rang each successive time, Rusty lifted his head and tensed. Then he settled down to wait for his master's return.

***

That evening, Tom stopped at a pet shop and bought a batch of edible dog toys.

At the butchers, he had them give him two huge bones. He couldn't believe how much he was looking forward to seeing the dog. Now that his heart had thawed a little, he felt he'd go with it.

The door to his flat was ajar and he felt a coldness. It wasn't lost on him that that's exactly what his "customers" experienced. Inside was a total mess.

"Rusty," he called "here boy."

Everything breakable was broken. A pile of excrement sat in the middle of the room. All his opera records were smashed.

With a sense of dread, he entered the bedroom. Rusty looked asleep, the blanket pulled up to his neck, his head resting on the pillow. Tom pulled the blanket back and let out a soft sob.

The dog had been gutted from end to neck. Tom sank to his knees and began to wail. As the anguish ripped him, it registered slowly that Rusty's tail had been removed. His eyes could see that his mind couldn't decipher the message.

He got shakily to his feet and stumbled to the wardrobe. The Armani suits were shredded, he tore them aside, the shotgun was gone. That this was near exactly what he did himself only added to his frustration.

Going to the shop, he tried to stop the tears that kept blinding him. He bought a bottle of brandy and a half dozen bin liners. Rusty he wrapped in a clean sheet and buried him in garden. All the time he swigged from the brandy. The third cross he placed on the mound of clay. Slowly, he packed the debris into the bin liners and used the work to freeze his heart.

The phone rang.

"Yea."

"Tom."

"Yea, who is this?"

"We were so sorry to miss you, we called but you were out."

"Did you have to gut the dog?"

"Thing is me old china, though he entertained us hugely in your absence, alas – he took a piece outa my colleague."

"What did you cut his tail off for?"

"Ah tut-tut, we were too subtle for you . . . and a man of your learning. You're familiar with the expression 'hair of the dog'."

"You fuck."

"Now, now, sticks and stones. We confiscated your shooter in the interest of your own safety. I trust we won't need to trouble you further – you got our message."

"Yea, that you're a sick psychotic bastard."

"Stay away from Mr Colbert, you wouldn't want to meet us. Must rush, tootle-pip."

And the phone went down.

It rang immediately.

"Yea."

"Tom, this is Liz, are you alright?"

"Yes."

"Tom don't stay there, a couple of thugs are on their way."

"They've been. I was out but they left their calling card. You know them?"

"Oh yes, I know them, Terry and Bill, two bogus cockneys with a sadistic streak. Are you all right, would you like me to come over?"

"No Liz . . . and thanks a lot, I gather those cowboys have some connection with your husband."

"My husband! Well, yes, he's that . . . it's so weird to hear you call him that . . . they're his errand boys,"

"I see, okay, thanks again, Liz."

He rang a major league villain he'd met in prison. A man he'd helped out once. Now he asked if the addresses of Terry and Bill might be provided.

They could, but it would take twenty-four hours.

Tom looked round his broken home. It seemed totally altered, he knew he'd never play his beloved opera in this place any more and decided then he'd look for a new address.

Back out to the garden, he stood over Rusty's plot and thought, "I'll grieve now . . . for this and all the other losses. Then I'll move on to the business at hand."

He thought if pain is some yardstick for growth, then he'd done all the growing he was going to do.

***

Robbie was drinking Pernod. The way it clouded over when the water hit was a source of endless interest. Didn't taste too bad either, bit sweet, but wow, did it kick or what. He thought he might hang out in Paris when the deal came through.

In his mind, he was cruising along Boulevard St Michel when the "bone breakers" arrived. They looked decidedly pleased with themselves.

He switched off Paris.

"How's the nose Mr C?"

"Never mind my friggin nose. How did it go? Did you put the fear of God in the bastard?"

Terry shouted to the barman.

Two pints of best landlord, and another Canary's Abortion for my friend.

"So how did it go dammit?"

"Tut, tut Mr C, impatient boys don't get dessert. You didn't quite put us in the picture, did he Bill, didn't play honest John, did he?"

Bill lifted a heavily bandaged hand to his pint, couldn't manage and used the other hand. The merry eyes were far from merry. He mouthed as he wiped foam from his upper lip.

"Had to get a bleedin' tetanus shot, didn't I, be bleedin' lucky I don't get rabies."

"He bit you, the convict bit you?"

"Steady Mr C, the dog it was."

"Dog . . . wot bloody dog."

"See Mr C . . . oh that rhymes . . . see, thing is, you didn't tell us he'd a dog, a flaming Alsatian, too. Game bugger, I'll give you that."

"What about the convict?"

"Well like we're trying to explain Mr C, the client wasn't home but his dog was . . ., and he had a piece of old Bill here . . . gave him a right nasty nip. But no worries, we done for 'im."

Bill gave a nasty chuckle.

"Yea, we done for 'im all right, slit 'im from head to tail and put 'im in bed then. All cosy like, sheets pulled up to his snout . . . lovely it were . . . bled a bit though . . . just a tad unpleasant, didn't half pong."

Robbie drained the Pernod, it made his eyeballs bulge.

"Am I supposed to be pleased with this fiasco or what? You really screwed it up."

"Mr C, I'm a little peeved at your attitude especially as Bill went to the bother of bringing you a small gift."

"Gift, wot bloody gift?"

Terry nodded to Bill who reached inside his jacket and took out a gaily wrapped parcel. He said,

"Heads you win."

Terry said,

"and . . ."

Robbie tore the wrapping off and looked at the contents in horror, he whispered,

"Tails . . ."

***

Bridie was to most people, a person on the dark side of the moon. Not that she marched to the beat of a different drummer, she was the very melody. But all agreed, she had a gift with flowers. She stood now in her small garden and admired the ocean of flowers she'd cultivated.

> Lilies
> Clematis
> Poppies
> Bluebells
> Gladiola
> Roses

"You are all my children," she said. And went inside. The house, a two storey semi-detached in Streatham was compulsively tidy but overflowing. She'd kept everything she'd ever got. Upstairs in a small white closet were a myriad of baby clothes. On very bad days, she'd rummage there and talk to the child she'd never have.

When she'd been told she'd never conceive she'd begun buying the clothes. Madness demands its attendant rituals. On these days she'd convince herself that

Gerry was alive. That he'd simply gone out and would "be home for his tea".

She'd then prepare his favourite, moussaka with pita bread and taramasalata, piled with olives and feta cheese. As evening fell and she knew she couldn't make it happen, she'd sweep all from the table and grind all the food underfoot. The pattern was set, she'd drop a few pills and wash them down with booze . . . if she didn't blackout and collapse, she'd hit the town and the town always hit back.

And hard.

Bridie enjoyed "shock" value as opposed to shock treatment. She'd had the latter but wasn't too fond of it. It left her too disorientated and her grip was tenuous at best. No, she liked the expression on people's faces when you did the completely unexpected.

Shop-lifting got a rise out of most. After two husbands Bridie was more than financially secure and had a second house in Kennington. It was rented to a civil servant. The gun Sevy had given her was in the fridge. Next to the Kerrygold. It gave her a frisson of excitement each time she opened the door. Seemed appropriate too that such an icy object should be kept in cold storage. The only time she'd held it, a shudder ran down her spine. What was the fascination they held for men she pondered. Not only were they ugly, but they made her feel similar. Tom came stomping into her mind.

As always she acted right on impulse. She called a mini-cab and went directly to him. His front door was ajar. She felt her heart palpitating. This kind of shock she didn't like as it was outside her control.

Pushing the door she asked, "Tom . . ."

He was sitting in the middle of the room with a lost expression. Even in prison he hadn't looked like that. She approached him slowly and he turned.

"Kendra?"

"No Tom . . . it's Bridie."

"Oh, hello Bridie."

"What's happened Tom . . . where's your dog?"

"He's in the garden, under the third cross."

Then he told her everything . . . from Liz's visit to prison to the present events. He looked up at her and said,

"But don't worry. I'm not going to cry. I've done that. I was a bit lost there. I kind of forgot what to do next but I'll be fine now, I just needed to spill my guts."

And the lost look had gone. He fingered his face.

"Do you like the yard?"

"You look like Terry Waites."

"Before or after his release."

Bridie made him some eggs and then persuaded him to lie down. After he was asleep, she began to clean the rooms. For the first time in her life, she felt a growing sense of purpose. A thought was shaping in her mind and she sensed the beginning of a major change. Most of all she felt needed. She knew that maybe once in a lifetime, a man like Tom crashed out and even then, only every so briefly. A privilege it was she believed to have been the one who picked him out and up. Further, she prayed she'd be able to wipe the slate clean of the blight that overtook him.

Not altogether sure that it was the song to symbolise what she'd expressed, she sang it mainly as it gave her a sense of loyalty.

"It must have been cold there in my shadow."

As "The Wind Beneath My Wings" grew in volume, her plan began to crystallise. Tom's dream was a kaleidoscope of images:

Rusty in a prison cell.
Kendra asking why the dog had no tail.
His father demanding his ring back
Shotguns out of reach
and
him, voiceless screaming silently.

Thus he woke, drenched in sweat. Rivulets had coursed down his back. A New York Yankees T-shirt was saturated. An aroma of fresh bread and frying reached him. Sometimes, such a combination can be the guise of hope. It calmed him, getting slowly out of bed, he felt battered and bedraggled. As if the living daylights had been pounded from him. The roof of his mouth tasted like bile with intent. He shook himself.

Dressed and showered, he felt part ways restored. Out to the living room and it was transformed. Vases of fresh cut flowers, new bright curtains and the scent of ventilation. Bridie was waiting with a nervous expression.

"What do you think Tom, are you angry, did I overdo it?"

He smiled.

"It's bloody marvellous, maybe I won't move after all. Smashing job, you're a little treasure."

"And Tom. I didn't shop-lift anything. I paid cash money."

"Good girl, so are we going to eat or wot?"

They did.

For after, Bridie had brought brandy and they sipped this.

"What will you do Tom?"

"Terrible things I think, but it's a bit unclear. I'll keep it simple and horrendous."

"Oh I nearly forgot. A man rang you and I wrote down these addresses . . . here."

He looked at them. Terry lived in The Borough, and Bill at The Oval. Quite an accent away from Bow Bells he thought.

Bridie bit her lower lip. Tom said,

"Don't bite your lower lip. In little girls it's cute, in women it's downright ridiculous."

"And your little girl, Tom . . . I can't stomach that animal . . . well . . ."

"Do you still have that gun, Bridie ?"

"Oh . . . no. Sevy took it back. I'm sorry."

"No worries, I want something more basic. If the logistics were right Bridie, I'd crucify the three of them. Right on Clapham Common . . . now wouldn't that be a sight to see."

Bridie thought of the gun sitting in her fridge and marveled at how easily the lie had come.

***

Robbie laid out his kit. A small gold-plated box with a mirror, straw, two full vials and an old fashioned razor blade. The coke was already prepared and lay in five lines. A glass of water was next to his daboddle of dreams like a plain reminder of reality.

He snorted the lines and then dipped his fingers in the water. With a groan he allowed the drops to enter his nostrils . . . he muttered, "Fuckin' nirvana on a good day."

The intercom beeped and put the heat crossways in him. It was very new. He'd gotten it the day before at a boot sale. Just the touch he felt to signal his new found status. The Korean was in, he'd given a verbal agreement by phone and in two days the papers would be signed and the cheque handed over.

"A very big, very fat cheque," he said.

He flipped the switch on the intercom.

"Yes Mrs. D."

"It's Mr. Naylor, he won't wait any longer, he says he's coming through . . . he's the bailiff."

As the coke soared, Robbie felt a brotherhood of man feeling.

"By all means Mrs. D, ask him to do so . . . and have the afternoon off eh . . . go shopping."

"With what . . . I might remind you of my wages . . ."

He flipped her off and swept his kit into a drawer.

As Naylor entered, Robbie rose to greet him. He was feeling positively saintly and reckoned he might even send a cheque to Mother Theresa. A glow he felt emanated from him.

To Naylor he looked indeed all lit up. Two sheets to the wind. He asked,

"Bit early for it is it Mr. Colbert?"

"Never too early for cordiality my friend. We've met before."

"Too right by halves, you know why I'm here."

"I do indeed and let me say on a personal level, you're very adept. Might I drop a note of commendation to your superiors."

"You might drop me a note of payment."

"All in good time my impatient friend. Some beverage perhaps."

"Let's get on with it Mr Colbert eh, I don't have all day."

"Are you a family man Naylor; are there a brood of junior sheriffs at home, waiting to repossess you?"

Robbie's high began to crumble. The very power of the drug was enhanced by it's brevity. He said in a high voice.

"Two days . . . that's it and I'm home free."

"I'm afraid the time is up" . . . and he slapped a form on the desk.

"For God's sake Naylor, gimme a break. You want something, a show of good faith is that it? Well here, (he began to unstrap his watch) take this, it's a Phillip Patek. Bet you've never had one of those. What do you use, a Timex . . . or a Swatch . . . yea, one of those functional jobs. So live a little. Show it to the little woman, get her juices flowing. There's more where that came from. JUST GIVE ME TWO LOUSY DAYS.

Naylor began to feel uneasy and thought he might need back-up. The man looked positively deranged. Naylor began to move towards the door.

"Mr. Colbert these premises are no longer your property."

Robbie flung the watch and Nayor beat a rapid retreat. He didn't notice the woman sitting quietly in the outer room.

Robbie let loose a string of obscenities and began rummaging in his desk for something to ingest. The woman came quietly in, picked up the watch and waited. He looked up,

"Who the hell are you?"

"Are you Robert Colbert?"

"No, I'm the fucking Aga Khan, who the hell do you think I am, what do you WANT?"

"I believe you may be able to help me. I have a special dilemma."

"Don't we all honey, well spit it out."

"I have a child that needs to be sexually abused. I hear you're just the man for the job. That it's a specialty of yours."

Robbie froze. What colour there was in his face drained away. He sat down slowly and asked quietly.

"What is this, who put you up to it?"

"I'm the little girl's aunt."

It took him a few moments to put it together and when he did, he gave a bitter smile.

"The convict's sister, the crazy bitch. Yea, I heard about you. Didn't they have you in some madhouse. Get early release did you . . . lemme tell you sister, you pull many more stunts, you'll be back on the funny farm."

"You have a filthy manner, but what else could I expect from a child molester. A pervert."

He stood up.

"That's it, you're outta here. I don't need this garbage today."

As he moved towards her, she reached in her bag and pulled out a gun. He thought it must be a toy, it looked so plastic.

"You're kidding. I'm supposed to buy that's real, gimme a break."

She squeezed the trigger and the intercom leapt from the desk. He looked round in disbelief.

"Yah bad bitch, I only bought that yesterday."
And she squeezed again.
It felt like a sledgehammer to his right knee and he sunk to the floor.
Now he was truly afraid.
"For pity's sake, I never touched that little girl."
And squeeze.
His middle fingers disappeared.

Squeeze.
Squeeze.
Squeezed.

***

Tom was planning his next job when the phone rang.
"Hello."
"Daddy?"
"Kendra, hello darling'"
His heart pounded in his chest and the phone felt sticky in his hand.
"How did you know it's me Daddy?"
"I'd recognise you anywhere honey."
"Mummy is going to be away all day and she said you could bring me out . . .
will you Daddy?"
"What time is it now darlin'?"
"Am . . . eleven I think."
"Start counting, at 12 o'clock, I'll be giving you the biggest hug you ever had.
Are you counting?"
"One
Two . . ."
He dressed fast, rang a mini-cab and was on his way. Five minutes after he left,
a police car pulled up to his door. Kendra was waiting at the window.
Seven years old now, she was her mother in tiny exact detail. He felt his breath
hold in his chest as he saw her. She was wearing a bright blue tracksuit with "Eurodisney"
on the front, and came racing into his arms.
As he held her he thought, "if I could hold her thus forever."
And already she was pulling away, laughing.
"Your beard tickled me Daddy."
They went to:

Kew Gardens
The Zoo
McDonalds
And
Burger King.

Tom couldn't believe one little girl could put away so much

> Ice cream
> Chips
> And soft drinks.

As a thief, he had to admire the glossy wholesale thievery of those outfits. The day was drawing to a close and a silence shaped above father and child. Kendra was sucking emptily on her Coke. He asked,

"Like anything else darling'"

"No thanks, Daddy."

"Are you upset about anything?"

"It's my first Communion next month."

"You'll be a big girl then."

"We have to make our confession and if we don't tell all our sins, we'll burn in hell till our skin falls off and we'll still be roasting. Sister Adele says it's like being burnt with a match only a million and million times hotter."

She said this in the rushed total concentrated way that child does. Her little cheeks were flushed as if she could a ready feel the heat.

Tom would have liked a few moments with the highly imaginative Sister Adele. He wondered what sins a seven year old girl could be burned for.

"I have a secret Daddy. It's a big bad thing."

Tom tried not to smile.

"Well honey, you can tell me. I won't tell anyone. Cross my heart and hope to die. That's what daddies are for, to tell all those things. Then the badness is wiped away."

"Alright so."

She took a deep breath, looked around, then with her head down, she began to tell.

"I told Mummy a big fib, . . . I said the man . . ., did things to me . . . like we were told about in school . . . you know . . . girls and touches . . . to always tell a grown up. So . . . I pretended and told Mummy the man did."

Tom was stunned. Thoughts chased each other in mad sequence.

". . . Robbie hadn't touched her

. . . they taught this at school?

. . . she didn't call Robbie her daddy!"

He lent over and put his hand under her chin, lifted her face gently,

"It's okay, Kendra, it's okay . . . no one's going to punish you."

Tears rolled down her small face. Between sobs, she said,

"Will Mummy be very cross, I only said 'cos I thought she'd send the man away and you could come home."

He wanted to weep himself, to stab somebody . . . anybody. To hide her away so the world would never touch her. But already she was drying her eyes and asked,

"Do I look terribly Daddy?"

"You look beautiful."

When they got back, Liz was waiting at the door, an expression of gravity clouding her.

"The police are here."

On cue, two plainclothes officers and WRC appeared. They were producing warrant cards. One said,

"Might we have a word Mr. Kenny, I'm Superintendent Barnes, this is Sergeant Woods. The WPC will look after the little girl." All moved inside.

"What's going on?" asked Tom.

"Your wife says, I'm sorry . . . your ex-wife says you picked up the little girl at 12. Is that correct?"

"Yes it is."

"And you spent the full day with her? Did you leave her at any stage?"

"What do you mean leave her? She's seven years old for God's sake. Do you know the animals that are out there."

The WPC turned and had a brief word with Barnes. He nodded.

"Well Mr. Kenny, your child confirms what you said."

"You questioned the child?"

"It was necessary Mr. Kenny. We're only doing our job. You've been inside I believe?"

"Yes I have."

"Staying clean are we?"

"Well I dunno about you but I am."

The policemen exchanged a look.

"You wouldn't possess a handgun, would you Tom?"

"Ah, the Christian name now. No, I don't have a gun. You said, I'm an ex-convict . . . What's going on?"

"Between one and two o'clock today, Mr Robert Colbert was shot to death."

"Jesus," said Tom.

"Any idea as to who might wish harm to him?"

"Just about anyone who ever came in contact with him . . . he was that type of individual. Half of London I should think. Does that help?"

"We'll be in touch Tom, keep yourself out of trouble, there's a good lad."

After they left. Liz walked right up to him.

"Did you have anything to do with this Tom?"

"No."

"You're sure?"

"Look, I'm not shedding any tears over him but I had nothing to do with it . . . okay. Is Kendra alright?"

"She's exhausted, I put her to bed."

As Tom turned to go he said,

"One thing Liz, if I'd gone after Colbert they wouldn't have been round here."

"I don't understand."

"There wouldn't have been enough of him left to identify. Do you understand that."

***

On his way home, Tom thought about Bridie.

"She couldn't have, no way. I mean she's crazy but is she pathological? God Almighty, what am I doing . . . blaming my own sister."

Back and forth the inner debate raged in him and he stopped at a call box. Her answering machine said,

"I'm not home right now and if my luck holds, I won't ever be. Whatever your position in the world, you have a right to be here."

For an awful moment, he thought she was going to recite the whole of the Desiderata but the bleep stopped it. He left a message for her to get in touch – urgently. He thought about Colbert and didn't think the world was dimmed by his passing. Then he moved to Kendra and that was the usual mix of joy, pain and regret.

***

Terry and Bill were drinking gin. As to whether it added to their air of depression was debatable, but it didn't inspire levity. They were sitting in their usual pub at a corner table.

Terry said,

"I suppose we should drink that Pernod piss as a momento mori."

"Fuck 'em."

"Yea, do you think the convict had 'owt to do with it? Would he have the bottle to kill Colbert . . . What cha fink?"

"I think maybe tomorrow we should call on the convict anyway. Shake him up for a few sobs."

Bill had an ex-wife to support and money was a constant preoccupation. He'd recently sold his car and had to rely on Terry's. Marriage or such considerations never entered Terry's plans. He kept budgies and his own company.

Bill looked over Terry's shoulder and said,

"There's a woman at the bar, keeps looking at you . . . looks like you're about to score again.

"What's she like?"

"Got a body on 'er. I'll give her that and worth a few bob I'd guess."

Terry had a knack of getting women. This he saw as further evidence of his all round superiority. Bill was envious to the point of hatred.

"You'll have the knickers off that I suppose."

Terry stood, stretched so's the woman could have a full eyeful and walked slowly over, his smile in place. He had practised the smile to syncronize with the walk in his full length mirror. As he neared, the smile deepened.

The woman gave a tiny smile.

"Gotcha," he thought and said,

"You are one beautiful lady but I expect you're sick of hearing that. What are you drinking?"

"Would a vodka and slimline tonic be okay?"

"You don't need slimline, you've the perfect figure."

"Yo Fred, let's get some service over here, large vodka for the lady, a bucket of gin for morose Bill over there and a large Gordon's . . . fresh lemon."

The woman looked at him with shining eyes and laid two fingers on his arm.

"I like a masterful man. It's so rare."

He casually brushed her knee.

"You gotta let the buggers know what's what, if you'll pardon my French."

"Oh no, I like a man who lives life to the full. Who's not afraid to take what he wants."

Terry thought, "Bingo!"

Bill came over a little later and said,

"I'm going to call it a night, Terry. I'll be round early so's we can call on our friend."

Terry saw no point in introductions. He nodded and said,

"Mind how you go Bill, it's a jungle out there."

He ordered more drinks and felt lust grow in proportion. A little after ten, he suggested they leave. The woman agreed. Outside, he pushed her against the wall and rammed his hand under her skirt.

"No" she said, "not here, do you have a car?"

He smiled and led her to it. They got in the back and she said,

"Just turn your head a moment while I take my knickers down."

He did. Then he unzipped his fly and put his hand behind her head . . .

"Here's what you want bitch."

He forced her down and threw his head back in anticipation of the pleasure. A coldness hit his groin and a sharp pain . . . it was a few seconds before he realized it was the barrel of a gun, he shouted,

"What the fuck."

"Shut up or I'll blow your balls off."

He shut up.

The woman sat upright, the gun held in place. She said,

"I can't for the life of me pronounce the name of this gun but I don't think you'll mind. I mean what's in a name? I can assure you though it works. A Mr. Colbert could have vouched for it but alas, he's moved on."

Terry felt fear grip him and thought he was going to soil his pants.

"Now Terry, tell me, how did it feel to kill the dog?"

"It was Bill done that. I love animals . . ."

"Now isn't that the oddest thing Terry. I felt in my bones you'd say that. I wonder if I'm psychic."

He thought "bloody psycho more like" but kept it to himself.

She hummed a while and he wondered what on earth she was waiting for.

Finally she said,

"You'd like to fuck people I think, if you'll pardon my French . . . Are you uncomfortable Terry?"

"Well, if you could maybe . . . you know . . . move the barrel a tad, I feel a bit exposed . . ."

"I'll think about it Terry, okay . . ."

And she went silent again.

Terry had no interest in culture. Indeed he referred to the whole area as a dance floor for nancy boys. Once though, he'd heard Richard Eyre talk about arguments at home. He'd said,

"I was fascinated not so much by the obvious entertainment of the streams of violence but by the silences that followed:

> *epic*
> *giant*
> *immense*
> *terrible*
> *and*
> *terrifying.*"

Terry had said then,

"Wot a load of cobblers."

But now he understood exactly the meaning of those silences. A strong smell of sweat and fear oozed from him.

She spoke and he tried not to jump.

"Terry, I was at the hairdressers the other day, not that you're interested in that, but I was reading an issue of Cosmopolitan. Do you know what I read?"

"N . . . o" This came out as a faint croak.

"Sixty-two percent of Australians prefer surfing to sex. Eighty percent think of sex while surfing. And fifty percent think of surfing during sex."

This near finished Terry off as it convinced him she was completely whacko.

He heard her say,

"I saw my husband Gerry today."

And then she pulled the trigger.

***

Next morning Tom shaved his beard. As he did, Radio 4 played Ave Maria and he sang aloud with it,

> "*Dominua tecum*
> *In mulieribus*
> *Et benidictus*
> *Et benedictus*

Fructus ventris
Ventries tui Jesus
Ave Maria
Sancta Maria
Maria mater dei"

As his face emerged, the music rose in him a profound sense of yearning for what he didn't know. It was he thought the very not knowing that gave the feeling such intensity. An alcoholic in prison had tried to tell him what he reckoned a drink would accomplish.

"I might fill the hole in my soul."

Tom hadn't followed that exactly but a junkie had leapt in saying,

"That's it, that's nearly it . . . a fix is like kissing God."

Tom thought the nearest he'd ever come to fulfilling the yearning was his love for Kendra. It frightened him a little that it made him so vulnerable. But it was as constant as his heartbeat. Clean shaven, he studied his new appearance. Ten years had fallen away but his face looked hollow. All the words in the world couldn't fill it, he whispered. The Ave Maria finished and the news followed. It included the story about Terry being shot to death in his car. The police were anxious to trace a woman seen leaving a public house in his company."

"God Almighty," he said.

Bill had heard the same news. He instantly ran to check the locks on the door and window. Then to the bedroom and pulled the shotgun from under the mattress. Sitting in a hard chair near the door, he cradled the gun on his lap and began to slug from a bottle of scotch. In no doubt about his abilities, he knew Robbie and Terry were superior in every department. But not smart enough to stay alive . . . no, not that bright at all. He began to mutter,

"You won't take me so easy you bastard, come and get some of this."

As the scotch went down his bravado rose and he began to hope the caller would come soon.

***

Sergeant Woods was in the canteen. A tall man, inclined to fat, he eyed a jelly donut. The cake seemed to howl,

"Eat me."

He did some calorie calculations. If he had a mug of tea without sugar, maybe he could have a donut. The canteen assistant was well used to the sergeant's dilemma. It didn't help that she vaguely reminded him of his mother.

"Ah go on Sergeant. Nobody lives forever . . . it won't kill you."

"Easy for you to say Molly. If the Super finished early in Forensics, he'd have my hide, he says I'm too heavy now."

"That Super is a miserable git, no meat on his bones, he wants to spoil it for everyone else."

The Sergeant had the donut and a large mug of tea. Sitting down, he took a huge bite and sweetness enveloped him.

"Bliss," he thought.

Alas, as life goes, the Super arrived and came straight over.

"God Sergeant, stuffing your face as usual. You've got your mouth full and I've got my hands full . . . "

The Sergeant tried to swallow quickly and nearly choked.

"Ah use a napkin for heaven's sake! I got the report from Forensics . . . they rushed it through. What's the damn woman's name, Margaret, is it?"

"Molly, Sir."

"Whatever, hey you, bring me a glass of freshly squeezed orange juice."

Molly ignored him.

The Super fixed his tie and began,

"This is getting out of hand. As we feared, the bullets came from the same gun. It gets better, this Terry worked for one Mr. Colbert. Him and another small time villain named Bill."

The Sergeant had to open his mouth to dislodge the donut remnants and it had the appearance of a yawn.

"Sorry I'm keeping you up Sergeant, but this is of some priority. You'd need to get yer ass in gear laddie or it's back on the beat for you. Be back bouncing the bunnies in Brixton . . . wot? Where's that damn woman with my orange juice."

"Bone breakers," said the Sergeant.

"What's that?"

"Terry and Bill, they operate as muscle and specialize in putting the frighteners on. They've quite a rep in certain circles. Terry's the wide boy, vicious and cunning. Bill is the stooge, no less dangerous mind."

"What's the connection then?"

"Well, Bill recently parted from his old lady and Colbert too. Would there be one of them troit things."

"That's 'menage a trois'. You might be on to something there. Where do you place our Tom Kenny, the jailbird, in all of this?"

"The way I see it Sir, how about we grill all players. Shake the tree and see what falls."

"Remaining players that is . . . well, it doesn't look like any orange juice is going to be shaken anyroad. Let's get moving then."

Molly watched them leave and when they were well clear of the canteen she said in a dramatic voice,

"Oh Superintendent, your orange juice!"

***

Tom tried again to ring Bridie. Her phone was now off the hook. He contemplated going over there.

"And then what?" he thought, "Ask her if she's shooting half the male population of London. Still, it made a change from marrying them."

A more immediate problem was the certainty that the police would be around again . . . and again. If he was to do a job, he'd have to do it now before the heat really increased. They'd never expect him to go thieving today. He forced his mind to business and made half a dozen calls round the estate agents.

A place in Brompton Road had just been let . . . close to Knightsbridge. He didn't like to work this fast but time was becoming scarce. Out came the labourers gear and he tried to match his enthusiasm to his haste.

The two policemen walked casually to the fourth floor of Bill's building. The Super vetoed the lift as he said,

"No need to advertise our arrival, and the exercise will do you no harm."

The sergeant said nothing. They listened outside Bill's door. Another door opened and a middle-aged woman said,

"Oh he's in there all right, fell in drunk as usual last night, the smell of drinking in the corridors was appalling, just appalling."

Superintendent Barnes said,

"Well Sergeant, don't just stand there, give it a good thump."

He did.

Bill had fallen into an alcoholic stupor.

The knock stirred him and he came to in a panic, though the door was being forced. Without thinking he squeezed both triggers of the shotgun.

The blast took out most of the door and slammed the Sergeant against the far wall, killing him instantly. For a few moments, nothing moved. Superintendent Barnes, shocked and crouched, saw Bill's head appear through the shattered door. He was whimpering.

"It was Terry . . . not me . . . I didn't do nowt."

***

Tom marveled at the flimsy lock on the door to the apartment and in sixty seconds, he was inside. He knew the rents for these places were exorbitant and yet they wouldn't spend a penny on a decent bolt. Once inside, he leant against the door and listened for sounds. Twice he heard voices in places and had left instantly. Only silence here. He looked at his watch, ten minutes tops.

The living room was strewn with clothes and empty cups. A quick frisk there revealed nothing. Then to the small kitchen and opened the fridge. Milk, frozen burgers, large containers of Greek yoghurt. He took the tops of these and put his hand in . . . extracting jewellery wrapped in cellophane. A matching set of male and female Rolex into his pocket.

The second carton held a batch of Krugerrands. Not as valuable as they'd once been but a nice earner. He spotted a tin of pure ground coffee . . . and they had a percolator. The temptation to brew up was nigh overpowering. But he knew what he did in people's homes was bad enough. Somehow he felt that using their cups or food was in the realm of desecration. A chill hit the back of his neck and without waiting to look round, he dived to his left. A baseball bat crashed down on the coffee tin, flattening it like rotten fruit. A large black man in some ceremonial African dress was wielding it. He swung round to get another shot and Tom scurried to his feet. The man had tribal scars on his face and an expression of concentrated murder. He held the bat with a practised ease. Tom faced him. In prison he'd learnt the rules of fighting.

– There are no rules.

Do whatever it takes to bring them down and ensure they're in no mood to rise. Tom feinted to his right and the man in his eagerness for damage lunged there. As he did, Tom dropkicked him with all his might and that was that.

Tom let out a long breath of fear and relief. Then he noticed the woman standing at the kitchen door. Also in ceremonial dress, she was tall with a face of striking composure and dignity.

Shame washed over him. He said,

"I'm so sorry . . . he'll be okay . . . just a bit sore . . . you have nothing to fear from me . . . I'm going."

He didn't even know if she spoke English and with a deep mortification he began to shuffle past her. All he wanted was to get out fast.

He'd moved past and was half way across the living room when he heard a horrendous scream and she came rushing at him. Her assault knocked him backwards and she fell over with him. Then her nails went for his face and narrowly missed his eyes as she tore down. Burning lacerations exploded on his cheeks as she sank her teeth in his ear and bit deep. He screamed and smashed his fist into her face. She went over backwards and was still.

Trembling with shock, pain and outrage, he dragged himself to his feet and shouted,

"What the fuck is wrong with you people? Jesus, didn't ye ever hear of passive resistance." He pulled himself over to a cupboard and tore it open, grabbed a bottle of whiskey. He drank deep and shuddered.

Moving towards the bathroom, he looked in on the black man in the kitchen. The man was doubled up, whimpering softly. Tom said,

"I swear, if you get up, I'll kill you. I'm not able for any more of this shit."

He picked up the baseball bat in case any more of the family were lurking.

Tom had heard your whole life flashed before you when you're right up close to death. What he found was two incidents rushed into his head with astounding clarity. What they were related to or why they should surface now, he couldn't figure. A blast of madness perhaps.

The first involved his father telling him a joke.

"A man tells his wife he has only six months to live. She answers 'never mind dear, with summer coming, you'll never find the time passing.'"

And secondly, when he was 19, he'd gone to the Big Irish Dance on a Saturday night. You couldn't fail to score according to local heroes. He'd said to the first girl who danced with him,

"Might I have the last dance?"

She said,

"Honey, you're having it."

In the bathroom, he was horrified to see two long ugly gashes in his cheek and his ear looked like it was mangled. All were bleeding freely. He found some band-aids in the cabinet and managed to cover up most of the carnage. He now looked like Frankenstein unbinding. And he cursed out loud for the instinct that had him shave his beard, saying,

"Well, fuck-it-all to hell, wasn't I busy."

There were some Tylenol and he swallowed a handful, washed them down with a Whiskey. The room spun and he thought he'd better get going. If he passed out here, maybe the Africans would eat him. As he got to the door, he took out the Rolexes and tossed them on the sofa, saying,

"You sure earnt these back."

He almost fell out on the street and used the bat to steady himself. A car was directly in front of him and the door opened.

Bridie leant out. Tom didn't know if he was hallucinating and said,

"What the hell are you doing here?"

"I followed you, I wanted to see you at work. You look like something chewed you."

"They did."

"So, was it worth it?"

"What . . . was what worth it?"

"All that for a baseball bat, wouldn't it be easier to buy one . . . Oh by the way, you're bleeding all over the footpath."

He got into the car and an overwhelming compulsion to sleep came at him. He said,

"I'd love to sleep."

"So do."

And she put the car in gear.

It was hours later before he came to full consciousness. A vague memory of Bridie's house in Kennington and her helping him inside. Something about her Civil Servant lodger chasing Arab boys in Morocco or was it the other way round.

Sitting up now he saw Bridie at the table, watching him. His face was freshly bandaged and his ear had a dressing. The sleep on the sofa had restored him partially. As he turned he felt something stick in his side. Reaching down, he took out the bundle of Krugerrands and let them drop to the floor.

Bridie brought him soup and French bread. He said,

"I didn't know you had a driver's license."

"I don't."

He thought,

"When . . . when will I learn to stop treating her like a normal person."

And he asked conversationally,

"So Bridie, did you shoot anyone today or is it a bit early yet?"

She smiled.

"The third musketeer took care of himself."

"I don't follow you, but then, I never did."

"The Bill fellow, the police went to see him and he blasted one of them to smithereens. They've got him in custody now."

Tom felt a chill with the relish she said this. Her loving emphasis on "blast" and "smithereens" was a horror show to hear.

He had like most convicts devoured crime novels. The hard-boiled work of Raymond Chandler was forever in demand. So too was Micky Spillane but you told yourself,

"This is prison, not the public library. Am I going to go highbrow? In every sense, you took what you got."

Chandler had written about murder and,

"Giving it back to the kind of people that commit it for reasons, not just to provide a corpse and with the means at hand, not hand-wrought duelling pistols or tropical fish."

He looked close at her as if her eyes could spell out who she was.

"How do you feel?"

"Feel . . . I feel fine, it was so easy and the rush, I nearly passed out from it. I tell you Tom, it's better than sex, well better than any I ever had with my deadbeats."

Her use of the present tense and the suggestion of further action appalled him.

He hung his head and she said,

"Tom, they deserved it. That Colbert was a child molester."

"No, no he wasn't."

"Yes he was, you told me so yourself."

"I was wrong. Kendra made it up to bring me back with Liz."

Bridie lost it for a moment, panic then horror washed over her features. Then whatever demon had taken up residence reasserted control. Cunning turning to malevolence replaced these. She said,

"Liz, it always comes back to that bitch. She deserted . . . no abandoned you then married that creep. Yes . . . yes. We may have to fix that bitch too."

"Good god Bridie. Are you gone stark raving bonkers? Kill Liz? This has to end . . . and now. You need serious help."

Bridie stood up.

"I can't believe you'd defend that . . . cow . . . you call me names. I can't believe how ungrateful you are . . . don't fuck with me Tom. There are things in my life you don't want to know. To think I brought you a present too.

She snatched her handbag. Rummaged in it and took out a brightly wrapped parcel. For a frozen moment he thought she was going for the gun. This more than anything else made him realize how far gone he believed she was. She's always been out there way beyond the boundaries of mere eccentricity. He didn't think there was any coming back for her . . . or him.

"So are you going to open the gift."

He took it and slowly unwrapped it. A gold cross with three jewels encased on the top. He didn't know what to say and she said,

"Three jewels, for the third Cross, like you told me . . . remember, Tom."

He stood up. Bridie seemed as if she might move to hug him but, let her hands fall useless to her sides.

"I brought you some clothes from your place Tom, while you slept. Don't go, I'll go to my own home. You're safe here."

"Give me the key Bridie."

She rummaged again.

"I dunno where I left it. I'll bring it by in the morning . . . okay Tom."

With a low tone he said,

"Bridie, stay away from Liz. I'm going to help you with all this mess. You're not responsible."

She moved to the door and before she went, she said,

"Don't threaten me Thomas. I don't like that. I'm very annoyed at your whole attitude . . . you've changed . . . and that's a terrible pity."

Then she was gone.

The gashes in Tom's face throbbed and he felt the onset of a massive headache. Fatigue pounded his bones and he wanted to sleep for a week. Moving to the phone, he rang Liz.

She sounded on the verge of hysteria and demanded to know what the dickens was happening. He hoped he could stay calm and not enrage her further.

"Liz, I'll come round in the morning and explain everything. If Bridie calls, don't let her in, on any account."

"Bridie . . . what's she got to do with this, what's this about?"

"She's been drinking again, you know how crazy she gets, okay."

"You and your family."

He wanted to let her have a piece of his rage or frustration but bit down and let it go.

"I'll talk to you in the morning. Goodbye."

He went into the kitchen and it took a while to locate some booze. Finally he found a bottle of Southern Comfort and began to work on it. Tomorrow, he thought, tomorrow I'll make a decision about Bridie. He stretched himself on the couch and resolved he'd shower and change in ten minutes. In a quarter of the time he was sound asleep.

**

In the police canteen, Molly was wiping down the counter and weeping quietly. Over and over she thought of what she'd said to the sergeant.

"It won't kill you."

She knew she'd never be able to see a donut without wanting to weep. If the Superintendent looked in, she had a gallon of fresh squeezed orange juice for him. Aloud she said,

"I don't think he will . . . not now."

***

A ferocious crash pulled Tom from his sleep and before he could sit up, policemen poured in through the ruined door. He was grabbed from the sofa and thrown to the ground, his hands locked behind him. Cuffs clicked on his wrists, elbows banged his head and a heavy boot sank into his groin. Throwing up, he was dragged to his knees and a fist took out his front teeth.

Superintendent Barnes said,

"Now now lads, easy does it."

Tom spat out the vomit and managed to ask,

"What the hell is this?"

"Mr. Thomas Kenny. I am arresting you for the murders of Robert Colbert and Terry Neill. I'm also charging you with assault and battery, breaking and entry plus robbery, from a holiday home yesterday."

"What are you talking about?"

The superintendent moved close to Tom, grabbed his hair and said,

"As the result of a tip we went to your home in Clapham late last night and found a Glock automatic, the murder weapon I believe, and a roll of coins from the robbery yesterday."

Tom said to himself.

"She took the bloody Krugerrands when she gave me the cross . . . crucified me all right."

They dragged him out with his shoes scraping the carpet. A keen-eyed constable bent quickly down and palmed the golden cross. As he slipped it into his tunic, he thought,

"Probably fake but you might get lucky – you could never tell."

***

The island of Ponos
Greece.

4 months later.

At Harry's outdoor cafe, an American woman had been left behind by her tour. She'd felt exhausted in the morning and decided not to accompany them on a day cruise to Hydra. Bored now, she was in the mood for company.

She looked round and saw a blond haired woman sitting alone. Rising she approached and asked,

"May I join you?"

"Be my guest."

"I'm Edie . . . Edie Barton from Trenton, New Jersey."

"Nice to meet you."

Edie was pleased to hear the British accent. London was next on their itinerary

314

and she might learn some useful tips. Plus, like Edie, she was inclined to plumpness and that gave them something in common. *The Daily Mirror* was open on the table. A headline about some murder trial. Edie said,

"Nobody's safe anywhere these days."

The woman closed the paper and said,

"I never read that type of thing. Crime disturbs me."

Edie felt a slight rebuff she wasn't a woman easily discouraged. Anyway, the British were snotty, it was part of their history, like Burberries. Charming too.

"What's that you're drinking?"

"It's a frappe, cold coffee."

"Oh you mean like iced coffee."

"No, like cold coffee."

Edie felt the charm might be wearing thin and looked round. It was brave the gauntlet of predatory Greeks or brazen it out. "What the hell," she thought and said,

"I thought all you English people only drank tea."

"You were misinformed."

"Are you travelling alone?"

"Well Kendra, my little girl, she's at boarding school. I'm expecting my husband Gerry in a few days."

"Why that's wonderful."

"He's my second husband actually."

Edie loved the 'actually', so authentic.

"I'm with you honey, second husband's are better, they try harder."

This usually met with laughter and Edie laughed to set the mirth in motion. She laughed alone.

"Well honey, family is important."

"I only have Gerry and Kendra. I had a brother but he died, poor Thomas. My Kendra was nearly set upon by one of those perverts but we found out in time."

"But my gawd, how awful. It's a jungle out there."

Edie was indeed horrified but more so at the can of worms she'd opened.

She though the woman might be unbalanced. Eccentricity was charming too but something about the woman's intensity alarmed her. For no reason other than intuition, she knew the woman was lying, certainly about her husband and child. She'd have bet her American Express Gold Card this woman had no children. There was a look, and it was absent here. She noticed the woman's hand reach to an odd cross around her neck. It was quite ugly and appeared to be fashioned from a nail of some sort. To distract her, she asked,

"What a most unusual piece of jewelry."

For the first time the woman became animated and said,

"Actually, it's known as 'The Third Cross.' Do you know the story?"

"No honey, I haven't come across that, I'd be fascinated to hear it."

All at once the woman's face lost all interest and her eyes withdrew to some other place. She said in a cold voice.

"No . . . no it's quite boring really. I found it in a market in Istanbul. It's just a piece of junk."

She snapped it from her neck and let it fall to the table, saying

"Nothing of consequence."

THE TIME OF SERENA-MAY

For Philomena-Catherine Kennedy
Grace indeed

If you want to make God laugh, make plans. Frank and Cathy Marshall had one. They enjoyed the sound,
"The Marshall Plan."
They had everything, almost.

> Jobs
> Home
> A dog
> each other

They didn't have a child. Entry to that special club of parent was denied. No carrying of snapshots in the wallet.
Always that moment in conversation.
"Do you have children?"
"No."
It hung there like sin, a failure, a definite lack of something. Worse, the other person then rushed in with the bland reassurance.

> "You're as well off . . .
> More time to yourselves . . .
> Plenty of time yet
> Oh, the pain you're saved
> The world's too crowded
> Wise choice."

And Cathy died a little each time.
She was 5'4" with a thin, hardy body. Black hair cut short and blue eyes. A snub nose guarded a full mouth that verged on a downward slide. The effect was close to prettiness, but the eyes could lead the face to moments of beauty. In her own words,
"What I've got isn't great, but I know how to use it . . . sometimes."
Her voice was deep and her Irish-London background gave a lilt that averted hardness. A scattering of Irish expressions littered her face and speech.
"I'm as skinny as a tinker, but I move fast."
Her job as a personnel manager suited her temperament.
"I don't work hard. What I do is I work well."
At 30, she'd one divorce behind her. No children. A party she'd reluctantly attended was winding down and so was she. An empty glass in her hand, a man had

approached.

"Are you Cathy?"

"What?"

"It's not a difficult question."

She gave him the hard look. Sufficient usually to "ice ice." He appeared unaffected.

Tall, six feet or so. The age between late 40s and shaky 50s. Brown eyes, the wide set model. A bad nose, either it had been broken or should have been. His mouth was a thin line . . . verging on meanness. A slight smile promised some redemption.

"Yes, I'm Cathy . . . so?"

"We have a friend in common. Deirdre. Deirdre Rankin."

"Hardly a friend."

He sighed and said,

"You know, I thought it was odd an attractive woman should be standing alone. Now I'm beginning to think it's little wonder. I'll leave you to it."

She liked his voice, deep and smokey. Only years of cigarettes and harsh whiskey could do that.

"Or," she thought, "was that harsh women."

"Hang on, are you going to get me a drink?"

"Something bitter, no doubt."

But he took her glass.

When he returned she asked,

"I saw you earlier with the boys, the ones who try to look as if their wives don't belong to them. Did they warn you about me?"

"They said you were a ball-breaker."

She laughed.

"Interesting description, it conveys a colourful mental picture."

"And are you?"

"Stick around and find out."

He looked thoughtful at this and asked,

"Would you be free for a little dinner some evening?"

"A little dinner, what . . . are you on limited expenses, is that it?"

"Cathy, you have a problem with direct questions, did you know that."

"I don't. I have lots of problems with the people who throw them . . . and no . . . no, I would not like a little dinner. Is that a clear answer."

However he felt about it, his face kept it under wraps. He drained his drink.

"Right then, I'll be off."

"I'd be free on Tuesday to go to the pictures."

"What's showing?"

"What do you care, you'll be too busy trying to keep your hands off me."

The startled smile he gave did indeed redeem his face.

It began thus. Two years later they got married. Now Cathy was forty-one years old and nervous. Heinz, the dog, bounced at her feet. His expression said, "I know you've got things on yer mind lady, but I've got to pee . . . so are you letting me out or what?"

She let him out. He was small, black and neurotic, in short, a London dog. They named him for being "57 varieties" as his pedigree contained at least that.

She rang her mother.

"Hello Mam."

"Hello Catherine. Please, I asked you to call me Dolores."

"You're my Mother, why can't I call you motherish things?"

"It's so aging Darling . . . and I do think you've outgrown 'Mam' at 40."

"I didn't know there was a cut-off period. So what, you're hoping to be like my sister, is it, like in the shampoo ads?"

"Don't be facetious, Darling, there's a good girl."

Dolores was English. She'd married an Irishman and even yet was in cultural shock. Since his death, it seemed she'd decided to regain her Englishness. Her accent achieved new shades of plumminess daily. Cathy was torn always between the wild call of the Irish and the etiquette of the English. Mostly, it left her tired.

"Are you following the series, Darling?"

"For Heaven's sake Mam, am I supposed to volley back that Kilkenny are in the All Ireland hurling final. Give us a break. Let Rupert Brooke lie."

"Who?"

"Mother, I'm pregnant."

Silence. Cathy waited then conceded her Mother was an expert in this.

"Mother, are you there, did you hear what I said?"

"Well really Catherine, I don't know how you can do this to me."

"To you . . . ! To you."

"At your age, you should be ashamed of yourself. What on earth were you thinking of?"

"England, most likely."

"I don't know, Catherine, I don't know how I'll be able to cope with this . . . you realize that, at your age, the child won't be right."

Cathy hung up. Fear crawled all down her back, and then a blistering anger. She wanted to sweep the things from the breakfast table. Frank walked in.

"Where's the dog?"

"I hung up on her."

Frank raised an eyebrow and headed for the coffee.

Frank was among the few smokers left in England. Or so it seemed to him. There was a rumour of a lady in Milton Keynes, but she probably did it for money. Cathy had stopped and tended to the zealous vigilance of the ex-smoker. She was particularly rough on early morning cigarettes. This was Frank's favourite. For peace, he usually waited till he was out of the house. Cathy gave him a searching look, said,

"Frank, you look fifty today."

"I am fifty . . . remember, but good of you to mention it."

"No . . . no, I mean usually you don't, but today you look old."

He drank the coffee, black and bitter, it burnt his tongue. In fact, much as the cigarette would do shortly. No reply he felt was fitting.

"You're probably gasping for a cigarette, Frank, you can't wait to get out of the house and away from me."

He stood up, said,

"No darling, I think I miss you already."

Grabbing his jacket, he headed for the door.

"Frank . . . Frank, do you think I'm too old . . . too old to have a baby?"

"Christ!"

and he remembered Jack Nicholson's line in *Terms of Endearment*.

"Almost a clean get-away."

But he kept it to himself.

He moved and put his arms round her.

"Are you angry Frank?"

"Good Heavens, I'm delighted. I'm scared but delighted."

"Me too."

They didn't hear Heinz hurling himself against the door, he couldn't believe they'd forgotten his breakfast. What they listened for was the sound of a new and tiny heartbeat. Frank said,

"You'll be eating coal now, I guess. Don't you get cravings and such."

"Makes your teeth whiter, or is that boot polish? We'll be O.K. . . . won't we Frank?"

He didn't know, and said,

"I dunno."

Cathy hugged him tighter, and he moved his head to look at her.

"I'm late, Cathy, I better go or I'm in trouble."

She laughed and said,

"I'm late, that's what has me in trouble."

Frank managed and owned a small computer company. Trouble was looming from a completely unexpected quarter. For years it had been a poor joke that video display units were dangerous to health. Now it was actually beginning to appear they were. A report from the London Hazards Centre. Many employees were now paying the cost of indiscriminate use of technology in the form of repetitive strain injury, stress and eye damage.

Further problems, such as back pain, skin irritation were also being claimed. R.S.I. had already been recognized at British Telecom. Two former data processors were given £6,000 compensation, plus interest. The move now was for regulations stating that staff working on screen will have their area checking for hazards, especially their distance from the screen.

It was a nightmare to Frank. He'd only just begun to show profit, and the threat of claims was imminent. The initials R.S.I. made him choke. America, he believed, was the culprit for abbreviating everything. As if shortening things would soften them. Take the pain out with the length.

The Marshalls lived at the Oval. Owning their own flat beside the tube station.

Frank could hear the cricket. At least he could hear the crowd. As he walked to the tube, he was hailed by his friend, Jim Barnard.

"Never trust a man with two first names," was Jim's habitual plea. Whatever humour this might have once echoed was long over. They'd grown up together, and longevity more than loyalty maintained their friendship. Jim drank . . . a lot and often . . . and increasingly without control.

He was tall and gangly. It didn't suit him, but he had a build that weight would simply lopside. A thin face with thin eyes, he was capable of warmth that his features denied. A startling feature was his hair, black and luxurious, rampant even. In truth, a terrific crop, and would have appeared so on anybody but Jim. He was a man who deserved to be bald. Few do. You looked at Jim with his riot of hair and felt baldness might not always be a bad thing.

He worked in the City. As Frank's office was off Charing Cross, they infrequently met.

"Top of the morning to you Frankie boy!"

A whiff of alcohol came from him and he had only haphazardly shaved. The hair, as usual, was a disgrace. Today it looked like a poorly styled hair piece and a rather cheap model.

"Good morning Jim."

"I see there's another claim for R.S.I. in this morning."

"Not right now Jim, O.K. I've other things on my mind. Cathy's pregnant."

"Who's the father?"

He took one look at Frank's face and regretted the bolstering drink.

"Sorry Frank, I'm not myself . . . that was in poor taste . . . CONGRATULA-TIONS."

Frank gave him a moment then asked,

"Had a few belts before we came out . . . did we?"

"Well, I dunno about a lot, but I certainly had a wee dram. The old Presbyterian ethic. Go to work on a jar."

"That's an egg, Jim, go to work on an egg."

"Ah . . . I must have misheard . . . did I tell you Helen was found. Jesus . . . bet you didn't even know she was missing."

Frank stopped at the entrance to the station and lit a cigarette. The nicotine slammed his brain and burned his mouth. Exactly as he hoped. Jim looked at the newsagent's display and said,

"Do I buy a rag which I'll really enjoy, or the sort of quality one hopes to be seen reading."

"I don't think the world cares what you read, Jim . . . so Helen's saved, is she?"

"Yea . . . and in a loud way. It's a theory of mine that if you can't have fun, have religion . . . well, let's go, Dad, eh."

Frank ground out his cigarette.

"Jim, don't call me that . . . O.K."

Jim didn't buy a paper. He said he'd read over somebody's shoulder and irritate the hell out of them. Frank said, "Well, Jim, I guess it's nice to have a plan for the day."

"You know, Frank, I dunno is it the light in here, but you look old? Probably just the light."

"Isn't this your stop?"

They didn't say goodbye or even the mandatory London "see ya later." Frank felt for the book in his jacket. Graham Greene's *The End of the Affair*. He knew it almost by heart . . . it had a poetic bleakness that chilled his heart. It was, he felt, what he'd feel if he ever lost Cathy. She'd asked him if his eye ever roved, and he'd fallen back on the old Paul Newman adage,

"Why settle for hamburger when I've steak at home."

He'd always remember the smile she'd given.

"Good answer, Frank. No . . . it's a great answer. How do you think I'd be if you had yourself a floosie?"

"A floosie?"

"Well, if the word's good enough for John Steinbeck, I don't see why you should have trouble with it. So . . . answer the question . . . carefully."

"Am. . . I don't think you'd be . . . what's the word? . . . compassionate."

The fire had lit her eyes.

"I'd burn her house to the ground first. What do you think, I'd sit home knitting?"

"And then?"

"Oh, then I'd cut your balls off."

And that ended that chat.

***

"Try the fava," said Frank, "it's split-pea pulse."

They were celebrating their news with a meal in a Greek restaurant.

Cathy asked,

"What Rev . . . ith . . . o – ICEFTEDES . . . or indeed . . . let me try to say this O.K. . . . SPAN . . . A . . . KO . . . RIZZO."

"That's good, so's your pronunciation. That first job is Chickpea Rissoles, and the other is spinach rice . . . you might like briam, it's a kind of vegetable stew."

"Why, cos I'm Irish? Is it on meself or are they a tad obsessed with chickpeas?"

A Greek in traditional costume played bouzouki and Cathy gave him a look.

"Jaysus, I hope that fella won't be twanging while we're trying to eat."

The waiter brought hot pita bread and Tzazitzi dip. He recommended they try the Sponakopittas, spinach pastries, and put two glasses of ouzo before them.

They drank.

She said,

"Ah, paint off a gate . . . will you want to know, Frank, if it's a boy or a girl?"

"No . . . I'd prefer not to know."

"Me too. There's a test they can do . . . to see if anything's wrong with the baby . . . "

She looked down at her hands and added slowly,

"You know . . . if there's anything wrong . . . they can terminate."

She'd begun to wring her serviette. These were the old-fashioned kind. It wound her fingers like a shroud.

"Good Lord, no. I mean . . . no."

She smiled and reached over, touched his hand.

"Thanks Frank. So what's a sheftalia or kleftiko? I dunno about eating them, but it's fairly fulfilling just trying to say them."

"Right, now the first is rolled minced pork sausages with onions I think, and the other lad is very tender meat on the bone. Here, dip the bread in this melitzzanos. It's an aubergine dip."

"Gee, Frank, I love it when you talk dirty. I'd say you'd prefer to have a boy, would you? Don't men want heirs and stuff like that."

"A boy! He'd probably grow up and kick the daylights outa me. Mind you, I'll be over seventy . . . not that that's any protection nowadays. In fact, it seems near obligatory. I'd have to learn the names of football teams too. God, I don't even know who Gasgoine is married to."

"He isn't."

"See . . . my point exactly."

***

The months of the pregnancy, Frank held his breath. He thought if he relaxed, something would go wrong. If the gods saw you weren't in good form, they seemed less inclined to send trouble. As if they didn't need to grab your attention. Frank suddenly noticed other pregnant women and wanted to give them smiles of encouragement. But such behaviour in London could get you nicked or married. It would certainly get you noticed and that's the worst thing.

Cathy seemed to develop like a character from an American soap. All the clichéd things. She blossomed, bloomed and never looked better. Physical discomfort was at a minimum. The hospital visits for the scan were terrifying, she went convinced they'd find something amiss, and she feared her terror would communicate itself to the baby. But all continued well.

Her mother rang with dietary suggestions and tips on where to buy baby clothes. Jim's drinking increased and his wife left. He took to ringing Frank and leaving odd messages. His favourite was the advice given to politicians about to make their first speech.

> "Say what you're about to say
> Say it
> And then say
> That you've said it."

Heinz, the dog, suspected treachery. They were too nice. He could live with "the edge" stuff. You never knew if a clout or a biscuit was following. The Russian roulette of it appealed. But a continuous diet of care and consideration made him highly suspicious. They were either:

A) out of their minds,
OR
B) about to disappear.

B) he could handle as humans were easy to track, they needed so many things. A) he'd always considered, but this constant blandness was driving him to distraction. He considered running away, but humans always looked in the wrong places. Ulterior motives played a large part with them and he could never grasp the concept. Getting away with outrageous behaviour was useless if it happened all the time.

No, something was in the air and he knew it bode ill for him. All he could do was stay vigilant and be ready when it happened. Cathy was being downright pleasant and even fed him tidbits from her plate. Frank looked on with an idiot smile, and Heinz knew this couldn't last. Hard times were coming, but he couldn't figure from where. If he knew anything of human behaviour, it was that they were never consistent. Meanwhile, he'd test them to the limit and see what shook free.

Cathy bought a book of names. As she sifted through them, she said to Frank,

"Jim left another message. He said if monkeys are so free of stress and worries, how come they're in cages?"

"He's deep, I'll give him that."

"He's a wanker is what he is . . . so, any boys' names you're keen about?"

"Jim?"

"I thought Sebastian would be nice, it has a sort of majesty."

"Jeez, Cathy, no way, they'd murder him in the playground . . . I say 'Sebastian.'"

Cathy put the book down.

"Frank, are you going to be objectionable all evening. I mean, don't feel you have to give me any help."

"Well, there was the guy who named his son after all the players in the Arsenal squad."

"This is a suggestion?"

"And fading rock stars, didn't they call their kids names like 'Dandelion' and 'Root-beer' . . . I'll be honest with you, Cathy, I have some sort of block when I try to think of boys' names. Maybe I'm afraid to tempt fate, or deep down I'm hoping it's a girl."

Cathy sighed.

"Well, girls' names then. Can you give me some of those."

"I'm sort of partial to Rachel."

"Didn't you have a thing with a Rachel?"

"Hardly that. I went out . . . once, with a Rachel, maybe twice."

"Scratch that, Buster, it's Dandelion before bloody Rachel."

"Now who's being awkward."

No progress was made and finally Cathy flung the book aside. Frank picked it up, asking,

"Who writes these friggin' books?"

The author was Serena Cole . . . and Frank looked at Cathy. She smiled and nodded. Only later did the horrible thought cross her mind that maybe it was the surname he meant.

***

Frank was a cautious man. Rarely did he throw caution to any wind. Computers suited him exactly. He fed a program in and it delivered. Control was very important, if he could have composed his own epithet, he'd have settled for,

"Here lies a man
under-whelmed by life."

***

Religion was not a major part of his life. Brought up a Catholic, he'd fallen away and subscribed to the Mediterranean form of church going,

1. They baptised you.
2. They married you.
3. They planted you.

Cathy had a more fundamental belief and clung closer.

Frank was coming down Great Portland Street when the Jewish synagogue caught his attention. For no reason he rang the bell and was admitted. In the vestibule was a huge lit tableau showing the counties and towns of slaughter. There was a silence such as Frank had never experienced. All around too was the sorrow and grieving that has never ceased. . . and a peace.

Frank remembered a line from childhood:

"Before you were born
I knew your name."

All the names here that would never now be uttered. He said quietly,

"God, will you give us this little baby."

Perhaps the very place put *Fiddler on the Roof* in his mind, and he paraphrased the song,

"Would it make such a huge difference to some vast eternal plan if this little baby is given to us, and that it's well and healthy."

He did offer up 10% of his earnings or indeed offer to do good works in exchange. If it was a question of trade, of barter, he felt he'd nothing to use. Then he simply sat and let a melancholia envelop him. Coming out to the street, he felt subdued and quiet. The gut-grinding fear had dissolved and he didn't know if all was going to be well. He did know he could face it, well, most of it anyway.

At the office, Jim had left a message, in the form of a Q and A.

Divorce lawyer.

"What do you call a married woman who says her marriage is wonderful?"

"What?"

"A client."

Frank rang him, but no reply. The last time they'd talked Frank had tried to get him to face his drink problem. Jim had answered in an Aussie accent,

"No worries bluey, my problem's trying to divorce me."

***

In a blur it seemed, the day arrived. The doctor had told Cathy to come to the hospital on September 1st, the day the baby was due. They intended inducing the birth if it didn't happen naturally. Frank couldn't credit they could forecast so specifically. He wondered if this doctor had ever chanced the pools.

That morning Cathy had her bag packed. They were having breakfast, sort of. A mountain of toast, mega pot of tea sat between them, untouched. Twice, Frank had gone out with Heinz to the garden and devoured cigarettes. He'd have mainlined if such were possible. Back inside, Heinz eyed the toast, if they weren't going to bother, he'd be glad to help. But today, he felt they noticed him without actually seeing him.

Frank picked up the paper, began to read aloud,

"Mike Slater, hooking in the fast bowlers second over got a top edge and was caught by Graham Gooch. Australia were nine for one. England had squeezed another 27 runs out of their last three wickets. Fraser scored 28 off 92 balls, only one short of his highest score."

"Frank!"

"What!?"

"You've got to be joking, you're reading me the cricket scores . . . I don't believe it."

"England only have three hundred to show for 23 half centuries this series."

"I hate cricket."

Frank put the paper down, took a slice of dead toast and began to gnaw it. Heinz's ears leapt.

"I thought it would take our minds off things."

Cathy laughed out loud,

"Short of an earthquake, I'm fairly tunnel-visioned today."

"What will you wear?"

"Wear? . . . oh, something big. I don't think it's a dress occasion. Are you going to shave?"

Frank fingered the stubble and thought, "jeez, it itches."

"No, I always had a picture of me stalking the corridors, chain smoking in a waistcoat, waiting for news."

"Sounds more like a poker game. It's not like that anymore."

Frank fed some toast to Heinz and said,

"The likes of Bruce Willis, they video the event."

"Yea . . . but who would you show it to . . . have people round for a showing . . . Good God, I certainly wouldn't want to see it."

The doorbell rang and Frank looked at his watch.

"It's too early for the cab . . . isn't it?"

"Mebbe it's a stork."

He opened the door, and couldn't quite figure out the vision before him.

A man stood there in a dobro. Those white belted suits worn by Tae Kwon Do teachers. His feet were bare. He suddenly crouched in an attack position and emitted a shrill yell that sounded,

"The dee ho han . . . yoo . . . hai . . . eeeee . . . cho . . . chan,"

and brought his right hand swooping down.

Frank's eyes settled on the hair.

"Jim, what on earth are you playing at."

Jim looked disappointed and now, more than a little drunk.

"I wanted ye to know the baby will have a guardian and that I'm here for ye."

"You could have phoned, Jim, this isn't a really good time."

"But look, I have something for Cathy."

He reached in his tunic and extracted first a half bottle of vodka, he looked sheepish. . . said,

"Sorry . . . it's not that."

And then found the gift. A small crystal on a gold chain.

"Thanks very much Jim . . . listen I hate to rush, but . . . "

"Hey . . . Frank . . . Buddy-Mio . . . baby . . . I'll come with you guys. Lend the old moral support . . . eh."

"I don't think so Jim . . . look, I'll call you later and we'll meet . . . O.K."

"Frank-ster, whatever . . . I'm here for ye . . . night or day . . . "

Frank had the door almost closed when Jim asked,

"Are you familiar with George Meredith?"

"Am . . . "

Jim threw back his head and recited a quote he had obviously rehearsed,

"Each one of an affectionate couple may be willing, as we say, to die for the other, yet unwilling to utter the agreeable word at the right moment."

Frank wasn't sure if he'd finished so he asked,

"That's it?"

"Aye . . . hark well, 'The Right Moment' laddie. Go tell your lassie now."

Cathy was pleased with the crystal and signified this with a small smile. The cab arrived and as they moved towards the door. Frank took her hand, said,

"I love you."

***

At the hospital she was put in a small room and hooked up to a machine that monitored the baby's heartbeat. Frank said to the nurse,

"Does it give the test results?"

The nurse, with an Irish accent, said,

"Well, now, what an original line. We've never had such humour before."

Frank's hands were sweating, he was nigh deafened by his own heartbeat.

To his amazement, the tea trolley came and gave them a cup each.

Cathy took his hand and said,

"You go and smoke nineteen cigarettes, but tell me a sad love story before you go."

"A sad one?"

"I'm Irish, sadness is part of my nature."

"Did you ever hear of Rider Haggard?"

"A Country and Western singer?"

"I think that's Merle. No, he was a writer. He wrote *She* and *King Solomon's Mines*."

"I saw *She* at the pictures, with Ursula Andress."

"Yea right. As a young man, he was stopped from marrying his sweetheart, a girl named Lily Jackson. She married a stockbroker. Haggard spent time in Africa and was convinced that he and Lily would be reunited, either in another spiritual dimension, or through reincarnation. Haggard married an heiress. Then, years later, Lily's husband ran off with all their money and Haggard re-housed her. But Lily's husband had infected her with Syphilis which killed her."

They hadn't noticed the nurse at the door who said in a broken voice, sobs barely contained,

"Poor Haggard."

And Cathy added in a tiny voice,

"Poor Lily."

They both looked set to weep oceans.

Frank left to catch up on some serious smoking. He hadn't the heart to quite finish the story, especially not today.

Haggard had a son, Jock, whom he worshipped. The little boy died after an attack of measles and Haggard was abroad at the time. From then on, all vitality left him, and he never mentioned the boy again. Such was his devastation that no one else was allowed to utter his name at any time.

As Frank thought of it now, he felt fairly overcome himself and whispered,

"Get a grip, old son, could be a long day."

The tears he didn't then shed would be fully used by the day's end.

***

They took Cathy to the labour ward at six that evening and they'd decided on a caesarean. A nurse gave Cathy's jewellery to Frank. It nearly gave him a coronary.

As if she'd died and these were her last things. He wrapped them in his hankie, then took them out and held them in his hand . . . finally he put them back in the hankie and tied it rather badly. He wanted to weep and take the hankie out one more time. He stood outside the labour unit and a nurse said,

"Won't be long."

He was dizzy from caffeine, from nicotine. A hand touched his shoulder and he jumped. Dolores, Cathy's mother. So grateful was he to see a familiar face that he wanted to take his wallet out and throw fifty-pound notes at her.

"Settle down, Frank."

"God, I'm glad to see you."

"That makes a refreshing change."

Little love had been lost between them in the past. The waiting made anxious allies and she slipped her hand in his. Every time the door swung, they jumped.

Then, two nurses came wheeling an incubator out. A tiny form inside. A nurse asked,

"Are you Mr. Marshall?"

"Y . . . es . . . I think so, yes . . . of course."

"Congratulations, Mr. Marshall, you have a daughter." And his world changed utterly.

He looked at the tiny thing . . . which looked right back. But something about the baby seemed not right. He didn't know a blessed thing about babies, but something looked not as it ought to be.

He turned to the nurse.

"Is Cathy . . . my wife . . . is she O.K.?"

"She's fine, Mr. Marshall, you'll see her in a moment."

Then it seemed as if another small army of nurses rushed out and then Cathy. She looked dead. His heart pounded and then her eyes opened, he whispered,

"Poor baby, she has an English face."

Frank couldn't shake the bad feeling. The baby looked fine and he couldn't see anything wrong. But there was a limpness to her, he just knew that wasn't right. Cathy was brought down to a single room, and then Frank was asked in. Tubes and antennae seemed to be attached all over. Her face looked ravaged.

"I'm so thirsty, Frank . . . where's our baby?"

The door opened and a man entered with the little bundle in a pink towel. Frank wondered if they kept an equal amount of blues and pinks.

"Jeez," he said, "who cares."

The man said,

"I'm Dr. Stevens, the paediatrician, could everyone please leave except the parents."

Frank didn't like this at all. It had an ominous ring. A childish urge to flee with the nurses and Dolores was strong.

The door closed. Frank moved to Cathy and made to take her hand. The tubes made it difficult, he held one of her fingers. It felt lifeless.

The doctor looked on the baby with tremendous affection and said,

"She's a beautiful wee thing, but alas, she is mildly Down's Syndrome."

Cathy threw her head back and screamed. She began to thrash in the bed and Frank was terrified the tubes would be torn free. His mind fought to understand what he'd heard

– Down's Syndrome

He couldn't differentiate between all the names that fill people with dread,

– Cystic fibrosis
– Cerebral palsy

They raced and leapt in his mind, like demons of the unknown, whisperers of trepidation.

The doctor said,

"I am so sorry, here . . . she's a lovely little thing, do you wish to hold her?"

And he held out the bundle to Frank.

Frank took her and was lost or found forever. Whatever term they use, bonding or union, it happened then.

Tears rolled down his face and fell on the baby's cheek. As long as he lived, he'd swear the baby gave him a quizzical look. The doctor gave an outline of what the condition meant. Whatever merits he had, and compassion was certainly among them, he was very long winded. He used four sentences to cover one, and tended to pause for long intervals. The gist of what Frank heard was that the girl would be slow. She'd do all the things babies do, but later. Six months behind in walk, speech, and mobility.

All the while, Cathy cried quietly. The doctor excused himself and said he'd be available the next day for any queries they'd have. Frank said to Cathy,

"She's beautiful, Sweetheart, will you hold her?"

Cathy put out her arms and held the baby. She immediately began to kiss and cuddle her.

"Frank, will they call her names in the playground?"

"Not a second time anyway."

"Are you disappointed in me Frank, did I let you down?" Pain tore his heart and he said,

"I never thought she'd be so beautiful, she's the image of you . . . it will be alright, Sweetheart."

By the time he'd to leave, Cathy was enjoined with her child . . . she asked,

"Did the doctor say she may . . . may lead an ordinary life?"

Frank couldn't remember, he said,

"Serena-may . . . do anything she please."

Cathy smiled.

"That's her name then, Serena-May. Let's give her the start of endless possibilities. Did you like the doctor, Frank?"

"I'll tell you, Sweetheart. However slow Serena may be, she couldn't possibly be as slow as him."

And left her laughing.

He hated the doctor, more than anyone he'd ever hated in his life. The desire to throttle him, to give him full-fisted blows to the head was near overpowering. He knew why, to kill the messenger and obliterate the diagnosis. Insanity, he knew that, but he said aloud, "What, I have to be rational now."

In the office, one of the girls had taped The Serenity Prayer. Frank said the short version,

"Fuck it."

A nurse approached. He didn't want to hear any words of sympathy.

"Mr. Marshall, your wife is in a private room, I hope you realize the cost. I don't want anyone running to me later, crying they weren't informed."

Frank took a deep breath, it didn't help.

"You think I'm going to do a runner, is that it? I've just been told my little girl has Down's Syndrome, my wife is in a shocking state, and you're worried about money."

And then he began to lose it big time, pulling out his wallet, drawing out notes and credit cards.

"Here . . . here take whatever you floggin' need, but so help me God . . . !"

Doctor Stevens appeared, put his arm round his shoulder, and said,

"Come on, there's a good man. Nurse, collect Mr. Marshall's things."

He led Frank into his office and sat him down, produced cigarettes.

"Doesn't do for it to be known I smoke, but what the hell eh."

They were the old fashioned unfiltered type, that would punch holes in the stomach of a mule. Frank took a drag and felt the piledriver kick.

"Jesus . . . " he said.

The doctor smiled.

"The real thing, eh, they don't put a warning on the packet, just give you a miniature shovel."

"My mother-in-law, is she all right?"

"Yes, I spoke to her and I suggested she go home and see the baby in the morning. I'm going to call you a cab and we can talk tomorrow."

"I wanted to kill you."

"You, and most of the nursing staff. Now let me call that cab."

By one of those vicious little turns of fate, the cab driver's radio was playing, Alison Moyet . . . "All cried out."

Frank muttered, "not yet . . . no . . . not yet."

A figure was huddled on his doorstep. Jim, in a swarm of flowers, chocolates, a huge Snoopy doll. His head was resting on Snoopy's shoulder, he was snoring loudly. Frank shook him gently, and he came to, roaring,

"Elvis has left the building!"

Then he shook and got to his feet, grabbed Frank in a hug.

"Congratulations, old Buddy-Mio."

"You know?"

"Hey, I rang the hospital, told them I was Cathy's parish priest. Put the fear of hell fire in some Irish Jesse."

"So you know it's a girl?"

"Is that Snoopy pink or wot? Jesus, tell me it's pink . . . at least, tell me you see a Snoopy. If that's a rate, I'm full fucked."

Inside, the dog went nigh hysterical with welcome. He wanted to sulk, but said the hell with it.

"Yo, 57 gifts for everyone."

"57?"

"Heinz . . . wotever, get yer mitts round that boy. You've got a sister . . . opps, sorry Frank . . . isn't he supposed to know?"

"He's a dog Jim."

"And life's a bitch."

The he began to sing in a very loud voice,

> "Well, they blew up the chicken man
> in Philly last night
> down on the boardwalk
> they're getting ready for a fight."

"Jim . . . jeez, Jim, hold it down a bit, O.K."

"Whoops, sorry, ol' Bruce Springsteen just begs for volume. You're a daddy . . . the hell of it is . . . you already have the look. God knows you've certainly got the moves."

Jim produced a bottle of brandy.

"So Frank, my man, Amigo, are we going to toast the baby's health or what?"

Frank didn't move.

"Yo, Franky . . . let's get shaking bro' . . . is something wrong? Should I have not come?"

"The baby, she's . . . Jesus . . . she has Down's Syndrome."

"Could be worse, there are some worse things."

Frank jumped up.

"Don't patronize me, you Scottish bastard. I don't have the luxury of climbing into a bottle. Have you the slightest idea of what Down's Syndrome is?"

Jim put the bottle back in his packages. Only now did Frank realize he wasn't wearing the judo outfit. He'd dressed for the moment. In a very smart three-piece wool suit. Not so smart as he'd recently slept in it, but still impressive. Him reached down and rubbed Heinz's ear. He said,

"My niece has Down's Syndrome, she's 19 now and attends college in Glasgow."

"Oh, God Jim, I'm sorry . . . Christ, am I a horse's ass. It's been a rough day. I didn't mean what I said about the bottle."

"Oh, you meant it alright. It's a bit out of control right enough. I sold the house to a fellah in the pub last week. I couldn't remember a bloody thing about it till he called round. Mind you, I wondered where the wad of notes came from . . . his deposit it seems . . . and I've drank it since."

"But surely, that's not legal, I mean . . . "

"It's a friggin' mess is what it is."

He stood up and gave the Snoopy doll a close concentrated look, then he planted a kiss on its soft snout.

"Frank, you know what I'd have really liked . . . course we'll never know now, but . . . I'd have liked to be the wee lass's Godfather. But that's impossible now because of something else which I'd like to discuss with you at a later date."

Frank stood up.

"You're . . . you're my friend, Jim."

"Naw, I'm your friend? . . . you're my best friend . . . you're also my only one, but that's my choice. I'll see you tomorrow."

They shook hands, like civil servants, a meaningless gesture and scarcely civil.

Frank cleared up a bit, fed Heinz and then slumped in the armchair. He thought of Cathy and the way she thrashed in the bed. The image was burned in his brain. A drink might have momentarily helped, but he was afraid. He looked to attack whatever was doing this to the very beat of his heart, and could see nothing.

Frank shook his hand at the roof, too weak to make a fist, and cried,

"Would it have killed you to leave that little baby alone . . . "

Frank woke late and crashing into his mind came the words, Down's Syndrome, like a lash.

"Jesus," he said.

Paralysis hit him, and he thought,

"If I just sit here, don't move, maybe everything will be O.K."

Heinz began to hop at his feet, and obviously paralysis was not on his agenda. Frank moved and began the morning things. Showered and shaved, he looked better, he felt woesome. First, he said, I've got to find out what this thing is. Rooting through the bookshelf he found an old dictionary, and under "Down's Syndrome" the first word he saw was "retardation" and dropped the book as if he'd been burned. Which in many ways he had.

***

En route to the hospital, he bought flowers, and didn't know what to buy Serena-May, and realized he'd called her by her name.

Cathy was sitting up, the baby asleep in her arms.

"I adore her," she said.

Her eyes were lit with wonder, and she said,

"A girl of twenty-two had a Down's baby a few days ago. She's hysterical and won't take her baby. I thought my age was to blame. Are you mad at us, Frank?"

"I will be if you ever say that again."

"O.K. So did you eat?"

Apart from eating Jim, he couldn't remember.

"Well, I know Heinz did."

"Do you think he'll like our little baby?"

"He bloody better hope so."

A woman stuck her head round the door.

"Mr. Marshall, a moment please."

Frank was beginning to dread these summonses.

"What, now?" he said.

The woman had the obligatory white coat with stethoscopes and instruments bulging from every pocket. She had a clipped manner.

"I'll need a blood sample from you, shall we say five minutes?"

"No . . . no we shan't say . . . what, it's like you need a light is it. Saw me passing and thought, Ah, I'll have a sample of him. Don't you people ever ASK? Or explain anything. Who the hell are you? I know you sixty seconds and you're into my veins. I'll tell you what you can do . . . you can flaming hop it . . . shall we say that?"

The woman backed way off. He wanted to follow her and physically shake her. He went down the corridor and found the smoking lounge. It was crammed with women.

"Mornin' ladies."

And tried to quiet the tremor in his hand. The one in his heart would require something more powerful than nicotine.

Returning to Cathy, they were joined by Doctor Stevens. He asked if he could hold the baby, and again, his tremendous feeling showed in his face. He said,

"Isn't she a beauty . . . I don't know how much you know about Down's Syndrome, but I'm going to presume it's very little and inform you accordingly."

Frank felt a rush of chronic anxiety, and said,

"That's a good presumption."

The doctor continued to gaze at the little baby as he spoke.

"We've come a long way since the old days when these little mites were locked in the attic or abandoned in institutions. Most Down's now live a full life, go to school, date, are a part of the community."

Frank thought of Jim, an ordinary normal man and his abandonment of the community, or was it vice versa.

"Ordinary people have 46 chromosomes. The Down's have 47. A feature of these children is a great love for music, and an amazing capacity for love. They are affectionate beyond belief. Your little girl . . . have you decided on a name?"

"Serena-May."

"Serena . . . is that to do with serenity?"

"We sure hope so."

The fear had been whispering at Frank and before he could consider, he blurted out,

"Will she know us, I mean . . . will she know we're her parents?"

Cathy began to weep.

The doctor looked stricken.

"Good heavens yes . . . oh, yes indeed. It might help you to meet the parents of Down's."

"No," said Cathy, "I'm not herding her in with others."

"You don't have to decide anything now. I know it's heard to believe, but you'll wonder later what all the grief was about. These Down's sometimes have heart trouble, but hers is strong and sound. In fact, physically, she's in great shape. There are all sorts of special services available, and it's good to know what's available. If I might add, I think this little girl is blessed to have you both. It's an eerie thing, but these Down's are never born to troubled families, and they certainly never cause it. On the contrary. So, I'll leave you to enjoy the wonder of this enchanted lady."

Cathy looked closely at her baby.

"Does she look Down's to you, Frank, would you know by just looking at her?"

He didn't know and said,

"I dunno. Aren't the Japanese eyes supposed to be a sure sign?"

Cathy laughed.

"Not to the Japanese . . . oh, Frank, isn't this awful, we're examining this baby for flaws."

As if on cue, a tiny tear slid down the baby's cheek. With his index finger, Frank gently took it and said, "If only I can always do that. Anyway, her eyes are almond, that's supposed to be sensual."

"Is it? How would you know things like that, are you watching wans with cats' eyes."

"There's Charlotte Rampling."

"Yea, and what about her?"

A nurse came and Frank headed for work.

***

Call it "serendipity" or plain down home coincidence. Or perhaps a touch of fate deciding to perverse, not to mention outright vicious.

Susan, Frank's secretary, was delighted about the baby. American fiction was the grand passion of her life. She and Frank competed as to who could introduce the other to a new writer. Frank had long since led the field in presenting her with the dual gifts of Raymond Carver and Jess Harper.

But now Susan felt she was about to sweep ahead. She'd been scanning her reviews studiously, and it seemed the critics on both sides of the Atlantic were falling over to heap praise on a new novelist. Plus, they all mentioned how blackly funny the novel was. Couldn't miss, she reckoned. When Frank arrived, the staff stood and applauded, flowers and congratulations were abundant.

Mortified, he fled to his office. He couldn't see how he deserved praise when the truth was that all this was Cathy's due. The book was left on his desk.

The Virgin Suicides
By

Jeffrey Eugenides.

"Jeez, what a title," he said, and read the review of the book. Sounded like a contender. The humour was stressed and he could sure use a touch of that. So he flicked through the pages.

Fate launched its lash.

Frank's eyes latched on to this passage,

"We were happy when Joe, the retard, showed up. As usual, he was grinning with the face he shared with every other mongoloid. He came murmuring with his oversize jaw and loose lips, his tiny Japanese eyes. We knew that retards didn't live long and aged faster than other people. We had him sing the song he always sang. We clapped, he was too dense to appreciate it."

Frank had read this standing at his desk. He slowly crumpled into his chair and shut the book. Then he picked it up and dropped it into the waste paper basket. Tears began to roll down his cheeks as he fumbled for a cigarette. His tears wet the filter and he couldn't get it to light. He said,

"Fuckin' thing."

Frank rummaged in his desk and found Graham Greene's *The End of the Affair*. For months he'd been bringing it to work. Someone had once described the novel as,

"Emotion recollected in hostility."

Frank saw it as a near perfect account of unbelief. The central character Bendrix is broken by Sarah's death, and oddly thus finds a tormented type of faith. Out loud Frank read the end lines of the book, believing that volume might ease his heart.

"I wrote at the start that this was a record of hate. I found the one prayer that seemed to suit the winter mood. 'O God, you've done enough. You've robbed me of enough, I'm too tired and too old to learn to love, leave me alone forever.'"

His intercom began to buzz and he knew it was going to be a long busy day. Just before he lifted the receiver, he recalled Job crying out in the desert,

"Why me, Lord, oh Lord . . . why me."

The Lord replied,

"Because you really piss me off."

***

At lunchtime, Susan came with coffee and sandwiches.

"You seem a bit down, Frank."

He nearly leapt at her, the word "down" was all out of proportion. She continued,

"It's your age, you're afraid you're too old to be a father?"

337

"Actually, Susan, I wasn't thinking that at all. But good of you to lodge the serpent in my head. The way I see it is, if I give her twenty of the very best years I can, maybe it's time enough."

Susan was hoping for a commendation for her book choice, but didn't really feel she should ask outright. Pride in knowing her place was sometimes operational. Plus she felt he was more than a little testy. Her mother had been right,

"Never, ever tell a man he's aging or balding."

***

Frank's mind was still in a literary lock. Ezra Pound who'd said,

"We're all writing the same poem."

and muttered,

"Not today Ezra."

Susan said,

"The sandwiches are corned beef. I think you'll find them rather delicious."

"Whatever," he answered.

A bemused Susan took her leave. She'd read in *Cosmo* that first time fathers were to be regarded as clinically insane, and she now full believed it.

Frank muttered as he peeked between the bread,

"Friggin' bully beef, Jeez I hate that."

And the sandwiches joined the new light of American literature in the bin.

Frank remembered his visit to the synagogue in Gt. Portland Street. He clearly remembered he'd emitted a sigh as he'd left. The Talmud said a sigh can break a man in two, and boy, he thought, did they ever get that right or what.

A knock at his door and his Mother-in-law entered. She looked like she'd been on the bottle. He couldn't be sure but thought she was wearing the same clothes as at the hospital, and . . . that she'd slept in them.

"Your secretary said you were eating lunch. Though how you can stomach anything . . . I'm sure I don't know. Men have no sensitivity."

Frank said,

"You're welcome to a sandwich,"

and he made a vague gesture towards the bin.

"I couldn't eat, I may never eat again."

Now he was sure she'd had a few belts of something.

"Your secretary seemed upset. God knows we're all upset. I doubt any of us will ever be happy again."

Frank thought he'd had enough of this shit.

"Dolores, what are you talking about?"

She burst into tears.

"That poor, damaged baby, what will become of her, will she have to be institutionalised. How are we ever going to look people in the face?"

The word "damage" sliced through his guts. Dolores sat and was crying loudly. He pulled up a hard chair and sat in inch from her face.

"Dorothy."

"Delores."

"I'm only going to tell you this once. If you ever call my daughter 'damaged' again, I'll show you exactly what the word means. If you've any intention of bringing this garbage to Cathy in the hospital – forget it. Now sober up and don't ever dare pull the stunt like that again. Am I getting through to you, Dolores?"

She nodded her head. He retrieved the sandwiches, found a large envelope and pushed them in.

"Now here's some lunch. You'll like it . . . corned beef."

"I like beef."

"There you go then. I'll see you later."

***

"Irrationally held truths may be more harmful than reasoned errors."
T. H. Huxley (1825-1895)
from *The Coming of Age of the Origin of Species.*

Every moment he could spare during the next week, Frank spent at the hospital. Cathy had moved into a dimension of near euphoria. That she adored the baby was a constant wonder to behold. Streams of visitors poured in and out. A nurse said they might need to install a revolving door.

Cathy rarely mentioned the Down's, except to note after each visitor,

"They didn't notice anything."

and if they were close friends and she told them, she said triumphantly,

"They said they can't see it. Some of them have seen Down's, and say they can't see it in Serena-May. Oh, Frank, nobody knows."

He didn't challenge any of this. Whatever got you through, he was all for that. A strange thing was happening for himself. When he was at the hospital, with Serena-May, he never thought of her condition. As soon as he left, he thought of nothing else. He'd devoured books, articles, people, in his mania for knowledge.

The books had mentioned a feeling of revulsion. That it was an instinctive feeling to experience this towards a Down's child. It came, they said, from primitive times when such a baby could not be cared for. Bonding would take a period of time and not to worry. Frank couldn't believe this. From moment one, he'd felt total love and bonding had occurred instantaneously. Fear . . . yes. Christ, he'd been afraid, but not of the baby . . . of the unknown.

Jim had come to visit. He was sober, suited and gift-laden. He'd borrowed the key to the house to tend to the dog, and instructed Cathy on the technique of bonding dog and baby. Cathy had said,

"If he doesn't bond, he emigrates."

Jim hoped she was referring to Heinz. He'd also promised not to sell the house. Cathy wasn't sure of the meaning of this, and Frank feigned ignorance.

Helen, Jim's ex-wife, also visited. Not of course, at the same time. She'd been wearing a huge silver crucifix and brought a smaller version for the baby. She said,

"A handicapped baby is a gift from God. Bernadette of Lourdes was a special child."

Cathy resolved there and then never to burden Serena-May with the true handicap of being labeled "special."

A nurse told Cathy how delighted the staff was at her love and acceptance of Serena-May.

"But she's my daughter."

"Mrs. Marshall, believe me, a lot of parents can't accept Down's Syndrome. In America, mothers have taken their children to plastic surgeons to alter their eyes."

"But the Down's Syndrome remains."

"Yes, but it can't be seen."

If Cathy had heard anything more obscene she couldn't recall it. It was stressed by many people about the love capacity, joy giving, and sheer endearment these babies had. She wondered if this were indeed the case, hadn't they got the prognosis wrong. They said a Down's Syndrome baby had one chromosome too many. Perhaps it was everyone else who had one less.

Dr. Stevens had come to see her one evening, and said,

"There is an area I'd like you to be aware of. Especially for a single child set of parents. A massive loss of self-esteem is involved. They feel they've failed with the one chance they had."

Cathy considered for a moment, then said,

"As if this was the best we could do. We got one shot at it and look what we produced."

"Exactly. I've known such parents to literally hide the child in a pram when they're out walking."

"I don't feel that now. God, do you think Frank does?"

"That's the point I wanted to make, Mrs. Marshall."

"Please call me Cathy, that Mrs. makes me feel so old."

"Fine . . . Cathy. There'll be times when you can't cope and your husband will be the strong one . . . and, of course, vice versa. No one can help you as much as each other. Also, it tends to come in waves. A long period of acceptance, then the doldrums."

"Do you think Frank has accepted . . . the situation?"

"I do know one thing, he loves that child passionately, and he loves you."

Cathy said nothing, then added, more to herself,

"What else is there?"

PART II

Never rely on what you think you know.

"Tell me again, does the diaper fold to the right?"

And Cathy came, whipped it on the baby in jig time.

"Don't worry, Frank, you'll get the gist of it."

The baby was home.

Frank thought he could do most things and mostly well. The whole caring for a baby was foreign and you couldn't really learn a lot from books. Literally, "hands-on" training. The baby didn't know you didn't know, and trusted you. That was worse.

Frank said,

"I feel kind of odd changing her diaper cos she's a girl . . . a bit embarrassed."

Cathy laughed.

"Well, it's only you and me hon. I don't think we can count on Heinz. I don't think you'll have much time to fret about mortification."

"God, there's so many things, I keep thinking I'll neglect some vital thing."

"Serena-May will let you know. You won't have to wonder if she's hungry, you'll hear her roaring."

Frank gave Cathy a long look.

"What."

"I was just wondering. Having Serena-May, do you think we'll change?"

"My mother says about me that I bring out the best in people."

"Well, that's true, you do."

"But that they bring out the worst in me."

"Ah, the old Irish back-hander, isn't it. They praise but always the little sting in the tail . . . did she say anything about me."

Cathy laughed.

"That's the oddest thing. I don't know what it means, but she said you make heavenly sandwiches. Do you, is this a hidden art?"

"It's the little talk before that adds the spice, plus, they were bully beef."

"You hate that."

"Touché."

And Serena-May gave a cry . . . "Feed me, Guys."

Cathy told Frank of babies with Down's Syndrome who were left at the hospital.

"How do you mean . . . left?"

"They don't bring them home."

"Ever."

"No."

"Good God."

"People do adopt children with Down's Syndrome. There's a woman in America

341

who'll only adopt those."

Heinz couldn't believe this tiny person was here to stay. For the first few days, he sulked and ignored his food. They ignored him so he had to pack it in. Instinct told him survival depended on an uneasy peace. So he tolerated her. Not graciously, or with any dignity, but felt he'd no choice. Maybe there'd be bonuses in the whole business, but it wasn't looking too hot. Already his daily walk had gone for a burton. Still, he reckoned, it could have been worse, they might have brought a whole tribe of these little people.

***

Frank was standing in Charing Cross Station when he noticed a group of children. An adult in charge of them said something and went to purchase tickets. They stood huddled together, a portrait of vulnerability and innocence. Then it clicked with him . . . Down's Syndrome . . . and his heart burned. He wanted to rush over . . . and do what? An overpowering sensation of love and tenderness crept down his whole body. He could have wept.

If things had been otherwise, he'd not have given them a second glance. Serena-May was changing him in ways he'd never have expected. Perhaps the old idea was right, you learnt compassion from pain, especially your own pain.

Cathy was learning too. They'd arranged a date for the christening, and the women she wanted as Godmothers weren't available. Time was running out, and she thought maybe it was fitting she ask Deirdre Rankin. Frank had mentioned her name the very first moment they'd met. Too, she'd sent Serena-May a beautiful present. She rang Deirdre at home.

"Deirdre, hi, this is Cathy."

"Cath! How lovely to hear from you, how is the baby and Frank?"

"Oh, they're wonderful."

"You're so lucky. As you know, I never had children, but I'm sure she's a total joy."

"The reason I'm ringing is . . . I'd like you to be her Godmother, if you can. We'd be delighted if you would."

There was a long pause. "Deirdre, hello . . . are you there?"

"Am . . . Cathy . . . I'm afraid that wouldn't be possible, under the circumstances."

"What . . . I don't follow."

"I don't think I'd be able to take responsibility for a child . . . well, let's just say of Serena-May's type."

Cathy was stunned, and it took a few moments before she could reply.

"Isn't it odd, Deirdre, I've known you all these years and I never knew of your disability."

"My what . . . did I hear you correctly . . . did you say disability?"

"Think about it honey."

Dolores had begun to spend her days at the house. Frank said to Cathy,

"It's good of your mother to help out, but she needn't come every day."

"You don't want her here?"

He didn't.

"It's not that, I mean, I appreciate her help, it's . . ."

"I'll tell her you don't want her."

"Jeez, Cathy . . . forget it. I love her being here, it's so challenging."

And it was certainly that.

One morning Dolores was doing what appeared to be housework, but it was fairly minimal. Frank asked,

"Should Serena-May's eyes roll like that?"

"I don't know."

Frank went to the phone as Cathy appeared.

"What's going on?"

"I'm ringing Dr. Stevens, the baby's eyes are rolling."

"For heavens-sake, Frank, get a grip, the baby's eyes are fine, it's normal. But you've got to stop this ringing of the doctor. Morning, noon and night, you'll drive him light."

Sheepishly he put the phone down. It went like that, whole periods of peaceful time then moments of pure panic. They'd feel hopeful and confident of Serena-May then crash out on a chance remark.

Normal ordinary things that babies do had Frank charmed and terrified. He didn't know if this were ordinary or the Down's Syndrome manifesting itself. He said to Cathy,

"Isn't she such a happy baby."

And Cathy freaked.

"You're saying she's placid, is that it, I don't want her to be bloody placid."

"Well I tell you Cathy, she's around you, I don't think we have to worry about that."

When Cathy took Serena-May for a check-up the doctor looked serious.

"Is something wrong, Doctor?"

"No, I was thinking it's a double tragedy, really."

Her heart pounded, the fear rushed to wallop her.

"I don't understand, have you found something?"

The doctor pursed his lips. Cathy prayed.

"God oh God, let it be something I can live with, don't let my baby have pain. Oh Jesus, don't let her die."

The doctor said,

"What I meant was, with the Down's Syndrome it's a double tragedy with her being a girl."

Afterwards, Cathy cried a mixture of grief, rage and relief. A thousand replies she might have come back with and all useless now. Chief among them, the one she regretted most was,

"You insensitive bastard."

***

Jim drained his glass, said,

"I tell you Frank, people never forget and rarely forgive."

They were in the Cricketeers on a Sunday morning. The place was hopping.

"That seems a bit harsh, Jim."

"Let me tell you Frank. A namesake of yours, Francis Bacon, are you familiar with his work?"

"I've seen some of it."

"Yea, well, when he had nowt, he was caught shoplifting in Harrods. Twenty years later, when he was world famous, they refused him a credit plan. All he ever really wanted was to look at the flaming tapestries hanging there. But you see, after all that time, they still had his balls in a meat grinder."

"Gracefully expressed, Jim."

"I'll never forget you Frank, for bullying me into being Godfather to Serena-May. I can't tell you how good it made me feel. At that time, I needed a boost so badly. I love that wee bairn. I think of her all the time, God . . . I even dream of her!"

"You've been very good to her, Jim . . . and to us."

Frank nearly said,

"And you actually sobered up there for a bit."

Which Jim had, but it hadn't lasted.

"That little girl Frank, she's pure love. If there's something wrong with her, we could all do with it. Doctors, Social Workers, they all talk about her condition . . . yea. How many of them talk about her. David Butler said,

'The function of the expert is not to be more right than other people, but to be wrong – for more sophisticated reasons.'"

Frank liked that a lot, he wanted to write it down. Instead he went to the bar and got drinks.

Settling again, they sipped in silence for a time. Jim began again,

"Remember, before, Frank, I told you I couldn't have been Godfather to your child . . . well, when Helen left, I went wild. But you already know that. What you don't know is the nature of that wildness."

Frank wasn't sure where this was leading. No place good he reckoned. He thought he'd lead him off at the pass. A confession was the last thing he needed.

"Well, Jim, we've all sown our wild oats."

"Frank, you have an annoying tendency to leap ahead and grab the wrong conclusion. I'm not talking about women. You catch my drift now?"

"AIDS," thought Frank, "doesn't the fool know it's rampant?"

"You don't want the sordid details, Frank . . . or do you? Never no mind, I can't hardly remember, but I do know I hit the gay bars . . . in search of company."

Frank didn't know what to say.

"I dunno what to say, Jim."

"One morning, fighting my way up from a Cointreau hangover, I noticed the blotches . . . I've had them checked, they're Karposki's and that spells only one thing . . . the old one way ticket. Good night, Irene."

"God Almighty."

"I don't want to be facetious, Frank, but I don't think God has anything to do with it."

"But there's treatments, other diagnosis."

"Yo, Barkeep, bring a couple of malt whiskeys . . . make em big ones . . . and one for yerself."

Frank was glad to hear they'd be large. Jim continued,

"There's some lines of Sylvia Plath that fit how I feel those nights after Helen left. I can't quote them exactly, but I've got the drift. I certainly got the message,

> 'I am inhabited by a cry
> nightly it flaps out
> looking with its talons
> for something
> to hook onto.'

"Each night, I'd drink and the loneliness of the house was pure terror, so I'd go stalking, like some sexual predator. Jesus, did I ever hook onto a big one. The greatest plague since the Middle Ages and I went out and grabbed it. But there is a point to all this, Frank, and believe it or not, I'm nearly ready to make it."

He took a huge swallow of his drink and grimaced as the spirit hit his throat, then set the glow in his chest.

"Ah, the spirit moves me. Did you ever see a movie called *Fried Green Tomatoes*?"

"Must have missed that one?"

"You shouldn't have. Jessica Tandy's character tells how she had a baby and they said it wasn't right. It would be best if she gave it up. But she always believed there was a special God for children. The child lived for 30 years and never gave her a day's trouble. He was the joy of her life. She was impatient to die so she could be re-united with him."

Frank loved the story, he couldn't wait to tell Cathy. He was also, he realized, more than a little drunk. Jim moved his hand in a slicing motion.

"Now, finally, the point of all this. As a child, I had it all, brains, roots family, sporting ability. As the yanks say, I was voted the one most like to. I did good in college, got a good job, married a beauty. See what I've become. Or Helen, similar story to mine. Nowadays she roams Hampstead Heath telling nannies that Jesus loves them. Most of them don't even speak English!

"So Frank, your little girl, all the things they say about her, don't burden her from the out. If I know anything she'll surprise them all. You love her, that's the ticket. I wish she was mine."

Frank felt a maudlin mood hover. He said,

"The social worker came yesterday. She said when we spoke to Serena-May, we should accompany the words with hand signals. When we say hello, we should use the salute sign."

Jim fumed, then asked,

"And Cathy, what did she say?"

"Oh, she waxed eloquent, she said, 'Kiss my ass,' that Serena-May had Down's Syndrome, not deafness. They're telling us we've got to keep the child stimulated. Cathy asked if loving care and attention was any relation."

"Frank, you've got three kids of professionals,

     1. Assholes
     2. Wankers
     3. and finally, Social Workers."

Cathy asked her mother,
"When people look at Serena-May, can they see the Down's?"
"No, I asked a few people and they were stunned to hear it. Does it bother you now?"
"Believe it or not, I couldn't care less. It used to. Those first few months. I was so conscious for her sake . . . and mine. I can't believe she's going to be a year old. I feel it's me who's grown up. Sometimes I think I read too much. A book said that unlike other children, her teeth would appear willy-nilly. But her bottom teeth arrived like any child."

Dolores was watching Serena-May crawl. Heinz would cruise by and give her a half-heartened lick. The child would make a grab for him, but he'd learnt from experience. Once had been painful as his ear was tugged ferociously. No one could accuse him of over-loving the baby. But he kept his eyes on her and knew with a sigh that he'd have to guard her continually. It was a dog thing. He might not be wild about her, but he sure wasn't going to let anyone mess with her. Perhaps he'd grow absurdly fond of her, but he doubted it.

Still, he took what was going on and endless treats appeared just by staying near her. His baby vigilance had near restored him to his owners' full attention. "So," he'd reckoned, "the old glory days were gone and the number one position had fled, but it could be worse."

Dolores picked up Serena-May and her heart melted anew. As the child gave a devastating smile, it seemed as if her eyes would disappear with the breath of the smile. Serena-May waited expectantly for Dolores to begin.
On the first word
Row!
she began to gurgle and move.
Dolores recited,

    "Row row
    row the boat
    gently down the stream . . ."

Serena-May looked over her shoulder to see if her mother was getting this. Cathy, as usual, was consumed with a love that she felt was near certifiable.
The recital continued,

"Merrily merrily,
merrily merrily,
life is but . . ."

Big pause.
And Serena-May caught her breath.
Cathy and her mother choruses,

"A dream."

Such times. Cathy remember the morning when she'd been dancing with the
baby as the radio played,
"Save the last dance for me."
This was followed by a Garth Brooks song. The DJ told how the singer had a
baby daughter. He'd looked in on his daughter one night, and thought if he died,
would the little girl know how much he loved her? Thus he wrote,
"If tomorrow never comes."
The song had crucified Cathy. A tremendous fear, always dormant, was what
would become of Serena-May if she and Frank were gone. But the baby answered
that by demanding her attention there and then.

***

Part of Frank's attraction for Cathy was his seriousness. He'd loosened up a lot
in ten years, but he still expected news to be bad rather than good. A waltzing with
down-right solemnity was always close to him. And then he'd lighten up unexpectedly
and redeem all. It was the not knowing that added to his attraction. Cathy would
never have dreamed of telling him. Such knowledge would have tipped him over to
full seriousness.
Cathy looked now at Serena-May. She seemed to have inherited both of their
characteristics. Just as people would remark.
"What a serious little girl."
She'd launch one of her heart-kicking smiles and they'd say,
"Isn't she as content!"
Frank had said, only once,
"If she's a mix of us then it means she'll skip down the street and drop a piece of
litter without a care. But, later she'll sneak back and put it in the bin."
Cathy said,
"But you don't litter . . . do you, Frank?"
A description by Chateaubriand described Serena's face exactly,
"The more serious the face, the more beautiful the smile."
Cathy resolved yet again to return to reading. In Serena-May's time, she bought
the paper daily and hadn't once opened it. She thought she might just as well go

into the newsagent, pay them but not actually take the paper. Sort of cut out the middleman, which was the actual reading. Frank read reams of Down's Syndrome, but it depressed him. She noticed he'd skip over any photos in the books. It had taken her a long time to be able to observe children with Down's Syndrome.

The pain was still there, but so was an empathy she'd never known. As long as she could, she'd deferred ringing special services. It was Jim who said casually,

"Might be some help to Serena-May."

The realization that she might deprive the child of any or all advantage overcame fear. She'd picked up the phone. Her hands were shaking as she dialed the number. A woman with a cold voice answered. Cathy told her it was to do with Down's Syndrome and immediately the woman said,

"You want the mentally handicapped section. Hold on, I'll put you through."

Cathy had stood transfixed. The dreaded words had been said . . . mentally handicapped . . . she felt sick to her stomach. A woman came on and was as warm as the other was cold. The services and help were outlined, and somebody would call at Cathy's discretion.

After, she picked up Serena-May and great sobs tore from her. Now the reality was here. No matter what people saw or didn't see in the child, thought or didn't think . . . here was the cold precise classification. From here till doomsday she and Frank could clutch at, "mild."

"She has mild Down's Syndrome."

The term had become a talisman. It now lay shattered at the end of a telephone line. Serena-May grabbed her finger and gave a tiny smile. Cathy said,

"Row the boat, do you think doodle-een you could go a blast of two of that."

Serena-May could. Her face lit up in anticipation of the sound of her mother's laughter. Heinz headed for the garden, he didn't think he could take it one more time.

"Surely," he thought, "there's a cat out here that needs the living daylights shook from it."

The tenderness Cathy was experiencing exorcised all remnants of the phone call. Salinger defined sentimentality as showing a thing more tenderness than God would give it. Who knows what God thinks, but an observer might have felt that now and then, a smile touches the mouth of any deity.

***

Mongol: Mongoloid.
Mongol, Mongol, Mongol, Mongol, Mongol . . .
Frank tried the stunt of saying a word often enough to take its power away. As Lenny Bruce had attempted with obscenity. If there was a more obscene word than this, he didn't know it. Cathy had mentioned the time when Serena-May would go to school and she asked Frank,

"How do you think I'd be if they taunted Serena-May?"

"I know how I'd be."

"I'd burn the friggin' school, do you think that's extreme?"

"I'll carry the paraffin . . . I nearly said I'll carry the can."

"That too."

"If any of them nuns say a word, I'll strangle them."

"Nuns?"

"Yea, women in hoods who do a lot of polishing. I went to The Sisters of Mercy. Whatever else, mercy was the least of their assets."

Frank smiled and this was followed by his literary look. Cathy hoped it wasn't yet another Graham Greene story. Any mention of religion got him quoting Greene. But it wasn't him.

"Scott Fitzgerald said in Gatsby that everybody suspects themselves of having at least one of the cardinal virtues. I strongly suspect that one of mine isn't tolerance and I'm getting worse."

Cathy added,

"Well, I don't have any patience, and don't agree with me, I know already, it doesn't need endorsement. But with Serena-May, I'm never impatient. I don't know what I used to think about before, but now, it's our daughter. Good Lord doesn't that sound awesome." Heinz bounced in and thought,

"Surprise, surprise, they're talking about the thing again."

He went to his water dish and slurped loudly as he could. Usually it annoyed the hell out of them. But they gave him the sweet look that made him want to chew ankles.

Jim was surveying the wreck of his home. It looked like the aftermath of a tornado. He wasn't really sure what happened, but he had vague flashbacks of running through the rooms trying to destroy everything. One vivid picture was him chasing a naked person with a meat cleaver. Their sex was indeterminate, but he wasn't even sure if he had a cleaver. If it had happened, he hoped the person was fast. Some of the rooms he no longer checked just in case their speed hadn't been up to the mark.

He looked down at his feet. Tins of dog food for Heinz he'd never delivered. Reaching in his pocket, he sorted various sheets of disheveled paper. These consisted of writing he'd once been especially fond of or moved by. A piece he'd earmarked for Heinz he read aloud, by the philosopher Henry Beston,

> "We need another and a wiser and perhaps a more mystical concept of animals. For the animal shall not be measured by Man. They are not brothers. They are not underlings. They are other nations, caught with ourselves in the net of life and time. Fellow prisoners of the travail and splendour of birth."

He thought for a moment then crumpled all the sheets together and launched them across the room. They landed with a soft thud on a pile of dirty shirts and slipped down, lost to view. Aloud he roared,

"Who bloody cares, who gives a proverbial toss."

Dragging himself to his feet, he tried to focus his mind. He had a letter to write.

***

It took Frank a long time to even know how to refer to Serena-May's condition. He had been saying "Down's Syndrome,"
and learnt that Down's Syndrome was the term as Dr. Down did not have the syndrome himself.

"Lucky Dr. Down," said Frank.

Nor did he own it. Frank was glad you said the child has Down's Syndrome, not is a Down's Syndrome. It wasn't all the child was.

Or a child with Down's Syndrome. A child first.

He felt he should know who this doctor was who held their lives in such a stranglehold.

Dr. John Langdon Down, 1828-1896. An Englishman working in Surrey. He first listed the characteristic features. But he didn't understand the cause of the condition he had described. In fact, he thought it was a reversion to a primitive Mongoloid ethnic stock.

"Jesus," thought Frank, "was the old doc ever off beam on that one."

He discovered that two-thirds of all children with the syndrome are born to mothers under 35. Of all Frank read, the information that actually charmed him was unexpected. The reading, the seeking of information, he did to banish fear. It never occurred to him that any of would warm him.

The most enjoyment the child would get from anything was looking at the parent's face, and would be more important to the child than any toy or object.

Frank was nigh child-like himself, as each successive time he gathered and presented the data to Cathy. One evening she said,

"Frank, I'm dizzy . . . I'm in a spin of statistics and research and theories. The truth is. . . I'm sick of Down's Syndrome. Let's just give Serena-May the best we can and use whatever help is available . . . what do you think?"

Frank didn't answer, he picked up his mini library with both hands, shuffled to the bin and lifted his bundle high. As he turned to Cathy, he let the load go and said,

"They're outa here . . . let's tend to our daughter."

***

Frank had told Cathy of one morning when he saw despair walking. Cathy was in the hospital with Serena-May at the time. He'd come early to visit. As he turned in, a couple were walking towards him. The man was walking slightly in front, carrying a suitcase and two plastic bags. Not a word passed between them. Frank glanced at the woman, her eyes were glued to the ground and she had the shuffled walk of the truly lost.

An air of awful desolation hung over them. A nurse said to Frank, "They lost their baby." Later, when he'd told Cathy, she'd been horrified.

"Oh my God, Frank, what if that had been us. And all the baby clothes waiting as a shocking reminder."

Frank couldn't think of it. The picture was too horrendous. It was then Cathy had said,

"If anything happened to Serena-May, I don't think we'd survive . . . would we, Frank?"

"I don't think we'd want to."

A few weeks later, the letter came from Jim. It read,

> *Dear Frank,*
>
> > *Remember I mentioned to you the diagnosis I had been given. Well, I'm not going to hangabout and just wither away. I found a painless solution in one of Norman Mailer's books. So I'm history.*
> >
> > *But I've been busy, boy . . . have I ever. I told you once how I'd sold my house in a pub. I got to thinking, why not try it once more,*
> > *and*
> > *and . . .*
> *I've lost count of how many buyers. When they come looking for me . . . well, they better be good. What about the money? I opened an account for Serena-May (you'll find it enclosed).*
> > *Knowing you, Frank, and what an absolute prig you are, you'll refuse it. But it's not yours. It's that little girl who gave me more wonder in a short time than my whole life of "achievement." If she's handicapped, then God help us normal folk. I think she allows for our shortcomings.*
> > *Be adventurous once in yer life, Frank, feel what it's like to be an outlaw, take the cash. If I had to end on a quote, I feel something from Blake like,*
>
> *"An build a heaven in hells despair."*
>
> *A tad solemn methinks.*
> *In 1746 Vauvenargues writes,*
>
> *"The wicked are always surprised to*
> *find the good*
> *can be clever."*
>
> *Be clever, Frank.*
> *Got to go, old buddy. I hear the doorbell . . . ask not for whom the bell etc.*
>
> *– FEED HEINZ!*

Jim-Bo.

Frank shook the envelope and out dropped the bank book. He opened it slowly, looked at the amount and whistled . . . exhaled a long "Phew."

Serena-May was chirping, it was time for her breakfast.

BIOGRAPHY

Ken Bruen's crime novels have earned him many awards and nominations, including wins for the Shamus Award and the Macavity Award. Among his works are the Jack Taylor private eye series (set in Galway) and the Brant police procuedral series (set in South London). Ken Bruen lives in Galway and New York City.

Visit him online at www.kenbruen.com.

KEN BRUEN ZIPPOS

Available online at www.bustedflushpress.com. $36 each.

also available

Damn Near Dead, edited by Duane Swierczynski, introduction by James Crumley, $26, ISBN 0-9767157-5-9. Available in June 2006. Featuring original noir stories by Ken Bruen, Reed Farrel Coleman, Laura Lippman, Jason Starr, John Harvey, and many, many more of today's hottest crime writers.